Praise for *Imperial Passions – The Great Palace*:
"For those who read Stephenson's Imperial Passions – The Porta Aurea, and wanted more, the wait is over. Imperial Passions – The Great Palace, the story of Anna Dalassena, a most important and fascinating woman in Byzantine history, is delightfully instructive and engaging. Come ready to immerse yourself in a thrilling story both political and personal."
~James Conroyd Martin, author of The Theodora Duology

Praise for *Imperial Passions - The Porta Aurea*
"One book does not suffice to tell the fascinating story of Anna Dalassena, one of the more intriguing medieval ladies around. Ms Stephenson ends her narrative while there is still a lot of life ahead of Anna. I hope she will be kind enough to furnish us with a sequel as well-written and researched as *Imperial Passions* is!" Historical Novel Society Indie Reviews
Shortlisted for Chanticleer Book Awards 2018 Chaucer Award for Pre-1750s Historical Fiction

Praise for *Tales of Byzantium*:
"Elegantly described details, sharply observed characters. . . three very intriguing windows into a part of history largely unknown too many readers." Historical Novel Society Indie Reviews

Winners of Indie/B.R.A.G. Medallions:
Tales of Byzantium
Imperial Passions - The Porta Aurea
Byzantine History in the 11th Century - A Brief Introduction

IMPERIAL PASSIONS - THE GREAT PALACE

EILEEN STEPHENSON

Blachernae Books

Blachernae Books

Rockville, MD

www.eileenstephenson.com

Publishers Note:

Imperial Passions – The Great Palace is a work of historical fiction. Apart from the well-known actual people, events and locales figuring in the narrative, all names, characters, places, and incidents are a product of the author's imagination or are used fictitiously. Any resemblance to actual people, living or dead, or to businesses, companies, events, institutions or locales is completely coincidental.

Cover design by Jennifer Quinlan

Imperial Passions-The Great Palace / Eileen Stephenson, 1st Edition

Print:

ISBN: 978-0-9996907-2-7

E-book:

ISBN: 978-0-9996907-3-4

❀ Created with Vellum

For Caleb, Stephanie, Molly, Nathan, Luke and Abigail

MAIN CHARACTERS

Dalassenus Family

Anna Dalassena – wife of John Comnenus. All deceased: her parents Helena Dalassena & Alexios Charon, grandparents Adrian Dalassenus and wife Theodora*.

Anna and John's children: Manuel, Isaac, Marie "Marina", Eudokia "Donya", Theodora, Alexios, Adrian, Nikephoros "Niko"

Constantine Dalassenus – Deceased. Adrian's oldest brother, Anna's Uncle Costas. Children: Deceased - Xene*.

Damien Dalassenus – Uncle Costas' son

Romanus Diogenes – Great grandson of oldest sister of Constantine and Adrian Dalassenus. Married first to Anna "Anya" Alusiana. Children: Theophano "Thea" and Constantine "Costas"

Ducas Family

Constantine Ducas – husband of (1) Xene* Dalassena and (2) Eudokia Makrembolitissa. Children: Michael, Andronikos, Constantinos, Anna, Theodora, Zoe

John Ducas – Constantine's younger brother; m. Irene Pegonitissa. Children: Andronikos, Constantine

Comnenus Family

Manuel Comnenus – Deceased. General under Basil II

Isaac Comnenus – eldest surviving son of Manuel

Catherine of Bulgaria – Isaac's wife and daughter of deceased tsar of Bulgaria

Marie "Marika" Comnena – daughter of Isaac and Catherine

John Comnenus – younger son of Manuel. Husband of Anna Dalassena

Eudokia "Donya"* Comnena – Deceased. Sister to Isaac and John; m. Michael Dokeianos (deceased). Their children: *Theodore*, George*, *Helena and Anastasi*a

11th Century Rulers of the Eastern Roman ("Byzantine") Empire to 1057

Basil II – emperor for almost 50 years until his death in December 1025

Constantine VIII – Basil's dissolute younger brother; deceased in 1028

Zoe – Eldest surviving daughter of Constantine VIII; empress upon his death. Deceased ~1050. Married: (1) Romanus III Argyros, (2) Michael IV, (3) Constantine IX Monomachos.

Michael V – Michael IV's nephew and adopted son of Zoe and Michael IV. Deceased in 1042 after being blinded by city mob.

Theodora – Zoe's younger sister and ruling empress following the death of Constantine IX Monomachos. Deceased 1056.

Michael VI Bringas – bureaucrat named emperor by Empress Theodora on her deathbed. Forced to abdicate August 31, 1057 in favor of Isaac I Comnenus. Deceased by 1059.

Other Characters

Eudokia Makrembolitissa – friend of Anna Dalassena; 2nd wife of Constantine Ducas

Michael Keroularios – Eudokia Makrembolitissa's uncle; patriarch

Marie of Bulgaria – orphaned niece of Catherine of Bulgaria

Michael Psellus – court functionary and historian

Katakalon Kekaumenos – renowned general

Peter Kekaumenos – soldier and nephew to Katakalon Kekaumenos

Gagik – abdicated king of Armenia, later in service to empire

Nikephoros Bryennios – renowned general

Nikephoros Botaneiates – renowned general

Michael Maurex – droungarios/admiral in Byzantine navy

Palace Eunuchs: *Thomas, Georgios,* Nikephoritzes, *Ignatios*

Michael Attaleiates – eminent judge; later historian

Marie Kourtikios – physician

Maria of Alania – princess of the Kingdom of Alania

Irene – cousin of Maria of Alania

Michael the Chartoularios – bureaucrat

Constantine Leichoudes – priest

Martina – refugee from Anatolia with her children George and Thekla

Michael Taronites – young soldier from the dynatoi

Nikephoros "Niko" Melissenos – young soldier from the dynatoi

George Palaiologos – young soldier from the dynatoi

•Asterisked names indicate that no record of the individual's actual name has survived.

Italicized names indicate a character created for this story.

Note: At the time this story takes place, the use of surnames is inconsistent. Not everyone had a surname, and of those who did, not all of them took their father's name. For example, Anna Dalassena's father, Alexios, only had the nickname of "Charon" and no recorded surname, while Anna took her maternal grandfather's surname.

GLOSSARY

19 Akkubita – The main banquet hall at the Great Palace. It had nineteen apses: nine on both sides, and one at the far end from the entrance for the emperor. It was originally built in the old Roman style with dining couches in the apses.

Anatolia – Also known as Asia Minor, this is the geographic area currently occupied by the Asian side Turkey. It extended east to the borders with Armenia and Mesopotamia in 1025 and was divided into about 16 Themes, or provinces, during Anna's lifetime.

Black Sea - The Black Sea has been known by several names over history, sometimes by the name Euxine Sea, the hospitable sea.

Chrysotriklinos – The main throne room, audience and occasional formal dining hall at the Great Palace. It was a large octagonal building with the main entry door of silver. Records indicate that the inside was covered with magnificent mosaics, lavish with gold, as well as gold lamps, and a throne of gold. There was a private entrance to the Boukoleon Palace for the monarch's use.

Domestic – A military leader. The Domestic of the Scholai was the leader of the Scholai elite taghmata, a regiment, and was the most senior military leader in the Byzantine Empire. The leaders of the six taghmata generally had the title of Domestic.

Droungarios – A military leader, usually referred to the admiral of the imperial fleet, but could also be the leader of one of the elite regiments, such as the Vigla Taghmata.

Dux – The commander/governor of the more critical cities or themes on the frontiers of the Empire.

Dynatoi – The term used for the Byzantine aristocrats.

Eparch of Constantinople – the city governor's office. It had wide-ranging powers, from maintaining public order, to resolving business disputes, and tax collection.

Franks – The Norman soldiers, generally the younger sons of the Norman nobility, who left in search of land and wealth in the south. Many of them settled in southern Italy and Sicily.

Gynecaeum – Many families in Byzantium kept their women, as much as possible, in separate women's quarters for protection. While not a universal practice, it was common, particularly among the upper classes.

Great Palace – The imperial residence in Constantinople; originally built by Constantine the Great, but added onto by many emperors.

Hagia Sophia – The Church of the Holy Wisdom of God. This basilica was built in the reign of Justinian about 575 and is considered the finest example of Byzantine architecture. It was the main church of the Eastern Church until 1453 when the Mehmet II conquered Constantinople and converted it and many other Orthodox churches to mosques.

Hegoumenos/Hegoumena – The Greek term for the abbot/abbess of a monastery.

Hippodrome – The stadium located near the Great Palace where chariot and horse races were traditionally held, as well as some imperial ceremonies. Finished by Constantine the Great in the 4th century, it could hold about 30,000 spectators and by Anna's day it was at least 600 years old.

Icon – Paintings of Christ, angels, the Mother of Christ, and other saints, to be venerated by Orthodox Christians.

Iconostasis – A screen between the nave (where worshippers were located) and the altar, where the priest, bishops, and/or deacons would be located. There were "royal doors" that opened between the nave and altar. The screen was typically adorned with paintings of Christ, the Theotokos, angels, and saints, or Biblical scenes.

Maphorion – A mantle, or veil, worn by Byzantine women when they went out.

Mese – The main road in Byzantium, beginning at the Milion marker near the Great Palace and the Hagia Sophia.

Milion – A marker near the Great Palace and the Hagia Sophia, where the Mese began, near the heart of Byzantium. Originally quite large, a small piece of it can still be seen in Istanbul today.

Pascha – The Orthodox term for Easter.

Prinkipo – One of the Princes' islands in the Sea of Marmara where abdicated/exiled rulers and political enemies of the rulers of the Empire were sent, typically to be tonsured as a monk or nun, to live out their days in the monastery or convent there.

Purple Room – The room in the Great Palace where Byzantine empresses traditionally gave birth. This room was built with walls of reddish/purple marble from Egypt called porphyry. Children born in this room traditionally bore the moniker of "Porphyrogenitus" or "Porphyrogenita".

Semantron - A wooden plank that makes a sound like a gong when hit with a mallet. Used to call the orthodox to church services since church bells were uncommon in Constantinople.

Solidi – (Solidus – singular) The traditional gold coins of the Byzantine Empire. These were highly regarded for centuries for their stable quality and value, and were often traded into Western Europe where they were called "bezants". During the period of this novel, however, emperors debased the coins to fund profligate imperial spending, resulting in inflation and popular dissatisfaction with the empire's rulers.

St. John Stoudion Monastery – This was the largest and best known of the monasteries in Byzantium for hundreds of years. It was commonly referred to simply as Stoudion. Portions of the ruined church can still be seen in Istanbul today.

Strategos – Governor of a Byzantine Theme; often a general since they had defensive responsibilities, or possibly a large landowner in the Theme.

Taghmata – These were the Byzantine Empire's six elite regiments – Scholai, Exkoubitores, Ikanatoi, Vigla, Arithmos and Athanatoi.

Tesserae – The small bits of stone, colored glass or marble that make up a mosaic.

Theme – The regional "provinces" within the Byzantine Empire. Each theme's defined borders could be altered, with the number of themes changing over the centuries.

Themata – These were the provincial army corps. Each province had their own, composed of professional soldiers and local troops who held land in exchange for military service.

Theodosian Land Walls – These nearly impregnable walls were built during the reign of the Emperor Theodosius II in the 5th century, extending in an arc from the Golden Horn in the north, to the Sea of Marmara in the south. They were matched with equally strong sea walls. The land walls consisted of a main fortress wall with numerous towers and watch posts, a lower outer wall, with a trench between the walls that could be filled with water. These walls were an amazingly effective deterrent for centuries and only fell in 1453 to the cannons of Mehmet II and the Ottoman Turks. Most of the walls can still be seen today in Istanbul.

Theotokos – The Greek term used commonly to refer to Mary, the mother of Jesus. It is literally translated as "God-bearer". Mary is a frequent subject of Byzantine icons, but always pictured with Jesus.

Varangian Guard – One of the most renowned mercenary corps in history, the Varangians were Scandinavians, Anglo-Saxons and Russians who had wandered south in search of wealth. They dedicated themselves to serving the Byzantine emperor, however needed, beginning in the early 10th century until the late 14th century.

MAP OF THE BYZANTINE EMPIRE
- 1025

The following map of the Byzantine Empire shows the extent of the empire in 1025, the year of the death of Emperor Basil II and the year Anna Dalassena was born. During Anna's lifetime, much of this territory was lost due to exceptionally poor leadership in most of the years following Basil's death.

One place mentioned often in the story that is not on the map is Bithynia. This ancient name for part of the Anatolian peninsula was not the name of any Byzantine theme (a governing unit similar to a state or province) and covered various parts of Anatolia at different times. This area was generally on the western most coast of Anatolia, from the Black Sea area down to the Bosphoros and the Sea of Marmara. Eleventh century Byzantines still called that general part of Anatolia "Bithynia" the way Americans might refer to the "Midwest" or "the East Coast." People generally knew what area was being referred to even though it isn't specifically labeled on a map.

I have no certainty of the location of the nomadic tribes of Scythes and Pechenegs. They did roam quite a bit. I've put them on the map so that readers can get a general idea of where they came from.

The empire lost vast amounts of territory during Anna's lifetime. The Hungarian kings were often trying and succeeding, before losing again, at taking Croatia and Serbia. The Norman mercenaries in Italy had taken over all remaining Byzantine territory there by about 1070. The Seljuk Turks began raiding in Anatolia by about 1050, but swooped into Anatolia almost without any impediment following the Battle of Manzikert in 1071. Every one of these losses cost the empire in tax revenue and resources, especially manpower.

N.B. – The official name of the capital city of the Eastern Roman Empire was Constantinople. However, I realized, when reading the histories written in this period, that the people living in Constantinople almost never called the city by its official name. It was most often called by its old name of Byzantium, and sometimes the Queen of Cities. I suspect it was because the official name is a mouthful – six syllables in Greek vs. four syllables for the old name. I do use all three names in this novel.

Cartography by Julie Witmer Custom Map Design

Base map data from Natural Earth
    Byzantine themes and places - Cplakidas, CC BY-SA 3.0, via Wikimedia Commons
    Additional places by Eileen Stephenson
    Via Egnatia route - Eric Gaba (Sting), CC BY-SA 2.5, via Wikimedia Commons

BYZANTINE EMPIRE

1025 A.D.

ALANIA

The Black Sea

IBERIA

Trebizond

CHALDIA
Amisos
Neokaisarea
Ani
Amasea
IBERIA
ARMENIA
PAPHLAGONIA
KOLONEIA
Theodosiopolos
ARMENIAKON
Manzikert
Heraklea
Sebasteia
Chliat
Lake
Van
Constantinople
Ancyra
Nikomedia
CHARSIANON
Nicaea
Caesarea
VASPARAKAN
OPSIKION
MELITENE
LYCANDOS
MESOPOTAMIA
ANATOLIKON
CAPPADOCIA
Ikonion
Chonai
Aleppo
Antioch

SYRIA

CHAPTER 1

IGNATIOS THE EUNUCH STOOD AT ATTENTION OUTSIDE THE entrance to the Akkubita, the Great Palace's ancient dining hall with its nineteen apses. He gripped the tall staff of a protovestiarios topped with a golden double-headed eagle, obsidian eyes gleaming. A thrum of anticipation pulsed through the enthusiastic crowd until two servants finally pushed open the massive carved wooden doors. At this sign, Ignatios pounded the staff on the marble floor three times, its heavy sound reverberating around us, and made his proclamation. The guests grew silent.

"Christ has crowned your emperor," he called out, his voice echoing loudly. "Many years, many years to the emperor, Isaac Comnenus, the most pious emperor and autocrat of the Romans, and Catherine, the most pious augusta. Christ has crowned your emperor. Enter and make your obeisance."

Our jubilant voices rose up in the traditional response, "Many years, many years."

This banquet celebrated the crowning of my brother-in-law, General Isaac Comnenus, as emperor of the Roman Empire;

finally, a true leader on the throne after thirty years of inept and spendthrift rulers. Silk banners fluttered along the walls of the great banquet hall with images of St. George, St. Demetrios, the Theotokos. Others were of Constantine the Great, Theodosios the Great, Justinian I, and Basil II. Their reds and golds, silvers and blues glittered in the late afternoon sunlight.

I shivered with excitement as my husband, John Comnenus, and I processed through the massive doorway into the Akkubita, the first time ever for me. The patriarch, Michael Keroularios, strode ahead of us in his stiff formal vestments with Constantine Ducas, Isaac's supporters, and the Senate members following us. The procession passed by the eighteen marble-walled apses, nine on each side, where liveried servants stood ready to guide the invited to tables after they were presented to Isaac. Most of the guests would be seated in those eighteen apses for the great feast celebrating the coronation. John, brother to the new emperor, and I would be seated in the nineteenth apse with him and a few others.

John's arm trembled under my hand as we processed. His face was flushed, and he looked around nervously as we approached Isaac on his throne. Isaac had named him Caesar, the title signifying John's elevation to the empire's second in command. He'd told me that he worried any misstep could embarrass his brother and could even be a poor omen for his reign. I squeezed his hand and smiled at him. He looked back and the tremor in his hand relaxed.

The patriarch, carrying his crozier topped by a cross and snakes, was the first to greet Isaac who sat on the sparkling golden throne. He said a blessing over Isaac, bending to kiss him on the mouth. Isaac returned the kiss of peace, and the patriarch stepped to Isaac's side, where a more modest throne awaited him, a little behind the emperor's.

The protovestiarios announced us. "Caesar John Comnenus and his wife, Caesarissa Anna Dalassena."

John knelt to make his obeisance, kissing his brother's

purple-clad foot and then his gold ring with its cabochon amethyst, intoning "Many years." I followed him, doing the same, and we took our places standing behind Augusta Catherine. Constantine Ducas, the leader of the Senate, then performed his obeisance, as did his wife Eudokia, my closest friend. They moved to stand behind Isaac near the patriarch, who was Eudokia's uncle.

One by one, the others were led forward by servants, kissing Isaac's foot and ring, repeating the words "Many years." The generals who had supported Isaac's rebellion led them, followed by senators, other dynatoi, and some family. The homages were finally done as the last rays of sun disappeared. The gold throne was moved away, and those of us dining in the nineteenth apse with Isaac sat down at tables. Eudokia and I sat with Catherine, apart from the men and the only women in attendance at this feast.

The protovestiarios signaled the servants to bring platters of food to our table and pour the wine into crystal goblets. I was hungry after the long ceremony but protocol demanded that I wait for Catherine. She finally picked up an olive with her silver fork and ate it, freeing Eudokia and me to partake. The three of us tried not to gawk at the elaborate room with its gold chandeliers, but it was our first visit to this building. The graceful old structure showed its five hundred years in the faded luster of its marble wall panels, even though the former Emperor Constantine Monomachos had spent a fortune ten years earlier repairing cracked floor mosaics, replacing the old-fashioned couches with chairs, and adding new tables.

I felt a little overwhelmed in the midst of all this grandeur. "I never expected to have the honor of dining here. Augusta, you know you're sitting where Empress Theodora would have sat, and Isaac is where Justinian would have been."

Catherine's lips turned up in a smug smile. "Yes."

Eudokia looked at us, eyes wide. "I wonder if anyone has seen ghosts here."

Catherine looked around suspiciously. "I hope not. I expect most ghosts would haunt the Church of the Holy Apostles, around all the tombs of the old emperors."

The entertainment began soon after the servants had served platters of food. Musicians from Syria banged on their tambourines and drums, plucked lyres, while their singers recounted heroic tales. The favorite was "A Border Guard Building a Wall," about a brave akrites guarding the eastern border. Most of the men in the room sang along to that one, including Isaac and John. After that, jugglers deftly tossed balls, knives and clubs amongst themselves, grinning at the audience's *oohs* and *aahs* of appreciation. Tumblers then ran through the center of the hall, bouncing and climbing on top of each other into a stack five men high. Mimes cavorted around making fun of one and all, although not of the new Emperor Isaac. The hall grew noisy with the music and the many conversations going on in the dining apses. Servants skirted around the entertainers with platters and pitchers.

Catherine's face, with a jeweled maphorion covering her head, glowed in the lamplight. Isaac had transformed her from daughter of the defeated Bulgarian ruler killed in battle against the Romans into the proud Roman augusta, the wife of the emperor. I had never seen her happier or prouder.

Eudokia nibbled at a piece of bread. I raised an eyebrow at her, wondering at her lack of appetite.

"I'm expecting another child in the late spring," she said with a wan smile.

"Congratulations," I said. I gave her an encouraging smile while inwardly grimacing. Constantine Ducas was old enough to be her father and I knew he was not an affectionate husband.

"Yes, congratulations," said Catherine, her face taking on a shadow. "This will be your fourth child?"

"Yes, Augusta," my old friend said, eyes downcast. She never looked across at her husband on the other side of the room, sitting with Isaac, John, and the patriarch.

Catherine's only son had died a few years earlier in a plague epidemic, leaving just her daughter, twenty-one-year-old Marie who we called Marika. She still grieved her young son and I often saw the envy of pregnant women in her eyes.

"You are fortunate," Catherine said with a tight smile, quickly turning back to watch the mimes, who were making hilarious faces at the crowd, one pretending to be a lazy bear trainer outside the hippodrome and the other his clever beast, tricking his human for a few more tasty morsels.

Wine flowed, food filled bellies, and the guests relaxed at the performances, but Isaac was not one for carousing all night. He was now emperor and autokrator. He would get to work early in the morning. After a couple of hours of celebrating, he nodded to Ignatios, the protovestiarios, who thumped his staff again on the marble floor. Isaac rose from his seat.

Everyone stood, acclaiming again, "Many years, many years." John, Catherine and I left the hall with Isaac, escorted by the Varangian guards back to our rooms in the Boukoleon Palace. The servants saw the other guests out, to make their own way home through the city's streets.

⚜

I WATCHED AS ISAAC SURVEYED THE SINGLE ROOM OF THE treasury that held the empire's valuables, such as they were, an hour past dawn the next morning. The air in this underground chamber smelled musty and mixed unpleasantly with the odor of sulfur from the torches. His eyes narrowed when he reached to flip up the lid of a half-empty chest containing more cheap copper obols than silver miliaresion and gold nomisma and solidi. The few other wooden chests in the room held the same jumbled contents.

"This is all there is? I thought the palace had more than one treasure room. Are you sure?" Isaac asked Michael the chartoularios, or record keeper, of the treasuries, who had escorted him, Catherine, John, and me to this storeroom.

The chartoularios, a gray bureaucrat a few years older than Isaac himself, would not meet the new emperor's incredulous eyes.

"Yes, lord, it's all. You can check the other rooms, but you'll not find even a single obol. The rooms are so empty the mice don't even scurry into them. The eparch will bring in the day's tariffs later, but the palace does have expenses, so there won't be much left after paying them."

"What happened?" Isaac asked.

"Sir," the bland little man began, "I did only what the emperors or empresses told me to. They asked for money; my job was to give it to them and keep the records."

The muscles in Isaac's jaw looked tight under his beard. It had turned a sandy color from its previous foxlike red now that he was fifty years old. He did not say another word, gave a curt nod to the chartoularios, strode up the stairs and out into the warm September air.

Catherine, John, and I followed him onto the lawn outside. The fresh air dispelled the dank odors lingering from the underground vaults. I looked at the dozen or so men standing watch. The treasure house's meager contents did not warrant such protection.

Catherine spoke first, seething with disappointment.

"I cannot believe that is all there is."

"I heard rumors that the treasury had shrunk, was not as full as it once was, but nothing like this," I said. My inheritance of the Dalassenus family warehouse meant I was more familiar with the city's commercial elements than my husband or Isaac, both of them soldiers, were. And Catherine, proud daughter of Bulgarian royalty, had not the slightest notion of how wealth accumulated, desiring only to be kept comfortable. Still, even I'd had no idea how bad it was.

"Anna, when did you hear that?" Isaac asked me in a voice

angry with shattered illusions. His eyes seemed sunken in shadow, his cheeks ashen under his beard.

I thought back to the years when taxes had been raised. Our old warehouse manager, Samuel, like so many others, had been arrested on a false charge of theft and only freed when I paid the eparch what was, in effect, a ransom. Then there were the whispers about loans from the Venetians. It must go back at least that far.

I shook my head. "I'm not sure, five or six years. Could be seven."

The new emperor grunted in disgust.

"We can't change what's done," said John. "But we do need more than what's there now."

Isaac's face was carved in stone. Only yesterday, the patriarch had crowned him in a majestic service in the Hagia Sophia, with celebratory races at the Hippodrome and the evening's banquet following. Now I thought he must feel like he had won a horserace only to have the horse die under him.

He still had to pay the soldiers who had fought for him to win the throne. I'd lent Isaac a hundred thousand gold solidi, some of the money he had needed, but the men would rightly expect more from the victor. And the armies in the borderlands were in desperate need of rebuilding after a decade of neglect. I had little of my inheritance left now and felt angry and sick to think Isaac might never have the funds to repay my assistance.

Isaac ran his hand over the back of his neck and closed his eyes in thought. The three of us watched our new emperor for some sign of direction. We had all spent our entire lives viewing the emperor as somehow set apart from and above the rest of mankind. Already I could see the reality of Isaac's new role making us more deferential to him and reluctant to give our opinions.

I noticed one of the court officials approaching from the corner of my eye, bowing several times as he neared. It was Michael Psellus, the unctuous man who had negotiated with

Isaac just a few days earlier, trying to deter him from pushing the inept old emperor, Michael VI, off the throne. Psellus was a court fixture who had survived in the Great Palace longer than any emperor I'd known with a clever mix of servility and self-serving advice.

Isaac put a hand up to keep him at some distance before speaking to us in quiet tones.

"I need to get a clear picture of where matters stand. John, I want you to join me while we talk with Psellus and whatever other palace secretaries we can find."

"Of course," said John.

"Isaac, I need to be there too," said Catherine. She turned to me, waving her hand in dismissal, "Anna, I'm sure you need to see to your children."

Catherine, the daughter of a king and married to the older brother, had always been condescending. I may have hoped for better, but I realized now nothing was changed. I gritted my teeth and murmured, "Of course, Augusta."

҈

I HID MY INDIGNATION AND FORCED A PLEASANT FACE. Perhaps I was just Isaac's sister-in-law, but he had needed my inheritance to pay the soldiers fighting for him to reach the throne. I would not disappear into the background. I was determined to find my own place in the Great Palace.

The first place I needed to be was with the children. The eunuchs had hastily assembled a nursery in the Boukoleon Palace for the many children now living there. Aside from my own brood of six, John's orphaned niece Anastasia and Catherine's orphaned niece, Marie of Bulgaria, were there. My friend Eudokia had learned only the day before that she and her children would be joining us. The palace eunuchs had no experience with children since the last infant living inside the palace walls had been Empress Theodora, who had died a year earlier in her seventies. My pace quickened while contemplating what chaos might await me.

The situation could have been worse. Anastasia, whom we had been raising since her parents died, was changing baby Alexios's diaper with the assistance of my daughter Marie who we called Marina. Catherine's six-year old Bulgarian niece, Marie, squatted beside my son, trying to distract him with a toy horse. Alexios squirmed about, full of mischief, while the girls struggled with him until I gave him the maternal glare that all children recognize as serious.

Manuel and Isaac were wrestling, as boys their age do, until I sent them outside. I instructed a eunuch to find them wooden swords with which to practice. I made a mental note to find a retired soldier to train the boys. The twins, four-year old Theodora and Donya, were sitting with their dolls and were sticky with the honeyed treats they had been given. The next thing I would have to do was give the eunuchs and other servants instructions on the appropriate diet for children.

Little Marie, Catherine's niece, appeared beside me, looking like she wanted to help. I realized then I would go a little mad if I didn't think of something else to call her.

"Marie, would you like it if I called you Marie of Bulgaria since that is where your father was from?" I asked. It was a mouthful, but it would lessen the confusion among the many Maries, and it was the best I could think of in that moment.

She blushed a vivid pink with pride, then smiled and nodded, "Yes, Lady Anna."

"Lovely. Now, please find me two wet cloths with which to clean up these messy girls, would you?"

"I will be right back," she answered.

I looked after the child, smiling at her sweet earnestness. A small sense of accomplishment filled me as the nursery came to order, and I could almost, *almost* forget about the casual dismissal Catherine had given me earlier.

❦

THAT EVENING JOHN AND I DINED WITH ISAAC AND
Catherine and their daughter, Marika, in the emperor's rooms.
Isaac's brow was furrowed and his mouth was turned down as we
sat down, but he said little. John and Catherine were just as
tight-lipped, leaving Marika and me wondering what had
happened. After the servants were dismissed and we had some
privacy, Isaac erupted.

"If I had known what incompetent fools were sitting on
the throne, I would have rebelled years ago. I thought the treasury was bad, but then I saw all the dispatches from the governors of the eastern themes begging for reinforcements and
supplies, requests sent for years, I felt like going over to the
Church of the Holy Apostles and stripping the silver off Zoe's
tomb."

Empress Zoe, dead these past seven years, and her three
husbands had wantonly squandered the empire's wealth, but
even Catherine raised an eyebrow at such sacrilegious talk.

"I suppose you could, but it wouldn't make much difference
given how much you need," Catherine said.

"I'm not ruling it out. Yet. Catherine, I need you to review
palace expenses and see what can be cut back. It seems like I'm
tripping over servants every time I turn around. We need to pare
those costs to the bone."

Catherine's eyes widened, but she nodded. She had rarely
worried about money. I didn't think she had any idea how to
economize.

Isaac glanced over at me. "Anna, perhaps you could help her
with that."

"I'd be happy to," I replied.

"John, I want you to get the eparch of the city in here. Find
out how much he collects in taxes each year, each month, even
each day. And the harbormasters as well. For God's sake, make
sure we get every nomisma and obol owed. I'll go over the tax

records for the themes; I suspect some of the governors may have miscalculated how much to send to the capital."

Isaac stuck a fork in the fish on his plate, then flung the fork down in disgust. He stood and stormed out. The rest of us finished our meal in silence.

❧

CATHERINE AND I STARTED TOGETHER AT THE TASK ISAAC set for us, but she soon left the real work to me. She had no head for numbers, or sense of organization, and agreed to any suggestions I made. I was happier managing on my own without her interference.

The biggest challenge was the eunuchs. My experience with those of "the third sex" was limited to their choirs in the Hagia Sophia where they sang beautifully. Now, I realized the palace stewards—all eunuchs—controlled the money spent in each individual area and were loath to give up that control. Many of them took advantage of the lack of oversight, feasting and accumulating great wealth under their rulers' noses.

I accompanied a eunuch named Georgios on my first visit to the palace's valuable imperial wardrobe storerooms. He pulled open the door to one, which then almost fell on top of me because of a loose hinge. The garments the room held were of the first-quality silk, used only for the imperial family, or of the softest wool, often embroidered with gold and silver threads and decorated with gems. They should have received the utmost care. Cedar lined the rooms, with fennel leaves and lavender hung throughout to deter moths, although dust covered the dried herbs. Some of the garments hanging within showed damage from insects.

"These might need a little mending," said Georgios as I looked askance at the gaping holes where moths had feasted.

I raised an eyebrow and glanced at Georgios's soft, plump hands that appeared to never have held a needle. His own robe was the finest unblemished silk, and he wore gold rings on both manicured hands.

"How long has that door needed repair?" I asked.

He blinked at me, as though he only then noticed its dilapidated state.

"It's been this way as long as I've been here."

Most of the rest of the palace complex had similar problems. I came to realize that while eunuchs may have had opportunities for the sins of lust and fornication cut from them when castrated, it only made more room for the sins of greed, sloth, and gluttony to take root. My eyes almost popped out of my head when I saw how much they spent on trifles. The records showed exorbitant amounts had been paid for piddling purchases, as much as a gold nomisma for a few fish, when that coin could have bought the fisherman's entire boat. I ended up pensioning off several of the eunuchs, and none continued to have financial responsibilities. Except for Thomas.

Thomas wore no rings, and his clothes were plain. He was in charge of the eunuchs who were the palace's gardeners. Not a glorious assignment for any of those men, as I called them since they came into the world as men. There seemed to be only one qualification for the job of gardener. The surgeons who made them eunuchs were not always careful in their cutting, sometimes damaging other parts of the anatomy that could leave them incontinent. All of the gardeners assigned outside work suffered from this embarrassing problem, although Thomas perhaps least of all.

Thomas and his men kept the palace's grounds looking exquisite. The marble footpaths had cracks, but they did not allow a single weed between them. The rosebushes were trimmed and dead leaves whisked away. The rest of the palace complex, as old as it was, had some tired or shabby buildings, but the gardens sparkled.

I surprised him when I first visited his small office on a chilly fall day. It was little more than a shed, rakes and shovels resting in a corner at the back. Thomas sat on a stool scratching notes into a journal with his quill when he glanced up and saw me.

"Caesarissa," he began and stood up, his rough work clothes stained with dirt and sweat. The stool fell backward onto the floor. "Welcome. I didn't know you would be coming by. Please have a seat." He gestured to a stool on the opposite side of his worn desk while righting his own that had tumbled over.

I looked around. This was a workroom, not a comfortable office with cushioned chairs and braziers for heat.

"A little chilly in here," I commented.

"I'm outside most of the time. Not much point in wasting money on charcoal for heat then, but I can get a brazier for you."

"No, no, that's not necessary," I said, warming to this thrifty eunuch. "What were you just writing in?"

He looked down at the journal. "It's just my schedule of work for the year. To make sure it all gets done on time. Otherwise, it's easy to forget. We take care of the palace's kitchen gardens, and I have a schedule for that, too. I keep track of all my spending here."

I picked up the book and looked through its neat pages, adding the amounts listed in it together. It looked like he spent about as much in a year as the wardrobe master did in a month. Each month, indeed each week, had work scheduled with notations about what tools were needed for each chore. I looked into earnest brown eyes that reminded me of a loyal dog.

"I'd like to see the kitchen gardens. Would you mind showing me?"

I observed Thomas on our walk over. He looked to be about thirty and kept his brown hair almost as short as a monk's. The time he spent outside left his beardless face tanned. He was muscular, unlike the flabbiness of Georgios and many other eunuchs I had encountered. He chattered on about his planting schedule as we walked, but stopped occasionally to speak with one of the other gardeners.

The kitchen garden was located between the interior walls built by Emperor Nikephoros Phocas and the Great Palace's main walls. This area also held an old, rarely used church, not far from the promontory overlooking the Bosphoros. I heard squawks from a chicken coop in one distant corner and a humming beehive in another. A pair of apple trees still had a few leaves on them. The gardeners had turned the land over for winter, with just cabbages, turnips and some tired, spindly herbs still growing. The garden was so tidy I half suspected Thomas and his staff had frightened away the weeds until I noticed him surreptitiously pulling a tiny one that had dared to show its green leaves.

We sat on a sunny bench next to the old church. The building provided some protection from the north wind.

"The emperor is concerned that palace expenses are higher than they need to be," I said.

Thomas made a small grimace. "I suspect he may be correct in that. Caesarissa, I will do whatever I can to reduce what we spend on the gardens."

That startled me. "No, no, that's not what I was trying to say. I could see from your journal that you waste little."

I looked into his earnest face, so unlike the those of the other eunuchs accustomed to privileges and perquisites.

"Thomas, do you think you could take on additional responsibilities?"

⚜

ONE NOVEMBER DAY, CATHERINE AND I WERE WALKING from the Boukoleon to the Daphne Palace, where Isaac kept his office, when a familiar figure approached us. It was Gagik, the former Armenian king who had saved John's life years earlier and now served in Isaac's army. Flushed with excitement, he bowed deeply to Catherine before sharing his news with us.

"Isaac's appointed me dux of the Lycandus theme," he said.

Lycandus was not the richest theme in the empire, but the military governorship of any theme was a high honor. Also, it was not far from his old home in the city of Ani. Gagik had earned Isaac's trust many times over since he'd arrived in Constantinople a dozen years earlier.

"I'm pleased for you," Catherine said. "Congratulations."

He gave a lopsided grin. "Thank you. It won't be an easy post, not like the Opsikion theme. Turks have been raiding there, so I'll be busy. But it's in the east, in the mountains. My wife and I have missed living in the mountains. Maybe not home, but close."

I gave him my best wishes and watched him walk to the palace gates to share his news at home.

"I'm glad to hear about this," I said. "Gagik's been a good friend to us."

Catherine gave me a sidelong glance and shrugged. Isaac often included his wife in discussions about the empire's business.

"There weren't many candidates willing to take on Lycandus. The few who might have would have asked for more gold than Isaac could pay them. Isaac knew Gagik wanted the promotion and wouldn't be greedy."

This was one of the cold calculations emperors needed to make every day. All soldiers expect to be in harm's way, and no one forced Gagik to take it. He was an outstanding soldier and I silently wished him luck in this new assignment.

ISAAC SOON REALIZED HE NEEDED MORE DRASTIC MEASURES than just cutting palace expenses.

"That Old Man really went crazy handing out gifts to his bureaucrat buddies," Isaac said irritably one night, speaking of Emperor Michael VI, whom he had deposed. "That along with the higher salaries he paid his many friends siphoned away a lot of gold. He was stupid to think that paying those mannequins who contribute nothing, while not paying me and the other generals who are fighting wars, was going to work out well for him."

Isaac revoked those gifts and cut the salaries, receiving many loud complaints. The treasury's supply of gold coins grew, but progress was painfully slow. The news from the borderlands only increased the sense of urgency we all felt.

First, Isaac's old friend Katakalon Kekaumenos sent word that the barbarians Pechenegs were stirring up trouble in the north and begged for weapons and men. Then in the east, Catherine's brother, Troian, skirmished with Turks raiding and conquering even well-fortified towns. The Turks had begun raiding Roman lands when I lived in exile in Amaseia with my grandparents at Uncle Costas's estate near Amasea. A couple of rogue Turks had even attacked me there when I was sixteen. It was only the fortuitous appearance of Isaac and John that saved me from being kidnapped. I worried about the growing presence of the Turks in that region where my cousin, Damien, and his family still lived.

Isaac revealed another problem regarding finances one night at dinner. He'd sat down without his usual greeting, tight-lipped and flushed. Catherine and John joined Marika and me at the table but said nothing and avoided our eyes. Marika and I shared a questioning look, but neither of us knew what to make of the ominous silence that continued as dinner was served.

Deciding to venture into what could be dangerous territory, I asked, "What news today?"

"What news?" Isaac snorted. "Just the usual news that I get everyday about this miserable empire."

Catherine reached over to pat his hand, for once trying to calm Isaac. "It's not that terrible."

"Really? Not that terrible?" Isaac slammed his fist on the table. "Being handed an overdue bill for two hundred thousand gold nomisma is not that terrible? I suppose you have that much lying around somewhere?" His eyes flashed with anger.

Catherine cringed and pulled her hand back.

John looked at me and said, "We received a delegation from the Venetians today. They presented us with a bill signed by Emperor Constantine Monomachos and confirmed by Constantine Ducas as the leader of the Senate at that time. No one, including Psellus, who wrote the document, or Ducas, had thought to mention this debt to Isaac. Conveniently, both of them had excuses to be elsewhere today."

Everyone knew Monomachos had spent the most extravagantly of Empress Zoe's three husbands. I gaped at him, still shocked by the huge amount of the debt, although not as much at the complicity of Ducas and Psellus. Samuel, the old Jew who had managed my family's warehouse near the harbor until his death from plague, had once mentioned rumors about such a loan, but no one would have guessed so much. Isaac must have felt overwhelmed with this huge additional burden given the still meager contents of the treasury and the empire's other demands.

Isaac shook his head, teeth gritted. "I have no choice now," he said bitterly. "I'm going to have to raise taxes."

⚜

THE CITY RESIDENTS, ONCE SO OPTIMISTIC ABOUT ISAAC, soon grumbled and complained at the higher taxes, up by ten percent. The people of Constantinople were ever ready to express their opinions about any emperor, and God have mercy on you if you lost their favor. They weren't yet ready to riot, but John thought it wise for me and for the children to stay inside the palace walls.

John was constantly at Isaac's side, advising and supporting his efforts to correct the mistakes of his recent predecessors. Their long days meant the two of them returned to work after dinner. John often did not get to bed until the middle of the dark winter nights. By January, he had bags under his eyes and could be short-tempered at small provocations. It had been a demanding eight months since the rebellion had first started Isaac on the road to the throne, with rarely a day to rest. The strain of it weighed on my husband.

I was pregnant again, due in the late spring, and the fatigue of carrying a child sent me to bed early one cold night. I was asleep when John slipped into bed next to me but was soon roused as he could not find a comfortable spot, turning back and forth.

"Are you feeling sick?" I whispered.

"You're awake? I'm sorry, I didn't mean to disturb you." He wrapped an arm around me and sighed.

"What's wrong?"

More heavy breathing. "It's nothing. Go back to sleep."

Whatever was the problem, it was *something*. I would have no sleep until I found out what that something was.

"You need to tell me what's wrong. Now."

John lay there for a moment before deciding what to say.

"It's just this isn't what I expected. Work I expected, but all the politics, the backbiting, the people trying to manipulate you —that I didn't expect. And all of a sudden, I have friends who can't be nicer to me, all with their hands out. It was great until I realized these men never acknowledged me before my brother became emperor. I don't feel like I can trust anyone."

I lay there for a moment before responding in a low voice. "You can trust me."

He leaned in to kiss my cheek. "Yes, I know I can trust you. But everyone else? Sometimes it feels like even Isaac isn't being honest with me. And the money problems just get worse everyday."

"It's only been a few months," I said, stroking his hand. "You're learning how the government works; it takes time and practice. Isaac is learning too, and he trusts you more than anyone else. A year from now, you might be surprised at how easy it will seem. "

"I hope you're right."

I felt his tension ease and he pulled me closer. John's breath soon grew even and he slept while I lay awake in his arms. I hoped I *was* right, but my husband's naive misgivings worried me.

CHAPTER 2

Early 1058

I heard two familiar voices echoing down from the other end of a long corridor in the Boukoleon one afternoon. I had just left the nursery after checking on the twins who both had a slight fever and a drippy nose. The voices, though, came from an alcove overlooking the Marmara, where the setting sun glowed through the glass, stretching the couple's shadows out into the hall. The man's voice was wheedling, pressing; the woman's clipped responses betrayed her nervousness. I approached and peered around the corner.

Constantine Ducas held the arm of Isaac's daughter, Marika, bending close to her as she attempted to push away from him. A bolt of rage shot through me. Without thinking, without hesitating, I walked into the alcove thrust myself between the two of them.

"Marika," I said, glaring directly at Ducas, "I believe your mother is looking for you."

Ducas's eyes bulged at the sight of me. Sputtering, he struggled to maintain control, while dropping his hands and stepping back from Marika.

I had known Ducas since I was a child. He had been tall, handsome, and blond, with my cousin Xene in love with him. That was before he'd hounded her to her death. Now, his face was flabby with middle age, his hair thin and beard a dingy gray. No young girl would be in love with him again, least of all Marika. But that would count for little if he forced himself on her.

"Lady Marika, I so enjoyed our chat before the Caesarissa interrupted us. We will have to speak another time." He turned and left, pointedly ignoring me. His footsteps echoed as he retreated down the hall and took the stairs to exit the building.

"I can't believe what just happened." She stood white-faced with her jaw set tight, the same way Isaac did when he was upset. "That disgusting man was trying to kiss me."

Ducas had once told me that his ambitions were to one day rule the empire himself. I realized then that Marika was simply an easy step on the climb to reach that pinnacle.

I could feel her trembling when I put an arm around her. "Marika, you need to avoid him. You must always be sure to have a companion with you."

"He started telling me how pretty I am, how fond he is of me, how much he respects Papa. He kept getting closer until he grabbed my arm and was pulling me to him." She shuddered, still incredulous at the man's behavior.

"That's terrible," I said. "It's a good thing I happened by when I did, otherwise something worse could have happened."

"I swear he was going to kiss me when you arrived. It was so horrible." Marika grimaced. "He's older than Papa, and his wife is pregnant. How can he think I would want that?"

"He doesn't care about what you want, only what he wants."

Ducas would not hesitate to think up some reason to divorce Eudokia if the opportunity arose to marry Marika. Eudokia got pregnant with no trouble, unlike Xene, whose infertility had led

Ducas to plan to divorce her before her unexpected death. Other men had divorced their wives and forced them into a monastery so they could wed the daughter of the emperor. Marika needed a solution.

"We should speak to your mother about this, but don't tell your father, and don't tell Eudokia. It would only complicate your father's life, and I think the augusta and I can take care of this."

How to deal with Ducas and his ambition? He wanted himself and his children, whether Eudokia's or Marika's, on the throne. The situation reminded me of all I had learned from Uncle Costas on maneuvering in a chess game. We needed to move a strategic piece between Ducas and Marika.

Catherine was adamant.

"Ducas is not someone I want as a husband for Marika. Just because he supported Isaac's rebellion doesn't give him the right to marry my daughter. Even so, Isaac can't afford to offend him now when so many in the city are angry about higher taxes. We need to find a way to let him know he's absolutely unwelcome, without jeopardizing Isaac's relationship with him."

I made the suggestion of a dinner invitation he would not refuse.

A few days later, Catherine and I made sure we were walking to the Daphne so as to encounter Ducas on his way in.

"Senator," Catherine began, "would you and your lovely wife join us for dinner? Eudokia is such a delightful lady, and she and our daughter have become such close friends. You know they share everything? Really, everything. Almost as much as she does with me." Her regal formality, expecting instant agreement, did not invite discussion. "I've also requested that your wife's uncle, the patriarch, attend."

Catherine paused, letting her meaning seep in. She wore the gold embroidered gown and red shoes only an empress, the augusta, could wear. She looked and sounded every inch the proud daughter of a king and the wife of an emperor.

Ducas's fleshy face reddened and he gave me a brief but angry sideways glance.

"Augusta Catherine, thank you for the kind invitation," he mumbled, making a deep bow to her.

"I am so glad you and your wife will join us and the patriarch," Catherine said in a condescending imperial voice. This was one time I appreciated her superior manner.

Ducas bowed again, and we continued past him into the Daphne.

Catherine sniffed. "That should keep the old lecher on his best behavior for a while."

"Yes, but the best solution would be for Marika to get married."

"I know that," she said, pursing her lips. "But she refuses to consider any of the men I've suggested. Isaac won't push her, and even if he would, he's got too much on his mind now to think about finding the right husband for her."

The unfortunate difficulty was that Marika would not give up her dream of the young naval officer Michael Maurex. Michael may have been talented, hardworking, and ambitious, but he was lowborn and that was not good enough for Empress Catherine. She often spoke of Marika one day inheriting the throne with her husband. That man, she was sure, could not be a sailor such as Michael. Marika would consider wedding someone else only if Isaac insisted on it. If she waited too long, though, Marika could turn into a pawn for Ducas or some other ambitious man seeking the throne.

※

I USED THE EXCUSE OF MY OWN PREGNANCY TO AVOID THE dinner with Ducas and Eudokia, so I did not hear what had transpired at it until the next day.

"Ducas had an interesting idea last night," he said as he dressed, "one he didn't mention until after the patriarch left."

"He did?" I asked, feeling cynical. I thought it unlikely that anything good could come from Ducas.

"Yes. He suggested that Isaac approach Keroularios and ask for a portion of the Church's wealth. There's plenty of land and gold there, and Ducas is sure Isaac can convince Keroularios to give it up."

I raised an eyebrow at that. Patriarch Michael Keroularios had a forceful personality, not an agreeable one. He'd even had the temerity to excommunicate the Latin pope in Rome a few years earlier over some nonsense. I was skeptical that he would be willing to give up even a small portion of the Church's wealth. "What did Eudokia say?"

John looked at me blankly. "I don't think she said anything, but she was talking with Catherine when the subject came up."

I sighed. My dress needed letting out again. I seemed to get large sooner with each pregnancy, but at least my physician, Maria Kourtikios, said it wasn't twins this time.

I glanced at my husband and wondered if he believed the patriarch would consent to raid the monasteries' storehouses for their gold chalices and patens. Isaac needed gold, but I doubted the Church would willingly give it up.

"Isaac agreed with Ducas that this could be a good solution."

"Maybe," I said slowly, "but where will Ducas be if Keroularios disagrees? Isaac will get the blame, not him."

John frowned. "That's true. I'll mention it to Isaac. It's just he's so impatient to put money problems behind him and push back against the Turks and Pechenegs. He wants to fight battles, not fret over money."

⁕

THE GREAT PALACE SOON MADE UP FOR THE MANY DECADES without children inside its walls. Eudokia and I had our babies in the spring; my seventh was a son, Adrian, named after my grandfather, and Eudokia's fourth, a daughter, Theodora.

My cousin, Romanus Diogenes, left on assignment to Armenia at about the same time. His wife, Anna, whom we called Anya, was another of Catherine's nieces. With Romanus gone, Catherine soon had Anya and their two children in the palace with us.

One afternoon, Catherine appeared with two little girls who looked younger than eight or nine years old. The younger of the two, a sweet-faced child with red-gold hair, stood subdued and shy. The other girl was not so fair, but had sharp eyes that missed nothing.

"Anna, the King of Alania sent his daughter Maria to us, along with her cousin, to be educated and brought up as princesses should be." She glanced around the room at the dozen or so children scampering about. "So I've brought them to join the rest of the children."

"This is Maria," she said, indicating the pretty, petite girl, "and what did you say your name was?" Catherine looked down inquiringly at the other child.

"My name is Irene," she said, giving Augusta Catherine a bold direct look.

"Oh yes, thank you. Girls, this is Lady Anna. She is in charge of the nursery, and she'll be taking care of you."

I seethed inside when Catherine spoke to me as though I were a servant, even forgetting to use my title of Caesarissa. I should have been used to her haughtiness, but it could still infuriate me. Catherine glided away, the very picture of an imperial augusta, back to the Daphne Palace and Isaac's offices. As was her wont, she looked as relieved to be done with the children as Pilate washing his hands.

I took a deep breath to calm down and turned to the little girls. Even bold little Irene had a nervous look in her eyes behind her brave front. I bent down to speak to them.

"Welcome to the palace, Maria and Irene. I am Caesarissa Anna. Let me introduce you to the other children."

⬮

ACCOMPANIED BY A PAIR OF BLACK-ROBED PRIESTS, Michael Keroularios walked the short distance from the patriarch's residence, across the busy Mese, to the Great Palace to meet with Isaac. The patriarch was in his mid-fifties, impeccably dressed in his clerical robes with his dark hair now shot with silver. Isaac was much the same age, but despite the rich imperial garments he had a soldier's aspect. The two men greeted each other as equals with the kiss of peace. The rest of us in attendance, John and I, Catherine, Eudokia and Ducas, Isaac's old friend Katakalon Kekaumenos and his nephew, along with Michael Psellus as secretary, made deep bows of obeisances to the patriarch, kissing his ring and asking for his blessing. Isaac invited his guest to be seated in a chair equal to his own, recognizing the eminent position he held that exceeded any other in the world except the emperor's.

The rest of us stood in respectful silence while servants brought wine and bread for patriarch and emperor. Once the niceties of imperial etiquette were accomplished, Isaac broached the subject at hand. "Your Beatitude, thank you for joining me today. I hope you can provide me with some advice and assistance."

The patriarch put down the elegant blue wine glass he'd been served, and eyed Isaac with a calculating look. "Of course, my son. What is your difficulty?"

"How much do you know about the state of the empire's treasury?"

The patriarch shrugged. "I am not concerned with such worldly matters, my son. I trust the worldly to look after their own affairs."

Isaac's eyebrows rose and he looked as if he was considering whether the patriarch was being honest or deflecting a subject he didn't want to discuss.

Patriarch Michael looked around the room and made a banal comment about the weather.

"Sir, unfortunately, I am one of those poor souls condemned to be concerned about worldly matters," said Isaac with a somber air. "I have grave concerns about the condition of the treasury, and I hope you can assist me."

"I am sure there is nothing I can do to assist you." The patriarch gave Isaac an irritated look and began gathering up his robes. He nodded to the two priests who rose to attention.

"Sir, please hear me out," Isaac said. I suspected the patriarch would have preferred to be gone already, except that protocol demanded he remain while the emperor spoke.

"Those who have sat in this imperial seat in the thirty-two years since Emperor Basil died have not been good stewards of the empire's wealth. The treasury that was full to overflowing when he died is bare. They have squandered all the gold that Basil left."

"No doubt you exaggerate. It is impossible for the treasury to be empty. Ours is the richest kingdom in the world."

Isaac frowned. "The kingdom may have wealth, but none of it is in the treasury."

"I fail to see why you are coming to me with this matter. Again, I do not concern myself with worldly affairs such as taxes and treasury," he said with a dismissive wave of his hand.

I thought that was disingenuous. He had concerned himself enough with the world to help get rid of the last emperor. Of course, Michael VI had shown no respect for this proud patriarch, thus losing his allegiance. Keroularios grimaced and picked at a speck of dust on his robe, before glaring hard into Isaac's eyes.

Isaac's face turned as cold and hard as a piece of porphyry marble.

"Your Beatitude, the empire's treasury is empty. The Turks, the Bulgarians, and the Pechenegs are all attacking our borders every day. What money we have is not enough to pay our soldiers, much less supply them." Isaac paused to let his words sink in before continuing.

"Sir, I am asking you now, much as Christ said to 'ask and it shall be given to you.' I need gold for our soldiers. The Church has gold in its vaults and income from the lands the monasteries hold." He paused. "I've cut what costs I can. The taxes levied on the people are already high; I can't push them higher. There's no place else I can go other than the Church."

"There'd just be a few grumbles if you raised taxes; it would pass. Or what about the Venetians? I'm sure they would lend you the money."

"Your Beatitude, you know the taxes are already higher than they have been in a hundred years. And the Venetians are a big part of the problem. Psellus here can explain how they lent Emperor Monomachos enormous amounts for all the grand buildings he erected. We can't even repay them what we owe now, as well as pay our armies defending our borders, as General Kekaumenos can tell you, when we have so little income. No, I've given this shortfall much consideration. Our best option, our only option, is for the monasteries to share their wealth."

The patriarch stood, red-faced with anger. "No," he said in a raised voice and waving a dismissive hand. "Your greedy exaggerations do you no credit. We are the Roman Empire, and none is wealthier. This discussion is finished. I can assure you that neither I, nor the Church, will be giving you any of its wealth. It would be pure theft from the Almighty. You must find a different way out of your difficulties."

Isaac glared at the patriarch, outraged that the man would defy him.

The emperor's eyes narrowed, his voice low and dangerous. "I assure you, Your Beatitude, that I have looked for alternatives. None has presented itself. The Church will provide us with gold."

IT DIDN'T HAPPEN IMMEDIATELY. JOHN AND PSELLUS FIRST made up lists of the wealthiest monasteries with the largest tracts of land and holding the richest endowments from patrons. Psellus was diligent in his list-making. He had no love for the patriarch after the man had made dangerous accusations of paganism against him some years earlier. Psellus's smoldering resentment left him eager to destroy the churchman, and his thorough survey of the monasteries overlooked nothing.

Most monasteries were small, humbly endowed, with a few monks living quietly within their walls and serving the poor, with little to contribute to the treasury. But it was common knowledge that the best-known ones had received rich gifts of gold, precious objects, or vast farms and vineyards that were exempted from taxation once the monastery owned them. St. John Stoudion, St. Demetrios in Thessaloniki, Hosios Loukas in Greece, Mt. Olympus in Bithynia, and at least forty others. All, even those favored by Isaac and his family, received instructions from the emperor.

They were allowed to keep enough land to feed their monks and the local poor, but the rest was to be turned over to the imperial treasury. Each monastery was limited to a few fine gold and silver vessels to use in the Divine Liturgy, with the remainder sent to Isaac to be melted into coins.

Isaac wanted to be out fighting battles, pushing back the invaders threatening our borders. He hated spending so much time trying to find gold. He was angry with Catherine over any money she spent and asked me each day about where we could cut expenses. His words now held more vinegar than honey.

"These monasteries should be grateful to me. They will have fewer worries now that they no longer have so much gold to guard or so many fields to till," he said, his face dark.

Of course, the patriarch instructed the monasteries not to remit anything to the emperor, but the wiser hegoumeni made at least a small show of compliance. They would send some dented silver patens, bowls, chalices, a chest full of the copper follis with little value with a few random shaved gold solidi scattered amongst them. The fields turned over were distant from those monasteries and unproductive.

My husband, John, told me that he would be taking a troop of soldiers to Bithynia for a few weeks to, as Isaac said, "encourage compliance with the imperial edict."

"I'm not relishing this trip," John said glumly as he mulled over our chess game. "I hate scavenging in monasteries, but Isaac can do nothing without their gold. Keroularios should have agreed to help." He nervously stroked the small enamel-and-gold cross he wore on a chain around his neck.

I looked over the board with its game pieces—knights and castles, kings and bishops, pawns. The king had little ability to win anything without the other pieces. The king could lose some of his pieces, but the more he lost, the more difficult winning became. I thought about what pieces Isaac had lost in his chess game. His bishops were gone with Keroularios, and probably some of the pawns, angry at taxes. Isaac still held his castles and the knights—the generals who supported him.

I looked up at my husband's face, recalling how I had first gotten to know him over a chessboard. Now his once bright red hair was faded to a tawny color. John was in his forties, years younger than Isaac, but he looked even more anxious than his brother did. He thought of himself as a good man, faithful to the Church. The need to expropriate Church property made him miserable.

I tried to reason with him. "Ask yourself what the patriarch is doing with all that gold. Isaac is only asking the wealthiest monasteries to contribute, not the small, poor ones. Those monks took vows of poverty. Don't blame yourself or Isaac for what's happening."

John frowned and pushed away from the chessboard after toppling over his king and admitting defeat. "I don't blame anyone but Keroularios, but I still don't like having to do it."

꧁꧂

PASCHA WAS JUST A FEW DAYS AWAY WHEN MY COUSIN Romanus returned to the city, dusty and travel-stained from his assignment in Armenia. He strode into the nursery to excited shouts from his children, Theophano, called Thea, and Constantine, whom we called Costas. Moments later, he embraced his wife, Anya, before bowing to Catherine, who was there on one of her rare visits.

"Augusta Catherine, I apologize for not changing into more appropriate attire for a palace visit, but I was eager to reunite with my family. I hope you don't mind if they return with me to our home now." Romanus smiled down at Anya, his arm wrapped around her waist.

"Of course not, General," said Catherine. "My niece has been watching for you since we received word you were on the way. I believe they've been ready to leave for days."

My daughter Theodora was at my side then, tugging at my dress.

"Is Costas leaving?" She looked bereft. He was just a year older than her five years and still tolerated her following him around.

"Yes, dear, but he'll be back soon. You still have your sisters to play with." I gave her a quick kiss to comfort her before she wandered off, still unhappy at her playmate's departure.

Servants scurried about while the nursery's remaining children played. I noticed that Eudokia stood apart, a hand resting on her son Michael's shoulder. She looked miserable and ignored in a corner with eyes downcast. She brightened when my little Isaac came over to Michael and asked him to play. Easygoing Isaac was never much bothered by Michael's oddities.

And Michael was odd. A sweet child, but slow to grow, slow to learn, easily frightened. He was not half-witted, nor was he sickly—or no more so than other children. Maybe just weak in a world that scorned the weak. He might make a good priest.

Catherine left to wish her niece's family farewell, and the other children settled down. I walked over to speak to Eudokia.

"Are you all right? You look upset,"

Her mouth twisted into a half grimace. She shook her head.

"It isn't fair."

"What isn't?" I asked.

"To see your cousin and his family so happy, and mine . . ." she trailed off, looking dejected. "It's been weeks since Constantine bothered to see our children. I know he's with the emperor, but he won't spare a moment for them and barely any time for me. Your cousin, though, wouldn't even take the time to bathe and put on fresh clothes. He couldn't wait to get back to his wife and children."

"I'm sorry," I said, putting my hand on her arm. I was sympathetic. Eudokia had many blessings, but her husband wasn't one of them. Ducas's wealth bought her the finest silk gowns with exquisite embroidery, almost as fine as anything Catherine wore, and yet the gold bracelets encircling her wrists were more like shackles.

"Not your fault. I was my uncle's pawn. Now, my husband is sniffing around the emperor's daughter and looking for an excuse to divorce me and marry her. It's humiliating."

So she knew.

"That won't happen. Catherine wants a prestigious marriage for Marika, and certainly not one to Constantine. He's older than Isaac, and he's already been married twice. The Church won't permit a third one."

She gave me a skeptical look that I could not blame her for.

JOHN COMPLETED HIS TASKS FOR ISAAC AND RETURNED home by April. Isaac's persistence and John's military help went a long way to returning the treasury to a healthy state by September, the first anniversary of his crowning. The soldiers on our borders received long overdue back pay, along with desperately needed supplies. Isaac also made payments to the Venetians for much of what they were owed.

The patriarch still fumed about what he called the "raping and pillaging" of the churches, although he only spoke of it publicly in the ambo when Isaac was not at the Divine Liturgy. Isaac took to attending when he knew Keroularios led the services at the Hagia Sophia. No one expected the patriarch, even one as bold as this one, to dare speak against Isaac with him standing there. This ploy minimized the patriarch's vocal criticisms and his sway over the many devout people of Constantinople who did not understand Isaac's dilemma. The churchman still kept up a steady drumbeat of criticism of Isaac in private and with friends, and word of his diatribes did make it back to us.

We hoped that over time Keroularios would become more reconciled to Isaac's demands, but his outrage and anger festered. Eudokia told me he complained bitterly when she visited him. For his part, Isaac resented the patriarch's stubborn refusal to understand why he'd been forced to make such demands. They were like two dogs circling a piece of meat, snarling and nipping at each other. The rest of us just wanted to stay out of their way and avoid getting bitten. It was inevitable that eventually one of them would attack and the real fight begin.

Keroularios lunged first on a Sunday in late September, at the Divine Liturgy at the Hagia Sophia. At first it was only the men in the nave who noticed, whispering among themselves as they glimpsed him, heads swiveling to look again to be sure. The sound of whispering and muttering reached us high in the women's gallery. My mouth hung open in disbelief when I saw what he was wearing, as bold as an actor on a stage. Catherine, at first engrossed in her prayers, stood on the green marble empress's circle but soon bent over the balustrade to see what was causing the chatter. She gasped when she saw him.

The patriarch was processing through the church in his usual patriarchal regalia, accompanied by priests and servers with their censers and candles burning. The one difference was that he wore purple socks and shoes. Only the emperor was permitted to wear purple socks and shoes. No one, not even a patriarch, had ever presumed to wear them before. He was insinuating that he was emperor, not Isaac.

The other women with us were all soon peering over the railing to see what was going on, whispering among themselves as much as the men in the nave were. Isaac looked up at us from where he stood with John and the rest of his entourage and gave a nod toward the exit to the palace. We left immediately, following behind him as soon as we could retreat down the long ramp.

It was only when we were behind closed doors that he voiced the anger and frustration that had been building during the year he had been emperor. My brother-in-law's patience had reached its limit.

John and I, Catherine and Marie, the old general Kekaumenos and his nephew, Peter, gathered in Isaac's office in the Daphne. The gray-haired Kekaumenos massaged his maimed hand, mutilated in the same battle that had killed John and Isaac's brother-in-law, Michael Dokeianos, almost ten years earlier.

"You know he's just goading you, trying to force your hand," said the older man.

Isaac raised an eyebrow and nodded.

"You're right. The question is, what does he think I will do? And what is it that I should do?"

"I think you need to get him to abdicate now and ship him off to some remote island," drawled young Peter Kekaumenos. "He's just trouble." Peter was a stocky man, about my height, who had fought alongside his uncle when Isaac took the throne. He had a soldier's preference for blunt speech.

"I know it seems like Keroularios was trying to say he should have the throne, but maybe he had a different message. Maybe he was just trying to say that the Church should rule our behavior, not the emperor." John was looking for any excuse to avoid making matters worse. I felt almost embarrassed at his gullible comment.

"Well, I suppose it's possible," said Peter, "but I doubt it."

The men continued arguing, but after a few minutes I felt too tired to keep listening. I was exhausted from trying to manage the palace's operations, even with Thomas's help. The children in the nursery always needed attention. Baby Adrian had been up several times during the night, and then, just at dawn, one of the nursemaids had woken us saying Alexios had disappeared. That child was smaller than his brothers had been at his age of two, but he had more energy and mischief than the two of them ever had. John and I got up, sick with fear, and searched for him for at least half an hour before I found him throwing sticks and rocks into the Boukoleon harbor.

It was fortunate I found him when I did since he was about to tumble into the deadly water when I scooped him into my arms. I chastised him for scaring his mother, but my heart melted when I saw the fear on his face.

"Sorry, Mama," he said, wrapping his little arms around my neck.

After such a night, with little sleep and an early rising, I was exhausted. The men droned on, and my head lolled back on the chair. Within a few minutes, I was asleep, dreaming of chess games, the little marble pieces gyrating in my head as if in some victory dance.

Someone must have noticed that I had nodded off since I felt a poke.

I heard Isaac speak through a sleepy haze, "How can Keroularios think he could become emperor? It's just crazy."

"Pawns," I responded without thinking.

Every face turned to me, even though I was not exactly sure what I meant.

"What did you say?" asked Isaac.

"She said 'pawns'," answered Catherine. She gave me a thoughtful look.

The dream I'd been having still swam through my head, but the clouds dissipated. "Yes, pawns. The patriarch has no castles, no soldiers, unlike a king does. All Keroularios has are the pawns, the people of Constantinople who believe everything he tells them. They support him."

"That's true," said Isaac. "I need to get him away from them. We need to grab him when he's not in the city, so no one learns of it until after we have his abdication in hand. Then he can retire to a remote monastery somewhere."

Kekaumenos and his nephew exchanged glances.

"I'll start figuring out a plan," said Peter.

CHAPTER 3

Fall 1058 to Summer 1059

Keroularios knew well how to blaze up a smoldering fire. The people of the city, unhappy about Isaac's higher taxes, made a great show of begging the patriarch for his blessing when he passed through the streets, while Isaac dared not venture beyond the Great Palace walls without a guard. Keroularios would use any conversation, any sermon as an excuse to blame all the empire's problems on Emperor Isaac.

The patriarch did not again wear the forbidden purple garments, but paraded through the city as though he ruled, not Isaac. Never before had any patriarch made such an effort to overthrow an emperor. I could not sleep many nights with worrying that mobs might storm the Great Palace.

Keroularios had to be the most popular patriarch in decades. He had a distinguished demeanor and a beguiling influence. He strutted through the streets in his golden robes at the slightest excuse, wearing a beatific expression that belied his worldly ambitions. Priests surrounded him carrying icons and images of saints emblazoned on banners, sprinkling holy water as they passed the pious crowds.

Did Keroularios play chess? He was playing to win but had only pawns. Bishops, though powerful pieces, could not win without knights and castles. Isaac had all the knights and castles.

Isaac held his temper and tongue, biding his time and making no overt challenge to the patriarch. This goaded the priest to increase his criticisms from the Hagia Sophia's marble ambo, as the incense swirled around him. In his pride, he must have thought the emperor humbled. Isaac kept his eye on the man and quietly put his *knights* and *castles* to work in his defense.

His first move was to plant a spy in the patriarch's household to learn his schedule. An opportunity arose when the spy informed him that Keroularios planned to visit the Nine Angels monastery for its official opening ceremony. It lay outside the city's walls in the sparsely populated countryside. The patriarch planned to leave the city in early November, escorted by only a few monks.

Isaac's old friend, Katakalon Kekaumenos, gave control over his soldiers in the Imperial Guard to his nephew, Peter. This enterprising officer took a squad of ten well-armed men to arrest the patriarch and swiftly bundle him onto a ship waiting in the Golden Horn. Keroularios would be held there until he signed the abdication document. The monks with him were to be held in one of the towers in the city's walls until that was accomplished.

Peter and his soldiers carried out the assignment brilliantly, arresting and transporting the angry priest to the ship without being noticed. That part of the operation could not have worked out better. I felt a guilty pleasure at the thought of how Eudokia's uncle, who had condemned her to a marriage with Ducas, was now feeling the heavy hand of authority carrying him off to an unavoidable fate. Not very Christian of me, I suppose, but very human.

Peter reported back to Isaac late the same afternoon.

"That cranky old geezer is on the ship; we're anchored a few miles out in the Marmara. He's kept below decks, out of sight. I told him you wanted his abdication. He outright refused. He's totally unwilling, thinks the people will rally around him. I pointed out that they won't do that if they don't know what's happened to him. He almost spat in my face." The young man looked disgusted. "No question he's stubborn. Got any suggestions on what to do next with him?"

Isaac sat pensively on his throne, stroking his beard and glanced over at Kekaumenos. They had known each other since childhood and Isaac trusted his advice more than any other's.

Kekaumenos massaged his maimed hand before commenting. "Well, we can't let anyone know where he is. Peter, just keep him out of sight with only your most trustworthy men. He's bound to come to his senses in a few days."

Isaac nodded. "I agree. Peter, get back to the ship and explain to Keroularios that I demand his abdication. John, we can't forget his two nephews; they might start asking questions when Keroularios doesn't return. Send men to arrest them, but keep it quiet."

The men nodded agreement.

We all believed that Keroularios would soon realize how his position had changed and that his best recourse would be to accept it.

Two weeks later the impasse continued. Isaac had the patriarch moved to a lonely monastery housing a half dozen elderly monks on a tiny spit of an island Psellus had found in the Marmara. If anything, this made the patriarch's defiance worse. Peter relayed that Keroularios not only continued to refuse to abdicate, but tried to convince Peter to take his side.

"He told me that if God wanted him to leave his patriarchal

seat, He would have done so without the emperor's help. Then he blessed me and said he must return to his prayers. That man is stubborn as a mule. If he wasn't a priest, I'd be tempted to beat him the way I would a mule."

"He's behaving ridiculously," said Catherine, her mouth tight with outrage over his defiance of her husband, the emperor. "He has to realize that Isaac will not allow him to return. He's simply delaying the inevitable."

"Is there someone we can send that he might listen to?" asked John in his gentle voice, his forehead lined with concern. My husband desired peace between emperor and patriarch, though I knew he doubted it could ever happen with this patriarch.

I pressed my lips closed in frustration, even while conceding that John's suggestion might work. I looked around the room. Everyone else had a reason to dislike Keroularios. Psellus had his old grudge against him, almost as old as mine on Eudokia's behalf. Isaac and Catherine were outraged at the priest's blatant attempt to control the throne. Kekaumenos and his nephew gave Isaac their unquestioning loyalty as their emperor and friend.

Michael Psellus cleared his throat before making a suggestion. "I think John Xiphilinos might be willing to speak to him; I know one or two other priests who could accompany him. It's worth trying."

Xiphilinos had been a respected judge before becoming a monk about five years earlier, so it was a sensible suggestion. Psellus had his uses.

The next morning a ship carrying Xiphilinos and two other priests set sail for Keroularios's wind-swept island. They returned late that afternoon.

"Your Majesty, the patriarch is adamant he will not abdicate. He appears even more stubborn than before, preaching the word of God to us, fasting, his strength of will undiminished . . ."

Xiphilinos's voice trailed off apologetically. "We tried to convince him, but with no success."

Isaac flushed red at that. He dismissed the priests, leaving only family, Kekaumenos and his nephew, and Psellus in the room.

"I need ideas. I want that man off the patriarchal throne," Isaac said in a clipped voice.

Catherine scowled. "Can't we just appoint another patriarch and send Keroularios into exile? Someplace in the Aegean? Does he actually have to abdicate?"

"Perhaps, but who would be willing to take the post under such conflicted circumstances?" I pointed out.

Psellus quirked an eyebrow before speaking.

"Augusta Catherine," he began, "Lady Anna is correct; we could do that, but there would always be a question of the legitimacy of the new patriarch. We should avoid that. I do have another idea, though."

All eyes were on the secretary.

"Let's hear it, then," demanded Isaac.

"Keroularios has written and done many things in his position as patriarch over the past fifteen years. I think it is likely that in those many years he has done or written some things that we could argue were heretical. In fact, I believe I know of a few incidents in his writings that might qualify as such. I could dig through the records and assemble a case to put him on trial for heresy—and possibly treason. He might even abdicate if we just let him know of the case we will present rather than face a trial."

JANUARY 1059

OVER THE NEXT WEEK, PSELLUS COLLECTED WRITINGS that, put together, made a strong argument against Keroularios,

a case for both heresy and treason. I began to realize how unin-
formed I had been about the patriarch. Psellus was not the only
man he had threatened; Isaac was not the only emperor he had
schemed against. He had intimidated and threatened many men
in the city with trumped-up accusations to get his way. These
senators, dynatoi, even other priests and monks, were eager to
whisper what they knew or suspected into Psellus's ear. I was not
so naive as to assume all their stories were true, but the priest
had acquired an impressive number of enemies.

Once the case against Keroularios was prepared, Isaac sent
Psellus out to see if this threat might at last force his abdication.
This situation was dragging out for so long and it did not put
the emperor in a good light.

"Put your case to that old fool, let him see what we have
against him. Tell him none of this will become public if he abdi-
cates. He should relent once he realizes the amount of material
we have," Isaac said to his secretary as we walked down to the
quay beside the Boukoleon Palace.

The January day was clear and cold with a good westerly
wind, as good a sailing day as you could have in the winter
season. Psellus had a set jaw and a confident walk as he carried
the satchel full of evidence that would put an end to the career
of the man who had tried to destroy him.

"I'll do my best, Your Majesty," he said, bowing deeply to
Isaac.

Psellus stepped onto one of the emperor's personal ships and
we watched as it sailed with the morning tide.

<hr>

LATE THE NEXT DAY, PSELLUS RETURNED, BREATHLESS WITH
suppressed excitement.

"So what did he say?" asked Isaac, leaning forward in his
chair in anticipation.

Psellus began recounting his journey, but his first comment

did not give us any hope.

"Your Majesty, I presented our case to him, as you instructed. I covered all the evidence we collected in detail. It took all day to tell him what we had. It only caused him to become angrier, his eyes bulging out and face scarlet when he told me to take these accusations and throw them into the sea. He was not going to abdicate. He was outraged and intense about his determination to continue as patriarch."

"I can't believe it. We've given him so many chances and he's thrown them all back in our faces," Catherine burst out angrily. She turned to a window overlooking one of the gardens Thomas so diligently cared for, barren now in winter, just past the feast of Epiphany. Every muscle in her body was tense with frustration. "We'll have to bring him before the judges after all."

John deflated at this setback. Isaac's face turned an angry red. I felt exasperated as I realized Isaac had few options left, and none of them good.

Psellus held up a hand. "Wait."

We all looked at him.

"As we had planned, I spent the night at the monastery before taking the ship back today. It is my duty to inform you that the Patriarch Michael Keroularios died in his sleep last night."

IN THE DAYS THAT FOLLOWED, ISAAC LOOKED AS THOUGH A great weight had been lifted. John and Catherine were relieved that God's will had finally coincided with Isaac's. Michael Psellus and I, while usually not on the best of terms, exchanged furtive knowing glances. We shared a sense that maybe, in this instance at least, justice was somehow accomplished.

Eudokia had no great fondness for the uncle who had married her off to Constantine Ducas. Even so, she worried at the same time if, without her uncle as protector, Ducas would become more brazen in his efforts to put her aside and marry Isaac's daughter.

Isaac now curried favor with the people of the city by showing great respect for the deceased by holding a magnificent funeral service in the Hagia Sophia. He also named a new, more agreeable, patriarch, someone Psellus recommended: Constantine Leichoudes.

This recent conflict with the patriarch had dragged on for months, from September into deepest winter, far beyond the campaigning season. Isaac and John began planning for a spring attack on the barbarian Pechenegs who had started moving across the border near the Danube. The empire was fortunate in this. If the Pechenegs had invaded a year earlier Isaac would not have had the money to pay the soldiers or order supplies. Now he did. Word also arrived from the Hungary that its king was threatening our border near Serdica in Bulgaria. Isaac planned a campaign to demonstrate to both that the Roman Empire was now ruled by a soldier capable of making war.

One day in March, John burst in on me while I was in the nursery with the children. The weather had warmed, but there were still a few of them with runny noses from winter colds. Our niece Anastasia had recently married Peter Kekaumenos and left for her own household, so I'd lost her help. Eudokia was often there, but not that day. Her daughter, baby Theodora, born soon after my little Adrian, had been colicky, and she was keeping the child in her rooms. The older children were in their classroom for lessons, leaving me with the littlest ones when John appeared looking flustered.

"Isaac doesn't want me in this campaign," he said without preamble. "I have to stay behind and govern as regent in his place."

"John, that's wonderful. I know there's no one he trusts more than you." I hoisted a squirming three-year-old Alexios onto my hip to keep him out of mischief. The monkeys some people kept as pets got into less trouble than this son of mine.

John frowned, impatience in his voice. "Maybe, but he knows I'd rather be with him in the field. It means I'll have to put up with all the nonsense that goes on around here, the bloodsuckers yammering at me for favors, gifts.."

I bit my lip, trying to keep my patience. Isaac had to choose his own brother, the man he named Caesar, his second-in-command and presumptive heir until Marika wed. It made no sense to me that John would complain about it.

"You've been at Isaac's right hand your whole life, and he knows you'll rule as he would, that's why he trusts you." John always preferred the clarity, the black and white, of the battle-field to the shadows and false faces of court life. I couldn't blame him for that. But the title of Caesar came with responsibilities. John needed this experience if he was ever called to the throne himself. He had an important role to play.

"You don't understand. I just don't want this." His voice grew louder in frustration with me.

"It's not about wants. John, you're the Caesar. Who else is there?" I responded, stunned that he would even think to shirk this responsibility. "Kekaumenos? He's Isaac's friend, but his health isn't strong. Or Ducas? Who could trust him? Or would you prefer some self-serving bureaucrat, like Psellus?"

John folded his arms across his chest. "I'm not sure I care."

"Well, you can't turn Isaac down. You do that and he'll be so upset with you that he won't want you on campaign either." John's stubbornness irritated me. "After all he's done for you? What are you thinking?"

John had expressed similar feelings to me a few times in the year and a half since Isaac had been crowned, but never so bluntly. I thought he had just needed time and encouragement to become accustomed to the responsibility. Instead, he stood looking at me, more like a cranky little boy than a grown man.

"I know I can't disappoint Isaac." He fumed. "But I don't like it."

Sometimes I felt as though we were tugging on the same

rope, only in opposite directions, John pulling back to a soldier's life, while I pulled him toward his duty to Isaac and the empire. We hadn't expected or wanted our lives to go this way, but God had decreed otherwise. Uncle Costas had warned me before John and I wed that we could be pulled into palace power struggles. I hadn't believed him then, but he had been correct. Generations of the Comnenus and Dalassenus families had been raised to be loyal and defend the empire when they were needed. We could not shirk that duty, no matter our personal preferences. What his brother, the emperor, was asking was not so difficult; he had already been doing it alongside Isaac for over a year. John should have expected this could happen. His unwillingness infuriated me.

Alexios wriggled out of my arms and proceeded to chase after a cat I knew was faster than his short legs could run.

"John," I said, looking straight at him, my own voice rising, "Isaac thinks you're ready for the job he's giving you. You'll have me here to help you, and Catherine will be here. She's learned a lot, and there's always Psellus. You can manage it. Isaac wouldn't give you this responsibility if he didn't have complete confidence in you."

He pulled a face at me, rolling his eyes. "You think I should confer with you or Catherine before I make a decision? What kind of man do you take me for? What do you think people will say if they see me taking orders from women? You almost sound like you agree with me that I shouldn't be taking this on." His mouth was tight, and his eyes bulged out.

"No, of course that's not it," I said in a lower voice, surprised at his quick temper as well as my own anger. "I just meant . . ." I tried to think what it was I had meant. "I just meant that you'll always have my support and help. Of course, you don't need my advice. And Catherine is the empress, but it will be important for people to see you have her support. That's all I meant."

He raised his hand to stop me. "This is a stupid discussion. I thought you would at least understand."

We glared furiously at each other. He had never spoken to me this way before. He had to know he was the logical choice to stay behind. I could not imagine why he didn't understand that.

"I'm going for a ride," he finally said and left.

JOHN TRIED TO HIDE HIS RELUCTANCE TO ACT AS REGENT over the next weeks as the army made its preparations. He apologized for his angry outburst and admitted he could manage in his brother's absence, but he still seemed distant. I hoped that being on his own, without Isaac around, would build John's confidence. He never wanted to disappoint his older brother.

Isaac spent weeks mustering the needed men from around the empire, ordering the horses from Cappadocia, and paying the armorers for the weapons and equipment he needed, so he did not depart until several weeks after Pascha. The new patriarch and his priests came out on that warm spring day to bless Isaac and the army, praying for their success in the coming battles. The people of the city had become halfheartedly reconciled to Isaac since Keroularios's death. Many of them gathered outside the walls to cheer the emperor in his shining armor and the soldiers eager to fight back against the vicious invaders, flinging sweet-smelling garlands of flowers at them. The sun shone bright on the men and horses with the promise of sure victory.

After rising from the patriarch's blessing, Isaac embraced Catherine and Marie, me and John in farewell. He looked me in the eye, embraced me, and whispered in my ear "I trust you'll give John all your support. I know he needs it." I flushed with embarrassment, knowing that he realized John's ambivalence.

We all waved and cheered the army as it began the long journey north to the Danube River and the Pechenegs.

JOHN MET DAILY WITH PSELLUS AND CATHERINE TO GO over the many requests and issues requiring an imperial ruling. Those that were trivial appointments or judgments built his confidence, but more serious questions left him tossing and sleepless at night. How much to send to the eastern themes begging for soldiers and arms against marauding Turks? Did a criminal deserve execution? How to put off a dynatoi from a powerful family asking for a court appointment? And the most contentious of all were the religious disputes that bubbled up in distant parts of the empire.

John and Catherine appeared to be in agreement on most matters, but I sensed that my sister-in-law was impatient with the slow and cautious way my husband came to a decision. Catherine was efficient and quick to decide—sometimes too quickly. John's caution meant cases could drag on, but he avoided some mistakes. I thought they balanced each other, even if they exasperated each other.

In the meantime, I continued working with Thomas to manage the palace's expenses. With that and the nursery, my day was filled from dawn to sunset. I could not have managed without Thomas's sharp eye and years of experience in the palace.

"Caesarissa, I think we've gotten palace expenses to where they should be," said Thomas.

He sat across from me in the small room in the Boukoleon I used for an office. I breathed in the lovely scent from the rose-bushes blooming outside the window that floated in with the early summer breeze. We had worked together for a year and a half to cut unnecessary costs that had been eating up so much money, much of that due to pilferage and outright theft. We had brought the palace, not just the gardens, into respectable condition, getting doors and locks repaired, reinforcing sagging stairs and walls. The difficulty was that so many of the buildings were hundreds of years old, with chipped tiles, rotten beams, cracked marble, and filled with dank odors. Even the best maintained buildings will show their age when over a hundred years old. The funds were not there to accomplish more.

"Yes," I agreed, "but it wasn't easy. I still think about Georgios, trying to leave with the emperor's gold plates tucked in his boxes. I'm so grateful you caught him." Georgios, the wardrobe master, was one of the first eunuchs we had pensioned off in the early days of Isaac's reign, although there were others. We learned from that experience to not provide much opportunity for theft, hurrying the dismissed from the palace before items could be looted and disappear. "I've been wondering, though, if we might need to find replacements for a few of the staff who are gone."

Thomas gave me the speculative look he reserved when he had something to say that would surprise me.

"I agree. There are a few spots that we could fill. Can I make a suggestion?"

"Of course, Thomas. Anything."

He took a deep breath and let it out before continuing. "I want to suggest that we not fill them with eunuchs."

I sat back in surprise. The Great Palace had always been staffed with eunuchs. A hundred years earlier, Emperor Romanus had even had two of his six sons, one a bastard, castrated. The bastard had become parakoimomenos and chief minister to four emperors, and the other had become patriarch. Eunuchs made up the choir at the Hagia Sophia. "No eunuchs? But, Thomas, the palace has always had eunuchs. Why not?"

Thomas's face was red with embarrassment. "Church forbids castration but winks at it, and boys are still cut. This would stop if parents or slaveowners know the palace won't take them on. Besides, I know people say eunuchs can be more loyal to the emperor without wife or children, but we both know they can be just as evil or greedy as anyone else." He stopped, face flushed with suppressed anger and frustration.

I had never considered that perhaps eunuchs didn't want their status as the "third sex." I looked into Thomas's warm brown eyes, thinking about what lay behind his words. He would have been a fine father and husband, but that yearning had been thwarted before he'd had a chance to imagine it. A wave of sadness washed over me thinking of all the eunuchs in the palace, cut as babies or young children, and forced into a life they would never have chosen on their own.

"Yes," I said slowly, "you're right, no eunuchs."

⚜

REGULAR REPORTS ARRIVED FROM ISAAC ABOUT HIS progress with hunting down the Pechenegs. He had first gone north to the city of Serdica to conclude negotiations begun earlier with the Hungarian king. That king backed down from his talk of war after seeing Isaac's army, but this diversion took up over two months in the summer with traveling over three hundred miles to reach Serdica. We received word in late July that the army was moving northeast into the mountains where the Pechenegs were camped.

John and I dined with Catherine and Marika most evenings, where we discussed the day's events and the news from Isaac. One evening in late July, John made a surprise suggestion.

"I've been thinking that I should like to take Anna and the children to her family's farm as we used to do almost every summer. It's been over three years since we were there last, and Alexios and Adrian have never been. I think we could all use a holiday, don't you, Anna?"

Catherine put down her fork.

I stared at John, almost not understanding what he said.

"John, you have responsibilities as regent. Isaac wants you here." I asked.

"It's summer, and as I said, we've had no holiday in years. Catherine, don't you think you can handle most of the palace business while we are gone? You'll have Psellus to advise you, and I won't be gone long."

Catherine's eyes narrowed as she raised an eyebrow at John.

"John, Isaac expects you to be here at the palace the entire time he's gone," Catherine said.

"Yes, but things are slow now it's the hottest time of the year, people leaving the city. Of course, if you need me, you can send for me and I'll come immediately. I don't think Isaac would expect us to stay cooped up in the palace the whole time he was gone."

Given the distance between the farm and the city, "immediately" could mean four or five days. John was right that palace business had diminished, but I doubted that Isaac expected us to decamp for the farm in his absence.

John's face had a stubborn, pleading look on it, almost as though he would go with or without Catherine's agreement.

Catherine pursed her mouth as she mulled over his words. It was clear she was unhappy with John's request. Finally, she said, "If you insist, I think we will be fine in your absence. I insist that a messenger be sent daily with dispatches, and you will return within three weeks."

John's face suddenly looked the happiest I had seen in many months.

"Thank you, Catherine. We'll be back in three weeks. You can depend on it."

CHAPTER 4

August 1059 to November 1059

We were on the road to the family farm in Thrace a couple of days later. I felt conflicted, apprehensive at leaving in Isaac's absence but looking forward to the time away. This journey included a squad of ten Varangians for protection for Caesar John and his family, along with two nursemaids to help with the children. Our eldest, Manuel, hero-worshipped the tall blond soldiers from the north. He was fourteen, growing fast, and eager to become a soldier like his father and uncle. He and his cousin, sixteen-year-old George Dokeianos, had become generals to the troops of younger children swarming in the palace nursery. Nine-year-old Isaac practiced at being second-in-command, keeping his youthful cohort in order.

There had never been such a crowd at the farm, with the Varangians camped in tents and a few bedding in the barn. They took turns fishing with the older boys, keeping watch over the farm, and caring for the horses. George, Manuel and Isaac raced their horses while the girls and the littlest boys cheered them on.

On the whole, it was easy duty for fighting men more accustomed to wielding battle-axes than fishing poles.

I was glad to see John's mood lightening while away from the city, the palace, and the burdens of ruling. We both enjoyed the holiday, with more time together since most of the children were older and we employed servants this time to help with the chores. We often relaxed in the evening with a jug of wine after the children were in bed, holding hands under the stars as we had in our earlier years there.

Catherine sent messengers daily with news from court and of Isaac's campaign. We had been gone almost three weeks when I mentioned to John that we should start planning our return.

"No need to start yet," he said, sounding unconcerned. "I sent Catherine word that we'd be here at least two more weeks."

I blinked in shock. "John, you promised her we'd be back in three weeks. I think we really should return now."

"Well, I don't, and I'm the Caesar. There's nothing going on that she can't take care of. I wrote her that we are staying two more weeks and that's the end of that." His willful attitude did not invite contradiction. It didn't seem to matter to him that he had ignored Catherine's command to be back in three weeks. I had deep misgivings about his decision, but no choice other than to accept it.

John may have thought that extending the holiday would have extended the fun we had been having, but the weather turned unseasonably cold, with gray clouds from one end of the sky to the other. Without cold-weather clothes, Alexios and baby Adrian started having runny noses and fevers by the second week in September, the week John had told Catherine we would leave for home. I knew Alexios was feeling bad when he was content to snuggle in my lap like a lazy cat.

"I don't think I should travel with Alexios and Adrian now," I told John. "I don't want them out in this weather as ill as they are."

"Well, we can put off leaving another week. Catherine will understand," came John's casual response.

"No, John, you need to get back. Catherine's expecting you. Take the older children, one of the nursemaids, and half of the Varangians. We'll follow in a few days, once the weather clears up and the boys are better." I had to insist. I felt like Sisyphus always rolling his boulder uphill, pushing John to meet his responsibilities as Caesar.

Eventually, he agreed to my suggestion, but he had a sulky look on his face as he rode away.

۞

THAT SEPTEMBER WAS THE COLDEST IN MEMORY. FOR TWO long weeks, the boys sweated with their fevers and runny noses. The miserable weather never let up, with a chilly rain before turning into an unexpected wintry cold late in the month. One morning we even woke to a snowy dusting, although it soon melted as the day warmed.

Alexios and Adrian finally recovered to the point where they could travel, but heavy sheets of cold rain poured down, leaving the country roads muddy and impassable. I was about to tear my hair out in frustration while we waited another week, cooped up with two healthy boys wanting to get out and play. The wagon we would use could not get through the muddy roads, but eventually the rain ended. Once the roads dried out enough, we could be on our way.

One afternoon, I wrapped the warmest shawl I had around my shoulders and ventured out to survey the road with a couple of the soldiers who would escort us back to the city. I glanced first to the western mountains and froze at the sight of three men on horseback cantering to the house. The soldiers tensed, drawing their battle-axes against intruders. I watched as the men approached, but my tension soon ebbed. I recognized his silhouette even from a great distance.

"You can sheath your weapons," I told the two Varangians. "It's your emperor."

A thousand thoughts flew through my mind, wondering how he got here, what did it portend? I put on a welcoming face for these sudden guests.

"Greetings, my lord, we were not expecting visitors," I said, "but of course we are always happy to see you."

Isaac and his men reigned in their horses. Isaac's face looked haggard, cheeks sunken and eyes dull.

One of Isaac's men addressed me. "Caesarissa, the army is camped a few miles away, but the emperor recalled that you and Caesar John had a farm here." The man glanced uncertainly at Isaac. "He thought this might be a more congenial spot to spend the night."

"Of course, you're all welcome. I am sorry I can't feed the army, but we can accommodate the three of you. My lord, please come inside. The Varangians can show your men where to stable the horses."

Isaac gave me a thin smile of gratitude and dismounted. He bent down to kiss my cheek in greeting. He looked as burdened as Atlas carrying the weight of the world on his shoulders.

"Thank you, Anna. Would you have some wine? The journey left me parched."

"Of course, Isaac. Come inside."

Childish laughs came from the side of the house. Alexios had been tumbling about with his little brother, the nursemaid keeping an eye on them. The girl tried to settle the boys down once she realized it was the emperor who approached, but Adrian was not much more than a baby and kept reaching to pull Alexios's hair. Isaac patted the children's heads with a distracted air before we went inside.

I set cups on the table and brought a flagon of wine out with a plate of bread and cheese.

"I didn't expect you'd still be here. Catherine wrote that you and John were going for a few weeks. But you don't usually stay so late into the fall." Isaac spoke with an air of disinterest, as though going through the motions of polite conversation.

"John returned several weeks ago, but the two boys were ill, and I thought it would be better to wait for them to recover. Then came the cold and the rain, and we've been stuck here ever since."

Isaac leaned forward, his elbows on his knees, the cup between his hands, head bent so I could not see his face, not meeting my eye.

"Yes, the cold, and it did rain, didn't it?" Isaac stood suddenly, poured himself more wine, and walked to the window, where he could look out at the children, standing there for several minutes. The silence echoed in the room while the boys caroused outside.

I grew anxious at his words, his demeanor. My palms suddenly felt damp from the fear growing up my spine.

"Isaac, what happened? Did the Pechenegs . . ." I couldn't finish my sentence.

"We defeated the Pechenegs. They won't be causing trouble for a good long time." He sighed deeply. "No, it was the rain that defeated us, and the snow, and the cold."

"What? The rain?"

He spoke slowly. "It was on the way home. Rain so bad it poured down so we couldn't see more than a foot or two in front of us. For three days. Then the cold came, and by then the men had no dry firewood to cook, keep warm. It's still September; they didn't expect to need their heavier clothes. There was no place to shelter the horses."

He stopped, a soft groan of anguish in his throat.

"They died. Men and horses, some went to sleep and never woke up. Some became sick and died. Not all, but many. Then we had to ford a river, and the storms returned. I had crossed, but most of the army was still . . ." He paused and gave me a haunted look. "They were on the other side. When they tried to cross it, the water surged up, swallowing maybe two hundred men and horses. But the weather was not done with us yet."

"What do you mean?" I asked, gripping the arms of my chair.

Isaac raised his cup to his chapped lips, swallowing what was in it. He put the cup down on a table and began to pace.

"The next day, trying to learn how many men we had lost, how many we still had, we stopped to get a count of who was left. I was standing under an oak when black storm clouds rolled through fast from the east. A bolt of lightning shot through the air and split the oak, burning it to its core. I was standing near it, not too close, but five other men were closer. The lightning hit them. I swear I was close enough to feel the heat and energy shoot out of the sky. The bodies of the ones who died looked frightening, tongues singed, bodies too hot to touch, boots blown off their feet. Like they'd been in hell."

I reached a hand out to him. "Dear Lord, that must have been horrible. I am so grateful it didn't strike you."

He shook his head, tears in his eyes. "I . . . I feel as though it was my fault. That I was being punished."

"Isaac, you can't blame yourself for the weather."

"No? Perhaps not, but maybe God is punishing me. Punishing me for getting rid of Keroularios, for taking the gold from the monasteries, for everything. Who else but I could bring down this terrible wrath from God?"

"You mustn't think that, Isaac. Nothing you did was for you, so you could live a life in easy luxury. It was for the protection of the empire. How else could you defeat invaders? Soldiers need to be paid. The rain, the snow, the cold weather, everyone felt it. It didn't just happen to you. Even the lightning—it was God's blessing that you were not struck by it. "

"Yes, but I'm the emperor, the one responsible. It was my soldiers that died."

"Isaac, you have no reason to blame yourself. Sit down now

and rest while I prepare dinner. You've had a rough few weeks, but you've still defeated the Pechenegs. No one can take that victory from you. You've accomplished so much while you've been emperor. You have your men's loyalty because you care about them."

He gave me a look full of sadness. "I hardly feel I deserve it."

⚜

Isaac spoke little at dinner until I mentioned how long I had been at the farm.

"I was surprised when Catherine's dispatches told me you and John came here. Catherine sounded unhappy about it," he said, eyeing me over the rim of his cup. "You know I expected John would stay in the city. Did he forget that?"

I flushed warm with embarrassment at his statement.

"John just really missed our visits. Can I get you anything else to eat?" I asked, trying to change the subject.

Isaac frowned and shook his head. He rubbed his temples as though his head ached.

I gestured to the servants to clear the table, forestalling any more conversation about my husband.

⚜

I gave Isaac my room that night while I moved in with the children and their nursemaid. But the sound of him pacing lasted long into the dark hours.

I rose early in the morning to secure supplies for him, as well as to begin preparations for our own departure. Isaac still looked morose as I bid him farewell but he seemed to have recovered some of his usual energy.

"We won't be far behind you. I expect we'll be back at the palace a day or two after you get there."

He raised an eyebrow at that but said nothing beyond his thanks and goodbye.

I spent that day packing up everything we would bring back to the city. Clothes, toys, cheeses and olives, baskets of apples and walnuts. We left early the next morning in the wagon, escorted by the Varangians John had left behind.

Even though the mud in the roads had dried, they were a pitted, bumpy mess, making the trip longer than normal, increasing my eagerness to return. The spicy aromas from the city's many kitchens blew toward us as we neared the city on the Via Egnatia highway—cinnamon, pepper, cardamom, garum, all the scents of home. Then the Porta Aurea came into view, the golden gate into Constantinople, the Queen of Cities, with its bright golden statues of elephants and angels above the gate, shining in the sun. It was such a relief to return after almost two months.

"Lady Anna, Lady Anna," a familiar voice called. It was Thomas, hurrying toward us.

"Thomas, I didn't expect to see you here," I said.

"Yes, lady. Your husband sent me to watch for you, to let you know that you should return to your house, not to go to the palace. He will be waiting for you there." Thomas had an anxious look about him but said nothing other than that. He was expected back at the palace.

The road from the Porta Aurea, the Mese, would have been an easy journey straight to the Great Palace. But the route home to Blachernae had many twists and turns through narrow streets and neighborhoods I had seen little of in the past two years. The houses and shops on the way looked much the same, if shabbier to eyes grown accustomed to imperial luxury.

Our gatekeeper, an old soldier named Demetrios, swung open the gate to our house on our arrival.

"Welcome, Caesarissa Anna. Caesar John is in the garden with the other children," he said with downcast eyes.

"Thank you, Demetrios," I said, noticing that he was not his usual gregarious self.

I descended from our wagon carefully, swinging the boys down. It would be strange to both of them. Alexios had been a baby when Isaac became emperor, and Adrian had been born in the palace. My stomach felt tight, wondering why we were here and not there.

I took the boys' hands and walked into the house, its smells both familiar and musty after our long vacancy. Pushing aside the curtains to peer out to the garden, I saw John with little Donya and Theodora. Marina, Isaac, and Manuel were nearby arguing over a game.

John looked up and saw us, a nervous smile on his face.

"Marina," he called, "come take Alexios and Adrian. I need to speak with your mother."

Inside with him, I finally spoke.

"John, what's wrong? Why are you here and not at the palace?"

He looked at me as if trying to come up with words.

"John, what's happened?"

He wouldn't meet my eyes. Finally, he swallowed hard and started to speak.

"You know you always said you would prefer to live here, not at the palace." His eyes darted around the room, evasive.

"What does that have to do with this situation?" I asked, irritation building. "We have responsibilities in the palace."

"Not any more." John's face turned red, then he blurted, "Isaac said I should just go home."

"Just go home?" I had to sit down.

"He was very angry that we left. You shouldn't have told him."

I looked at him as if he had lost his mind.

"Shouldn't have told him what? That we were there for more than a month? Catherine already told him we'd gone, and he could easily guess how long we stayed since I was still there."

His mouth shrank into a circle, his chin hard as a rock.

"Did you want me to lie to him? Do you think he wouldn't have learned the truth?" I said, my voice rising in anger. John was trying to blame me, when it was entirely his responsibility. "I did try to keep him from learning how much you delayed our return."

He had the decency to look away.

"Isaac said I wasn't needed at the palace anymore. He said to just take the children and return here."

Isaac must have been livid, or he would never have sent his brother away. As close as they had been John's whole life, this was a devastating break. John was close to breaking down in tears. I had to back up and push my own exasperation at my husband's actions aside. I pulled John close to me.

"Isaac will get over this. You know he will. He was under a lot of stress after losing so many men in the storms. He needs a little time, and you'll be back on good terms with him." I tried to comfort my husband while the children played outside, shouting in their games. Isaac loved his brother, but John had disappointed him far too much this time. Coming right after the terrible losses in Bulgaria, Isaac was taking it out on his brother. John would have to work to regain Isaac's good opinion.

❦

JOHN VENTURED TO THE GREAT PALACE ALMOST EVERY DAY for the next few weeks, trying to repair the break between them. It wasn't easy, but Isaac was courteous, and he did seem to soften, or so John said. One evening, he returned with an escort and a chest filled with gold coins.

"Isaac sends this, with his thanks. He didn't want you to think he forgot what he owed you now that the treasury is on a stronger footing," John said,

The emperor had been generous, the box holding a bit more than I had provided two years earlier. I worried it may have meant he was trying to loosen the ties he had with John and me, or it could mean he only now had the means to make the payment.

In the palace, I had longed to be where I was now, at home with our seven children. Now, I found I missed the many other young faces I had spent two years with in the nursery. My own children missed their old playmates.

Besides that, I had found managing the staff and day-to-day operations of the Great Palace unexpectedly fulfilling. The old buildings held priceless porphyry, icons, and mosaics and witnessed many generations of emperors and empresses. It had been an honor to return some of it to good condition. Some buildings, in truth, needed to be torn down. But for much of it, I'd reached a point over the summer where its operations ran as smoothly as a water mill rotating endlessly on its axle. Thomas's help had been invaluable, and I missed his friendly face. In mid-November, I decided I needed to visit the palace.

After an absence of over three months, I was surprised at how happy I felt to be back inside the palace walls. The nursery hummed with the chaotic activity of children playing or nibbling on treats the eunuchs had brought. Eudokia and my niece Marika greeted me excitedly with embraces and many questions. They were looking after the children, who all greeted me with smiles.

The nursery felt warm from unseasonable winds blowing from the south and held the familiar smells, good and bad, of the children in it.

"Caesarissa Anna, I've missed you," said dark-eyed Marie of Bulgaria. She was a sweet, earnest eight-year-old now.

"I've missed you too, Marie, so I thought I should come for a visit. Tell me, how have you been? And how have your lessons been?"

She seriously explained what she'd learned from her tutors, pushing back a strand of dark hair slipping across her face.

"Aunt Catherine is so busy I hardly ever see her," Marie of

Bulgaria whispered in her soft voice. I put my arms around this little orphan who needed more hugs than she would ever get from Empress Catherine.

Maria of Alania and her cousin Irene also greeted me. Maria's beauty, even at that age, was exceptional. Her flawless skin, red-gold hair, and rosebud mouth were complemented by a courteous manner and friendly disposition. Irene was a sturdier, more resilient, version of Maria.

Eudokia's oldest, her son, Michael, approached and asked after my son Isaac, who had always been his favorite playmate. He was such a shy child; he must have really missed my son to seek me out. I felt bad disappointing him with the news that Isaac was not with me.

Eudokia and Marika pulled me aside to talk of the latest events. Inevitably, John's abrupt departure from court was the main topic.

"Papa was upset about Uncle John's absence from the city, but he was even angrier after he spoke to Mama. I'm not sure what she told him, but I know she thought Uncle was little help. I don't think I've ever seen Papa so mad."

I swallowed hard at that, blaming myself for not resisting John's suggestion for the trip.

"Marika, I don't think there was anything that serious that came up while they were gone. Your mother may just have felt overwhelmed with both John and the emperor gone," said Eudokia. She was diplomatic in her efforts to smooth over the affair. Knowing Catherine, though, her irritation could have magnified every perceived lapse. It meant John would have to reconcile with both Isaac and Catherine. I wasn't sure my husband could manage that.

I bid farewell to Eudokia and my niece and went in search of Thomas, finding him back in the workroom where I'd first met him.

Thomas's face held a line of perspiration along his upper lip, and his damp tunic gave evidence of heavy work. He looked up as my shadow from the doorway darkened the workroom.

"Caesarissa Anna," he exclaimed with a smile, "what a surprise to see you. I had no idea you were coming here today."

"I gave no warning. I wanted it to be a quiet visit, nothing formal."

"Well, I'm happy to see you again. I've missed our talks, and," he said, looking more somber, "there have been changes since you left in August."

"I'm glad to see you as well, Thomas. What sort of changes? I see you're back here now." I sat down on the stool near his desk, breathing in the natural scents that clung to the tools stored in it. They reminded me of my grandmother's gardens, pungent with the earth and herbs, roses and fruits.

"The empress had some, uh, different ideas. She thought it was better for me to focus again on the outdoor areas, and she brought back some of those you had pensioned off."

I blinked at that. Catherine had never intimated that she was unhappy with my decisions. In fact, she never evidenced any interest in the palace's operations beyond what I reported to her. Someone must have influenced her. Thomas's face betrayed his disappointment in the demotion.

"I'm so sorry to hear that, Thomas. I'm sure she'll realize soon enough how valuable you are."

"Perhaps, but since you left, she, and now the emperor after his return, spend a lot of time with Michael Psellus. That one prefers the palace the way it used to be run. Both Psellus and Constantine Ducas prefer that."

"Ducas?" This was another unfortunate turn of events because of that holiday John had insisted on.

Thomas frowned. "You didn't know? The emperor has been spending most of his days with Psellus and Ducas."

I shook my head, disgusted. That would have to change. Thank heaven that John seemed to be getting back in Isaac's favor.

"Your roses are blooming so late?" I asked, looking at a chipped ceramic bowl brimming with stunning crimson and ivory roses on the desk.

He smiled, his fingers brushing the soft petals. "I thought they'd be done after the cold weather we had in September. Then the last few days, with hot winds blowing up from Africa, these blossomed as though it was summer again."

I took my leave of Thomas then, walking the well-worn marble paths leading to the Daphne Palace to meet John and pay my respects to Catherine and Isaac. I wanted to do whatever I could to smooth over relations between the brothers.

It was a surprise when I arrived at Isaac's office in the palace to hear the sounds of laughter. There were, to be sure, others in the room when I arrived, several supporters of Isaac's, including Psellus and Ducas. But the lighthearted atmosphere lacked the sullen tension that John said had marked his visits a few weeks earlier. Isaac gave me a brief but warm welcome, and Catherine's greeting gave no evidence of a lingering resentment.

John told me on our return home that day that Isaac had invited him to join his hunting party the following day.

"I think you were right," he said, "Isaac just needed some time to get over his irritation."

That was the best news. I slipped my hand into John's and smiled up at him, the simmering irritation I'd been feeling for weeks now cooling and forgotten.

☙❧

JOHN CREPT FROM OUR BED BEFORE FIRST LIGHT, EAGER TO join Isaac and the other men in the hunt. I lay half-asleep, half-awake while the sun slowly edged above the horizon, blissful in my enjoyment of the quiet before the house roused. I fell back over the edge into sleep, dreaming of a chess game I had played with Uncle Costas, and woke to a cock's crow. Uncle Costas, an esteemed general and my grandfather's oldest brother, had died fourteen years earlier, and I rarely thought of him now, other than to pray for his soul in church. Fully awake, I struggled to think what chess game it was that the dream recalled. We had played so often the games blurred together.

It made no sense to just lie there, so I got up and dressed for the day. Glancing in my clothes chest, I saw the corner of the wine-colored cloak Uncle Costas had handed me when he left for the monastery, buried at the bottom under my dresses. I pulled it out then, the scent of it bringing back his memory. The old wool felt stiff between my fingers, and suddenly I recalled the chess game in the dream. It was somehow about his daughter, Xene, who had been married to Constantine Ducas. In the dream it seemed he had been trying to explain something to me about the game, but like most dreams, his words evaporated in the light of day.

Isaac was the king on the chessboard, John his knight. I was just a pawn, moving to defend the king. But I also moved in opposition to another would-be king. Constantine Ducas. I had promised my cousin Xene on her grave that I would avenge her death at his hands. That was the true reason why I had given Isaac the gold I had inherited from my grandparents to pay his soldiers since, without it, Ducas might have taken the lead in the rebellion. Now Ducas was still just a senator and still married to Eudokia, instead of Isaac's daughter, despite his efforts at seduction. It was so gratifying to know I had thwarted his every maneuver to gain the throne. *Yes, Xene, I have avenged you.*

It felt good to start the day remembering that, even though I was just a woman, I had stopped Constantine Ducas.

THE DAY PASSED AS MOST DAYS DID, WITH CHORES AND hungry children, lessons and scraped knees. My oldest, Manuel, and I sat down at the chess board in the cloudy afternoon, storm clouds and rain rolling through. At fourteen, he played a fine game, as good as my grandfather's had been, although not as good as Uncle Costas had. Scents from the kitchen foretold of the fish stew we would soon enjoy at dinner.

"When will Papa be home?" he asked, moving a knight to counter my bishop. He was a handsome boy, just showing the signs of his first beard coming in, a rich brown with red lights glinting in it.

"I'm not sure. It might not be until late, possibly not until tomorrow. He might stay the night at the palace if they return late."

My son gave me a searching glance before speaking again.

"So is he getting along better with Uncle Isaac?"

We had not spoken to the children of why we returned home from the palace after spending two years there. But Manuel was old enough to overhear conversations and gossip. From the worried look on his face, he was old enough to have concerns about what he heard.

I gave him an encouraging smile. "Manuel, they're brothers. Brothers fight, and brothers make up. But in the end, brothers are loyal to each other and stand together. You need to remember that when you're grown and your own brother Isaac fights with you."

He laughed. "It won't be Isaac I'll be fighting with, he's too easygoing. It'll be Alexios."

I chuckled at that. Alexios, at three, spent most of his day finding ways to torment his brothers and sisters, but especially Manuel.

"You have to be loyal to all your brothers—and sisters too. Family is always the most important," I said.

It was then that I heard John arriving in the courtyard, calling for the stable boy to take his horse.

He rushed into the house, searching me out.

"Isaac's taken ill. We're needed at the palace." His face was dirt-streaked, beard soaked and eyes red-rimmed.

"Taken ill? What happened?"

"He chased a boar to the shore of the Bosphorus. There'd been rain, but suddenly lightning started, and before we knew what was happening, it struck next to Isaac, and he fell from his horse. The horse must have been hit worse—it's dead. Isaac started foaming at the mouth, didn't seem to recognize anyone. We found a boat and brought him back to the palace. He's with the physicians now."

I called the servants together while John hastily assembled some clothes.

"The Caesar and I must leave for the palace. I'm not sure when we'll return, but I'm leaving Manuel in charge in our absence. You are to treat any instructions he gives you as though they came from me. Does everyone understand? And I ask also for your urgent prayers for the emperor's recovery."

They nodded agreement; none of them were likely to cause Manuel problems, but I wanted to be clear. I put a hand on Manuel's shoulder. He stood taller, and his face held a serious demeanor.

"I don't expect we'll be gone long, but you know to contact Maria Kourtikios if anyone takes ill, and send word to us at the palace if that happens. Do you have any questions?"

"No, Mama."

The boy was already as tall as I was, growing towards manhood, proud to have this responsibility. I kissed his cheek in farewell.

It was dusk by the time we arrived at the palace, but it was lit up as though for a great festivity. Eunuchs were scurrying in with wine and food for the dynatoi pressing in to learn any news. John and I, Caesar and Caesarissa, received preferential treatment, escorted into Isaac's rooms by two well-armed Varangians. Catherine and Marika looked anxious as they conferred with one of the physicians, who wore the uniform of the venerable Hospital of Sampson, located closest to the palace.

Psellus came over to greet us, obsequious as ever.

"Caesar John, Caesarissa Anna, good that you're here. The

emperor is resting now. The physician gave him a draught to help him sleep."

"Has there been any improvement?" John asked. He held my hand tight in a sweaty grip.

Psellus looked down, the picture of concern. "He's bruised from the fall from his horse, and the lightning left burn marks on one side. He seems to be aware of people, but he's not able to hear right now."

John pushed back his hair nervously.

"The empress asked me to clear the room, although I'm sure she wants you both to remain. Excuse me while I see everyone else out."

Psellus moved to escort the other visitors to the exit while John and I went to speak with Catherine.

"We'll have someone stay with the emperor all night," said the physician, "although he should sleep well with the medicine I gave him. With God's help, he will recover by morning. It wasn't a direct hit and some people recover quickly."

Catherine stood listening, twisting a ring on her finger over and over.

"And if he doesn't? What do we do then?" she said, her voice sharp as a knife.

"My lady, we will have to look him over again in the morning to know. As I said, many do recover, but it is in God's hands now." The physician bowed to her and excused himself.

"Catherine, do you want Anna and me to stay with Isaac? We can take turns, and you can get some rest and be ready if he needs you in the morning," said John.

"And I'll help too," said Marika. "Someone will be at his side all night."

Catherine's foot tapped on the floor nervously before she nodded agreement. I glanced around the almost empty room as the three of them conferred on our schedule for attending to Isaac. A couple of servants were clearing the remains of the meal. Michael Psellus had not quite emptied the room; he stood talking in grave tones with Constantine Ducas and his younger brother, John, near the door. I couldn't help but wish that Ducas would just disappear or go far away.

⚜

ISAAC REMAINED STUNNED, CONFUSED, BUT HIS HEARING did start to return slowly. The physicians had him drink concoctions, some of which seemed to help. We all took turns staying with him, helping the physicians care for him, coaxing him to take even just a little broth, eat a corner of bread. Catherine sat often at his side, more gentle than I had seen her before, wiping his brow with a cool cloth when the confusion came over him. She spent hours praying for his recovery in the Chapel of the Theotokos when not at Isaac's side.

The late November days grew ever shorter, the north winds blowing the warmth back to Africa. One evening as I sat with Isaac, he was tossing, trying to get comfortable. His limp body looked shriveled from its former sturdy bulk, weak as a newborn.

"Isaac, here, try and take a little broth," I said, my voice louder than normal so he could hear.

He sipped a small amount before leaning back against the cushions.

"Thank you, Anna, but no more. It's too much effort to drink."

"I'll give it to you in spoonfuls, then. You just open your mouth."

He gave a tired smile and let me dribble some of it in before saying, "Enough for now."

I set the bowl aside and wrung out a cool cloth to wipe his tired face. His eyes closed and for a few minutes I thought he had fallen asleep before they opened and he peered at my face.

"Anna, tell me honestly," he began in a hoarse whisper, "did I do something to deserve this?"

His question startled me. "No, Isaac, you did nothing. What makes you think that?"

"Was it wrong of me to rebel against Michael Bringas?" he asked, speaking of the old man he had overthrown who had ruled so badly as emperor for a year. "And what about Keroularios? Is God punishing me now?"

"Oh, Isaac, you know Michael Bringas was a fool who should never have sat on the throne. And Keroularios may have been patriarch, but he was no saint." His hand lay on the side of the bed. I reached over and squeezed it.

His eyes were haunted. He swallowed. "I'm not sure. All the men I lost in the Danube, the men killed when lightning struck the tree I stood under, but I wasn't. Then to feel the power of the lightning strike me here near the palace, like the hand of God warning me of what punishment my sins will warrant if I don't repent. It felt like my final sign."

Many would agree with Isaac about such ominous signs, and I struggled to find words of encouragement. "Not punished, Isaac, just tested."

A half smile passed over his tired face, "I'm not sure I'm passing the test."

He drifted into a restless sleep then.

෯෴෯

I LEFT ISAAC'S BEDSIDE IN THE EARLY MORNING HOURS when John came to relieve me. Isaac roused at John's arrival and smiled at his younger brother. After a few hours sleep myself, I returned to Isaac's rooms at midday, waiting in the antechamber, and learned that the hegoumenos of the monastery of St. John Stoudion was with him. The monks there had raised Isaac and John after their parents had died. Priests and monks had visited Isaac almost daily since he became ill, but this was the first time Stoudion's hegoumenos had been there.

There appeared to be affairs of state that required discussion, with Psellus, Constantine Ducas, Kekaumenos, John, and several other councilors being escorted into his chamber. Eudokia arrived, explaining her husband had sent for her. The meeting in Isaac's chamber went on into the late afternoon when Psellus left and returned with Catherine and her daughter. They both looked worn out after their days of care and worry. Until now, Catherine had always carried herself with such a regal air.

The door opened to Isaac's chamber, and his visitors all filed out except for the hegoumenos. I had been listening to Eudokia's whispered questions about the emperor's health when I noticed John, who usually would stand close by me, instead moved to the other side of the antechamber, talking with a few of the men. I tried to catch his eye but he appeared distracted and did not even glance at me. Michael Psellus cleared his throat to speak.

"My lords and ladies, the emperor has asked me to make an announcement. His illness is such he believes he has few remaining days on this earth. He has decided that to atone for his sins and make his soul ready for passage into the eternal tomb, he will now abdicate the throne and enter the monastery of St. John Stoudion as a simple monk for his remaining days."

"No, Isaac, you can't do this," Catherine cried out to the closed door that stood between them. "What's to become of me?" she moaned as she sagged to the floor.

Marika clutched her mother's arm, tears streaming down. I moved to embrace them when the thought hit me that this would mean that John, as Isaac's Caesar, would become emperor, and I his empress.

But Psellus had not finished.

"The emperor is thus abdicating today and has chosen Senator Constantine Ducas as his successor."

I heard the words, but their meaning made no sense to me. How could Ducas be named Isaac's successor? What of John? I looked at my husband, whose face spoke of his guilt, darting glances at me before shifting his gaze to the mosaic floor with the image of a snake coiled around the throat of a stag. It felt like a snake had coiled around me as I had the sick realization that the words I had heard were true. John knew the kind of man Ducas was better than anyone aside from me. John knew what he had done to Xene and John had still let this happen. John, my husband, had betrayed me. I could hardly breathe.

CHAPTER 5

November 1059 to May 1062

I painted a smile on my face and congratulated Eudokia, but I could not look at the new emperor. I returned to our rooms with John trailing behind me. Once inside, I shut the massive oak door and locked it.

"What happened in that room with Isaac? How is it you're not emperor now? You are, or were," I said with disdain, "the Caesar." My voice was cold with the effort to control it, to not scream at him.

"Isaac tried to stand this morning and walk across the room but couldn't manage it. He spoke with the hegoumenos later and made his decision. He . . . he said he didn't think he'd ever recover the strength to rule again." John was pale, stumbling over his words as he tried to placate me.

"So why not you, then? Or one of your sister's boys? Theodore is certainly of an age. Why that disgusting man and not a Comnenus?"

John's eyes shifted away. "It's not my fault. I would have

suggested Theodore after I told Isaac I did not want the throne," he pleaded.

"You what? You turned him down?" His words made me sick with disappointment. I should have expected that, but I still could not believe the words I heard.

John turned red with anger. "Anna, you know I didn't want to be emperor. Isaac wasn't surprised when I told him. And then . . . and then Psellus spoke up before I could say anything else and suggested Ducas. The men there all seemed to like his suggestion well enough, and before I could say anything it was decided. It wasn't my fault that Isaac chose Ducas."

I looked at him as though I'd never seen this man before. I thought I had married a soldier like the men in my family, willing to take on whatever task the empire asked of him. Not someone trying to escape blame by saying it wasn't his fault. I looked at him: *It wasn't his fault.* My disappointment in John was far greater than knowing Constantine Ducas was about to be emperor.

I put my head in my trembling hands, so aghast was I at his words. "How could you do this? What man turns down the throne and lets someone like Ducas take it?"

"Why is it so hard to believe?" he shot back. "You know I didn't want to rule. Not everyone wants power, wants a throne. Besides . . . what about your own Uncle Costas?" he added with a furious voice. "He turned it down when Empress Zoe wanted him to be her husband. I just made the same choice."

I had forgotten that incident in the white heat of my anger, forgotten that my dear uncle had turned down a throne just as my husband had.

"Don't you dare compare yourself to Uncle Costas. My uncle was an old man, over seventy and feeling too old to rule. That's not you."

"I don't think it's different," he said, chin jutting out.

We stood glaring at each other for a long time before I finally turned away and said, "I'm returning home. I need to think of our children." I turned away, thinking I had to get back to my sons. I would raise them to never shirk their responsibilities.

John did not immediately respond.

"I need to stay here. Ducas has asked for my help with the transition."

I almost laughed at that foolishness. "You think he wants your help?" I asked bitterly. "You don't think he's just keeping an eye on you, Emperor Isaac's brother, in case you have second thoughts?"

He blinked at me. "Ducas will see only a loyal subject in me, not a rival," John said defensively.

I'd had enough of my oblivious husband.

"I'll be at home," I said. "I'll send a message to Thomas for anything I leave behind."

John's face flushed, and a tremor shook his hands. "I'm not sure when I will be back," he mumbled.

"Don't rush," came my cold response.

৩৩৩

I SPENT THE FIRST FEW DAYS AT HOME TRYING TO CALM myself and grappling with the terrible fact that Constantine Ducas was now emperor. Thomas sent my things home along with a note about what Catherine and Marika had decided. They had entered the Myrelaion monastery, not far from the Great Palace, and a place where other empresses had retired to. The monastery overlooked the Marmara and held some lovely gardens, but that would be a small consolation for Catherine who born the daughter of the Bulgarian king and had been the wife of a Roman emperor. She and I had never been close, but the two of us now shared the sting of social obsolescence since both our husbands had given up the crown. Perhaps we could commiserate with each other.

Their rooms were those of castoff royalty—large, airy, and

reasonably comfortable. A carpet softened the stone floor, and cushioned chairs were ready for visitors. A warm glow came from a brazier. The last imperial residents had been the daughters of Constantine VII, the one called Porphyrogenitus, a hundred years earlier, who had been put away there by their own brother. It was a comfortable setting but modest compared to the opulent Great Palace. Catherine and Marika had enjoyed the palace's luxuries for only two years but had lived lavishly even before that.

Marika's tranquil greeting at the monastery's entrance surprised me. Her face showed little anguish or grief, and she had not been tonsured, her hair in a braid hanging over her shoulder. She was dressed soberly but not in the typical attire of the nuns in this monastery.

"Thank you for visiting, Auntie. Mama will be happy to see you."

"How are you both?" I asked quietly. "Ducas certainly made sure you moved here quickly."

She raised an eyebrow at that. "I was more than happy to get away from that man and his pawing hands. I don't know how Eudokia manages him; she's a saint. At least here he won't bother me anymore."

I eyed her neatly plaited hair. "But no tonsure?"

She gave a wistful smile. "I'm not sure I'm ready to take that step. Mama was tonsured right away, but I want to wait."

Marika was only twenty-three. There was no rule that she had to have her hair cut and take vows; many women moved to monasteries to live out their days without it, not taking the final step until they were on their deathbed.

Catherine entered the room then, looking smaller than she had in the fine embroidered silks she had always worn, even before Isaac became emperor. The nun's black garb covered all of her except face and hands. Her only ornament was an enameled and jeweled cross hung around her neck on a thick gold chain that she nervously fingered, rubbing the gems in it as if praying for good luck to appear.

"Anna, so kind of you to visit," she said before the tears started falling.

"Catherine, I'm so sorry. I know this has been a terrible trial for you and Marika."

I spent the next hour sympathizing with her on the unfortunate events of the past few weeks. She had lost not only her position as empress, but her husband. They were both committed now to celibate life in their own monasteries, apart, even though Stoudion was just a mile or so away. She could not visit him, nor could he see her. After years of those two trading barbed comments, it seemed Catherine had finally recognized her love for Isaac, and it was far too late.

Yet my sympathy for Catherine ebbed by the end as her conversation became a monologue of complaints about the accommodations, the food, the hegoumena's expectations for her attendance at multiple services each day. I made my excuses to return home and stood up to leave.

"I'll accompany you to the gate, Auntie."

Marika closed the heavy oak door behind us and we walked down the deserted peristyle to the entrance. The center garden had rosebushes, now dormant for winter, a few frostbitten cabbage plants, and the subdued gray-green of sleeping lavender. The sounds of the nuns' hymns came from the monastery's church.

"Auntie," Marika began, then stopped.

I looked at my niece, wondering why she hesitated.

"Marika, what is it?"

She stopped and looked at me, a plea in her eyes.

"Do you think he remembers me? Ever thinks of me?"

She could only have been speaking of Michael Maurex.

"I . . . I don't know. I haven't seen him in at least a year," I stuttered.

We began walking again and reached the gate. She leaned close and whispered.

"If you see him, please tell him I think of him. I think of him fondly. Promise me you'll tell him that."

Marika's face hungered for hope.

I embraced her, "Of course, dear, I will." There seemed little chance I would see him and less chance that my telling him would help matters. At that moment, the world looked filled with little but misery.

※

JOHN WAS HOME AND GLARED ANGRILY AT ME WHEN I arrived back. After a quick glance, I brushed past him into the workroom that held my household account books and sewing. He would be unhappy with me ignoring him, but then, at that moment, I wasn't happy either.

He followed me in, shutting the door behind him.

"The emperor's coronation is tomorrow."

I opened one of my leather-bound account books, pretending to peruse its columns of numbers, and then looked up at him.

"We are expected to be there for it. Both of us."

"You'll have to make excuses for me. I won't be able to attend." My voice sounded icy, even to my own ears.

"There can be no excuses, Anna. If we aren't there, talk will be that we don't support Ducas. He'll become suspicious of our intentions, the intentions of the former emperor's family."

"Perhaps you should have thought of that sooner. I still don't want to attend this farce. You know as well as I do that Ducas is not qualified to rule. The Comnenus family are not puppets to be pulled on a string hither and yon."

"Eudokia specifically asked for you," he said.

"She will understand why I can't be there."

"She might. But she needs you now. She's pregnant and overwhelmed. She has no idea how to manage as empress."

She had long been my closest friend, and I knew she was a dreamy sort, not one to take control or even delegate to me, as Catherine had done. The silence drew out between us as I thought about Eudokia's request, my eyes not seeing the numbers anymore. Ducas would be preening like a rooster, strutting as though he'd actually accomplished something other than manipulate that social-climbing bureaucrat Psellus into suggesting him as Isaac's successor. Eudokia, on the other hand, was a gentle dove trying to keep her husband satisfied, though easily overwhelmed. I had to grit my teeth when I spoke.

"I will return to the palace, but only until her child is born."

John was visibly relieved. "Excellent. Get the children ready, and we can be there before dark."

※

JOHN DID NOT MENTION IT THEN, BUT THE TITLE OF Caesar had already been taken from him. The new Caesar John was the emperor's younger brother, another man I had no love for. I'd known his wife Irene since childhood but never really liked her. She was a whiny sort who would never be much help for Eudokia.

The coronation of Constantine X Ducas went smoothly. The gown I was given to wear at the ceremony was not as fine as the one I'd worn just over two years earlier, but I was no longer the emperor's sister-in-law. John's place in the procession to the Hagia Sophia was distant from the new emperor's. It looked like an afterthought that he was included, a cursory demonstration of the former emperor's family's support for the new ruler. My husband professed no concern about the snub but flushed angrily when I brought it to his attention.

I brought Thomas to Eudokia's chambers for an introduction a few days after the coronation. I recounted my first meeting with Thomas in his small office and assured her he was someone she could rely on once I returned home.

"Thomas, I'm feeling a little restless today. I think I'd like to take a walk to see where you work," the new empress said, standing slowly with her hand pushing against her back, as many pregnant women did. "Anna, will you join us?"

The three of us strolled along the pathways between the palace's many grand old buildings to the modest structure Thomas worked in. The two of them were soon engrossed in lively conversation and I dropped behind them. The mid-December gray sky felt heavy, and glancing down, I saw my painful knuckles were red with chilblains. I tucked my hands closer into my heavy woolen mantle and watched the other two slip around a corner out of sight. I stopped, suddenly too discouraged to want to keep walking. The entrance to the Chrysotriklinos, the emperor's golden reception hall, was in front of me, the symbol of my defeat, my enemy's victory.

My grandfather's words flashed through my head like a sudden vision. Words he said in a history lesson about Emperor Basil when he already suspected our family was about to be exiled.

"Basil was young then, not much experience. Good soldier, yes, but he didn't know the enemy's tricks. Learned them at Trajan's Gate. Never made those mistakes again."

Trajan's Gate had been a terrible defeat for Emperor Basil, but he recovered and defeated the Bulgarians years later. Was this my Trajan's Gate? Grandfather also said, *"The key to eventual victory is to survive and learn from defeat."*

I still lived. I would learn from this defeat. I would pray that victory would someday, somehow, be mine. I would look ahead.

Heartened with the memory of my grandfather's words, I walked over to join the two people I trusted most: Eudokia, my enemy's wife, and Thomas, my enemy's servant.

Eudokia soon agreed to dismiss some of the servants Psellus had managed to bring back into the palace. It was impossible to be rid of them all since Psellus was like a snake whispering in the emperor's ear and would not hesitate to cause trouble for her if all were gone. He was a leech, stuck to Ducas's side constantly, always praising the emperor for his "wise" rulings without advising wise decisions.

The Nativity passed, and in the time between the Epiphany and the start of Lent an announcement was made that little Marie of Bulgaria would be betrothed to Caesar John Ducas's son, Andronikos. Marie was a great heiress, inheriting lands and wealth from both her parents and had remained in the palace when her Aunt Catherine and cousin Marika left for Myrelaion. The child seemed a bit bereft, with what family she had now gone, so perhaps this betrothal was for the best. Andronikos was about sixteen, just getting his first wispy beard, and a nice-looking but nervous lad. They seemed to like each other, but the betrothal would last for several years until Marie was old enough to wed.

By Epiphany, I had news of a different sort. I was pregnant with our eighth child. It must have happened just before Isaac's accident, and I can't say I was as overjoyed with it as I had been with our other children. It did little for my vanity to be nauseous in the early months of pregnancy and relegated to the lower ranks at court. Eudokia remained a great friend and never condescended to me, as some might have. But John's refusing the throne still embarrassed me. I wasn't vain about clothes or cosmetics, the way women often were. No, my vanity was that I had presumed I had defeated Ducas, never expecting that Isaac would abdicate and John prove to be so feckless. Instead, Ducas had won, and now I had to live with that defeat.

☙❧

EUDOKIA'S CHILD WAS BORN IN LATE MARCH, JUST AFTER Pascha in the imperial birthing chamber with its walls of purple porphyry marble. The emperor arrogantly named this third son

Constantios, the same name as a son of Constantine the Great, as though he was just as great a ruler as that first Constantine. The boy was the first porphyrogenitus, a child of the emperor born in the purple room, in a hundred years, and Psellus chortled that it was a good omen for the dynasty. Constantine strutted around about it, preening like a peacock.

A month later, the imperial family attended the Divine Liturgy at the great church of St. George of Mangana on St. George's feast day, April twenty-third. The emperor and his family and favorites traveled on the magnificent imperial galley moored at the quay beside the Boukoleon Palace. They sailed around the cape to St. George's church, making a grand appearance for the populace. John and I were required to attend the services but we were not invited to travel on the galley. I was more than happy to be in my sedan chair, enjoying the mild spring air, while John followed nearby on horseback.

Traveling through the streets in the rose-colored hours of dawn felt odd that morning. My glimpses through the chair's curtains showed groups of burly men in clusters. Some stood by the Milion monument outside the Hagia Sophia, then others gathered near the Hospital of Sampson, the Hagia Irene, and farther along the road to St. George's. It seemed odd that they were doing nothing, not going about morning work routines, just waiting and watching, but we arrived at the church without any difficulties.

Two hours later, the services in the church were coming to a conclusion when the low rumble of voices in the distance floated through the windows of the women's gallery, where I stood with the other women near Eudokia. In the nave below, a red-faced senator approached the emperor and Caesar John Ducas, whispering urgently. The three men rushed out of the service, and Varangians soon appeared to collect the empress and her children, sweeping me along in the confusion.

Outside, the shouting grew louder, accompanied now by the clamor of metal striking metal. Men with short swords were skirmishing with the emperor's guards in the street outside the church. A few of Eudokia's other women began whimpering. Eudokia gathered her frightened children close as we were hurried down to the quay where the anxious emperor searched in vain for the imperial galley. It had inexplicably disappeared.

"Your Majesty," called a young magistrate I recognized as Joseph Trachaneiotes. "Sire, here, please get on my boat. We can get you away safely from this mob faster than waiting for your galley."

Constantine Ducas turned back to see the fighting between Varangians and the mob, his face pale and terrified.

"Yes, let's go," he said in a shaky voice. The frightened man boarded the boat with alacrity, leaving others to help Eudokia and her children.

John pushed me onto the boat before it pulled away from the shore, then going back to join the fight. Several of the rebels raced to the quay thinking to stop us from leaving but they were too late and were cut down by the guard.

This attempt at rebellion lasted less time than a race day in the hippodrome. Caesar John marched up the Mese that afternoon arresting the leading conspirators. Many were dynatoi from the wealthiest aristocratic families in the city. Even the city's eparch, its most senior administrator, had joined it. Unfortunately for them, none had the least idea how to execute a rebellion.

The emperor sat as judge at the trials that started a week after St. George's Day and gained a reputation for generosity. He was praised for not using the death penalty for the rebels. Of course, all of the convicted—and all *were* convicted—relinquished to the crown all of their property and wealth, their wives barely allowed to hold onto their dower properties. The amateur rebels at least had their lives, poverty-stricken though they might be. Ducas's reputation as a greedy miser began then with all those confiscations. He feared another rebellion and became suspicious of the people of Constantinople after that, rarely showing himself in public.

John convinced me that for our own safety we should remain at the palace until after our child was born. Best to wait until the dust settled from that failed rebellion to be certain the emperor knew we were not involved. John also hoped for a military assignment, but no emperor would be foolish enough to give it to him, Isaac's brother, especially after just putting down an uprising. Instead, the rest of the court treated him as the political non-entity he had become.

OUR SON, NAMED NIKEPHOROS AFTER AN UNCLE OF JOHN'S, arrived in late July. We remained in the palace until the end of the summer's heat in September.

I sat down with Thomas the day before returning home. We'd been working together for several years now, and trusted each other's judgment. Thomas's growing responsibilities meant a move to better offices than he'd had when we first met. With his support, Eudokia became more confident in her ability to manage the palace's operations with his support.

"Thomas, after I'm back at my house, you know you can talk to me anytime if you have any concerns. The empress is my closest friend, and I would want to know if she's having any difficulties. I know you'll be a great help to her. Still, unusual circumstances could occur, and I would want to know, even need to know." I wondered if he understood what I was asking.

Thomas blinked at me, his brown eyes searching my face for a minute before responding. "Lady Anna, you know I'll keep you informed. It's the least I can do."

I visited Isaac once at Stoudion for news I could give to Catherine and Marika. I knocked at the monastery's gate in early October and was surprised to see the former emperor's face appear in the portal.

"Isaac, it's me, Anna," I said. "I wanted to see how you are."

"Anna?" He squinted at me, and his face broke into a broad smile. "Of course, come in. I'll ask someone to watch the gate for me."

I slipped in through the gate while Isaac spoke to another monk. I shook my head at the thought of my brother-in-law, once the mightiest ruler in the world, deciding it was better to be a doorkeeper in a monastery than to live in a golden palace. How things had changed in just three years, but other emperors had come to far worse ends.

"Anna, let's walk in the garden." He stood there, leaning on a cane, beckoning me.

The autumn leaves drifted down from trees while the other plants looked bedraggled and tired at the end of the growing season. I gave Isaac news of Catherine and Marika, and of my own family. I noticed how his right leg was still not recovered from the fall from his horse when the lightning had dealt him a glancing blow. He stopped every few steps from the pain it caused. Eventually we settled onto a bench.

"Congratulations on the new son," Isaac said. "John visits me every few weeks and told me of little Nikephoros. That's a fine name for the lad."

John had not mentioned those visits, although I had suspected them.

Isaac paused before continuing. "Anna, I hope you can forgive John for declining the throne. John told me it disappointed you."

He looked into my eyes. "I should have realized it years ago. He wasn't made for ruling an empire. Some people are; John isn't one of them. You would have been a fine empress, but we both know he could not have been emperor."

Isaac's face showed the fatigue of age and living with an injured leg that would not heal. He peered at me now, looking for a sign that I understood. I realized he didn't know how Ducas had driven my cousin to her death. How much I desired to avenge Xene. How sick I felt to see Ducas as emperor.

"I expect you're right, Isaac." I knew in my heart that he was right. John was not meant for a throne. But Ducas was worse; he only ruled because he lusted for the throne and had done whatever was necessary to get it.

A glance at the sky showed heavy dark clouds rolling in. I would have to hurry to get home before the downpour started. We said our good-byes. My last sight of him was his peaceful face in the portal before it was shut. The first frost arrived a few weeks later and we were told he came down with a fever and a bad cough. John rushed to the monastery's infirmary and sat beside his brother when the former emperor was released from his earthly bindings.

◈

MY ANGER AND DISAPPOINTMENT WITH JOHN WANED, watching him play with our children and I began to understand the wisdom of Isaac's words. Our children filled our days with their needs and John was a wonderful father.

Manuel turned fifteen and began training with the emperor's tagmata troops. He'd grown as tall as John, with dark reddish-brown hair and freckles across his cheeks, now partly hidden with his first beard. He was soon bringing home tagmata friends, other young men training with him. Most I did not know, but one looked familiar to me.

"Lady Anna, do you remember me?" asked a tall brown-haired boy, thin, with an angular face.

Searching his face reminded me of a long-ago night when I'd had to pay to get our warehouse manager, Samuel, released from another emperor's custody on trumped-up charges. This young man had needed my help when one of the eparch's men had tried to pilfer some of the coins he'd brought.

"Michael Taronites? Yes, I do remember you," I said, embracing him. "It is wonderful to see you again. How is your family?"

We exchanged pleasantries, and he joined us for dinner that night and soon became a regular visitor. The reason was not difficult to fathom. Our oldest daughter, Marina, was almost fifteen and had blossomed into a lovely young woman with wavy chestnut hair and a fair complexion. I noticed how they often managed to sit beside each other at meals and how attentive he was to whatever she said.

"How well do you know Gregory Taronites?" I asked John one afternoon.

He looked up from the repair he was making to a table leg our five-year-old Alexios had managed to damage while playing.

"Taronites? Well enough. A good sort; got into a bit of trouble with the Orphanotrophus back in the day. But didn't everyone?"

"I've been wondering if his son, Michael, might be a good husband for our Marina. You know she's of an age to be betrothed."

He gave me an incredulous look, like any father contemplating the loss of a daughter to another man.

"Yes, she'll be fifteen next year, a good age to be wed. I always promised myself that my daughters would not wait as long as I had to. Michael seems a fine young man, and he comes from a good family. I have the feeling he and Marina will be pleased about it. They always seem to be glancing at each other. Don't you think his family will be happy to have a connection with us since Isaac was emperor? The connection would be a mark of prestige for them." I stopped, letting him think about it for a minute.

"Do you really think Marina is ready to be married?" he asked.

"Most girls are at her age." I paused. "Why don't you discuss it with Gregory and see what he thinks?"

MY COUSIN ROMANUS DIOGENES SERVED UNDER ISAAC'S old friend Nikephoros Botaneiates and was stationed in the borderlands of Bulgaria near the Danube. He returned to the city in time for Marina and Michael's wedding at the end of April and stopped by our house before returning to Bulgaria, as angry as a hornet's nest. My cousin was still the handsome man he'd been as a youth, but ten years as a soldier had left him lean and muscled, tanned and tense.

"All I hear from people in the city is about how high the taxes are. If that's the case, then why can't the emperor send my men the pay they are owed and the equipment they need? I just met with him and received a pittance of what I needed and what my men were owed. Does he want to see what happened to Belgrade happen to the rest of Bulgaria?"

Belgrade stood near our border with Hungary. Isaac had decisively put down an attack from the Hungarians on his last fateful campaign, pressuring their king into signing a treaty. Emperor Constantine Ducas, however, neglected the borderlands, leaving them open to attack. It wasn't long before the Hungarian king realized Ducas would not respond as Isaac had and recaptured the city.

John reddened as he explained the venality of the man on the throne. "The emperor has favorites. He promotes them to positions with generous allowances. His brother gets especially generous payments, twice as much as Isaac paid me when I was Caesar. I suspect the emperor sees these as a hedge against another St. George's Day rebellion."

Romanus rolled his eyes. "He has to pay for loyalty?"

"The money goes both ways. Did you know the emperor sits as the judge at trials?" I asked.

"I'd heard that. Ridiculous," answered Romanus, shaking his head. Then he gave me a second look and asked, "But wait, he's doing it for the money?"

John cleared his throat and explained, "Rumor has it favorable decisions go to the highest bidder. Some people even bring lawsuits to win favor with the emperor, leaving the loser impoverished."

Romanus's face turned red. "What kind of justice is that?"

"Corrupted justice, which is no justice." I said tartly. John avoided my eye at that.

My cousin shook his head, looking sick at heart. "I don't know what I'll tell my men when I get back. They're loyal to me, but they need to eat, they need equipment. I promised I'd return with more than just the trivial bag of coins the emperor gave me."

John frowned and said, "How much longer before you leave? I may know some people who can find what you need. No guarantees, but I'll see what I can do."

In the end, John's contacts did find much of the equipment Romanus needed, but no additional gold. The emperor kept a miserly eye on the treasury, as though its contents were only for himself. I couldn't help but think of how little Constantine Ducas cared about his soldiers compared to how much Romanus did.

CHAPTER 6

Summer 1063 to late 1064

My heart stopped when a ghost walked through our gate on a hot summer day. It looked like my Uncle Costas, dead almost twenty years now, bedraggled and worn as though risen from his grave, and speaking with our gatekeeper. Behind him stood a clutch of other wraithlike figures, tired and sad-eyed. Rising from my desk, I peered more closely at the man leading the group. It wasn't Uncle Costas; this man walked with the distinctive limp of his son, my cousin Damien. Twenty years had aged him into his father, whose face was etched in my memory.

They were soon all in the house, wan smiles on their travel-weary faces. Damien had brought his sons, Constantine and Alexander, and their wives and children, and his daughter, Sophia and her family. She had been a babe in arms when I left their home in Amasea but was now a woman with a husband, child, and a babe in arms herself. Fourteen in all.

"Irene left this earth about a month ago," Damien responded to my question about his wife, wiping his eyes. "She'd been sick for a few months but made me promise to take the children and leave after she died. She didn't want us staying in the house, or in Amasea, after everything that's happened."

I'd had food and drink brought outside to the shady terrace, where it was cooler, and handed a cup of wine to Damien.

"What do you mean? What's happened?" asked John who had joined us.

"You didn't hear what happened in Theodosiopolis? It must have happened maybe two months ago."

John and I shook our heads.

Damien put his cup down, lowered his head and began rubbing his eyes as though trying to blot out something while we waited. Reluctantly, he began to speak.

"I'm not surprised there's been little news. By now, most of the survivors are in the Damascus slave markets; very few got away. I am surprised, though, no merchants or traders brought word."

"Survivors of what?" I asked.

"The Turks." He gave us a hard look. "They've been raiding on the eastern borders for at least four or five years now, bolder every year, but this was far more than a raid, it was an invading army. The city's flimsy walls crumbled before them. The city was sacked, most of the men were killed, the women and the children who could walk were taken to the slave markets. The soldiers smashed the infants' skulls against walls, throwing their bodies into a pile with the men's. A bloodbath, and the whole city put to the torch as they left. A pair of terrified survivors straggled into Amasea before Irene died. She'd been anxious because of the raids even before that, but with that news, she made me promise to leave."

"There were what, about thirty or forty thousand people living there? Where was the army? They didn't know this was happening?" asked John, alarm in his voice.

"The army? You mean the mercenaries they hire for those jobs?" Damien spat out in a way reminiscent of his father's dismissive attitude toward imperial functionaries. "They're all

Franks and only show up when they get paid. Their only worry is for their own arses. Not like when your brother was strategos and we had our own soldiers. I don't understand how the emperor could let this happen."

"What happened next?" I asked softly, feeling sick at the news.

"We buried Irene in the cemetery at the church of St. George, but only stayed long enough for the first nine days of mourning. I sold the farm for a pittance since others are also leaving, but it was enough to get us here, with a bit left over." Tears filled his eyes again, and his chin trembled. I moved to wrap an arm around him. John's eyes glazed with a mixture of horror and despair.

Damien wiped his face on his stained and worn sleeve and struggled to speak. "Now, we're here. I never expected I would have to beg your help, as your family did of us so long ago."

Damien's family spent the next few days recuperating from their journey, trying to decide what to do next. We managed, but the house was cramped. Our summer trip to the farm was scheduled for just a few days hence. I spoke with John about the farm before I made a suggestion to Damien.

"We've had a tenant farmer for years, but Simon's wife died a couple of years ago and he's getting on, even though he manages with help from a couple of boys from the neighborhood. I remember you never liked living in the city, did you?"

Damien shook his head. "Too many bad memories of how my father and sister were treated. And with Ducas on the throne, as bad as he treated my sister Xene, he'd treat me worse."

"John and I wondered if you and your family would like to move to our farm? You may want to build a bigger house or add onto what we have, or even see if there's land nearby you'd like to buy. We'll still want to be there for a month in the summer, but otherwise you'd have it to yourselves. You can stay as long as you need to."

Damien grasped my hands, full of gratitude. "I'll speak to my children. I can't think of a more welcome solution."

⁂

JOHN AND I STAYED AT THE FARM INTO SEPTEMBER, helping Damien and his family get settled and expanding the house to accommodate everyone. We were back home by the end of the month. One evening a week or so later, we were talking about Damien's family.

"One of Damien's grandsons, Alexander's son Constantine, is interested in joining the Excubitors in a few years. I promised I would sponsor him when he's ready," John said.

I smiled at that. "Uncle Costas would be pleased to know his great-grandson, his namesake, would follow in his footsteps."

The floor began vibrating then, as though a giant was walking across the house, with a low groaning that sounded wrenched from the bowels of the earth. The shaking intensified so that John's face blurred, dishes fell, chess pieces rolled off their table, the chess table itself rising into the air. I stood, panicked to find and protect my children.

"John, the chil—" I started to speak when I stepped on an ivory pawn, slipping and falling into oblivion.

I next heard voices, felt a cold cloth wiping my face that, for some reason, hurt as though I'd fallen onto it from a horse.

"Ouch, stop that," was all I could say.

"Anna? Anna!" John's insistent voice came from far away.

I forced an eye open to what looked like many images of John and our children staring down at me, faces pale with fright. I closed them again and remembered the earthquake.

"What happened?"

"You slipped, and your head fell against the chess table. The table flipped and fell on you. I got you out of the way of anything else that might fall and brought the children in here. They're all safe. Only you were hurt."

The tremors started again and several of the children screamed. Isaac wrapped his arms around the two girls while Alexios pulled his two little brothers close. I shook in terror so that John covered me with his body until the world stopped trembling again.

Somehow we got outside to the courtyard. The cook and kitchen lad, the gatekeeper and stable boys were there, eyes round with fright. Screams, crying and calls for help came from outside our walls. John took Isaac and went to see what could be done to help, sending a stable boy for our physician, Maria Kourtikios, since my right leg was in terrible pain where a deep purple bruise covered almost its entire length.

The city was in chaos. Thank the good God, we heard the next morning that Manuel had survived the earthquake in his barracks, and Marina and Michael Taronites were also safe at their house.

It was over a day later before Maria Kourtikios could finally see me since so many injured and dying needing her attention. John made sure I was cared for, but he kept busy helping our neighbors dig out from the rubble. Our house was newer than most others and had withstood the shaking better than many. The oldest buildings had not fared well, with roofs collapsing, walls sagging over the street, fires starting from fallen oil lamps.

Maria Kourtikios wrapped my ankle in a tight bandage, telling me to stay off it for at least a week.

"You're fortunate." She dabbed ointment on the scrapes on my head where I'd been hit. "So many others died, were terribly hurt, or lost their homes." She pressed her lips together, the pain of what she'd seen in her eyes. "Even the Great Palace. You know how old those buildings are; it's a miracle any of them still stand."

"Was anyone injured there? At the palace, I mean," I asked, not sure if I was hopeful or worried.

She frowned, thinking about it. "No idea. The physicians at the Sampson Hospital took care of them. No one of note, though. The emperor and his family survived. You knew the empress was near her time, didn't you?"

I nodded. Eudokia was expecting her sixth child any day now.

John stopped in our room. He looked exhausted from running the household, helping neighbors, repairing the damage around our house. His red hair had long since turned sandy, and now there were streaks of white in his beard. His clothes were covered in dust and stained.

"Maria, thank you for coming. I know so many need your attention. I've been worried about Anna." He gripped my hand like a drowning sailor clinging to a rope, and I found myself gripping his hand back. He may not have had the strength to be emperor, but he'd been strong during the earthquakes, and I was grateful.

I spent weeks recovering, slowly regaining my strength, before the whole family made the journey across the city to the church of St. Thekla where Isaac was buried, to give thanks for our survival. The city for many days echoed with the rhythmic gongs of semantrons calling the faithful to services for the dead, or services of thanksgiving for survival.

I visited the palace the first week in November to see Eudokia and her new baby girl, Zoe, her second child born in the purple room and so a porphyrogenita.

"It was terrible. The walls rattled; the floors shook. The waves in the Marmara were so high they swept into the Boukoleon. I'd like to move into a different palace, but most of the other buildings are even older and suffered worse damage. Part of the wall Emperor Nikephoros Phocas built caved in, and the little church of St. Paul caught fire. I don't know if it can be repaired."

Even weeks later, the earth would occasionally tremble like an angry reminder from hell. Everyone in the city was on edge, but I'd heard the destruction was worse to the west, along the north shore of the Marmara and other parts of the empire.

"Your new baby is beautiful," I said, cradling little Zoe. The child had Eudokia's curling blond hair and deep blue eyes, and even her face gave no evidence of the Ducas family traits, just her mother's. "How are the other children in the nursery?"

"They're well. It isn't announced yet, but Constantine decided that Michael should be betrothed to Maria of Alania. The marriage won't take place for a year or two, when they're older."

Maria's father, the king of the Alans, would be elated to have his daughter wed to the emperor's heir, the first foreign princess to marry a Roman heir in hundreds of years. Maria would be a beautiful empress, but Michael was a child compared to her, although they were the same age. The lad was not maturing. It would be years before he would grow his first beard.

"And Thomas? How is he faring?" I asked after handing Zoe to her nurse.

"Thomas had the servants start putting things back to rights as soon as the quaking stopped. There's still much work to be done, but Constantine was impressed with his efforts," she said with a tremble in her voice. "He even complimented me on promoting Thomas." Eudokia looked more relieved at that accolade than proud. Ducas was as stingy with compliments for his wife as he was with coins for the soldiers in the imperial taghmata.

⚜

ROMANUS DIOGENES RETURNED TO THE CITY OVER THE winter to see his ailing wife, and to again importune the emperor for his soldiers' pay and supplies. The emperor scowled at the request, and the coins were not enough, but John again helped my cousin develop back channels to supply needed equipment.

Manuel, at nineteen, was finishing his training, and like any aspiring young soldier he was eager for an assignment that would offer opportunities for advancement. John and I took him to visit Romanus and his family after Epiphany; an introduction masquerading as a family social call. Romanus had met Manuel several times over the years since he and I were cousins, but it had been a few years since his visit.

The family greeted us at their door, their house at once familiar and foreign to me. My grandparents had owned it and raised me there after my parents died. Romanus and his wife bought it from me after Grandfather died. Romanus's wife, Anya, had changed the house to suit her needs, but I still walked into ghosts with every corner I turned.

Romanus stood lean and taut as the strings on a lyre, his handsome face shadowed when glancing at his wife. Anya had experienced severe headaches and dizziness for the past two years and had chosen not to remain in the Great Palace after Isaac abdicated. In any case, Ducas would not have wanted anyone in ill health nearby. Anya had lost a good deal of weight and leaned on her husband's arm, but otherwise was in good spirits. Behind their parents stood Thea, who was fifteen, and Costas, who was twelve. Both children had inherited their father's robust good looks rather than their mother's sparrowlike features.

John had impressed on Manuel the importance of this meeting beforehand. My cousin served under the dux of Bulgaria, Nikephoros Botaneiates, a distinguished general in his mid-sixties. Romanus's campaigns in Bulgaria against the Pechenegs had been successful, especially compared to the armies in Anatolia, where the Turks were slithering in. John wanted Manuel to learn from a successful leader rather than pick up bad habits from a losing one.

Anya and I and her children stayed inside while the three men went outside to confer. Braziers kept the room warm, and we sipped mulled wine while we chatted. Thea had matured into a friendly and courteous young woman since I'd last seen her in the palace. I could tell she kept a surreptitious eye on her mother, should she need assistance. Costas was still a child, but looked bored and impatient in the company of women, despite an occasional glare from his mother.

We all sat down together after the men returned from their talk.

"Manuel, it was your mother's family that helped me get my start in the army all those years ago. My mother and I had almost nothing left, and they helped me get what I needed. I know we were all related—cousins, uncles, and grandparents— but none of our other relatives lifted a finger," Romanus said. "And it was a little later when your Uncle Isaac thought I would make an acceptable husband for his niece, my Anya, that your mother did the matchmaking. So I have many reasons to be grateful to her."

Anya beamed at that reminder. The plain woman's prospects of making a good match, even with a generous dowry, had diminished after her father rebelled against the emperor. Romanus's prospects had been equally poor, with a good family name, but no money and a father also tainted by an accusation of rebellion. It had been my first effort at match-making, and I had to say, it was remarkably successful. Romanus and Anya never appeared less than happy around each other.

The earth shook then, just for a moment.

"Blessed Theotokos, these tremors are terrible. I pray every day that the earth would finally settle down," said our hostess.

"We all do," I said. "Did you have much damage when it first hit?"

"A little, a small fire in the kitchen and damage to the walls by the street, all repaired now. But did you hear about Raidestos? So much of that city crumbled and has to be rebuilt. The emperor refused to send money to help them," said Anya.

Romanus made a grunting sound from the back of his throat. "Is anyone surprised? If he won't pay his own soldiers to stop the Turks from destroying his cities, he won't be paying for any rebuilding. Manuel, you'll be fortunate to join me rather than the Anatolian armies; no one over there cares enough to beg, borrow, or steal what his soldiers need."

Manuel's head swiveled around toward Romanus at the sound of his name, his cheeks reddening. I realized he'd been looking at Thea, who appeared to be blushing just as furiously. Manuel had met Thea on the day she'd been born and had known her ever since. But perhaps he had never really looked at her. Now, he reminded me of how John had looked at me when we first met.

"Yes, sir. Pardon me, sir, would you repeat that?" my son stumbled out.

Romanus raised an eyebrow and grinned. "Nothing important."

※

MANUEL JOINED ROMANUS WHEN HE LEFT AFTER PASCHA to return to the Danube forts. He could not be gone long since the Pechenegs and other barbarians kept testing our frontiers, probing for weak points. Before they left, however, Manuel and Thea were betrothed with the wedding planned for autumn. It was a good match for both our families. Fortunately, although distant cousins, they were just outside of the seven degrees of kinship, so it would not require the patriarch's approval. It was agreed that Manuel would move into Romanus's house after the wedding rather than set up house on his own, so that Thea could stay there to help her mother.

That summer started out idyllic, with sun-washed days and many cool star-filled nights. Our daughter Marina had given birth to our first grandchild, a girl they named Anna, who we called Annetta, and a delight for us all. The one cloud overshadowing it was Catherine's death in mid-June. She had lived quietly at Myrelion since Isaac's abdication four years earlier, mourning his death and morose over the loss of her few glorious days as empress of the Roman Empire. Her daughter, Marika, remained quietly in the monastery following the funeral, though still without the tonsure or vows of a nun.

At the end of September, horrific news filtered in from Armenia in the farthest eastern lands of the empire. The Turkish sultan, Alp Arslan, had besieged the great city of Ani, following a foolhardy raid on the rearguard of the sultan's army by the dux that Ducas had appointed for the city.

The siege did not last long. The Turks broke through and slaughtered tens of thousands of citizens, the streets were said to have run with blood. The survivors, some fifty thousand souls, were sent to the slave markets.

The news of this disaster was devastating. I did not understand how the Turkish sultan could have been marching an army —an actual army of tens of thousands of men—through Roman territory with no impediment from the empire's soldiers. Where was Arslan going if he was originally going to bypass Ani for another target? Ani was a great city with strong walls. It had to have been a traitor who gave it away to these barbarians. Emperor Constantine Ducas made light of the tragedy, and pretended it didn't matter. It was so clear now why Damien and his family had left Amaseia, just a fortnight's journey from Ani.

A couple of weeks later, John blanched after opening a letter from Manuel.

"We're being invaded from the north. Manuel says Scythe tribes crossed the Danube and are ravaging the countryside. The Bulgarians tried to stop them, Botaneiates tried to stop them, but he was defeated. He says the tribes are heading to Thessalonike, and Romanus's army is moving to hold them back. Botaneiates's army was in Nicopolis when the barbarians crossed the river where it narrows at Vidin. There are hundreds of thousands of them. I can't believe this."

My heart skipped a beat.

"Manuel wasn't injured, was he?"

"No, no, he says he was with Romanus a hundred miles to the east." John put the letter down and began pacing. "We need to do something. Ani was bad enough, but Thessalonike? How can Romanus defeat them if Botaneiates failed with his larger army? The emperor must do something about this."

I held my tongue, hiding my bitterness of the fateful choice John had made when Isaac abdicated. Ducas's miserly ways meant Romanus's army never had the money or equipment it needed. John would not have let that happen if he had succeeded his brother, and his choice then might now result in our son's death.

"If the emperor thinks no one knows or cares about it, he'll do nothing," he said. "We need to confront him about this."

"We?" I asked.

"I know other men who have sons fighting with Botaneiates and Romanus. I know they'll want to come together and speak to the emperor about sending help. He won't listen to just one or two of us, but he'll pay attention to a dozen or more of us. He has to."

I wasn't sure about that, but something needed to be done.

In the end, John and his friends found over two dozen men of the dynatoi whose sons were fighting in Bulgaria, or, often almost as important, they owned land that the barbarians were devastating. I and a few other mothers and wives insisted on joining them when they approached Ducas in the Chrysotriklinos, the golden throne room, just three days later. I stood at the back of the room with the other women, gazing at the glittering chamber. The room was much as it had been on my first visit years earlier, filled with beautiful mosaics and sunlight flowing from the dome over its center. Even Psellus was still there, as he had been on that first occasion when I was a girl.

John strode to the front with Katakalon Kekaumenos, the most senior of the dynatoi. After making their obeisances, they addressed Ducas.

"Illustrious emperor of the Romans, we have received grave news from Bulgaria of invading barbarians defeating of our armies, bringing death and destruction to our people. We hear there are hundreds of thousands of the invaders swarming the land, stealing everything they can, and killing or enslaving our citizens. We have sons fighting there and would urge you to send reinforcements to those armies."

Ducas's eyes narrowed as he contemplated this call to action and what its cost would be. I noticed the robes he wore were new, not from the old stock of the palace's wardrobes of imperial attire that Isaac had used. The soft silk fabric almost floated on him, its exquisite gold embroidery complementing the deep purple color. A heavy gold ring with a cabochon ruby graced his right hand. Isaac had shunned the frivolous expense of new robes and jewelry when he sat on the throne, instead working to rebuild the army. Only the crown Ducas wore was the same as before.

"I appreciate you bringing your concerns to our attention. I will instruct the patriarch to celebrate a liturgy for the relief of our soldiers, for if we have God on our side, who can defeat us?"

John and Kekaumenos gave each other sideways glances before continuing.

"With respect, sire, while we are sure the liturgy will benefit the armies in Bulgaria, they will benefit even more from additional soldiers and weapons. And the pay the soldiers are owed," said Kekaumenos.

"I will take your request under consideration," Ducas said, waving his hand in dismissal.

I glanced at Psellus as we filed out of the throne room, dejected at the emperor's lax attitude about the threats to the empire. His own court robes looked a bit tattered and patched, his shoes well-worn.

The men returned to our house to discuss this miserable outcome and determine what their next steps should be. Isaac was fourteen now and served food and drink for our guests. I stood next to John as the men gathered, grumbling about the outcome, and suddenly was filled with an urgency to speak.

"Excuse me, but I have a suggestion," I spoke loudly over the men. The beards turned to me, surprised that a woman would speak up in their group.

"I have a suggestion," I repeated. "We all know how close the emperor is to Michael Psellus. Is there something we can offer him, some gift, to encourage him to whisper in the emperor's ear?"

Kekaumenos chuckled. "Lady Anna, that very thought was just coming to me as well."

The men came up with enough gold coins, and Kekaumenos threw in a small farm he had been awarded in Macedonia years earlier, land that would be looted by the barbarians if they got there before the army did.

"It's never done me much good before. Not the most productive land in that area, but maybe it'll help now," he said.

The tokens we gave to Psellus did finally get the emperor to undertake a defense, although his actions were laughable. First, he tried the usual route of sending the leaders of the barbarians rich gifts to bribe them to leave, but with his usual stinginess, those gifts were as nothing to such a large horde. Next, he decided to go on campaign against them, assembling one hundred and fifty men for that effort. One hundred and fifty men against hundreds of thousands. He rode out of the Porta Aurea, at the head of this troop of one hundred and fifty soldiers, to the hoots and hollers of so many citizens that I wondered how he maintained his imperial dignity.

In the end, it seemed that the emperor's first suggestion of the patriarch leading a liturgy to beg God to relieve our people may have been the most effective. Much as the weather had turned against Isaac five years earlier, the weather turned against the invaders. Torrential downpours and flooding followed by epidemics and starvation ended their progress through Roman territory. Most of them perished in the trek back to their own lands, some dying as the flooding Danube consumed them when they tried to cross its swollen currents. Although Ducas and his one hundred and fifty soldiers had done nothing to defeat this invasion, the accidental victory allowed him to return to the city in a triumphal procession.

☙❧

GAGIK, THE LAST KING OF THE DESTROYED ARMENIAN CITY of Ani, returned to the city from his theme of Lycandos, to learn that he was being reassigned to being the dux of Charsianon, a much larger theme in the east. He visited us to pay his respects.

"You would not believe the chaos in the borderlands," he said. "It was bad before Alp Arslan destroyed my homeland." Gagik stopped then, a catch in his voice, his face bowed and in shadow. A few glints of silver shone through his black hair, much as I saw in my own mirror.

"We were so sorry to hear the news," I said, reaching out to pat his hand. Words felt inadequate, but they were all I could offer.

"Yes, and appalled at the tragedy," added John.

Gagik sighed deeply. "Thank you. You'd think after being away from the city for twenty years, it wouldn't be so painful. But it was my childhood home." He stopped and shook his head. "I'm afraid it won't be the Turks' last conquest if the emperor doesn't make some changes soon."

John raised an eyebrow. "What do you mean?"

"It's chaos in the themes of Iberia, Chaldia, Koloneia, Vasparakan. Really, all the themes in the east are in upheaval. What used to be random Turkish raiding parties have grown into full-scale invasions. No city or town is safe. I don't know where Alp Arslan was going before he turned around and attacked Ani, but it could have been anywhere, maybe Manzikert or Koloneia. Manzikert would have been closest, but Koloneia is richer."

"What about our army? Aren't they stopping them?" I asked.

Gagik frowned. "No, not at all. The emperor has starved the themes of money and military supplies, and the best soldiers have all left, leaving a motley core of untrained and lazy troops. From what I hear, it's worse than in Bulgaria. I can't blame the soldiers too much—if the emperor doesn't care, why should they? A lot of the soldiers are mercenaries, and cheap ones at that. The good ones, like the Norman, Roussel de Bailleul, are not above a little brigandage to assure themselves of adequate pay."

"What about where you'll be in Charsianon?" John asked.

"I think not so bad. In Lycandos, I kept the troops I had always on their guard and plan do the same there. It's farther from the border, but after Ani, no place is safe. The minute the patrols stop, the Turks are there."

"And the money?" I asked.

He shrugged. "I'll do what I can with the miserable few coins the emperor provides."

CHAPTER 7

1065 to 1067

L IFE WAS LIKE A CHESSBOARD, AND I WATCHED AS THE
pawns, knights and kings moved into formation for the next
generation. Weddings followed Epiphany and into the Paschal
season that year for the younger generation, but there was one
sad death.

The first wedding was for Manuel and Thea. In the weeks
preceding the wedding, our twins, Donya and Theodora, often
traveled to the Diogenes house to assist their future sister-in-law
with preparations. I doubted that two twelve-year-old girls
would be much help, but they begged so persistently that I
agreed. Thea had no sisters with whom to share her excitement
and her mother's health was not robust. It went well until a week
or so before the wedding when the two girls returned, Theodora
rushing to her room in tears.

I soon pried the story of what happened from Donya.

"We were sitting with Thea and her mother, embroidering
her gown, when Theodora said something about us doing the
same thing for her when she marries Costas," said Donya.

My eyes went wide at that comment. Theodora had been fond of Romanus's son, Costas, since childhood, always wanting to play with him when they were in the palace's nursery. I had not realized the affection still lingered.

"Then what happened?"

"Well," said Donya, wrapping a strand of her blond hair around a finger the way she did when nervous, "Thea's mother said that she would be happy to help with embroidering Theodora's dress, but she probably would not be marrying Costas. Theodora asked why not, and Lady Anya said that the Church forbids marriages where two siblings marry two other siblings."

I let out a long sigh. I had not realized the strength of Theodora's affections. She was now of marriageable age but still only twelve.

"Thank you, Donya. Lady Anya is correct about that. Sometimes the patriarch will approve such marriages, but not often. I will explain that to Theodora."

Later that day I did speak with Theodora. Her eyes were red-rimmed, and her hair tousled.

I smoothed her hair, taking hold of her hand before speaking.

"Theodora, tell me about this idea of marrying Thea's brother."

The child burst into tears and sobbed, "I know I can never marry him."

I wrapped my arms around my young daughter, trying to calm her.

"My dear child, you are still too young for us to decide on whom you should marry. I know many fine young men who would make you a good . . ." I started.

"No, you don't understand, I only want Costas. No one else." She spoke with sniffles and youthful defiance. "If I can't marry him, I will become a nun."

Theodora didn't have the best temperament to become a nun, so I suggested an alternative.

"You're awfully young to make up your mind this way. As I was saying, there are many fine men you could marry, men you would be happy with. How do you know you would be happy with Costas? He may not even want to marry you, and he's only thirteen, awfully young for a boy to be married."

"I'm sure he wants to marry me," she said, her chin set with youthful determination.

"Has he said that?" I was skeptical that a thirteen-year-old would have said that.

"No, but I know he does."

I refrained from rolling my eyes with a massive effort. I looked down at my strong-willed girl, trying to think of some way to calm her.

"I'll tell you what I can do. When you're both a bit older, if you're still sure you want to marry him, we'll speak to his parents and see if they would be willing to make such a request to the patriarch for his consent. Your father and I would also have to request it. If that doesn't work out, you will also have to be willing to consider other young men. If we can find no one else you might consider, then when you're twenty you can be tonsured and enter a monastery." I again smoothed the beautiful red hair that would be cut off if she did that. "Can you agree with that?"

Her teary blue eyes looked up at me, and she nodded.

A FEW WEEKS AFTER MANUEL AND THEA'S WEDDING, JOHN and I attended the wedding of Marie of Bulgaria and John Ducas's oldest son, Andronikos. John Ducas had amassed a great deal of wealth since his brother became emperor, and Marie was a great heiress, so the festivities were some of the most lavish I had seen since Romanus wed his Anya, also a wealthy heiress.

My cousin and his wife had been invited, but Anya's health declined after their daughter's wedding, so they were not there.

John Ducas's mansion was not far from the Great Palace, with the women's celebration in one wing of the building and the men's in the other wing. I congratulated Marie on her wedding, and praised her to her new mother-in-law, Irene, who stood beside her. Marie was a lovely and happy bride at fifteen. Irene had always been thin and wan, but now she was more haggard, although she looked happy at her son's match.

"Marie, I'm so pleased for you. Irene, your son was fortunate in his choice. Marie was always such a help when we lived in the Great Palace. I know you'll have a wonderful daughter-in-law."

Irene gave a weak smile. "Yes, I think so too. I'm looking forward to having another woman in the family."

The reception line moved on, and I found myself alone, looking for someone to talk to. Swarms of women clustered around Augusta Eudokia, and of course the bride. I was not so important anymore, but I knew who my friends were. I picked up a plate of food and began chatting with General Nikephoros Botaneiates' wife, Vevdene. I admired the beautifully embroidered maphorion that covered her hair, which had to be gray since her creased face testified to her advanced years. She was at least sixty but still made lively conversation and shared what her husband had written her about the situation in Bulgaria, where Romanus and Manuel would soon return.

"The general settled things down in Bulgaria since that terrible barbarian invasion. He doesn't expect them to return for years, if ever, given how many died in their retreat."

"That's good news," I said, grateful to hear that.

Vevdene inched closer to me, whispering, "Between us, I think the general is expecting a promotion, a better title and new assignment elsewhere. A real crown for his last years." She stopped then, winking at me. "You know what that might mean for your cousin?"

I blinked at her unexpected news. So Romanus would likely

be promoted to strategos of Bulgaria. "Oh, that is wonderful," I said. "Be sure to give my congratulations to the general when the announcement comes."

She gave me a conspiratorial wink, and we drifted into other conversations.

I gazed around the room and saw a group of young women circling Maria of Alania, soon to be wed to the emperor's son. She had grown into a beautiful young woman, even prettier than Eudokia had been at her age. One of the girls, Maria's cousin Irene, saw me and broke away from their cluster.

"Lady Anna, it's good to see you here today." The accent Irene and Maria had brought with them from distant Alania had lessened over the years to a soft lilt.

"You too, Irene. How are the preparations coming for your cousin's wedding? After Pascha, isn't it?"

She gave a brief glance at lovely Maria of Alania, surrounded by the excited chirping of a flock of young girls. "They're coming along well. The emperor is sparing no expense for it."

I sipped from my wine while a servant offered us food from a tray of olives, cheeses, and pastirma.

"And how are your children? Did any of them accompany you today?" Irene asked.

"The children are well, but none of them were invited to these festivities."

"Oh," she said, looking disappointed. "I had heard that Manuel was sent with General Diogenes to Bulgaria. What of the other boys?"

Interestingly, she asked only about the boys, not the girls.

"Well, my son Isaac is starting his training with the Excubitors soon, but the other boys still have a few more years."

"Is he? I remember Isaac very well." Irene's half smile and sudden alertness told me her memories were fond ones. "Please be sure to tell him I asked after him."

We parted then. I glanced back at Irene as she returned to her cousin's side, recalling how even as a child she had been so much more determined than Maria. Any desire she had for Isaac would do her little good if the emperor would not agree to it, though.

When the time came to depart, I waited in the central hall of the house for John, who was still making his farewells. He emerged from the reception room with someone I hadn't seen in years, Michael Maurex. We'd first met him when my family returned to Constantinople over twenty years earlier. The young man had filled out, strong and full of energy and now wore the uniform of an admiral. He had the polish and confidence that only success brings.

"Lady Anna, it's so good to see you again," he said, brushing back hair still as thick and black as it had been when we first met.

"Michael, I'm glad as well. We haven't seen you, but we do hear news of your many promotions."

"Yes, you're a real rising star in the navy these days," said John. "Isaac certainly knew what he was doing when he sent you to the Droungarios all those years ago. Now, here you are, invited to the wedding of the emperor's nephew."

John left to see to our ride home. Turning back to Michael, I recalled the promise I'd made to Marika.

"Michael," I began hesitantly, wondering if mentioning Marika's request was stupid or foolish, but I plunged in. "Do you recall Isaac's daughter, Marika?"

His face took on a serious look, somber even. He looked away briefly before looking again directly at me.

"Yes, of course I do. I think of her all the time, always. How could I forget her, even if she is a nun?"

"She isn't," I said. "A nun, I mean. She was never tonsured and said no vows, so she isn't a nun, even though she still lives at Myrelion."

His eyebrows rose at that, mouth agape.

"She wanted you to know that she still thinks of you fondly. I promised her I would tell you if I saw you again." I remembered that years ago Isaac had brought Michael Dokieanos to Myrelion with him on his visits to his sister when she lived there, spurring a marriage proposal. "I doubt you would be allowed to visit her alone, but I'd be happy to accompany you there if you're interested."

Michael's face was blank, as though he did not understand the words he was hearing.

"Would you like to visit her?" I asked, wondering if this conversation was a mistake. If he said no, how would I explain that to Marika?

He grinned at me then, grasping my hand.

"Lady Anna, I would be delighted—no, beyond delighted—to accompany you to Myrelion."

❦

IT WAS A BLESSING THAT MANUEL AND THEA'S WEDDING occurred when it did. Anya's delicate health took a turn for the worse in a chilly spell during Lent and she developed a fever. The poor woman soon began coughing, which grew worse until she could hardly breathe. Romanus, and his children Thea and Costas, as well as Manuel, were at her bedside, praying for a recovery, but the physicians could do little to help. She slipped away into eternity two weeks before Pascha. John and Manuel kept watch over her body with the bereaved Romanus the night before her funeral, trying to comfort him. Romanus wept as the priest intoned the final blessing on his wife's body.

The wedding of the emperor's oldest son, Michael, to Maria of Alania a few weeks later was the extravagant affair Irene had led me to expect. As the daughter of a king, the bride was allowed the privilege of wearing red slippers, but her gown was blue, symbolizing her lower status than her new husband's. The sheerest of silk veils covered her heart-shaped face and red-gold hair. People were already starting to say she was the most beautiful woman in the world.

Michael stood stiffly at his betrothed's side during the service, head bent but sometimes looking up nervously at her. He had the barest hint of a beard on his chin, occasionally reaching up to scratch it. He was handsomely attired in imperial purple embroidered in gold, but it did little to improve his gawky physique. I chided myself for the coarse thought that the marriage might not be consummated that night.

The entertainment opened with jugglers prancing and tumbling around the hall before the banquet started. Soon dozens of dancers with jingling cymbals on their fingers and musicians with their harps, flutes, and drums began their performance. Venison, lamb and boar, geese and shellfish, cheeses, olives, nuts, and fruits imported from Africa where they had already ripened covered the tables. Wines imported from Macedonia and Crete filled our cups. There was so much of it left over that the beggars outside the palace's gates would have feasted almost as well as we did. After so many years managing a household, as well as in my time in the palace when Isaac was emperor, I could estimate the wedding's tremendous cost. Romanus would have been enraged that the emperor spent more on this celebration than he spent in a year on the army for the soldiers guarding the empire his son would someday rule.

My thoughts turned to Isaac's daughter, Marika, still ensconced in the Myrelion monastery. I had accompanied Michael Maurex on visits there before he sailed with the navy to the Adriatic to fend off the Normans in Italy. The two of them had time alone together while I paid my respects at Catherine's tomb in the monastery's church. Catherine might not have appreciated the assignations her daughter was having with the naval commander, but the joy on their faces said it was the right thing to do. The issue was how to extricate Marika from this confinement in Myrelion's walls without raising the emperor's suspicions.

❦

MANUEL SURPRISED US SHORTLY BEFORE HE AND ROMANUS left for Bulgaria with the happy announcement that Thea was expecting their first child, who was due in the winter. It was welcome news for my cousin, Romanus, still melancholic since his wife's passing.

I made plans for our annual summer trip to the farm, this time with only five of our children. I told John of a change to our plans a few days before we left. We sat on the terrace talking, and in the bright sunlight I noticed how his hair had faded almost to white. He was over fifty now, slowing down, but still as eager as ever to depart for our holiday. He cocked an eyebrow at me at the alteration I suggested and shook his head.

"Anna, I hope you know what you're doing."

The day before we left, I stopped by Myrelion to bring Marika to our house to be ready for our departure early the next morning.

"The hegoumena did not object to your joining us on holiday?" I asked.

"No, I'm not sure she realizes that the emperor would want to know if I left. He hasn't bothered to check on me in a couple of years. She's the third one we've had in charge since my father abdicated and Mama and I came here. And that instruction may have been mislaid."

"Really?" I wondered about that.

"Yes, it definitely was misplaced," Marika said, sure of herself. "Possibly even burned."

I decided it was best I did not know how that might have happened. "Did you bring the necklace?"

Marika pulled out a small wrapped package, unfolding the cloth to show me the jeweled and enameled cross with its thick gold chain that her mother had worn as a nun.

"Excellent," I said, pleased at the success of the first part of my plan.

We left at dawn. Nine-year-old Alexios was thrilled since this would be his first time on horseback for the entire journey, while his younger brothers could only take turns riding up front with the driver. Donya and Theodora were in the litter with Marika and me, chattering and excited to be with their cousin. As always, we traveled the old and busy Via Egnatia for the first two days before turning north onto less traveled roads.

Toward the end of our second day's travels we stopped as we always did at an inn in Heraklea Thracia for the night. This harbor town perched on a hillside next to the Sea of Marmara, its narrow roads leading down to the sea, where the water sparkled summer blue in the late afternoon light. The friendly townspeople knew we stayed with them each year, so the stop would excite no particular interest. The inn held a collection of sturdy if plain buildings, overseen by an attentive innkeeper whose discretion could be trusted. As we emerged from the wagon, sore from the jostling road, Michael Maurex emerged from the shadows and pulled Marika to him.

"Good to see you made it on time," said John. "All went well in the Adriatic?"

"Yes, very well. Been here two days already. Couldn't take a chance and miss you," said Michael. "The priest's in the church just down the road from here. He'll need you to approve the marriage as Marika's oldest male relative, but that's all."

I looked at Marika. "You don't want to wait until tomorrow? Get a bath and some rest before your wedding?"

She shook her head, smiling at her sailor. "I've waited long enough. I'm ready now."

We left the driver to see to the donkeys and horses, and the whole family walked down to the sea, to the church of St. George overlooking the harbor. There in its shadowy interior, beneath images of St. George killing the evil dragon, Marika and Michael were finally wed so many years after their eyes first met.

Marika pressed the small package containing her mother's gold cross and chain into my hands before she and Michael parted from us. She would live the rest of her life in his Marmara estate another day's journey west, far from the city.

"I'll get this back to you as soon as I can," I promised, elated at the joy I saw on their faces.

"No, you must keep it if the emperor ever asks for proof of my death. I'm leaving Constantinople's palaces and politics behind. I'll never need it again." She embraced me. "Thank you for everything you've done. We are so grateful."

৩৯৫

I ENJOYED OUR HOLIDAY MONTH ON THE FARM MORE THAT year than I had in many years. I felt great satisfaction at helping Marika and Michael finally wed despite all the odds against that happening. If Ducas had had his way, she would have only left Myrelion in a coffin.

Damien and his family had adjusted to farming in the drier climate of Thrace and produced an abundant crop that year.

One night, Damien sat down with John and me, in the glow of a lantern with fireflies flitting in the air around us.

"I wanted to speak to you about this farm. I want you to know that if you ever considered selling it, my sons and I would be interested in buying it," he said.

John smiled but shook his head. The farm may have been my inheritance, but he loved it more. "We could never think of selling. It's been in Anna's family since before she was born. Of course, you're welcome to stay as long as you want."

Damien nodded. "I thought that would be your answer, but let us know if you change your mind." He paused and took a sip of his wine. "On another subject, you'll recall my grandson, Alexander's boy, Constantine, wanted to be a soldier? He turns fifteen in the spring, wants to start training, but he decided he wants to be in the navy. Hard to believe, but he fell in love with the sea on our journey to the city. Could you take him back with you? Stay with you until he can start next year?"

John and I glanced at each other. We would be happy to take in this young Constantine Dalassenus. The emperor had no fondness for that name, but Michael Maurex should be willing to take him on.

"We can," said John. "We have tutors and training for our boys. He can join them. We might know someone willing to take him on."

"Alexander will like that. The lad's impatient and not suited to farming." Damien winked and said, "Reminds me of my father."

I laughed at the recollection of my dear Uncle Costas.

❧

WE RETURNED HOME IN SEPTEMBER, AND I MADE MY WAY to Myrelion the next day to tell my tale.

"Hegoumena, I must tell you that we lost my niece during our holiday," I said, wiping a tear from my eye.

"Oh my," she said. "What happened to Lady Marika?"

"It was so short; we were so sad to lose her," I murmured with a catch in my voice, implying a brief illness. "She said she felt blessed to be leaving behind the city and its palaces for a better place. She left me this."

I opened the package I carried, removing the gold cross and chain that Catherine had worn as a nun. "It was her greatest treasure. She said she wanted me to have it."

The nun's face softened at the sight of the jewelry. I could tell she recalled how precious this had been for Marika after her mother died.

"My dear, you have my deepest sympathy for your loss. I'm glad she was with family when it happened. I only hope a priest was there to bless her?"

"Yes, Hegoumena. Yes, I was there when she received the priest's blessing. Her body rests now in Thrace."

I managed to leave soon after, grateful I avoided any outright lie. I also did not mention that the emperor might want to know about this. Better that he should not be reminded of her existence.

EARLY 1066

MANUEL RETURNED HOME IN TIME FOR THE BIRTH OF HIS first child, a daughter they named Anna after both of her grandmothers, giving her Thea's mother's nickname of Anya. Romanus returned at the same time and looked pleased with his first grandchild, a small blessing for him in a year with too many other concerns.

"Every year it's the same thing. I plead with the emperor for money; he gives me a miserly amount. I tell him that the soldiers are owed more than that; he says they'll have to wait. I scurry around the city, hunting up whatever supplies I can scrounge for the army. Never enough, but something. How long does he think we can do this?"

John shrugged. "He's been doing it for six years; probably not changing now."

I kept my head bent over the mending I was doing. It was February, and chilblains left my hands reddened and sore. I had little choice about it since our seamstress had recently died.

"Let me know what you need," John said, "and I'll see what I can do. But you're fortunate to be in Bulgaria. I think it's much worse in the east. After Ani, the Turks have grown much bolder, attacking cities and towns. Carting off people to the slave markets, the cattle and horses gone, monasteries stripped of every chalice and icon."

That was a sore subject with Romanus. His father's family came from Cappadocia, and he'd inherited lands there. Those raids were not far from where he'd lived as a child.

"And what is the emperor doing about it? Isn't he supposed

to be the protector of his people? If he doesn't start hitting back, he won't have much of an empire left," Romanus said, red with anger. He stood and walked to the brazier to warm his hands.

"The people in the city know about it, there's talk in the street about it a lot. The emperor must realize people know but he does nothing," I said. "You'd think he at least cared about the taxes the people can't pay because they're dead or gone. Or maybe noticed the beggars drifting here from the eastern themes, seeking refuge. But he doesn't leave the palace often, just for liturgy at Hagia Sophia. I think he's afraid of the people rioting."

It was a relief to say what I thought about the emperor to Romanus. And it was the truth, even if John thought I shouldn't talk so much about Ducas. Bringing up Ducas only irritated him, reminding him of the consequences of his choice.

"Bad enough he's left me in charge in Bulgaria, but without the promotion and title Botaneiates had. Said I still needed to prove myself," said Romanus. "Cheap as he is, the delay is just to save money."

John looked troubled at this rehashing of all that was happening. He tried not to be confronted with the shambles Ducas had made of the empire, but it could be avoided no longer. He stood and placed a hand on Romanus's shoulder.

"We'll go out in the morning. Manuel can join us. We'll get you resupplied."

SEPTEMBER 1066

OUR HOUSE WAS IN THE NORTHERN BLACHERNAE PART OF the city, tucked near its walls. The endless hum of traffic from the Mese and the busier streets and markets never reached us in this quiet section. As my grandmother taught me, we never turned away a beggar knocking at our gates looking for bread, but few of them ventured into this corner of Byzantium.

I sat in the courtyard one hot early September day, hoping for a cooling breeze while I again addressed the mending of clothes. I had hired first one seamstress and then another after the death of the one I'd had for many years, but sent both away. One had carelessly broken my expensive needles, and the other drank her wine without water before falling asleep during the few days I had employed her. A knock on the gate alerted old Demetrios, our gatekeeper, while I was repairing a seam that had ripped. He spoke briefly through the grille before shoving back the bolt to let the visitor in.

A shabby woman with two thin children, maybe about eight and ten, huddled nervously just inside our walls. Demetrios came to me, explaining they were begging for food.

"The woman speaks almost like an Armenian," he observed before going to the kitchen to find something for them.

Curious, I walked over to them.

"Good morning, I'm Lady Anna. My gatekeeper will bring you something to eat, but please come sit in the shade while you wait. It's much too hot to stand in the sun."

The woman murmured a few words of gratitude and guided the children to the bench where I'd been sitting.

"What are your names?" I asked.

"I am called Martina," the woman said, "and my children are George and Thekla." Her accent was not quite like Gagik's Armenian, but similar, from the eastern part of the empire.

"You're not from here?"

Martina bent her head, eyes down. "No, Lady. We're from Chaldia."

"How did you come to Constantinople?"

She began to weep, her mute and hungry children staring at her with large brown eyes.

"The Turks. They attacked our town. The children and I were outside the walls when they attacked. We hid in a cave for two days until they were gone. When we came out. . ." Her weeping grew louder, and I put an arm around her, trying to console the poor woman.

Finally she calmed, wiped her face with her dusty sleeve, and continued.

"When we came out, the town was empty. My husband dead, along with most of the other men. A few other people were still alive, some like us who had been away."

"What happened then?" I asked in a whisper, horrified at the poor woman's plight.

Demetrios arrived with water and a plate of bread, cheese, and olives for the destitute travelers.

"I couldn't stay there. I knew where my husband had buried a box with the coins he'd saved. Dug them up with my own fingers since the Turks had taken everything, and we left. I was too afraid to even stay long enough to bury him." She bowed her head, rubbing her face as though ashamed. "We walked to Amisos and got passage. My husband has family here, and I thought they could help. But the city is so large. I thought we could just ask for someone who knew him but Byzantium has so many people, no one knew of him. We've been here a month and have nothing left."

"I'm so sorry," I said, thinking frantically about what I could do to help. "We have a room above the stable you all could stay in. Then we'll see what can be done."

Martina's gaunt face teared up again as she pressed my hands in thanks. I had Demetrios show them to the now empty room where I housed any of the traveling monks who found their way to our gate looking for charity. I picked up my sewing again, shaking my head at the poor woman's tragedy. Pricking my finger as I sewed, I began to wonder if Martina might have seamstress skills.

❦

I PAID A VISIT TO THE PALACE FOR THE FIRST TIME IN months when the cool winds blew into the city in October, turning the air crisp. The emperor had taken his family to a seaside villa on the Bosphoros for the summer, trying to escape jeering from the increasingly unhappy people of Constantinople, but they were now back. Eudokia never complained of the spiteful words hurled at her husband. I doubted she knew much about what was going on in the eastern themes. Perhaps she hoped they were only foolish rumors. My new seamstress, Martina, and my cousin Damien could have explained the truth of them to her.

She greeted me in the Boukoleon Palace in the perfumed rooms of the nursery. It held only a few children now, many fewer than when Isaac had ruled. Most of the ones who had been there six years earlier had grown up and were having children of their own. Sweet Marie of Bulgaria, married only in January, was due to have her first child within the next month. Eudokia sat on the floor playing dolls with her youngest, Zoe, a three-year old copy of her mother's blond good looks.

"I'm glad to see a friendly face. Everyone seems out of sorts these days. Constantine complains about his back hurting him; the servants look angry. Psellus says I can't leave the palace—too dangerous. I feel like I'm in prison here."

"I'm sorry I haven't been to see you sooner. I've been spending time with our new grandchild. With her own mother gone, Thea is by herself with the baby, no husband or father around, just her little brother, who is no help." I paused and then became curious about what she'd said.

"How long has the emperor's back been hurting him?"

"Most of the summer, but it's worse recently. He complains as though no one has ever suffered so. I think we'd still be at the villa if he weren't in so much pain. He wanted to consult the physicians at the Hospital of Sampson." She stopped and rolled her eyes. "Michael Psellus likes to say he's a physician, but he's useless."

"I'm sure the physicians at Sampson will be of some help," I said, full of politeness, before changing the subject. "How are Michael and his new wife? Any sign of a grandchild for you?"

She shrugged and looked down. "No, Michael is fond of Maria, but nothing yet."

Being fond of Maria was one thing, bedding her was another. Most seventeen-year-old boys, with as beautiful a wife as Maria, would have been so eager that a child would be on its way by now.

"Why does Psellus say you can't leave the palace?" I asked.

"He said the people in the city were upset about fighting in Italy, or maybe someplace else. He was vague about that. He said people were making the problems into something bigger than they really are, so it's just some troublemakers." Eudokia stopped and looked at me with a raised eyebrow. "You don't agree?"

I took in a deep breath and proceeded to recount the stories of Damien and Martina. I also hinted at Romanus's complaints about the lack of money and supplies in Bulgaria and that soldiers' gossip I'd heard said Anatolia received even less.

The empress hardly moved as I spoke.

"I guess the emperor doesn't tell you about this?" I asked.

"No, he doesn't, nothing at all," she said, shaking her head. She looked thoughtful for a minute, then said, "This could be a problem for Michael when he inherits the throne, couldn't it?"

I nodded.

Just then a eunuch entered the room. "Augusta, the emperor is asking for you."

Eudokia handed Zoe to her nurse. "You'll have to excuse me. Constantine asks for me often since he's been having his back problems."

We parted, and I went to visit Thomas. He was at his desk in a corner of the Daphne Palace.

"Lady Anna," he exclaimed, a broad smile on his face. "Haven't seen you in a long time. Welcome back to the palace."

"Thank you, Thomas. It's good to see you. How has everything been here? Any changes?" I shooed a gray cat off the stool and sat across from my old friend.

He gave me a long look and then moved to shut the door, something he rarely did on my visits. The only light in the room came from a small window.

"You've heard the emperor is not well?" he asked in a low voice.

"Yes, the empress told me. Just back pain, she said."

"Yes, it would be painful, I expect. I don't think the physicians have told him yet, but I overheard them talking yesterday. They all agree there's a tumor, a cancer, that's causing the pain, but no one wants to give him the bad news."

"Oh," I said, my mind churning. "Anything they can do for him?"

"They don't know, but they didn't seem optimistic. Probably only poppy juice. They don't think he has much time."

Constantine Ducas deserved a painful death, but the empire could not manage with a boy emperor like Michael and the Turks on the frontier.

"I appreciate you letting me know. I'm not sure young Michael is ready for the responsibility of ruling."

Thomas snorted at that. "He's not ready for much of anything, not even marriage."

"What do you mean?"

"They haven't done it. Not yet." Thomas gave a knowing wink. "They haven't consummated the marriage." He had a disgusted look on his face. As someone whose ability to marry and have a family had been cut away, he found this ridiculous.

"What? How can you know?" I asked. "Has someone been spying on them?"

"No blood on the sheets. That's what the servants cleaning their rooms say. Besides that, he never touches her, looks scared of her."

"Scared of Maria? She's not exactly an Amazon; she wouldn't frighten a mouse."

"If you ever see them together and she touches him, which she will do sometimes, ever so gently, he practically jumps out of his skin. No, they haven't done it, I'm sure of it."

"I doubt he's ready to deal with the Turks if he can't manage to bed his own wife," I said. I recalled Eudokia's expression and short answer that said she had to suspect her son's timidity in the bedroom.

Thomas waved his hands as if to ward off the Turks. "That's another thing. A lot of the eunuchs and servants in the palace came from the east—Paphlagonia, Chaldia, Armeniakon. We hear from family members about what's going on out there. And what do we see the emperor doing about it? Nothing. The people in the city are getting upset and it's obvious why Ducas is avoiding the city. Why else stay away for the whole summer?"

That explained the angry looks Eudokia had noticed.

I left the palace that day feeling that I'd gotten the official story from Eudokia, but the true story from Thomas.

1067

MANUEL AND ROMANUS RETURNED FOR THE WINTER A month later, exhausted but glad to be home. Donya and Theodora, just turned fourteen, had gotten into the habit of joining my visits to help Thea with the baby. Even when the men of the house were home, though, we found excuses to come and spend time with little baby Anya.

Romanus welcomed many of his Excubitor soldiers to his house during the winter months, building their loyalty to him and a sense of camaraderie among them. One of them was Nikephoros Melissenus, a striking young man about Manuel's age. He immediately caught Donya's eye, and after a few swishes of her skirts and bold smiles in his direction, she caught his eye as well. His family was Anatolian dynatoi, with many generals so it was a good match. My growing experience with betrothal negotiations meant they went smoothly, and their wedding was in February.

I worried that Theodora might be disappointed to see her twin wed with nothing yet for her. She saw Costas on most of our visits. He was cordial and friendly, but I could tell most of the affection between them was on her side.

"Do you still have your heart set on Costas?" I asked her a few days before the wedding.

She looked at me as though I had lost my mind. "Of course. Nothing's changed. You had to wait a long time to marry Papa. I can wait too."

❧❧❧

THE EMPEROR'S HEALTH DECLINED SLOWLY OVER THE months following the physicians' diagnosis. He was not even able to attend the Divine Liturgy at Pascha, sending his wife and heir in his place. Eudokia said there was little aside from poppy juice that alleviated his pain, and even then he was miserable. She was often at his side, as were Caesar John, and, of course, Michael Psellus.

After Pascha in mid-April, Ducas was clearly in his last days. I visited Eudokia at the palace to offer her my support. She looked exhausted.

"He has me at his side night and day. Only when he's sleeping, as he is now, can I leave him. The physicians give him more and more poppy juice for the pain, so he sleeps a great deal."

"I'm sorry. This is a difficult time. Is there something I can help with?" I asked.

"I can't think of anything," she said, pushing back a loose strand of hair.

"Have you thought about what will happen after he's gone? Will there be a regent for Michael? I know he's of age to rule on his own. . ." I trailed off, reluctant to voice what everyone knew.

"We haven't discussed it, but he's probably spoken with John and Psellus about it. I know," she said hesitantly, "Michael needs more time to mature, needs my help, guidance for a few more years."

I was silent for a moment before asking, "Do you want to be regent and rule the empire? Or do you want John to take that responsibility?"

She looked at me and shuddered. "John? As regent? He'd probably send me and my daughters to a monastery to die the way Isaac's wife and daughter did. No, I want to rule as Michael's regent."

"Ruling is a great responsibility, but if you want it, you must act quickly. You'll have to convince your husband to designate you as regent for Michael, otherwise you'll be in Catherine's old rooms at Myrelion before summer."

⚜

THOMAS SENT WORD IN MAY THAT THE PHYSICIANS SAID the emperor would likely die that day. John and I left immediately for the palace for the deathwatch. Half the senate was there when we arrived, gossiping and eager to witness the transition. Finally, Caesar John, Eudokia, and her son entered the hall where we all waited, accompanied by the patriarch and Michael Psellus. Caesar John made the announcement.

"I have the sad responsibility to announce that my dearest brother, Emperor Constantine, today left this world for a world of eternal life. Let us all pray for his soul." He turned away, wiping tears from his face.

The patriarch then led the prayers for the dead, reminding us all of our own mortality. The crowd tamped down their curiosity about the succession for the few minutes as he spoke.

Psellus then moved to the front.

"Before he died, Emperor Constantine designated his wife, Empress Eudokia, as regent for their son, Michael, for as long as he requires her steady guidance. He has the utmost confidence in her judgment and wisdom. To that end, he had her swear an oath before the patriarch and others not to remarry but to faithfully guide his children and to allow no other claimants onto the throne than his own descendants."

Eudokia had succeeded in claiming the regency of her son, but the price Ducas demanded was foreswearing remarriage. No less than an oath sworn before the patriarch to ensure her obedience.

In the past, empresses sometimes remarried, finding new spouses among the empire's generals willing to fight wars for their stepsons until they came of age. Some would take the throne for themselves. Michael, seventeen and showing no martial inclinations, would never lead an army. My friend would need excellent advisors to stop the Turks and rebuild the Anatolian cities they had destroyed, but it appeared it would not be someone she could wed.

THE CITIZENS OF CONSTANTINOPLE HAD NO LOVE FOR Emperor Constantine Ducas. The announcement of his death generated only derision and calls to "bury his filthy bones somewhere else" or worse. I could tell the glee over his death shocked Eudokia to the point that he had no service for the dead at the Hagia Sophia, no carved marble sarcophagus in a magnificent city church. In fact, a few nights after he died, the emperor's body in an ordinary wooden coffin built for someone else was put on a ship docked outside of the Boukoleon Palace. The ship sailed with it to a monastery dedicated to St. Nicholas some distance from the city, in a small town on the Sea of Marmara. His brother, Caesar John, was the only devoted family member escorting it.

The end of Constantine Ducas's reign as emperor was not the end of the empire's problems. By late June came the news that Caesarea, a great and prosperous city over three hundred miles inside the empire's borders in the Charsianon theme, had been sacked. That city, which hadn't seen an invasion in hundreds of years, had let its walls deteriorate. There had been no need for them. The Turks seized it with little effort. The city was put to the torch, the monasteries robbed, and any survivors enslaved.

Gagik was the dux of the Charsianon theme, and Caesarea had been its capital. He had taken his soldiers to another town where he'd expected an attack, and so had not been there to defend it. The emperor had not sent enough money to pay for as many soldiers needed to ensure the safety of the entire theme.

I knew Eudokia would be desperate to get insight on how to deal with the situation. She wouldn't get it from Caesar John or Psellus; their advice had only worsened the situation.

"John, what would you think about coming with me to the palace and speak with Eudokia about what's going on in the east? I know she could use solid ideas from someone with military experience," I asked one evening as I poured us both some wine.

He looked up at me, a look of irritation on his face. He looked tired. His hair was almost white now. He'd gotten heavier over the past few years, moving slower, not as quick to wrestle with our youngest sons.

"Anna, don't be so quick to volunteer me. The empress has many soldiers she can call on, why should I—" he stopped abruptly.

I looked at him, ready to hand him his cup. His face colored from a blotchy red into purple. His eyes rolled up in his head and he slumped to the side with one arm twitching.

"John, John!" I called, rushing to him before he fell to the floor. "Help! I need help!"

CHAPTER 8

JULY TO OCTOBER 1067

JOHN WAS GONE. HE WOULD NEVER SLEEP NEXT TO ME again. He would never take us on holiday to the farm again. He would never play with our children again. His gentle voice would never call my name again. We never think about how all the things we love doing, one day we will be doing them, without realizing it, for the last time.

I lay awake at night remembering the first time we played chess and he looked so deeply into my eyes, the years of longing when we waited to marry, the making of our children, how he stood by me when my grandparents died. All the memories I had from over twenty years of marriage. I could not have asked for a more loving husband than John had been.

Thea was soon at our house, making the funeral arrangements, sending a messenger to bring Manuel home and another one to the priest and our friends in the city. I sat beside her, agreeing to her suggestions, while John's last contorted expression haunted my mind. I wept and prayed that his last moments had not been too painful.

The summer's heat meant the funeral could not wait for Manuel's return since that would take at least a week. As it was, the earliest it could be scheduled was on Monday. Thea and my daughters did the customary sweeping of the house. They bought a length of the finest white silk for Martina to sew into his shroud. She must have been up all night working on it since it was ready for visitors arriving on the second day after he left this troubled world. I consented to his burial in the small church of St. Thekla, where Isaac was interred. Isaac had built and sponsored the little church years earlier, and I knew John would rest happily beside his beloved brother.

Thea lent me the dark mourning garments for John's funeral that she had worn when her mother died. Martina would sew my own later, but John's unexpected death meant I had nothing. I wept at the thought of wearing a widow's garments. I found one of his forgotten boots under the bed and threw it at the wall, furious at John for dying and at myself for my anger at John. The night before friends would come to pay their respects, I stood in the garden behind our house, gazing up at the stars, smelling the roses in full bloom and sad that John would miss all the life still pulsing in the world. Waves of love and regret washed over me, bringing me to my knees. The wind rustled the leaves, almost like John's soul pushed them aside on its way to heaven. I yearned to summon John's ghost back and tell him he'd left us too soon.

I rose at dawn, struggled into the unfamiliar attire, adjusting the belt to fit my larger waist. Thea and Manuel had only the one child to my eight, so it needed letting out. My fingers fumbled at it in the dim light. I glanced at the bed I had shared with John for so long. I sat down on it, tears falling at the memory of how often he would sleep later than I did. So many times I gave into temptation, slipping back between the sheets to warm myself beside him, his arms wrapping around me. I should have done it more often.

I dried my eyes and went downstairs to be sure all was ready.

A sheet covered John, which I pulled back to expose his face, my hand brushing his cold, unmoving cheek. Bowls of flowers throughout the room sweetened the warm air, while olive and laurel sprigs were spread beneath my feet. Clatter from the distant kitchen told of our cook readying the food and drink visitors would expect.

My son Isaac appeared in the doorway, the concerned look on his face that everyone had been showing me.

"Mama, how are you? Can I get you anything?"

I looked at my son, blinking at his question before shaking my head. This boy's temperament was most like John's, warlike in battle but avoiding pointless quarrels as his father did.

"No, thank you, Isaac," I said, putting on a slight smile at his concern. "Just let me sit here in the quiet with him for a few minutes."

He left to check on the kitchen's preparations.

I gazed at John's face, my heart aching at the thought it would soon be beyond my ability to see.

"John, I forgive you for not taking the throne when Isaac gave it up. Can you forgive me for wanting you to take it?" My tears stained the fine white silk burial shirt he wore. I knew that he should have ruled, yet I knew he did not have it in him to grasp the crown as Ducas had.

"Mama," said a small voice behind me.

Alexios was there, his red hair plastered down with water, his eleven-year-old freckled face polished clean for the day. His eyebrows were raised in surprise.

"Papa didn't want to be emperor when Uncle Isaac gave it up?" Alexios had been just five when those events shattered my life and would not have known. John and I rarely spoke of it, and never around the children.

I gave my son a long look. The truth and my emotions had been bottled up too long.

"No, son, he didn't want to. He had no wish to rule over others or deal with palace politics. It wasn't in him. But sometimes you have to take on a responsibility you don't want. I thought your father should have taken the throne. It was the one thing we disagreed on. Instead, Constantine Ducas let the empire fall apart. Your father would never have let that happen."

Alexios swallowed, looked down at his father's cold body, then back at me. He suddenly embraced me.

"Mama, I promise I will never disappoint you. No matter what." My son's voice, usually so full of mischief, never serious, was hoarse with grief and maturity.

I put my arms around his slim body. "Thank you, Alexios. I know you won't."

❦

EUDOKIA WAS AMONG THE FIRST VISITORS THAT DAY, accompanied by Thomas and an escort of Varangians for protection. The two of us resembled a pair of crows in our black mourning. Eudokia knelt first beside John's casket to say her prayers before stopping to speak with me.

"I am so sorry, Anna. This must have been a shock to you."

I nodded, unable to speak. My friend embraced me in consolation.

"You know I would be happy if you rejoined me in the palace. I've missed talking to you every day as we used to," Eudokia said as she grasped my hand. "I wish it weren't so, but we can support each other in our widowhood. I realize it's too soon to decide, but you know I would welcome you."

"Thank you. I'm just trying to get through each day now. Waiting for Manuel to return," I said. "But thank you."

She nodded and turned to leave. Thomas stopped to give me his condolences, his soft brown eyes regarding me with gentle concern.

"Lady Anna, my deepest sympathy. Lord John was a wonderful man." He pressed my cold hand between his two warm ones, before turning to kneel at the bier to pray.

A long procession of mourners filled the house all day. Many of our neighbors stopped by, expressing their gratitude for John's help after the earthquakes a few years earlier, kneeling to say prayers beside the bier. Soldiers that John and Isaac had served with, some hobbling in on canes or missing a limb, all praying beside my husband's body. Our physician, Maria Kourtikios, was there, reminiscing about what a stoic patient he had been. That made me laugh since John always complained about her painful stitching of his wounds.

I thought the last of the visitors were gone late in the afternoon when a dark figure loomed in the shadows at the doorway. Gagik stepped into the room and gripped my hands.

"Lady Anna, I was so sorry to hear the sad news of your husband's death. I just arrived in the city to speak with the empress about the situation in Caesarea. I haven't even been to the palace yet. Tell me, how did this happen?"

"It was very sudden, unexpected. We were just talking when. . ." I choked out, but could not speak anymore.

Gagik knelt to pay his respects and kissed both my hands in the Armenian way of consolation. "I understand. I am sad the Comnenus brothers are gone now. They helped me so much when I first arrived here. I am certain they are together now in heaven."

"It is also my prayer that they are," I said as I wiped the tears from my eyes. Looking at Gagik I could see his clothes were dusty and travel-stained, deep crevices of pain etched on his face. Caesarea. I walked him out to the garden with its long twilight shadows.

"You must tell me of what happened in Caesarea," I said. "The news is beyond terrible."

"Whatever you heard, it was worse. Such a beautiful city desolate. I'd gone north where we heard there was an attack planned. It was a ruse. The Turks attacked when they knew I was gone and disappeared before I could return." His own eyes now glistened with tears at the memory of the destruction. "Thousands dead, even more taken to Damascus. Everything of value gone."

"I am so sorry," I said, laying a hand on his arm. "You shouldn't be blamed for this."

"I hope not. The emperor has starved the army in Anatolia for years. What soldiers I have are poorly paid and armed. I wrote many times asking for more, but no help comes. I'd worry about losing my position, but no one else would take it."

"I can speak with the empress, if that would help."

"Please, whatever you can do," he said.

๑๕๑

THE NEXT DAY WAS SUNDAY. AGAIN, I KEPT WATCH OVER the body in the dark hours of that last night with John after over twenty years together, now ended. Isaac and Alexios spent some of those hours with me, reminding me that while those years might be behind me, our children remained.

The priest arrived early Monday morning to begin the service and lead the procession to St. Thekla's. Neighbors and friends lined the road, weeping and saying prayers for the dead as we passed. My children wailed loudly on the walk to the church, while I wept in silence, my face covered with a sheer black veil.

The panels of the iconostasis inside Isaac's intimate church held holy icons of Jesus and the Theotokos, St. Paul, and his disciple, the pagan Roman he converted, St. Thekla. Their golden halos glowed in the candlelight. Our children and I were in tears as the priest said the last prayers. It felt as though a part of my soul was missing, and I kept trying to find it. I barely noticed the mourners who returned to the house for a meal in John's remembrance.

I was in my office two days later, making an effort to focus on what we would have to live on now that John's stipend from the palace was gone. I had a good income from the warehouse, but I still had five unmarried children to consider. We had already gotten Isaac outfitted for his military service; that was an enormous expense that would come up again in a few years for Alexios, then Adrian and Nikephoros. There was the farm, and Damien said he would be interested in buying it. I loved the farm but visiting it would not be the same. My eyes blurred with tears and I couldn't add and subtract the numbers.

Clattering of hooves in the courtyard got my attention. A horse and rider, Manuel, were there.

"Mama," he said in a gruff voice before embracing me. His face was tearstained, sweaty, and exhausted. "I came as quickly as I could."

"I know. We couldn't wait any longer for the funeral. But you'll be here for the third-day services tomorrow. Can you stay longer?"

He nodded. "The strategos said to stay as long as I needed to," he said, referring to Romanus by his new title.

"Come inside and see everyone first. I know you'll want to get home to Thea and the baby. Your wife has been such a help after your father died; I don't know what I would have done without her."

Manuel was home for the third day memorial and the ninth day as well. I hadn't expected him to stay for the fortieth day service but he did. I finally became curious when he showed no sense of urgency about returning to Bulgaria.

"Romanus must be hoping you will be returning soon," I commented one day in early September as we sat outside under the arbor attempting to play chess.

He shrugged but said nothing.

"Manuel, what's wrong? I am happy you are here, but I would have thought Romanus would want you back by now."

He sat back in his chair, his gaze darting around as though checking for something. Then he leaned forward to whisper.

"The strategos was happy I could leave so I wouldn't be implicated if it all goes wrong."

Chilling words for a hot summer day.

"He's reached his limit. The emperor's starving his troops, leaving us to make do with whatever we can scrounge. Bad enough, but when Romanus heard about the Caesarea disaster, it drove him mad. He has family near there and no idea what's happened to them. He's rebelling and bringing his army to the city," Manuel said in a quiet voice. "I may be able to help him from inside the walls. We'll know in the next few weeks."

Everything Manuel said about Caesarea was right. It was a disaster, one created by Constantine Ducas and his miserly ways when it came to the empire's soldiers. But Ducas was dead, and Romanus was rebelling against a young man too reticent to consummate his marriage, and against his mother and regent, who was my best friend. I knew Romanus was justified in his actions, but I worried about how this might harm Eudokia and her son. Romanus was not a brute, though, who would execute a woman and her children.

"How soon?"

"I expect to hear in the next few days. He was pulling together all the support he needs."

৩১৫৩

MANUEL'S IMPATIENCE GREW AS THE DAYS PASSED WITH NO word. Finally, the worst news arrived: one of Romanus's men had betrayed him and was bringing him back to the city in chains. It was a sick reminder of Grandmother telling me of Romanus's father when he rebelled against the Orphanotrophos, was betrayed, and ended up dead himself rather than betray his own friends.

We were on the Mese when the wagon came through with Romanus in it, in chains but still standing tall. I expected the people to throw rotten food or other garbage at him, but the populace was quiet. The only comment I heard came from a burly man unloading heavy barrels of wine outside a tavern.

"I wish someone had rebelled a long time ago."

I went to the Great Palace to make my case, first speaking with Thomas. He had a comfortable office, reflecting the empress's reliance on him.

"Thomas, can you tell me where they are holding the strategos? What is being planned for him? Can I see him?"

Thomas frowned. "He's in the old Baths of Zeuxippus. He's not been harmed, but Caesar John wants a show trial for him before the Senate, maybe in a week or so. The Caesar is furious about this rebellion; it puts his nephew's right to the throne in question. He wants the general executed."

I closed my eyes, sick at that thought. "I understand. But can I see him?"

Thomas screwed up his face for a moment, thinking. Finally, he said, "I can give you a few minutes with him."

We took a circuitous path around the palace to a small back entrance into the old baths. The Baths of Zeuxippus had long since been converted to a prison. I ran my fingers over the cracked and worn marble where the old Latin word "Frigidarium" had been carved on the wall outside the room where he was held.

"Romanus?" I whispered into the shadowy room, the only light coming from a high window.

His head rose at my voice. "Anna?" He stood and embraced me.

"Yes. How are you? I've brought some food, clean clothes, and a blanket for you."

"Thank you. I'm doing as well as you can expect. How are Manuel and Thea? And Costas?"

"So far all are well. I have only a little time. I've heard you will be tried before the Senate within the week."

"I guess they want at least a public trial before executing me." He snorted in derision. "They'd rather get rid of me and keep the Turks."

"I can get you a lawyer."

"What for? It won't make a difference. I rebelled. I'm not going to deny it. The verdict will be the same no matter. They have the testimony of that Armenian who betrayed me." He sounded determined, and angry.

My heart sank. "But you're not a traitor. You can't give up." Romanus was a good man; he deserved better than an emperor as weak as Michael was.

"I know I'm not. I'll defend myself with the sword of truth. No one will leave that trial saying they don't know how bad things are. The senators will know that if, or when, they execute me, they'll have lost their last best chance to turn back the Turks. I don't want to die, but at least I won't be around to see the Roman people destroyed."

I could not blame Romanus for being disillusioned, but I was not resigned. Romanus was right about everything going on in the east. I knew he was the only one who could turn back the surging Turkish armies that destroyed our lands, leaving only empty cities and weeping orphans. I had to think of a way, the right way, to make that happen.

፨

SLEEP DID NOT COME EASILY, MY MIND FULL OF IDEAS AND schemes, until the simplest and easiest solution became obvious. I rose early the next morning and dressed in the fine silk mourning dress Martina had sewn for me. I gave instructions to her and the other servants and then sent for a sedan chair to take me to the Great Palace to visit Empress Eudokia.

When I arrived, the empress was meeting Emperor Michael and her counselors, who would include the Caesar John Ducas and Psellus. Her situation must have felt like being in the grip of a giant pincer, with the Turks attacking in the east, Romanus rebelling in the west, and the advice she was getting from Ducas and Psellus being no better than what they had given Constantine Ducas when he ruled.

I waited patiently in her rooms, rehearsing to myself what I planned to say. It was a crisp fall day with red and yellow leaves brilliant against a clear blue sky, the air fresh. This path into politics felt like cutting fabric for a new garment. I was making the first slash. It had to be right.

Eudokia finally joined me, her lovely face shadowed with concerns. She was in her late thirties now, and when she removed her maphorion, a little silver glinted among her blond tresses, braided and looped at her back. We embraced in greeting.

"Do you recall when John died and you offered me a place here in the palace as one of your companions?" I asked.

Her eyes lit up with expectation. "Oh yes, of course. Have you decided to accept my offer? I would be so happy if you were here."

"I think so, if you'll still have me."

"Of course I will. Why wouldn't I?"

"Well, because Romanus Diogenes is my cousin, and my son is married to his daughter. I wasn't sure how you would feel about that."

"Anna, we've known each other a long time. I know I can trust you," she said. "Caesar John may not be too pleased, but he doesn't expect women to make trouble."

"Thank you, I'm grateful the offer is still available." I paused, swallowed, and pressed on. "I am so sorry Romanus has caused you any concerns. You know he's had the same worries about the Turks that we've had, but more so since he has family nearby Caesarea, in Cappadocia. He's been leading the army in Bulgaria and hoped that he could lead that army over to Anatolia. He wanted to use it to push back the Turks. It sounds like the Turks have gotten much bolder since you and I spoke about them last year."

The empress nodded in agreement and frowned. "So much worse. You can't even know how terrible the reports are. Psellus only lets a little of the truth trickle out into the city. "

I said nothing for a moment and let her thoughts dwell on the devastation.

"Do you remember my cousin? I think you met him once or twice at our house, and perhaps when his late wife, Anya, was serving Augusta Catherine?"

She paused and thought about it, a smile of recollection glowing on her face. "Yes, I do recall him, although we never spoke beyond a polite greeting. I remember Anya but I didn't realize she had died."

"Yes, it was a couple of years ago. You know Romanus is to be tried next week," I said.

"Yes, in front of the Senate and three judges."

I gave her a direct look. "Perhaps your son, and you, as the empress regent for your son, should attend. The charges against Romanus are serious, but you should hear what he has to say. You may decide his actions were warranted."

Eudokia peered at me thoughtfully, an eyebrow raised.

She gave a slow knowing smile. "I believe you're correct. My presence as regent would lend credibility to any decision the court arrived at. Yes, I definitely think we need to attend the trial."

CHAPTER 9

OCTOBER 1067 TO JANUARY 1, 1068

THE FOLLOWING WEEK, I SAT ON A STOOL BESIDE THE thrones Eudokia and Michael were seated on in the Senate, gazing around at this antique building for the first time. Beautiful marble panels covered the walls, similar to those found in the Hagia Sophia. The well-worn floors still had intricate mosaics swirling in red-and-green patterns that edged multicolored rectangles. Four enormous chandeliers, each with at least twenty oil lamps blazing, hung from the ceiling.

The room quieted, and the senators—there had to be at least two hundred of them—and judges stood in silent respect for the empress and her son as they took their places opposite the spot where Romanus would be held. Everyone in the room sat after Eudokia graciously inclined her head, signifying permission, while Emperor Michael looked at the crowd with wide eyes. Caesar John Ducas and a few of his retainers sat nearby. There were three judges hearing the trial but the primary one was Michael Attaleiates, a man held in high esteem by all for his fairness. Each judge wore their traditional close-fitting red hoods and sober dark robes.

Two imposing soldiers escorted Romanus into the accused's box on the Senate floor, with two more not far behind them. A chorus of boos and hisses from the usual bootlickers greeted him as he came into view. My cousin's face did not move from its stern expression at this rude greeting. He stood above average height, with dark hair, tanned skin, and piercing blue eyes. He looked every inch the general he was in the dress uniform I'd sent him. General Romanus Diogenes made a deep obeisance to Eudokia and Emperor Michael before turning and bowing to the judges.

Judge Michael Attaleiates read the charges.

"Romanus Diogenes, Strategos of Bulgaria, you have been charged with conspiring to rebel against the empire, the Emperor Michael, and his lady regent mother, the Augusta Eudokia. You have also been accused of attempting to plot to bring the empire's enemies, the Hungarians, into this conspiracy, bringing our enemies to the very walls of this city. How do you respond to these accusations?"

The room was silent as everyone waited. Romanus stood looking directly at the judges, his lips pursed and his hands clasped behind his back, before finally speaking.

"I am innocent, innocent of plotting rebellion against this empire, this Roman Empire, that I have sworn loyalty to for my entire life. My loyalty to my homeland is unwavering. What I rebelled against is the mismanagement, the neglect of the Roman people. I served the empire in Bulgaria for over ten years, first under the great general Nikephoros Botaneiates, and for the past two years as strategos myself. I've seen the miserly amounts that my soldiers received during those years in Bulgaria that were barely enough to keep them alive, and yet we continued to defend our homeland, our great Roman Empire, from the barbarians who would swarm over our borders, steal our gold and cattle, kill or enslave our people. Many of those soldiers gave their life for their country. Some of them survive but with terrible wounds, wondering how the Roman Empire can abandon them when they never abandoned it. Widows and their orphaned children come to me, asking for the widow's payment they are due, but we have nothing to give them. What would you have me say to them? What would you have me do?"

Romanus paused and looked around at the assemblage, trying to gauge their response. Many of the senators, well-fed and silk-clad, had little idea what our soldiers lived through for the modest compensation he described. Few of them had ever served in the military, never tramped miles through mountains and valleys in summer's heat or freezing rain to really know what those men managed to accomplish. Some of the senators had looks of dawning realization, some of skepticism, some of real shock at what they were hearing. They had been happy in their ignorance. Caesar John's impassive face betrayed little interest in the accused's charges.

"For all those years, I said to the soldiers that the empire would make good on its promises eventually. Eventually. I did whatever I could to improve the situation, wheedling supplies and equipment wherever I could find some. I kept hope for a better day burning in their hearts, and they trusted me," he said with an anguished shout.

Romanus bowed his head, his voice cracking but filled with anger. "They trusted me even though I failed them because I could not get the empire to understand that it needed to pay its soldiers and supply its soldiers so they could fight another day, another battle." He lifted his head now, looking at the polished senators. "So they could stop the hordes from invading our great Roman Empire, something barbarians try to do so often. I failed them." Romanus gripped the railing and glared around at the crowd. Tears streaked his cheeks.

"My army and I remained loyal despite the shameful neglect. At the same time, news from the east, in Anatolia, kept coming to us. We heard of more and more raids on our once-secure cities and towns there. The Turkish sultans wanted our gold, our cattle and horses, our people to sell in the slave markets. Our women and children forced to abandon our holy Church." For the first time, Romanus looked squarely at John Ducas. "Surely, I thought, these attacks would be answered, the waves of attacks stopped. But no, no, we heard only of more and more of them. For a while, the attacks were only on the borders, distant spots that some thought were unimportant, could be forgotten. Strange that was not what I thought when Pechenegs and Scythians attacked on the borders my men guarded. My armies fought back those invaders."

Romanus's tears were gone, his voice grew louder and angrier. He had everyone's attention, especially Eudokia's.

"How was I to know that as badly as my soldiers had been treated, the soldiers in the east fared even worse? That was the only conclusion I could come to based on those reports. Over the past few years, I prayed that the news would report that the Turks had been defeated, defeated the way my armies defeated the Scythe barbarians, the brutal Pechenegs. That the destruction would end. Then came the news about Caesarea, a city over three hundred miles from the border. A city thought so safe and secure that its walls became decrepit because there was no need to fear invasion. A city just a few miles from my own ancestral home. Sacked, devastated, babies murdered, more women and children enslaved, monasteries looted of their precious chalices, their beautiful icons, their holy relics. Their buildings burned to the ground.

"At this moment, I lost all hope that the empire, this great Roman Empire of ours that reaches back a thousand years to Augustus, to Marcus Aurelius, to Constantine the Great, to Justinian, would come to its senses and end the madness of ignoring these attacks. I love my homeland and had to do something to stop them. If that meant I had to lead my army to the capital, and march into Anatolia, then so be it. There was no one else able or willing. I had to do what no one else would.

"So, yes, I did rebel, but it was not against the empire, only against those unwilling to fight for it. That is my guilt."

His speech had silenced the chattering senators, everyone holding their breath at Romanus's passionate defense. Many senators, long secure in their palaces in the city, were slack-jawed in shock at the dire image he painted. They had no idea the price soldiers paid for their luxurious and safe lives in their palaces. Most may not even have realized how dire the situation was.

Michael Attaleiates and the other two judges were pale, no doubt wondering how to condemn the one man who was willing to stop the Turks. Romanus's impassioned defense had enthralled Eudokia, while Caesar John Ducas flushed red-faced with anger and embarrassment. The accusations of imperial mismanagement and parsimony fell directly on him, his dead brother, and Michael Psellus.

The judges called for a recess so they could discuss the case.

Eudokia turned to me and whispered, "There is so much I had no idea about. Constantine never told me much of what was happening, especially when it concerned the army or money."

"I know. That was his way." I glanced at Emperor Michael who was chatting with Psellus.

"Your cousin was so forceful in his defense; I don't know how the judges can condemn him for what he did."

"Yes, but he did rebel, no matter how justified it was. I think the judges will have to find him guilty. But as empress regent you do have the ability to commute the punishment to something other than execution."

Eudokia glanced over to where Romanus was being held. He was looking directly at us. I thought at first he was looking at me before realizing he was staring at her. Her eyes met his. The two of them could not stop looking at each other, as though the rest of the world mattered not. A flush rose on Eudokia's cheeks.

Caesar John strutted over to where we were sitting. He spoke in a low voice so he wouldn't be heard by anyone else.

"Diogenes certainly made a dramatic speech, but it sounded

more like exaggeration and fantasy to me than what's really going on. Those Turks are nothing but gnats. An annoyance, of course, but nothing more than that to the Roman Empire. When we're ready, we'll just swat them away."

Eudokia broke her gaze with Romanus and turned to Caesar John. She raised an eyebrow, impatient with his excuses.

"Caesar, just when do you think we'll be ready? I'm concerned about the empire my son has inherited. I've met many times with you, with Psellus, and the rest of my late husband's advisors, and I've been told that we aren't ready. Nor have any plans been made for our defense. Will we have plans before they reach the walls of Nicaea? Certainly before Nicomedia, I hope."

Her biting sarcasm made the barbarian threat sound worse than I hoped it ever would be. If the Turks reached Nicaea or Nicomedia, just across the Bosphoros, then the situation would be infinitely more frightening. John Ducas gave a sort of grunt of acknowledgement before slinking back to his seat.

The judges did not make us wait long for their decision and were back in less than an hour. Michael Attaleiates rose to read the verdict, clearing his throat.

"The defendant, the Strategos of Bulgaria, Romanus Diogenes, has been accused of rebellion against the empire. General Diogenes has admitted in court that his plan was to bring his army to Constantinople and thence to Anatolia. He received no such instructions from Emperor Michael, the emperor's regent, Augusta Eudokia, or any other imperial official. He and his army should have remained in Bulgaria. This is precisely the definition of rebellion, which the general admits. Consequently, we do find the defendant, Romanus Diogenes, guilty of rebellion. As such, the penalty for rebellion is execution and forfeiture of his property and titles."

The crowd of senators began chattering at the decision. John Ducas looked pleased at this supposed vindication of his late brother's governing policies. But Attaleiates was not finished and raised his voice over the hubbub.

"At the same time, we recognize that the general was motivated by a great desire to benefit, help, even save the empire from the results of policies that, ah," he stopped, trying to think of the best turn of phrase, "that may have been shortsighted. Therefore, we ask that Augusta Eudokia, regent for her son, the Emperor Michael, consider commuting this penalty and maintain the general's life, his rights, his properties, and titles."

Like flowers following the sun, all faces turned to the augusta, anticipating her response. Her impassive face revealed nothing of her thoughts, but she gazed across the crowded room at Romanus. I had tried my best to save my cousin, but even I could not be certain what her response would be. My hands were sweaty in my lap, and my heart raced as we waited for her to speak.

"Thank you, judges, for your thoughtful verdict in this difficult case. I appreciate the wisdom and experience you brought to it, and I agree that the traditional punishment for rebellion would be too harsh a choice for General Diogenes. He spoke eloquently of his concerns for the Roman Empire, concerns that I share as regent for my son, Emperor Michael. Rebellion is a serious crime, but in this case the general wanted only to save us from our own mistakes."

John Ducas snorted at that before spitting into a corner. I glanced over at him and saw him giving me a black look, as though accusing me of thwarting his plans.

Eudokia ignored him and continued. "Therefore, I have decided to commute his sentence to one of exile to his ancestral home in Cappadocia. He will have a week in the city to clear up his affairs, but he will have to be gone by then."

I closed my eyes in relief at this. It was the best that could be expected for Romanus, but the situation in the east would remain chaotic.

❦

EUDOKIA WENT ABOUT HER USUAL DUTIES OVER THE NEXT
few days but appeared distracted, her mind elsewhere. She asked
people to repeat themselves, often staring dreamily out the
window.

The day before Romanus had to leave Byzantium he was
announced as a visitor. He swept into Eudokia's receiving rooms
dressed in a green wool tunic, breeches, and traveling boots, a
heavy winter cloak on his shoulders. He knelt before the
empress, looking directly up at her. His face was flushed, his eyes
intense.

"Your Majesty, I want to express my sincerest gratitude for
the mercy you showed me in commuting my sentence. You
should understand I would never have harmed you or your children. I was desperate to stop the destruction raining on the
empire, and I believed I had no other choice. Please forgive my
error. I hope you will someday find me useful in turning back
these invaders."

My cousin had Eudokia's full attention. Her lips parted with
a radiant smile.

"General Diogenes, your efforts on behalf of the empire have
been noted, and we are grateful for them. We believe the Turks
will only be stopped if the empire musters its forces and defeats
them. At present, we appear to be sorely lacking in qualified
leaders, so it may not be long before we will call upon you. How
long will it take you to return home?"

The two of them spoke for a few more minutes but I had
heard—and seen—enough. I thought it would not be long
before she would find a reason for Romanus to be summoned
back to Constantinople.

❦

Turkish attacks continued but on a smaller scale over the next few weeks. I sat beside Eudokia as her companion when she met with Caesar John, Psellus, and the other advisors who dithered about what to do. John Ducas had never commanded an army, nor was he inclined to leave the luxuries of the city. The neglect of the army for almost seven years meant that the best soldiers had retired or resigned in disgust. The soldiers sent east, with the exception of the critical dux of Antioch, Nikephoros Botaneiates, had little experience with major military actions. Any town fortunate to have strong walls could hold back the Turks, but the surrounding countryside would be denuded of everything of value, leaving the residents with nothing to live on.

They really had no one left to call on except for Romanus Diogenes.

Eudokia and I returned one afternoon to her rooms after another frustrating meeting.

"Those men have no idea what to do. They try to tell me that the attacks aren't so bad. Do they think I'm an idiot?" she asked while pacing the room. "I see refugees streaming into the city, I see the taxes paid to the treasury dropping to nothing from more and more parts of the empire. Do they think the Turks will magically stop? What kind of a mother would I be if I left an empire like that for my son?"

"What do you want to do?" I asked, knowing the answer.

She gave me an earnest look. "I think we should ask Romanus to return. I want him to assume command of the army in the east."

I waited a long moment before answering, giving thought to my words.

"In the past, when an empress ruled as regent for her son but needed a strong general to fight the empire's wars, it was often thought wise that the empress marry the general. Otherwise, that general might decide to take the throne for himself and eliminate the legitimate heirs. He would have obligations to the boy as stepfather that would not permit killing the child or sending him to a monastery. Emperor Basil's mother did that," I reminded her.

Eudokia nodded, eyes wide.

"In your case, your husband made you promise on his deathbed not to remarry. An oath before the patriarch, senators, and Caesar John. It would be difficult for you to be released from such an oath or to get the senators to agree to it. John Ducas would likely not be happy about it. He could make it difficult. At the same time, it would be the best way to guarantee Romanus's loyalty. You have to resolve those issues if you decide it best to marry again."

I paused to let the full meaning of my words become clear. "What do you want to do?"

"I. . .I am willing to marry again if I can be released from my oath. I would do it for my son, for Michael. But do you think," she hesitated, her face flushed, "do you think your cousin would be willing to marry me? I wouldn't want to force him to."

I looked at her. Even in her late thirties with six children, she was still a lovely woman, an empress who would make whomever she married an emperor. Any man would be pleased at such an offer. Recalling how Romanus had looked at her, I doubted he would feel forced.

"I think he would be eager to consider your proposal. But we will have to consider how to present it to your counselors— and the patriarch since he'll be the one to release you from your oath. That will be the difficult part."

⚜

THE DAYS GREW SHORTER AND THE WEATHER COLDER AS the weeks of Advent moved toward the Feast of the Nativity. A letter was sent to Romanus with instructions that he should return to the capital. I included a short note of my own to allay any suspicions he might have. Eudokia was anxious to see him again but as the weeks passed and the north winds blew in cold and snowy, no word came.

Eudokia grew more forceful with her counselors, insisting that the borderlands increase their soldiers, that there should be retaliation against the Turks. She embarrassed these men whose passive attitudes had allowed the realm to reach such a state. She discussed with them who should lead the army, how many men, what supplies should be sent, where the money would come from. She got them to finally stop ignoring the problem, although their efforts were feeble.

The morning of the Nativity dawned cold and clear, a crystal-blue sky with frost everywhere. The imperial procession from the palace to the Hagia Sophia began, the eunuch choir at the head, followed by the senators, Caesar John, then courtiers such as myself, and lastly Eudokia, Emperor Michael, and Michael's wife, Marie of Alania. We were almost to the Hagia Sophia for the service when a travel-stained figure pushed through to the front of the crowd and raised a hand in greeting.

Romanus had arrived.

❦

EUDOKIA'S CONVERSATIONS WITH HER ADVISORS intensified, emphasizing the need to field an army against the Turks by spring. Who would lead the army? The choices were appallingly few—only Nikephoros Botaneiates, already an old man nearing seventy, or Romanus. The empire had soldiers, but there were no others with the tested experience they had battling invasions. Eudokia asked her counselors a question.

"How can I be sure that either of them would stay loyal and not push my son aside?"

The men looked around the table at each other, tugging on their gray beards, making gruff sounds in their throats. Finally, one of them spoke the words Eudokia wanted them to admit.

"The usual way would be for you to marry him," said one.

She looked down the table, gauging how best to lead them where she wanted them.

"How could I marry him if I swore an oath to my late husband, before all of you here and the patriarch, that I would not remarry?"

The rest of this submissive group looked to Caesar John to express his opinion before daring to voice their own. I sat by Eudokia's side, her lady companion, watching his face contort as he considered his options. He recalled his brother's dying wish that his wife never remarry, but even he recognized that the empire needed a strong military leader. He knew what coins the treasury held, he knew what pitiful taxes were flowing into it, he knew that desperate and destitute souls were flooding the city.

"I could speak to the patriarch, get his approval to free you from that obligation," he said grumpily.

"Speak to him today, if possible," Eudokia said. "The other question is which of these two men I should wed."

One of the men, Basil Trachaneiotes, spoke up.

"I prefer Botaneiates. A strong general, proven experience, wife died last year."

"Yes, he has valuable abilities," Eudokia agreed. "But he's defending Antioch. This time of year, it could be months before he could arrive here. That would not leave him enough time to assemble an army before spring, and we need to do something about the Turks now. I believe General Diogenes is in the city now."

"Well, they're both good leaders, makes no difference to me which one you marry so long as they do the job," said Trachaneiotes. The other men around the table, except for John Ducas, nodded agreement.

John Ducas glanced at the other councilors, gauging what they wanted. Eventually, even he nodded in agreement.

"I'll visit the patriarch to see what he's willing to do."

☨

IT TOOK A COUPLE OF DAYS, BUT BY DECEMBER 31 CAESAR John had convinced the patriarch to consent to freeing Eudokia from her vow not to remarry. John Ducas did have to intimate that Eudokia might be willing to marry the patriarch's wastrel brother to gain his consent, but later her other counselors did away with that suggestion, and they all soon agreed it would have to be Romanus Diogenes.

Romanus entered the Great Palace in his full military regalia that night while most of the world slept and a light snow fell on the city. It was after midnight when he greeted Eudokia who stood in a candlelit chapel with a priest, waiting for him. He fell to his knees before her.

"Your Majesty, Eudokia, I promise you my life, my affections, and my sword, so that I may protect you, our family, and this great empire." He stopped and looked up at her shining face.

"I promise you will never regret your choice of me as your husband."

CHAPTER 10

January 1068 to January 1071

Eudokia looked as though a veil had been pulled aside in the days following her wedding. Her face glowed in a way I had not seen in all the years of her marriage to Constantine. Constantine had been old enough to be her father when they wed and, with his gout and the cancer at the end, had not aged well. Romanus was close to her age, handsome and vigorous. Anyone could see they were smitten with each other.

The morning after their wedding, Eudokia told her children that her counselors had recommended she remarry and that she had chosen Romanus since she believed he would be a good father to them and a strong leader for the empire against the Turks. The little one, Zoe, was only three years old and had never spent much time with her father. She seemed as happy as her mother at the news. Her sisters, Anna and Theodora, looked surprised but made the polite congratulations expected of them. The three boys—Emperor Michael, his younger brothers Andronikos and Constantios, all of them thin, unathletic, pampered—gazed up at their tanned stepfather standing tall in his armor as though an ancient god of war had entered their lives.

Romanus, now co-emperor with his stepson, treated Michael with respect, including him in discussions about armament purchases and planning for the spring campaign. The young man looked bored in these meetings, gazing out windows and tapping his foot on the floor in impatience to return to his studies with Psellus who still tutored him. Romanus had been training young men in the military for years and persisted in his efforts to interest all three of his stepsons in their martial responsibilities, but only ten-year-old Andronikos appeared interested in it.

The new Emperor Romanus wasted no time assembling an army to take into the eastern themes. No one doubted that the Turkish sultan would attack our towns and villages come spring. It was clear the troops stationed in Anatolia had not been enough to stop them in the past and that they lacked sufficient equipment.

"I don't think I've got the whole story about why the Turks have been so successful," he said one night at dinner. "It was years since I was last home to Cappadocia, but the soldiers I saw when I traveled there and back in the fall were. . .slovenly. Uniforms filthy, the men either gambling or drunk. An absolute disgrace."

He grimaced at the memory, shocked as only a professional soldier can be. Eudokia looked down at her plate, embarrassed at her ignorance of the situation.

"I'm sure it's just a small aberration, an accident you came across such men," said Michael, the loyal son. He shrugged in denial. "I know my father would not have tolerated such carelessness."

The boy sounded defensive and a little pompous. Romanus met my eyes across the table, both of us acknowledging that Constantine Ducas had either known of the army's condition or should have known.

"Michael, your father was emperor, but his health was not good the last few years," said Eudokia, trying to keep the peace. "He could not be everywhere. It is possible some of the strategoi were not as attentive as Romanus is. I'm sure your stepfather will soon remedy whatever shortcomings are there."

Michael flushed and picked up his goblet. His beautiful young wife, Maria, kept her eyes downcast. Her cousin Irene met my gaze with a raised eyebrow, complicit with the truth.

Michael stood abruptly and said what he said most evenings, "I must return to my studies. I expect I'll be late to bed tonight."

Maria nodded but said nothing, resigned.

❧

ROMANUS DECIDED HE WOULD HAVE TO LEAVE BEFORE winter's end to determine the condition of the Anatolian troops. He sent for some of his men stationed in Bulgaria, those on whom he could rely to train the eastern troops to meet his standards, including Manuel. And finally, after all the years spent begging Constantine Ducas for funds, Romanus could simply spend the coins he needed, paying soldiers and purchasing supplies.

One of the men Romanus convinced to join him was Michael Attaleiates, who had been the chief judge at his trial in the fall. The military brought judges along on campaign to dispense justice when soldiers got into disputes, but it was unusual for a judge of his stature to accept such an assignment. I suspected Attaleiates had grown tired dealing with the petty squabbles of arrogant dynatoi and tightfisted merchants, thinking a military campaign would be more interesting.

Eudokia tried to be stoic about her beloved new husband's departure, but she was often weepy. After so many years tethered close to a husband for whom she had few warm feelings, God had sent her a husband she loved but whose duties kept him far from her side. It did not seem fair, but it was still a bargain she could accept as long as he returned to her.

Romanus left on the first of March with about fifteen hundred of the most reliable of his Bulgarian forces and almost as many support staff such as doctors, cooks and servants, judges and priests, to keep the army fed and healthy.

Manuel visited me in the palace the day before they left. Thea and their daughter would remain in the house Romanus had shared with Anya, along with her brother, Costas. Romanus had made the wise choice of not bringing his son into the Great Palace since that could lead to accusations that he was trying to supplant Michael.

"Mama, I know I don't have to ask, but please be sure to keep an eye on Thea for me. I think she's with child again," Manuel said.

"She is? I'm so happy for you both. Perhaps this child will be a son," I said, elated at his news.

He laughed. "Maybe."

"Be sure to write me often with news. I want to know what you see happening. I know the official reports don't always tell the whole story."

My son, grown tall and strong as a bull, wrapped me in a farewell hug and returned home for his last night.

I accompanied Eudokia in the morning when she sent Romanus off with his army, across the Bosphorus to the city of Nicomedia and beyond, to the lands called Bithynia and Phrygia in olden times that we now call the themes of Optimatoi and Opsikion. There they would join the troops assigned to those themes and assess how best to move against the Turks. Letters from Manuel soon reached me from the same correspondence bags the emperor used.

To Lady Anna Dalassena
March 10

· · ·

MOTHER - THE EMPEROR WAS APPALLED AT THE CONDITION OF the troops we found at our first stop in Amorion. They were not the trained tagmata troops the Romans have long been known to field. They were a wretched group who were unpaid for over a year, resulting in many abandoning the army. The men who remained in service were miserable—filthy, undisciplined, and lazy. The trouble-makers were sent to Judge Attaleiates who dispensed justice. The officers in charge of the troops were drunken louts not fit to herd goats. The emperor lured some of the good soldiers back, either through promises of reliable pay or through conscription. Those of us who served with him in Bulgaria exhaust ourselves sunup to sundown to train them to his standards. They are truly raw recruits, but the emperor wants them to be ready to go on campaign by early May.
  Your son,
  Manuel Comnenus

EUDOKIA LOOKED PALE AS SHE READ HER LETTER FROM Romanus recounting the same harsh story that Manuel's told.

"Anna, I don't understand how Constantine could have let this happen. Romanus is so disturbed at the condition the army is in. Said the problems started long before Constantine took ill." Her brows drew together in consternation.

"Augusta, it's not your fault. Constantine Ducas made his own decisions, not you."

She frowned, gazing down at the letter still in her hand. "I still feel that I've disappointed my husband somehow."

"You haven't, and once he hears your news, he will be overjoyed."

Eudokia looked up with a pleased smile and rested her hand on her belly, where a child was growing.

To Manuel Comnenus
   April 20

Son, I hope this letter finds you well. Your wife's health is good and she expects her child in September, so it will be a long summer for her. Your brother Isaac is well in Bulgaria. I am grateful the emperor saw fit to assign him to an experienced army there rather than with the pitiful forces you have been forced to train in Anatolia. Fewer opportunities to develop bad habits.

The empress is ecstatic to be expecting another child, with the baby due a month or two after yours. This will be her third child born in the purple room. I am not as confident about how pleased the other members of the imperial family are. Caesar John Ducas looks thoroughly put out by it. I suspect he thinks the child will be a competitor for the throne of his older half brothers. It might be best if the child is a girl.

The empress's other counselors were pleased at the emperor's progress. They hired a Frankish mercenary named Crispin, who leads over one hundred fifty men to augment the emperor's troops. I was with the empress when the Frank appeared to offer his services. He looks to be a competent soldier, but I have my suspicions on how well he can be trusted, as I would with any Frank.

   Your mother,
   Anna Dalassena

৩⁕৩

To Lady Anna Dalassena
   August 19

Mother, it's been a cat-and-mouse game with the Turks. Our spies told us the enemy was withdrawing from the north to attack Antioch in the south. The emperor split the army into two

*parts, one part going north to Sebastea in case they attacked there
again, while we went south to the Syrian border where the threat
looked worse. The men sent to Sebastea have seen few battles and
complain about the usual campaign inconveniences. We only
encountered a few raiding parties before word arrived that the Turks
had attacked Neokaisereia in the north in full force. We left immediately to retaliate and are searching through some wild territory
with few roads. Am otherwise well.*

Your son,
Manuel Comnenus

҈

EUDOKIA'S EYES WIDENED WITH JOY OVER THE NEWS IN HER
letter from the emperor that arrived a week after mine from
Manuel.

"Emperor Romanus has won a great victory," she announced
to Emperor Michael and the other imperial counselors in the
palace that day. "Thanks be to the intercession of the Theotokos,
he tracked down and surprised the army of Turks who devastated Neokaisareia and defeated them. Our army killed many of
them, while freeing the prisoners on their way to Damascus and
recovering all the booty, from gold icons to small calves."

Many of the counselors in the chamber broke into relieved
smiles and congratulations.

I sat to the side of the room, in attendance as Eudokia's
companion at these meetings. I watched John Ducas, who sat
sullen and silent at the news. His allies among the counselors,
including Michael Psellus, squirmed uncomfortably in their
seats, unwilling to give Romanus any credit. It angered me that
these jealous men, who had ignored invaders until it was almost
too late, were unwilling to acknowledge the one man who was
doing something about it.

"This victory is to be announced today at the palace gates,

and I will ask the patriarch to hold a special thanksgiving service for it," said Eudokia.

"Augusta, that seems premature," said Psellus. "Shouldn't we wait until Emperor Romanus returns?"

"I agree," said Caesar John.

Eudokia sat on a throne at the head of the table beside her mute son, who sat on his own throne. She looked down at Psellus, her hand resting on her expanding belly, considering his suggestion.

"Lord Psellus, thank you for your suggestion," she said, her voice cold. "However, the emperor does not indicate when he will be able to return, and since it has been a long time since we've had such good news from Anatolia, I believe the people of the city will be grateful to learn this and deserve a celebration."

To Manuel Comnenus
September 12

My son, you have another beautiful daughter. Your wife chose to name the child Eugenia after Thea's grandmother. The child is healthy, and Thea is well. You have my congratulations and please let the emperor, your father-in-law, know he has a new grand-daughter.

The entire city was relieved to hear the news of the emperor's great victory. The empress had the patriarch hold a special service in the Hagia Sophia in thanksgiving for it. She is nearing her time and praying for a son. Her accommodations for birthing in the purple room are complete, and she waits impatiently. This victory and the empress's new child are seen as good signs that Romanus was the right man for the empress to choose. The only unhappy ones are, as you would expect, Caesar John and Michael Psellus. The two of

them look as though they've been forced to eat freshly dug raw turnips every time they see Eudokia with her expanded waist.
    Your mother,
    Anna Dalassena

To Emperor Romanus Diogenes
    October 10

Your Majesty, the Empress Eudokia gave birth to a son yesterday and has named him Nikephoros. He is a fine, healthy child with your coloring and a lusty cry that can only signify his future as a military commander. The empress recovers well and looks forward to presenting your new son to you upon your return.
    Lady Anna Dalassena

Eudokia soon returned to her rooms in the Boukoleon following the child's birth.

"I know an empress has to give birth in the purple room," she said as she relaxed in her usual apartment, little Nikephoros in her arms, "but I just don't like being there. I can't help remembering all the women who've given birth inside its walls. Sometimes the mother died, sometimes the baby died, and then those cold purple marble walls feel so eerie. I half expect to see ghosts flitting about when I'm in labor." She shivered slightly at the recollection.

I nodded in agreement but tried to cheer her up. "I know what you mean. You've been fortunate, though. It's been good luck for you, with three healthy babies born there."

She handed the babe to his nurse and turned to the letter from her husband that awaited her. She pulled loose the lead seal and red ribbon that kept the letter secure from spies and unfolded it. A look of disappointment crossed her face.

"Oh, Anna, they won't be back for many more weeks."

"What's happened?" I asked, dismayed myself at this news since it meant Manuel would not be home soon either.

"He's learned of the town just inside the border with Syria where the Turks stage their raids on us. He's planning to attack it, cut them off." Eudokia looked up at me, tears in her eyes. "What if something happens to him? He hasn't even seen our son yet."

I reached an arm around, trying to comfort her as I would any woman, still emotional after the ordeal of giving birth. "The emperor's a strong man. I'm sure he'll return safely to you soon."

She nodded, knuckling away her tears. "You're right, Anna. But I do miss him."

To Lady Anna Dalassena
November 25

MOTHER, BY NOW YOU WILL HAVE HEARD OF THE EMPEROR'S great victory at Hierapolis. The army proved itself in that assault despite many of our officers' lax efforts. They do nothing unless the emperor is there. The emperor is frustrated and angry at them.

Often, despite the emperor's best attempts to encourage bravery among his officers, they acquit themselves in a timid or cowardly fashion. He sent five thousand soldiers to Melitene who did nothing to retaliate when the Turks attacked. They huddled safe inside the city's walls while neighboring villages were destroyed. Do they want the emperor to fail, or are they incompetent? Neither is good.

None of this detracts from the emperor's accomplishments this year. I don't believe anyone could have achieved more than he has, given the state of the army in the east when we arrived. But at times

it seems as though he is swimming upstream against river currents
full of the spring's melted snow. We hope to return soon.
　　Your son,
　　Manuel Comnenus

◈◈◈

1069

PALACE GUARDS KEPT A LOOKOUT FOR THE EMPEROR EVERY
day after Eudokia received a letter from him announcing his
imminent return. Finally, at the end of January we saw imperial
banners snapping in the winter wind on the far shore across the
Bosphoros where the emperor waited for ships to ferry him and
his soldiers across. It was after midday before he arrived at the
quay beside the Boukoleon Palace. He had departed eleven
months earlier, only two short months after he and Eudokia
wed.

Romanus looked as though he had lost weight, and his eyes
were sunken in dark circles of fatigue. His armor hung loose
beneath his woolen mantle. He crossed the bridge from the ship
to where Eudokia waited for him, quivering with excitement. He
embraced her, and I could see them exchange a greeting but
could not hear the words. Worry lines creased Romanus's forehead as he moved forward to greet the officials waiting for him
with a forced smile, some of them cordial, others not so much. I
was angry to see that John Ducas would barely bend the knee
before his emperor.

The crowd dispersed after Romanus and Eudokia retired to
their rooms, where their new son waited to be introduced to his
father. I remained, searching the faces of the men disembarking,
looking for Manuel. I saw him and waved as he came down the
bridge.

"Welcome home, son," I said. His embrace was as strong as

before, but I felt his ribs protruding when my arms wrapped around him.

"Mama, I am so happy to be here. I sometimes wondered if I'd ever see the city again."

I glanced down at his reddened hands, the mark of chilblains. His beard was unkempt, his clothes stained, and he had lost weight.

"When did these start?" I asked, patting the bulging red welts on his hand. "Come to my rooms. It's warm there and we can get you some food and drink before you leave for home."

He followed me down a corridor to my rooms. He sat warming his hands by a brazier with glowing coals while I poured him a cup of wine.

Manuel sighed and shook his head. "The return journey through the Taurus Mountains was miserable. It was terrible cold, and we had only summer clothing. We lost a lot of men there, frozen to death." He looked away from me, as though trying not to remember. "Maybe two hundred."

"What? We've heard nothing of that. That's horrible."

"No way you would have heard. We traveled as fast as we could to get through it, fast as any messenger, given the snow. And I don't think the emperor wanted to let people know before we returned. Not everyone wants him to be successful. Let people enjoy the victories we had."

"I know. Caesar John Ducas and his allies would jump at any chance to criticize Romanus, discounting any of his victories. It doesn't help that Eudokia has a new purple-born son. But the entire city has been ecstatic about our victories over the Turks. The news has been a great relief to everyone," I said as I handed him a plate with bread, cheese, and apples.

Manuel raised an eyebrow at that before biting into an apple.

"This is delicious. We've been on short rations for the past couple of weeks. But as for the victories. . ."

I looked at him, wondering what he meant. "What's wrong? Didn't the army defeat the Turks?"

"Yes, on a few occasions," he said with a grimace. "But overall? No, the Turks probably did us more harm than we did them this year. Their troops are well trained and equipped. They've been raiding and stealing from us for years now. They've acquired a taste for Roman gold and silver. We hit them back for the first time in a long time, but it'll take more than one campaign to stop them. We won't be home for long."

My heart sank at this news. "That's unfortunate. The empress will be disappointed. She's sorely missed her husband."

He frowned. "Thea will be too. Can't be helped unless you want to learn to speak Turkish."

❦

THE EMPEROR KEPT BUSY OVER THE NEXT TWO MONTHS, accumulating supplies and equipment, assessing how many men would be mustered for the year's campaign, all while evaluating the empire's beleaguered finances. Tax revenues were diminished, and not just because of the Turks in Anatolia. Frankish adventurers marauding in Italy had whittled down the empire's oncegreat holdings there to one or two towns, while the Hungarian king laid claim to our land in Serbia and Croatia. All these losses amounted to almost one-fifth of the lands—and the tax revenues they brought in—compared to what the empire had when Emperor Basil II ruled.

Eudokia spent every minute she could with Romanus, attending meetings about military matters and bringing Michael. The young man was never eager to be there, but he was at least being introduced to the true responsibilities of a ruler.

The biggest problem was Caesar John and, to a lesser extent Michael Psellus, who clung to the Caesar like a leech. Psellus continued as Michael's tutor as he had under Emperor Constantine Ducas. Romanus had never dealt much with

Psellus before marrying Eudokia, so their acquaintance remained superficial.

Relations between Romanus and John Ducas finally came to a boil in mid-March when the council was going over the allocations for salaries paid to the empire's ruling elites. Ducas had received the title of Caesar from his brother, and it came with a generous salary. Other men had purchased their positions, paying a price based on the value of their expected incomes, provided to them annually in a ceremony on Pascha in mid-April. This year, as in the year prior, Emperor Michael would bestow the gold since Romanus would be on campaign. Romanus made the final decision about those amounts, although there was a general understanding about what they would be.

At this council meeting, one of the imperial secretaries read out the names of those receiving payments and what those payments would be, starting with the least and ending with Caesar John, who received the greatest amount. Romanus had decreased them all, with John Ducas's payment dropping the most. The council sat in mute surprise for a few minutes after the secretary finished reading off the names, which included all of them. Romanus sat at a table on a raised dais with the empress and Emperor Michael on either side of him. The remaining council members sat at a long table facing them, Ducas in the center of it. He stood to speak, red in the face.

"Your Majesty, these reductions are uncalled for. May I ask what you based them on?" he growled. He sounded like the gruff men who trained bears to perform in the hippodrome.

"Caesar John, we've all gone over the tax revenues on hand and the cost of the campaign this year. As you know, revenues are much lower and the cost of war is great, but taxes will drop more if we don't push back the Turks. We've little choice."

Ducas put his hands on his hips, frowning at Romanus.

"And why such a large cut in my salary? Will it improve on the pitiful results your army reported last year?"

Romanus became very still, staring down at the red-faced Caesar. He had spent almost a full year in the saddle trying to turn back a relentless enemy that John Ducas and his brother had ignored for years. Eudokia put a hand on his arm when he didn't respond immediately and he glanced at her before turning back.

"Perhaps we should discuss that in private," the emperor said in a chilly voice.

"No, let's hear it out now," said Ducas, chin jutting forward.

"If you insist. Your salary was by far the largest and I judged you the one best able to adjust to a reduction. Also, Michael is now nineteen, and he has three younger brothers, as well as myself as his co-emperor. You will, of course, keep your courtesy title of caesar, but with the decreased responsibility comes a decreased salary."

It did not sit well with John that Romanus included his own baby son with Michael's full brothers. The other counselors watched in rapt attention as the drama played out between the two men. Ducas turned slightly so as to face his nephew, Emperor Michael, ignoring Emperor Romanus.

"Your Majesty, it appears that my services are no longer required in the palace. I will retire to my estates in Bithynia for the moment."

Romanus glared at Ducas, jaw tight at the man's rudeness.

"Sir," he responded, "you may retire to your estates in Bithynia permanently. I do not want you back in the city again."

⚜

ROMANUS DECIDED THAT IT WOULD BE HELPFUL IF Michael Psellus joined the army on campaign that year. The bureaucrat could advise him as well as gain an understanding of the progress of the war on the Turks. Psellus had been in service in the Great Palace for over twenty years and knew how the government worked, but nothing about the military. The emperor also thought the man's distance from the city would diminish his connection with Caesar John.

Psellus had lived in Byzantium since birth, rarely venturing outside its walls. Even so, it came as a surprise when it turned out that he had a terror of horses.

"Mama, you would not believe how frightened that man is of horses. He'd better get used to them, or he'll wear out all those fine shoes he has for the paved city streets while marching with the infantry," said Manuel the day before the emperor planned to leave. "The emperor threatened all of us with demotion if we laugh at him, but he looks ridiculous trying to mount, much less hang on while the meek little palfrey he's been given is at a slow canter."

I had a hard time trying not to laugh out loud at the thought of him, in his proud courtier's dress and hood, trying to mount a horse. Humorous as that might be, I had a more serious subject to discuss with Manuel.

"You'll need to keep an eye on him. He and Caesar John have worked too closely for Psellus to foreswear that loyalty for loyalty to your father-in-law. I worry Romanus might be too busy or too trusting, maybe won't see what mischief they might be conjuring up."

Manuel gave me a more sober look and nodded. "I agree."

"Just keep an eye on them. Write to me as you did last year."

To Lady Anna Dalassena
May 5

MOTHER, THE EMPEROR'S CAMPAIGN THIS YEAR STARTED OUT *well enough. He enlisted new soldiers, trained them, and began moving the army east. Problems started when Crispin, the mercenary the imperial council hired a year ago, said he was told his pay would be more than he received. At first the emperor believed him, but then Psellus convinced Romanus that Crispin was just a typical lying Frank. Psellus was emphatic about this and he was the only one with us who had also been at the council meeting where his pay was decided on. Crispin took his men and left. I think the emperor was trying to conciliate Psellus, turn him into an ally, but I fear my father-in-law just fell into a trap. We needed Crispin and his men.*

We are moving onto Caesarea, where scouts report Turks rampaging through the countryside.

Your son,
Manuel Comnenus

EUDOKIA AND I SAT ON A BENCH IN THE SHADE OF THE spreading branches of a plane tree late in August. Her youngest daughter, five-year-old Zoe, sat on a blanket playing with her half-brother, baby Nikephoros. Zoe, the child who most resembled her mother, made funny faces at the baby and urged him to stretch to reach the silver rattle she put just outside his reach. I wiped at the perspiration that beaded my forehead before sipping at the juice servants had laid on a nearby table.

"How is Michael?" I asked. He had fallen the previous day from the horse he was riding when he went hunting with Alexios.

Eudokia looked down. "He's no worse for the fall. A few bruises, but nothing serious. I guess my son is not cut out to be a soldier. I had hoped that with Psellus gone, Michael might develop other skills besides poetry and oratory."

Psellus was proud of being Emperor Michael's tutor and only reluctantly agreed to go on campaign with Romanus. Eudokia and Romanus both wanted to break that connection, but the boy seemed glued to his tutor, even with Psellus being gone.

"Not everyone has a taste for horses and swords," I said. "Manuel's letter says Psellus thinks he knows everything about how to lead a military campaign."

The empress rolled her eyes. "Romanus says the same thing. Psellus can't ride a horse properly, almost never ventures out beyond the city walls, was never a soldier, and he thinks he knows more than my husband. Most of what he's done this summer is cause problems, and Romanus doesn't need that. I am sure Psellus won't be going on campaign again."

"Manuel wrote that the Turks raid towns and slip away so fast it's impossible to catch them."

"True, but the worst part isn't the Turks. It's the Roman soldiers," she said. "Romanus is disgusted with the officers who make no effort to fight back, or if they do, they're so inept that they get captured. The army fights well when Romanus leads it, but no one else seems able to manage it."

The baby had fallen asleep on the blanket so Zoe wandered to her mother, resting her head on Eudokia's knee.

"I worry that the emperor doesn't get good advice from his officers. Many of them owe loyalty to John Ducas," I said.

"I worry about that too." She sighed, stroking Zoe's blond locks. "I'm also worried about his health; he complains about not being able to sleep and about the heat. I'll be glad when he's back."

❧❦❧

THE EMPEROR RETURNED IN THE FIRST WEEK OF November. He received a warm reception from the empress and the people of the city, who celebrated his successes against our enemies. The dynatoi, many of them allies of Caesar John, gave him a lackluster welcome. John Ducas was still exiled to his Bithynian estates, but we could see from the Boukoleon's mullioned windows the messengers wearing Ducas family colors and known Ducas supporters sailing across the Bosphoros almost daily. I had a feeling nothing good was going on.

I stopped in Thomas's office one day at the end of November to learn what he thought of Ducas's activities. The eunuch now had comfortable surroundings following his promotion by Eudokia to managing half the palace's servants. A pair of braziers pushed back the winter chill. It was late in the day, and my stomach growled from hunger with the Advent fasting as I closed the door behind me.

"Lady Anna, it's so good to see you. Please sit down," he said with his customary courtesy.

"Thank you, Thomas. I'm glad for the warmth. I saw a few snowflakes on my walk here. I'm afraid my chilblains will return soon."

"Yours and mine too," he said, shaking his head. "Almost makes you want to move to Africa."

"Almost," I said. "Thomas, can I ask you about John Ducas?"

He gave me a quizzical look. "You can ask me about anything, you know that. What did you want to know that you don't already know?"

"I want to know what he's plotting. He must be up to something, and I know you hear all the palace gossip. Why do I see his messengers back and forth to Bithynia almost daily?"

Thomas had no beard to hide behind. He looked uncomfortable and cleared his throat before answering.

"The Caesar does not confide in me, of course, but you know he's protective of his nephews. He was always fiercely loyal to his brother and doesn't want the Ducas family legacy lost. I suspect he's worried the emperor will do something to prevent Michael from ruling on his own one day. The new child makes it possible Michael will be denied that opportunity."

I had suspected that from the time Eudokia became pregnant.

"He knows Romanus promised the empress to keep Michael on the throne. But even John Ducas has to admit the boy seems unsuited to it," I said.

Thomas nodded before continuing.

"Yes, there's that. But it's more than that; the Caesar is angry at the cut in his income. He got used to only the biggest and very best of everything. This year was not fun for him that way. He has partisans to pay and not so much in coin."

"John Ducas was being paid more than double what my husband was paid when he was in the same position." It must have bothered Romanus when he learned how much the Caesar received when the army had little.

Thomas gave me a long look and laid out the stark picture of Romanus's situation.

"Perhaps so, but he hates Romanus. You can see it in the Caesar's face. He hates the emperor for making his brother's widow happier than she was with his brother, for paying him less, and for being a threat to his nephews, especially with his new son. The Caesar hates the emperor for his good looks and his military skills. He hates him because the emperor is popular with the people when neither he nor Constantine ever were. He simply hates the emperor, and he's convinced, and in more cases than I'd like to admit, paid many in the Senate and the other dynatoi to do so as well."

My heart sank at his unsparing words, realizing that Romanus's greatest enemy might not be the Turks.

"So I have no certain knowledge of what he's plotting, but we can be sure he is plotting and it won't be good for the emperor."

1070

An emissary from the Turkish sultan, Alp Arslan, arrived early in January, just after Epiphany, to negotiate a truce with Romanus. He proposed a peace treaty for a term of one year that Romanus accepted. Eudokia was overjoyed at the thought of her husband home for a year.

I wished it had been as easy to reach an agreement with my daughter Theodora.

She frequently mentioned her desire to marry Romanus's oldest son, Costas, especially since my cousin had become emperor. I pushed back on that for the first two years Romanus sat on the throne since he was preoccupied with military affairs, his imperial responsibilities, and only briefly in the city. Now, though, he would be home for at least a year, and seventeen-year-old Theodora pushed harder. I had to broach the subject with him.

I found him alone one day in the large room in the Daphne Palace that Isaac had also used as an office. It was early January and cold, but Romanus managed with just a single brazier. I tucked my hands into my sleeves for warmth as I sat opposite him.

"Romanus, have you thought about a betrothal for Costas?" I asked. I would never have addressed him informally like that with other people around, but in private we were just cousins.

He looked interested and a little surprised. Costas and my son Isaac had been assigned to the Bulgarian themes but were home for the winter season.

"Costas hasn't mentioned an interest in marriage yet, but I suppose it might be time to consider it," he said, grinning and cocking an eye at me. "Anna, you know you have a reputation for arranging marriages—you did it to me twice, with Anya and then with Eudokia. What exactly do you have in mind?"

"You give me too much credit. I do so little, just nudging people in the best direction," I said, stifling a laugh. "This time is a little different."

"How is it different?" he asked, leaning back in his chair.

"My daughter Theodora seems to be enamored of Costas. She tells me that Costas feels the same way about her, although I have no certainty on that. You know the Church will not permit the marriage between the siblings of two people who are already married, although the patriarch might be convinced to approve it, especially if you, as the emperor, requested it.

"Of course, as emperor, I know you have many things to consider before approving such a request. I promised Theodora I would discuss this with you, but I told her it might not be in your best interest."

He looked across at me, thoughtful. "I appreciate you told her that; not everyone considers my interests."

"I agree, not everyone considers your interests." I shivered a little, as much from anxiety over political issues as from the chilly office.

"What do you mean by that?"

"Romanus, you know you have an enemy in John Ducas."

He snorted at that. "How could I not? He's been an oozing sore for me since the day I married Eudokia."

"He's plotting something against you, I just know he is. You need to convert more of the Senate and the dynatoi into your allies, not his. Otherwise, you'll have to watch your back all the time." My voice rose with the urgency of my concern.

"Anna, what can he do? He's stuck in Bithynia and has no army. I know he means me ill, even though I did let him keep the title of Caesar. What kind of precedent would it set if I arrested and executed him? If something happened to me, what then happens to my sons? I'm walking on the edge of a sword, trying to balance him, Eudokia, her sons, our son, my son, not to mention fighting a war and ruling the empire." He stopped and rubbed his eyes as though tired of it all. "I do appreciate your concern about Ducas. I'm doing the best I can. And I will consider your request for Theodora. Let me think about it for a few days and speak with Costas, and I'll let you know."

I thanked him and left the office, walking the long marble-floored corridor to the building's entrance. The murmur of the familiar voices of Michael Psellus and Basil Trachaneiotes, another of John Ducas's favorites, in an alcove caught my attention as I passed. Psellus noticed me approaching, nodded respectfully in my direction, but then pulled Trachaneiotes in closer and lowered his voice. Those two palace moths circled around the twin flames of power and money, and I doubted any of what they spoke would benefit Romanus. It was unsettling the way they reminded me of why my husband had chosen a different path.

⊗

ROMANUS AND I MET AGAIN AT THE END OF FEBRUARY.

"I've spoken with my son, and he is agreeable to a betrothal with Theodora, with a wedding planned for November. I'll see the patriarch in a few days and speak with him then about his approval for the marriage. We'll sign the betrothal agreement after we've gotten his approval, but it will have to be soon."

"Thank you, Romanus. Theodora will be ecstatic, but why must we sign the betrothal soon?" I asked.

"I haven't told him yet, but I'll be sending Manuel with an army to Anatolia this summer. I still need someone in the field there. It's time he had an army of his own to lead. Even so, I don't expect he'll encounter much trouble given the new treaty with the sultan."

"Of course. He'll need to sign the agreement for Theodora," I said.

"Yes, Manuel will leave right after Pascha. But that should give us enough time to arrange it." He stopped for a moment before continuing. "I did give this betrothal a lot of thought. Costas was willing, but what decided it was that I know I can trust you and your family. There aren't many others I can say that about."

⊗

ROMANUS TOOK ADVANTAGE OF HIS TIME IN Constantinople, talking with senators, attending services in the

Hagia Sophia, conferring with his counselors. He traveled across the Bosphorus to Bithynia to evaluate the troops he had mustered, sometimes staying for a week or more. The army in Anatolia began to shape itself into the fighting force the Roman Empire was known for. Eudokia's face spoke of her happiness when her husband was there, especially since she was now expecting another child, due in October.

Romanus promoted Manuel to general and commander before he left in mid-April at the head of a small army of ten thousand men. My son had earned the promotion, although some probably grumbled that he'd gotten it because the emperor was his father-in-law. He would have to prove himself in the field.

Manuel had been gone for about two months when Romanus appeared in the nursery, where Eudokia and I were with the children, his face pale. He pulled me aside.

"Anna, I've received a letter from the eparch of Sebasteia, where Manuel was camped with his army. The news is not good." He then showed me the letter.

To Emperor Romanus Diogenes
June 20

Your Majesty, I regret to inform you that a Turkish army attacked the Roman army camped near our city of Sebasteia two days ago. Many soldiers were killed, but most escaped death when they sought refuge within our city walls. However, General Comnenus, was taken captive. We will send you word on his condition as soon as we determine what the Turks plan to ask for his release.
Leo, Eparch of Sebasteia

· · ·

My heart stopped at those words. The letter held no words of his death, but his capture was almost as bad. I covered my face with my hands and groaned.

"Anna, he's a valuable captive. I'm sure they'll want to ransom him," Romanus said, putting an arm around me.

Eudokia walked over to join us. "What's happened?"

"The Turks captured Manuel, but that's all we know. I told Anna they'll probably want to ransom him," answered Romanus.

I sat down as thoughts tumbled through my mind. A ransom demand was likely. Thea would need to know about this. The eparch had written his letter almost a week past. The Turks should send a message about the ransom soon. I felt cold despite the summer's heat.

I looked up into Romanus's and Eudokia's anxious faces. They had known Manuel since he was born and loved him almost as much as I did. I knew they would do whatever was necessary to rescue Manuel. I also knew that any outcome was possible.

"Thank you, but I think I need some time alone." I slipped away into the palace's gardens, full of the sweet scents of roses and lilies, ending up near the Nea Ekklesia, the new church. It was almost two hundred years old, but it was newer than the rest of the palace's churches. I pulled open its heavy oak door and entered the cool interior, the smell of incense and wax candles left from the last service still there. Light filtered in through a few of the windows at the bases of the five domes, lighting up a blue-and-gold mosaic of the Theotokos with her holy child, and surrounded by golden stars and angels. I knelt weeping before her and prayed for the rescue of my firstborn son. After pouring out my heart, a calm acceptance of God's will washed over me in that empty church. I had done what I could.

Little news came from Sebasteia over the next month. Thea was distraught, often visiting the Great Palace for news before visiting the Hagia Sophia for prayers. The city Manuel was held in was high in the mountains, almost as far east as the empire stretched. Turkish raiding parties, not part of Alp Arslan's army, plagued the roads that led to Constantinople, while summer squalls on the Black Sea kept ships that a messenger would take from departing. I spent my nights pacing my room more than sleeping before we heard from Manuel.

To Emperor Romanus Diogenes
July 15

Your Majesty, I am pleased to inform you that I won my freedom from the Turkish army. The days I spent in their company were not ill-used. The Turkish commander, Arisghi, was in rebellion against his brother-in-law, Sultan Alp Arslan, after they had a disagreement. We spoke often over several days, and I convinced him that his future good fortune lay with the Roman Empire rather than with the sultan. We expect to arrive by the first of August and Arisghi will pledge his fealty to you and the empire at that time.
General Manuel Comnenus

My prayers had been answered. Thea was ecstatic.

The news of Manuel's escapade elated the city. No one had ever heard of anyone convincing a Turk to become an ally before. It reminded me of the stories of John's father, also named Manuel, who had a reputation for defeating his opponents with clever tricks.

The Turk moved into Manuel's house when they returned to the city. Arisghi was short, with a kind of dark, smushed-down face and a long black beard. He was not an attractive man at all.

He spoke Greek with a heavy accent, but at least he did speak it. He and Alexios struck up a friendship of sorts, and my son began learning to speak Turkish from him as well as picking up tricks of Turkish sword play.

Manuel presented Arisghi to the emperor and empress in a formal ceremony in the Chrysotriklinos a week after they arrived in the city. The entrance into the Great Palace, guarded by tall blond Varangians, the walk through many gardens, along corridors filled with timeless mosaics before reaching the golden throne room would impress anyone. The little Turk, long accustomed to a rough nomadic life, was struck dumb by the time he reached the foot of Romanus's throne and made his obeisance. He could barely squeak out the words of fealty to the emperor and the Roman Empire.

I accompanied the empress when she and Romanus congratulated Manuel on his accomplishment in his office later that day.

"You've done a fine job your first time out on your own. I wish I could have been out in the field with you," he said, clapping Manuel on the back.

"Thank you, sir. I can tell you I wasn't sure how it would all end once Arisghi's men cornered me and I was forced to surrender. But I kept my wits and noticed things. I could tell right away that he and the sultan were quarreling. One conversation with him led to another, and he soon realized his best option was with us."

Romanus grinned at him. "I still can't believe it, but I'm grateful. I'm just jealous that I couldn't be there."

"We'll be in the field together again next year, Your Majesty," Manuel said. "Next year we'll finally put a stop to the sultan's army, I know it."

"That's what I'm planning for," said the emperor.

꧁꧂

THE TREES THAT AUTUMN WERE BRILLIANT GOLDEN COLORS against the deep blue skies of sunny days, with fair breezes filling the bright sails of the ships in the Sea of Marmara outside the palace windows.

Eudokia's and Romanus's second child, a son they named Leo, was born a few weeks after Manuel's return. Romanus had not seen their first son until he was several months old, but this time he paced for hours outside the purple marble room where empresses gave birth. This babe had Eudokia's fair coloring— unlike Nikephoros, who was the image of his father. Romanus looked to burst with pride when he held this son, believing the child was a sign from God confirming that he was meant to rule the empire.

My daughter Theodora and Romanus's oldest son, Costas, wed in early November. The two of them looked happy enough at the altar, although I admitted to myself that Costas's enthusiasm looked pale in comparison to Theodora's. He'd agreed to the marriage, but I sensed something shading his happiness that day.

Michael Maurex returned to the city just before the wedding. His fleet had been in the Adriatic, destroying the ships of some Normans who had chipped away at our lands in Italy.

"Lady Anna, I'm so glad to see you again," he said in greeting when he saw me in the palace. "I promised my wife I would check on you. I didn't expect you'd be here, though."

"I returned as a companion for the empress not long after John died. How have you been? And your wife?" I asked.

"My wife is well and sends you her greetings. But for me, the last few weeks have been tough," he said, lips pursed in a grimace. "The Normans are swarming all over southern Italy. One of them, Robert d'Hauteville—they call him Guiscard the Weasel— is the biggest threat. He controls most of southern Italy now; we just have one or two small cities left. My fleet stopped him for now, but it would be easier to bail out a sinking ship with a wine cup than to completely defeat him as matters now stand. I'll be giving the emperor my estimation of the situation in a few minutes. He won't be happy, but I can't see how he can fight the Turks and the Normans at the same time."

"Are you recommending abandoning the cities in Italy?" I asked, crestfallen at the loss of these last remnants of the lands the empire had held for hundreds of years.

"I don't believe the emperor has a choice. They're almost gone as it is," he said, shaking his head. "Not enough money or men."

JANUARY 1071

EUDOKIA'S FOREHEAD WAS CREASED, AND DARK CIRCLES surrounded her eyes. She snapped at one of the nursemaids that morning in January and paced restlessly through her rooms before I could sit down with her to talk.

"Anna, I am worried. Worried about Romanus, about our sons. Do you know what John Ducas has done?" she asked, looking as taut as a lute string.

"I know he's sent no word of congratulations on the birth of your son. But his own boy, Andronikos, came and offered his best wishes and brought a gift."

She rolled her eyes at that. "Yes, he brought a gift. A gift more like something I would give a servant when they had a child. Andronikos is married to one of the wealthiest women in the empire, and his own father received huge gifts from Constantine when he was emperor. I know it's not as though we need anything, it's just that it shows so little respect for my husband. I woke up during the night and couldn't stop thinking John Ducas is trying to hurt us. Romanus says there's nothing he can do, but I've known John for twenty years. He is relentless. Romanus wouldn't listen to me, and we argued."

She wiped a tear away, overcome with worry for her husband and dismay at their argument.

I put an arm around her shoulders, trying to comfort her.

"I'm sure Romanus wasn't angry with you; he's got a lot to do preparing for the campaign this summer. For what it's worth, I agree John is not sitting quietly, simply tending his vines on his estate." A few ideas skipped through my mind. "Why don't I pay a visit to Andronikos's wife, Marie? She was always a favorite of mine when she was a child here in the palace. Perhaps I can learn something."

※

ANDRONIKOS LIVED IN THE MANSION OVERLOOKING THE Marmara that had once belonged to my brother-in-law, Isaac, and his wife, Catherine. After Marika's "death", her cousin, Andronikos's wife, Marie of Bulgaria, had inherited it. I walked into the magnificent house, filled for me with memories of Isaac and Catherine, their strong personalities so often at odds with each other. A servant brought me to the gynecaeum, where Marie presided over her children and the household.

"Lady Anna, I am so glad to see you. It's been too long," she said, embracing me.

"Yes, it has. We missed you at Theodora's wedding, but of course we'd understood. I was hoping to see your new daughter today and catch up with you." I handed her a small wrapped gift for the child, whom they'd named Anna.

A little girl tugged on Marie's skirt, her oldest child, Irene, with a small boy beside her.

"Irene, say hello to Lady Anna," said her mother.

Irene was named after her grandmother who had died not long before she was born. The child gave me a suspicious look before pushing her face totally into her mother's skirts. The boy, Michael, stood staring at me and clutching a small wooden horse.

"Do not trouble the child, Marie. But I'd love to see baby Anna. It seems to be a popular name. I already have two grand-daughters named Anna."

Marie shooed Irene to a nursemaid before grasping my arm. "Lady Anna, how could we not name our girls after you? You always helped all the children in the nursery when Uncle Isaac was emperor. Aunt Catherine had so many other interests, and we rarely saw her."

I blushed at that compliment. We walked over to the cradle Anna slept in, little fists pulled close to her cheeks.

"She's beautiful, Marie. Congratulations," I said. "I always made it a practice not to disturb sleeping babies. Why don't we let her be and we can talk? You're looking well yourself."

"Thank you. Yes, I seem to recover easily from childbirth."

"I did too, thanks be to the Theotokos. And how is Andronikos handling the responsibility of three children?"

"Much as he did with the other two—looking forward to being out with the army again." She laughed a little. "Like many men do."

"Yes, I guess many men are that way. Has their grandfather had a chance to see them?" John Ducas was her children's only surviving grandparent.

"No, since the emperor sent him to his estates, he can't come to the city. Andronikos is on campaign in the summer months, and I wouldn't want to go without him, so I don't know when Caesar John will get to see them."

"That's unfortunate," I said. "I know I would be miserable if I couldn't visit with my grandchildren." A true statement on my part.

"I agree. Andronikos does hear from his father almost every-day, though. Caesar John hears all the news of our children, and I know many of his friends visit as well."

"I would have thought he might enjoy the quiet of the coun-try. It sounds like he's just as involved as always."

She widened her eyes at that. "Oh, yes he is. He sees so many senators that you'd think he was still living in the city."

I smiled at Marie, sweet young woman that she was, the type who could easily end up the long-suffering wife, but I had learned enough. Caesar John still held an iron grip on his many affairs in the city, no matter that Romanus wore the crown. I took my leave and walked the corridor to the sedan chair waiting in the courtyard. As I passed one of the rooms, I heard the familiar voice of Michael Psellus.

"So it's set, then. You'll be going to Anatolia this year rather than to Bulgaria. I'm sure you'll find an opportunity to make sure he's seen as the fool we all know him to be. And the money your father sent will help convince others to help you in that," said Psellus in his gravelly, sycophantic voice.

"Yes, I know we'll get him this time. The first couple of years we didn't manage it so well. This year we will." Those words of betrayal were spoken by Andronikos.

I heard approaching footsteps and slipped out of the house then, unseen by the two conspirators.

CHAPTER 11

EUDOKIA SPENT THE WEEKS PRIOR TO ROMANUS'S departure trying to get him to send Andronikos Ducas back to Bulgaria. I told them both what I'd overheard but my cousin seemed to think I could not be sure they were speaking of him. True enough, the two plotters had mentioned no names, but there could be little doubt of whom they'd spoken. Romanus had trained Andronikos and fought beside him in Bulgaria and refused to believe the young man could be disloyal to him.

It was painful to hear their arguments about the Ducas boy, but both emperor and empress trusted me to hold my tongue about their private matters.

"Husband, you don't think Andronikos would betray you if his father asked him to? I've known him since he was born, and I believe he would." Her voice held a desperate tone.

Romanus gave her a skeptical look. "My dear, you don't understand loyalty between soldiers. And even John Ducas has to realize there's no one else capable of stopping the Turks. Politics is one thing, but in a fight to survive? I doubt it."

The muscles in Eudokia's face were taut, her eyes bright. "I don't doubt it. Please believe me, you must not let John Ducas's son go with you; you must not give him authority of any kind. I don't know what he'll do, but I do know he means you harm."

Romanus's face turned an angry red. "I must not take him? If you know so much about military affairs, why didn't you do anything about the abysmal state of affairs when your first husband was ruling? Really? Exactly how much do you know now that you can lecture me, someone who has spent his entire life donning armor, in the saddle, leading men, and fighting wars? Explain that to me."

Eudokia flushed with embarrassment at his accusation.

"I will admit I know little of war. What I do know is that Caesar John will do whatever it takes to get his way. And I know he means you no good."

Their argument turned the mood of the imperial chambers frosty with formality in the last days before Romanus's departure.

༺❀༻

THE EMPEROR'S SHIP LEFT THE QUAY OUTSIDE THE Boukoleon Palace at dawn on March thirteenth. Their quarrel not settled, Eudokia gave him a chaste kiss on the cheek in their rooms in farewell and did not accompany him to the water's edge.

"Anna, I am so worried about him. I keep waking in the night thinking about what John Ducas could be planning. Romanus is everything to me, no matter our disagreements. I don't know what I'll do if something happens to him. I hate that we've argued." She stood by a window, watching his ship cross the Bosphorus, tears streaming down her face.

It seemed the emperor felt the same way. His ship soon returned with a message and gift for Eudokia.

The gift was a soft gray dove that delighted Eudokia. She reached though the staves of its cage to stroke its small head.

"You know, Romanus sometimes calls me his 'gray dove,'" she said after reading the message, smiling at the bird. She looked up at me, her eyes bright. "He apologized for the cold words we had. I can't leave things as they are between us. Anna, let's pack up and go to Nicomedia ourselves. He's at the palace there, and we can stay with him for a few days."

We were soon on board one of the imperial ships, wrapped in heavy mantles and with sea spray chilly on our faces. I was secretly glad to be going since I'd only seen Manuel briefly before he'd boarded the ship with Romanus. I would never again take for granted my son's safe return after his capture the year before.

Our carriage arrived at the palace near sunset. Romanus stood in the sun's reddish glow at the building's entrance talking with some of his men, including Manuel. The surprise on Romanus's face when he saw Eudokia soon turned to joy, and he descended the steps to embrace her. I stepped away while they spoke in intimate whispers, hands clasped.

"Mama, I didn't expect to see you so soon," said Manuel as he enfolded me in a warm hug. "I am glad to see you, of course." He glanced over at the emperor and empress. "And I'm glad to see her. The emperor's been grumpy since we left. I hope she'll brighten his mood."

I took his arm so we could walk away from the rest of the men milling around the entrance, down to a garden beside it.

"The empress worries about what John Ducas might be plotting," I began and then told him about what I overheard Andronikos Ducas and Michael Psellus discussing.

"Romanus doesn't believe Andronikos would do anything to hurt him. Eudokia and I think he could and will."

I searched my son's face, looking for his reaction. He looked to the west, where the sun was lowering below the horizon, before responding.

"I haven't noticed anything suspicious with Andronikos myself. He comports himself well, gives no indication of disloyalty, but. . ." he trailed off, looking thoughtful. "Everyone knows loyalty is everything to the Ducas family. A threat to one of them is a threat to them all. I doubt John Ducas ever liked my father-in-law, even before he married Eudokia. Romanus is everything he isn't."

I shivered when a cold wind blew through just then. "Son, I know nothing my cousin does can ever win over John Ducas. Nothing." My teeth chattered with cold. "Promise me you'll keep an eye on the Ducas boy? Make sure he can't threaten the emperor?"

"Of course, Mama," he said. "I hope you're wrong, but I think you're right to be concerned."

"Thank you, Manuel. The empress will be relieved to know you're watching out for him."

Eudokia and I spent four delightful days in Nicomedia with Romanus and Manuel. The day after our arrival, the weather had an early spring thaw and we had clear days for the visit. Romanus kept busy, purchasing supplies, monitoring the training of new recruits, getting reports from scouts about Turkish activity, planning the details of the year's campaign. Romanus and Eudokia spent their evenings alone and each morning looked as happy as they'd been when they'd wed three years earlier.

Manuel and I ate together every evening, laughing and recalling stories from his childhood. I felt so proud of this son, tall and muscular, his hair and beard the same chestnut color as my hair, laugh lines around his eyes, but still every inch of him a fierce warrior. His tanned skin glowed golden in the lamplight.

"Son, please be careful this year. You can't scare your mother again the way you did last year," I said in farewell the last day.

"Mama, me? I was always fine. You worry too much," he said with a casual grin. Did every son say that to his mother when he left for war?

I embraced him and gave him my blessing before whispering in his ear, "And don't forget about Andronikos."

"Of course, Mama."

Eudokia gave a small speech to her husband and his officers assembled to see her off.

"Dearest husband and officers of the imperial army, you will soon be going into battle against a fierce enemy. I am confident you will be accompanied by the spirits of the soldiers gone before you who have fought for the Roman Empire—in Julius Caesar's battles, with Trajan's soldiers, to win Constantine the Great's victories. The souls of those murdered by the Turks call out for retribution, and they will be with you, strengthening your right arm in battle. Led by my imperial husband, Emperor Romanus Diogenes—God grant him many years—I am confident you will perform your duty to defeat this terrible invader and return peace and plenty to our beautiful, God-blessed land. Never forget the honor you bear serving the Roman Empire."

The soldiers gave her enthusiastic applause, and we departed in our carriage. Romanus rode beside us as escort the two miles to the shore where the imperial barge awaited, sails furled.

Romanus and Eudokia stood close together, delaying her departure as long as possible.

"Farewell, my beautiful gray dove," I heard him say to her.

"God keep you safe, my handsome prince," she said before kissing him.

Romanus glanced over at me, a fierce expression on his face. "Anna, you must keep my wife and children safe from harm. There's no one else I can entrust them to more than you."

"Of course, cousin. You don't even need to ask."

We boarded the ship and waved to Romanus as long as he remained in sight. It was only when he could no longer see us that Eudokia turned to me and wept in my arms.

❦

I ACCOMPANIED EUDOKIA TO THE COUNCIL MEETINGS where Romanus's frequent dispatches were read and discussed. The debates I heard going on around the table left me unsettled. Some of the men somehow remained blind to the threat the Turks meant to the Roman Empire. Others were obvious partisans of John Ducas, always ready to point out some perceived flaw in the emperor's strategy. None fully supported Romanus. Michael Psellus, the chattering bureaucrat, who, if he had ever picked up a sword would have hurt himself, was the worst of them. His petty criticisms of the emperor only revealed his ignorance of war. I realized his loyalty was always first to himself and then to whomever paid him the most.

I tried not to worry about Romanus, knowing he had Manuel's support and the support of his troops, many of whom would do anything for him. I knew that too many of the other officers, though, had ties to Caesar John. It concerned me, then, when Manuel wrote that he and Arisghi, now going by the Greek name of Chrysokoulos, and a small force were being sent by a different route to Sebasteia, where the two armies would meet again. Romanus was a capable man, but a feeling of foreboding settled over me during the long days of Lent.

A mud-stained and sweaty messenger arrived at the palace late on the day after Pascha. A messenger for me from the hegoumenos of the monastery of the Theotokos of Alypos, someone I did not know. My finger trembled as I broke the wax seal and opened the short note.

The monk had written that Manuel had taken ill with an ear infection and I must come immediately.

I packed a few items and left for Bithynia within the hour on the imperial dromon Eudokia insisted I take. I sent a quick note to Thea letting her know of Manuel's illness, trying not to frighten her. I didn't think an ear infection could be too serious, although the letter's urgency alarmed me.

The monastery was a day's journey from the city, and I arrived late on the sixteenth. The little Turk, Arisghi/Chrysokoulos, was at the entrance gate. I could barely understand his garbled tongue, but the terrible words I did discern were "You came in time." Inside the walls were several soldiers wearing imperial insignia. Romanus must be inside.

A monk hurried toward me, his head bowed and bald pate shining pink.

"Lady Anna, God be praised, you have arrived. A priest is with your son now."

I felt my knees buckle and leaned heavily against the stone wall, the blood draining from my body along with hope. "Tell me. What happened?"

"Your son arrived a few days ago on Holy Saturday. He was in great pain with his ear and feverish. I don't know how it happened, mayhap a tiny scratch; the physician does not know how. The ear was already swollen to twice its normal size. The poison in the infection soon spread throughout his body. We've done what we can but. . ."

But there was no chance. I could see that in his kind eyes. Dear God, how could this be?

"Father, can I see him?"

"I'll take you to him. The priest shouldn't be much longer."

He escorted me to the monastery's infirmary. One old monk lay in his bed, breathing heavily, while a younger one sat up with his foot elevated. Manuel was in an alcove where he had some privacy. Romanus stood outside it, pale and mournful. He looked up when I entered the infirmary and came to embrace me.

"Anna, I am so sorry about this. Manuel said he just woke up one morning with the ear throbbing and the pain just got worse and worse, the swelling worse and worse, and he ended up here."

My son, my firstborn, my handsome, laughing son, so strong in war and now losing a battle with an infection. I could not understand how God could let this happen. It was so unfair. He was a good man, the world needed good men; not the many bad men who still walked its streets. It made no sense to me.

The priest finished his blessing of Manuel. I crept into the alcove, sat on the stool beside the bed and took my son's burning-hot hand. His right ear was hugely swollen, almost resembling an elephant's ear. I reached to gently stroke it only to see him wince in agony.

"Manuel, it's Mama."

Feverish eyes in a red face turned to me. "Mama" he said, gripping my hand. "Mama, I'm so sorry. I don't know how this happened. It just started hurting one night and—"

"Don't tire yourself with talking." Tears streamed down my face at my poor boy, my golden son, once so strong. "I'm here now. I'll not leave you."

"You must tell Thea I love her and our daughters. Tell her I'm sorry. Please take care of them. I've disappointed everyone."

"No, you haven't. You have been the best son I could ever ask for." I wiped away tears that blurred at the sight my poor boy. "Your daughters will grow up knowing you were the best father they could ever have."

"Lady Anna, we should let him rest for a bit," said one of the infirmary monks.

"Yes, son, rest your eyes and sleep. I'll be here when you awaken."

He smiled faintly and closed his eyes, his breathing rough and unsteady.

Romanus and I sat beside his bed that last night my son lived on this earth, as he groaned and fitfully clawed at the swollen ear. Our tears flowed watching his fever dreams turn to nightmares, frightening him to half wakefulness. We wiped his head with a cool damp cloth for some small relief. Manuel's little Turkish friend, Chrysokoulos, watched from across the room with a somber face.

Finally, at dawn, he roused suddenly, gasped, his eyes wild

before they rolled back in his head in agony. His body went limp, his strong hand no longer gripping mine.

⚜

CHRYSOKOULOS ACCOMPANIED ME WITH MANUEL'S BODY to Byzantium, along with an honor guard Romanus sent. He would be buried at St. Thekla's beside his father and Uncle Isaac. Romanus sent a letter with me to Thea, apologizing to his daughter for not returning home with the body. He was the emperor, and the death of a son-in-law, however fond he might be of the lad, could not take precedence over the Roman Empire. The monks wrapped Manuel's body in a white linen shroud and placed it in a plain coffin for his return home.

Every step on that journey home was a step I didn't want to take, but the living have no choice but to go on. We arrived at the quay outside the Boukoleon not long after sunset the day of his death. Eudokia wept at the news and made an effort to console me. My grief was too fresh for consolation, though. A wagon brought his coffin to our house in Blachernae in the dark hours of the night, where it would wait for burial. Manuel and Thea had moved there after Theodora and Costas married so they could have Romanus's old house to themselves. I had to break the news to Thea, using words I had no practice speaking, but with her I had someone with whom I could grieve, someone who loved Manuel as much as I did.

Thea and I spent the rest of the night weeping and saying the prayers for the dead beside his body. The servants began preparations at dawn for the expected visitors but after two sleepless nights, I could only fall into my bed. I woke after midday and found my mourning clothes in the room. Eudokia must have sent them from the palace. It was almost four years since I'd first worn them when John died, and it was agony to put them on again.

I crept downstairs to the room where John had lain, and it

was almost exactly as before. Friends were comforting Thea, bright yellow spring daffodils surrounded the casket, food nearby for visitors. My other sons were there, my daughters and their husbands too. Chrysokoulos stood in a corner speaking softly with Alexios. Isaac came and embraced me with tears in his eyes.

"Mama, I can't believe he's gone."

I could only shake my head. My children soon surrounded me, murmuring words of shock, sadness, and consolation.

The rest of that day and the next, the day of the funeral at St. Thekla's, were a blur of condolences. It was only after the third-day service that I realized the little Turk, Chrysokoulos, was staying at the house with us.

"Do you expect him to be here much longer?" I asked Thea, puzzled by his presence.

She shrugged. "I'm not sure, but he and Manuel became great friends. He's stayed with us since swearing loyalty to my father."

I decided to speak with Chrysokoulos the next day, perhaps learn more about what happened to Manuel.

"Lady Anna, I do not understand your son's illness. Maybe from a scratch, but I saw nothing there. We traveled for two days, his ear looking worse and worse, when he said we turn back. Get to physician. Monastery was closest. But too late."

"Oh. Thank you." I started to turn away when he stopped me.

"Lady, Manuel and I talked. He say you suspect someone betray emperor. I say you probably right."

"Really?"

"Yes. Some say things around me, don't think I understand. I tell Manuel I think you right, some might betray emperor." He stopped, glancing around to be sure no one heard us. "Now Manuel not there to watch."

Manuel's death had pushed that worry from my mind. Now the little Turk brought it back.

"I have idea," he said. "Maybe you send Alexios to emperor. I take him there."

"Alexios? But he's not even fifteen. Why not Isaac?"

"Isaac leave soon for Bulgaria. Too suspicious. But Alexios so young, no one suspect he spy on them. So maybe a good idea?" He looked at me for agreement. "Boy is eager to go."

Now I knew what he and Alexios had been speaking of. In truth, it was not a bad plan, even though Alexios was still younger than most. Or maybe because he was younger.

I sent a letter to the palace to be forwarded to Romanus in Cappadocia, offering to allow Alexios to take the place of Manuel.

I made a decision about the house while I waited for a response. I told Thea she could, of course, stay there with their daughters. I would stay until the end of the forty days of mourning before returning to the palace as Eudokia's companion.

Thea looked around the house, tears brimming. "I do want to stay. We were happiest here."

I returned to the palace with the three youngest boys, Alexios, Adrian, and Nikephoros, in June. The ancient philosophers say we are all, at any moment, close to death's door, something we all have to accept. So while I wanted to curl up in a cocoon with my grief, my duty to them kept me sane.

It wasn't long after we returned to the palace that I heard back from Romanus about my offer of Alexios.

I sat down with Alexios to show him the emperor's letter. He'd let his hopes rise that he might soon be fighting in the army, perhaps with the added excitement of spying.

"So he doesn't think I'm ready," he said, mouth twisted into a scowl.

"He thinks you're too young. And he doesn't want me to risk losing another son."

"Chrysokoulos said you were worried about the emperor,

that you'd asked Manuel to keep an eye on the officers, especially Andronikos Ducas," Alexios said.

"That's true. Not everyone is as loyal to the emperor as they should be."

Alexios frowned. "Are you talking about Caesar John? Because everyone knows he hates the emperor."

The same words Thomas had used. "Alexios," I began. "And everyone knows Andronikos will do anything his father says. He's terrified of the old man. If I were Romanus, I know I'd be worried about Andronikos."

"Son, I have the same worries, but you must keep this to yourself."

He pushed back his red hair impatiently. "Keep it to myself? Everyone knows. All my friends talk about it."

Even the children knew. "Perhaps so, but it will do you no good to speak openly about it. Let others do that. This is a lesson you need to learn early and learn well." I looked him hard in the eye.

He backed off then, quiet for a minute, staring back at me, before answering. "I understand, Mama."

☙❧

EUDOKIA SHARED WITH ME THE CORRESPONDENCE SHE received from her husband before she had it read in the council chamber. We read these letters to determine how she could best discuss their contents with the council, many of whom were antagonistic toward Romanus and the rest ambivalent. The army's scouts reported Alp Arslan's forces besieged Edessa in Syria, so the emperor decided to use that opportunity to attack the Turks in their less-fortified towns of Manzikert and Chliat. Inevitably, criticism of his decision arose.

"Wouldn't it be better if the emperor attacked the Turks at Edessa?" asked Psellus. "He could finish all of them off there."

"The emperor chose Manzikert since it is the easternmost

fort held by the Turks. It's reported to be lightly manned since the sultan diverted most of his soldiers to Edessa. If we regain Manzikert easily, as he expects, it will cut off Turkish access to a large part of the empire. Edessa is outside our borders and difficult to keep armies supplied," Eudokia explained calmly.

Psellus pursed his lips and sat stroking his long gray beard. "I still think attacking Edessa would be the better option."

Eudokia gave him a sweet smile and said, "Perhaps next year you can take the army on campaign, then."

The bureaucrat, terrified of horses, turned red and looked back at his notes.

A week later, a letter arrived with more alarming news. The emperor had camped his army near Cappadocia, and during the night a fire broke out in the camp, although it only destroyed his horses, weapons, saddles and other equipment.

Eudokia looked up at me. "The fire only destroyed Romanus's horses, weapons, and saddles? No one else's?"

I looked at her. "That seems odd."

Eudokia rubbed her temples. "Yes. I don't want to believe sabotage, but this worries me."

"He wrote that he'll stop at his estate in Cappadocia to replace his horses and equipment," I said. "I hope it doesn't take long. Every day it takes is another day that gives the sultan a chance to find out where Romanus is going. Those Turkish armies move fast."

Eudokia had this letter read out in the council meeting. There were a few murmurs of sympathy from the dozen men in the chamber, but most said nothing, sitting silent and looking bored. Psellus kept his head down, using the time to write his notes.

Romanus's other letters told of visiting forts along the roads to Manzikert, inspecting them to be sure they could hold out against attacks. He also had problems with some of the mercenaries, who carried off the grain stores of local farmers, forcing him to discipline them. These were the normal problems any military leader would have.

Eudokia watched the ships coming to the Boukoleon quay each day, looking for any letter from Romanus as the summer passed. She was restless, often visiting a palace church to pray, and even her children distracted her for only short periods. I tried to reassure her.

"Romanus has the strongest army we've had in the east in many years. The Turks do not stand a chance against him now. Once Manzikert and Chliat are secured, he'll be able to turn them back forever."

She gave me a wan smile. "You're right, but so much could still go wrong. There are no certainties in war. I can't relax until I know for sure."

Early August brought more letters. In one of them Romanus spoke of coming across the bodies of Roman soldiers left behind after Manuel's battle last year near Sebasteia. I wept at that reminder of his last year, where Manuel turned defeat into victory when he convinced Chrysokoulos to change sides. Another letter spoke of the terrible devastation the Turkish raids caused to the city of Theodosiopolis caused—most of the people gone, either killed or enslaved; the buildings looted before being burned down; the hunger rampant among the survivors.

The horrific destruction Romanus encountered on the road to Manzikert appeared only to reinforce his intention to return control of the area to the empire. He wrote that scouts confirmed the fort at Manzikert had few soldiers manning it. The army he had assembled over three years was now well-trained and experienced.

Eudokia had this last letter read out in the council meeting, pleased at the confidence her husband had at the expected outcome. Most of the usual nay-sayers grumbled out a few comments—except for Psellus, who said nothing.

I OFTEN VISITED OUR HOUSE IN BLACHERNAE THAT SUMMER to spend time with Thea and her two small daughters. We consoled each other, one of us strong when the other could not be. Theodora was often there since, except for servants, she was alone in her house while Costas was in Bulgaria with Isaac.

Thea was inside with the girls one day in late August while Theodora and I worked in the herb garden. My daughter's forceful efforts to remove the weeds growing around the rosemary plant began to threaten the herb with extinction.

"Theodora, I think you've removed all the weeds," I said.

She looked up at me, startled and with tears in her eyes. She wiped her sleeve across her face and sat back on her heels, shaking.

I moved to wrap my arms around her, murmuring, "I know, we all miss Manuel."

She shook her head. "No, Mama. Well, it's not that I'm not sad he died, I am. It's not about Manuel."

"So what is it?"

She rubbed her fingers against her forehead, as though trying to rub something out of her mind.

"It's Costas."

"Costas? Is he hurt? Have you had news of him?"

"No, that's the problem. I rarely hear from him. It's been almost two months without word, and Isaac sends you letters almost every week. If it weren't for them, I would know nothing about how they are doing."

"Perhaps he's busy or maybe just doesn't realize you want to hear from him."

"I tell him I do in every letter I send him. But that's not all that worries me." She scowled as though remembering an unpleasant thought.

I wasn't sure I wanted the answer to my question but asked it anyway.

"What else worries you?"

She flushed so deep a pink that the freckles across her nose stood out. "I didn't tell you before, but we did not consummate our marriage until a week after the wedding. He said we should get accustomed to each other before we did that."

The two of them had known each other since they were babies.

"But you did consummate it?"

"Yes, we did finally. And then it was Advent, and Costas said we must abstain from it until Epiphany, but he'd be out late at night. There were a few more times before Lent, and we had to abstain again. There were more excuses for being out late. Then he left right after Pascha," she stopped, her hand over her eyes. "Mama, I wonder if he finds me ugly or doesn't love me. He says he does, but. . ."

"Sweet girl, you are certainly not ugly, and he wouldn't say he loves you if he doesn't." I hoped that was true, but avoiding the marriage bed did not bode well. "I'm sure things will get better once he's home again."

She nodded and dried her eyes. "I hope so."

I would have to speak with Romanus about his son when he returned. He'd told me Costas was willing to marry her, but perhaps there was someone else? Or some other problem?

৩৬৩

I AWOKE AFTER MIDNIGHT ON SEPTEMBER THIRD, a servant knocking on my door. "The empress requests your presence in the Daphne Palace, Lady Anna."

A midnight summons is never good news. I began saying my prayers as I hurried to dress.

Thomas greeted me at the door with a hard face, putting a finger to his lips to indicate silence. The walk from there to the Daphne Palace was short, guided by the small lamp he carried. We reached the office Romanus used, and Thomas quietly opened the door.

Eudokia was inside, resting her head on her husband's desk,

sobbing softly. A scruffy soldier was also in the room, clothes ripped in places, his exhausted face filthy, gazing on the empress with pity. . . and with fear.

I ran to Eudokia's side, taking her hand.

"My dear friend, what's happened?" I asked, barely able to get the words out.

"Anna, he's dead," she said and grasped me around the waist. "This soldier tells me the Turks killed my beloved husband at Manzikert."

It felt like we had been flung from a ship, left adrift in stormy waters. "Oh no, Eudokia," I said, stroking her shaking head.

The soldier spoke abruptly. "The fighting was fierce, terrible. The emperor right in the middle of it, leading the army. I saw him, but then I couldn't. Someone said he was down, heathen Turks killed him. All our men started to abandon the fight then. We all raced to escape like ghouls were chasing us. Found a fast horse and rode to bring word."

"Did you actually see the emperor killed? Laying on the ground dead?" I asked, grasping for some thread of hope.

He hesitated. "Not exactly, but I heard people say it."

"How soon did you leave the area? A few hours later or right away?"

He looked at me as if I were crazy. "Right away, Lady. Made no sense to wait to get hauled to the slave markets."

I caught Thomas's eye. "Take this young man someplace safe, where he won't be noticed. Get him food and drink and a place to sleep. We'll need to speak with him again in the morning. But don't let anyone else know about him or talk to him."

We couldn't keep the emperor's death quiet for long, but we needed to come up with a plan before word got out. Assuming he was dead.

"Eudokia, we mustn't despair. That man did not see Romanus dead. Battles are savage places where confusion reigns above all. John and Isaac always said that; my grandfather taught me that as a child. So this man might be mistaken. Let's not give up hope. Not yet."

Her grief-shattered face looked up at me, and she nodded. I helped her to her chamber, put her in the bed, and sat next to her on a chair in the dark, considering what to do next.

⚜

EUDOKIA WOKE FROM A FEW HOURS OF FITFUL SLEEP AT dawn, still weeping but calmer. The first person she asked me to summon was Emperor Michael.

Michael looked surprised to see his mother's tearstained face.

"Mama, what's wrong? What's happened?"

She looked away from him, as though she couldn't face him while saying the ghastly words. "My son, I received word last night that your stepfather was in a great battle at Manzikert in the eastern borderlands around Lake Van." She stopped to wipe her eyes, catch her breath.

"A soldier arrived with the news. He said. . . he said that my husband may have been killed. That's what he heard from other soldiers, but he didn't see him fall, so he might have been captured. We aren't sure yet."

Michael blinked at that news, pushing his hair back. He sat without saying anything for a minute, as though trying to grasp what this meant, before looking again at his mother.

"Mama, this is terrible news. I am so sorry to hear this. When did the battle happen?"

His words sounded concerned, but he did not look grief-stricken. Perhaps he was eager to rule on his own, without the oversight of such a formidable stepfather.

"It was over a week ago. I am calling a council meeting for tomorrow to discuss what our options are. I hope we'll have more news by then."

"I think you should also send for Uncle John."

Eudokia stiffened at that. She had tolerated John Ducas in

her first marriage, but she could not forget or forgive the rudeness and backstabbing he displayed to her second husband. Even so, timid Michael would be no help, and no other dynatoi had the influence to lead in this situation the way John Ducas could.

She sighed heavily and nodded. "I think you're correct. I'll ask Psellus to send a messenger to him."

"I can tell him. I was going to see him shortly anyway." Michael, who might now be the sole emperor ruling, embraced his mother and left.

"I wish I didn't have to send for Caesar John," she said.

"I know," I said. "He hates Romanus, but if Romanus is dead, the empire will need John Ducas."

❧

I ACCOMPANIED EUDOKIA THE NEXT DAY TO THE COUNCIL chamber. She had invited the leading senators to join the normal council members, and they gathered around the table, curious about the summons. I entered the room a step behind Eudokia, as apprehensive about this situation as she was.

"Senators and council members, this soldier, Petrus from Emperor Romanus's army, arrived yesterday with disturbing news."

The soldier, cleaned up and in decent clothes, came forward to relate his story. He was unused to such elite company and his voice quavered in places. He recounted his story, but this time, on Eudokia's instructions, made sure his listeners knew he had not seen Romanus dead.

"The fighting was fierce, the emperor leading the army, as was his way, and right in the thick of it. Then I looked for him, didn't see him, someone called out he was down. Men started saying the emperor's dead, falling back. I kept fighting but soon the field was almost empty. I had to go."

"You didn't see the emperor when the field was deserted?" asked one of the senators.

Petrus shrugged. "It was all confusion then. He might've been there, but I wasn't going to hunt for him when men said he was gone. I's lucky to find a horse and get away. Weren't many left, most scattered or slaughtered in the fighting."

The senators had been silent when the soldier told his story, but now broke into a torrent of questions, shouts, accusations. Eudokia stood up, forcing the counselors to stand up and stop talking.

"Senators, we need to discuss what our response will be to the sultan. If my husband is dead, then we must demand his body for burial. If not, we must negotiate his release."

"Your Majesty," said Nikephoros Palaiologos, a great friend of John Ducas's, "this is terrible news but we should have expected it. I never thought Emperor Romanus had a chance against the Turks. He shouldn't have been so aggressive against them."

Eudokia kept calm at this calumny, only saying, "Do you think you could have done better?"

"I'm sure I could have," he said, his chest thrust out. "What about Caesar John? He should be here."

"We've sent for him," said Michael, speaking on his own for the first time in a council meeting that I had attended. "We expect him in a few days."

"Have we received word from anyone else?" asked another senator.

"No, this soldier is the only one so far," said Eudokia. "I suggest we wait for any other news about the battle's outcome and for Caesar John's arrival. I am sure if the emperor survived the battle, we will soon hear from him, or if otherwise, other men will bring that news. In the meanwhile, Senator Palaiologos, perhaps you can start assembling an army since the Turks may arrive on our doorstep at any time?"

The puffed-up senator's eyes widened, apparently surprised to have his offer taken up, but he nodded agreement.

JOHN DUCAS'S BITHYNIAN ESTATE WAS SOME DISTANCE from the city, at least a two-day journey in each direction. So it was surprising when he showed up at the palace on the following day. The Caesar swaggered into the imperial audience chamber with Michael Psellus and his son Andronikos trailing in his wake, giving me a terrible sense of foreboding. Eudokia stared incredulously when she saw Andronikos who would have been with Romanus at Manzikert.

"Caesar, I didn't expect you to arrive so soon. I summoned you only two days ago."

"Your Majesty, I was already on my way here when I met your messenger. My son arrived with part of the emperor's army a few days ago. He has news of the battle that you and Emperor Michael should hear." Serious words said with an attitude of glee at someone else's misfortune.

Andronikos Ducas stepped forward, staring at Eudokia and her son as they waited to hear what he had to say. He looked away from them, then coughed to clear his voice before finally speaking.

"I was with Emperor Romanus at Lake Van, outside the fortress of Manzikert. The battle with the Turks began on August twenty-sixth. Before it started, the emperor assigned to me thirty-five thousand men to keep some distance from where the army would fight, held in reserve should he need us. He said he would send me a message when he wanted us." The young man stopped, seeming uncertain about what to say next.

"Go on, tell her what happened," said his father, nudging him with his elbow.

Andronikos looked at his father and stiffened. "The fighting was relentless, but we could see from a distance that the emperor had the upper hand at the start. His men began chasing the Turks back, but then it looked like the emperor went down. At least, we could no longer see him. Then a message arrived that the emperor was dead, so we turned around and left as quickly as we could."

Eudokia was near tears at this confirmation of the story of her husband's death, but she was calm enough to ask questions.

"What sort of message was it? Written? By whom?"

Andronikos looked around, as if trying to think of the answer. "No, not written. I recall it was a messenger who brought the news."

"Who was the messenger? I'd like to speak to him."

Andronikos swallowed hard and blinked. "I can't recall his name. He turned around and rode toward camp. I didn't see him again."

Eudokia slumped back in her throne, hand to her mouth, unable to speak. Michael gripped his mother's hand and was biting the nails on his other hand, a habit he'd never been able to break.

"Your Majesty," said the Caesar while looking at Michael, "when your mother wed Romanus Diogenes you were still quite young and perhaps needed a guiding hand. Over the past three years everyone has seen you grow in maturity and dignity. I believe it is time for you to rule on your own and without a regent now that your stepfather is dead. Of course, with the advice of your council."

Michael stopped biting his nails, released his mother's hand, and sat up a little straighter.

"And Your Majesty," said Psellus, "if I might suggest that your uncle, Caesar John, rejoin the council? I believe his presence, with his many years of wisdom and judgment, has been sorely missed."

Emperor Michael looked surprised but proud at this sudden elevation in his status. "Of course, Uncle John, I would be pleased for you to rejoin the council." He stepped down and embraced his uncle and cousin, with Psellus beaming at the three of them.

The four men soon left the audience chamber, forgetting Eudokia.

Eudokia rose and turned to me, tears flowing down her cheeks.

"Anna, I can't believe he's gone. It just doesn't seem real."

"I know," I said. I was crying too, and I wrapped my arms around her, trying to give some comfort. The thought that Romanus was gone appalled me, sickened me. It had been centuries since a Roman emperor had been killed in battle, and that was a terrible stain on any emperor's reputation. He was a great general, a strong soldier, and had assembled a formidable army. I needed to find out what truly happened that day.

The other thoughts churning in my brain were about Emperor Michael. No one could believe he had grown in maturity when he had not even managed to bed his lovely wife after almost five years of marriage. It certainly looked like John Ducas's flattery found its mark with Michael, though. And now the Caesar would return to the council.

CAESAR JOHN MANAGED, WITH A COMBINATION OF HONEY-coated words and generous gifts, to grasp control of the council and Emperor Michael within a day of his return. Michael often met with his uncle and Psellus, paying little attention to his mother. In any event, Eudokia cared little about that in her grief.

More soldiers straggled into the city, none with any other news about Romanus. Then, in mid-October, a travel-stained messenger arrived and demanded to see the empress. He carried a letter meant only for her.

Eudokia's hands trembled as she took the folded parchment with its red wax seal. Her thin finger broke the seal, and she opened it to read the words on it.

"Anna, Anna, he's alive!" she exclaimed. "God be praised, he is alive. He says he was captured, but he signed an agreement with the sultan who then released him. He's had to agree to pay a huge ransom, but he's on his way home." She clasped the letter to her chest, joy radiating from her.

"I must tell Michael about this," she said, standing and reaching for her maphorion to cover her hair.

"Eudokia, you do need to tell them, but. . ." I began.

She looked at me, an eyebrow raised.

"How do you think Michael and John Ducas and the rest of the council will react to this letter? They'll not be pleased. They seem like they would be. . . uninterested in having Romanus return."

She sucked in her breath, realizing the truth of what I said.

"Perhaps you should calm yourself, do not express great happiness at this news, then see what their response is. You have to think about what this might mean for your Diogenes sons. We should plan how you will let the council know."

Her eyes widened in understanding. She sat down again, running her fingers nervously up and down the maphorion's embroidered edge.

We spent a few minutes planning a strategy we hoped would work. Then Eudokia sent a messenger to her son, requesting a meeting.

❧

"MY SON, I HAVE RECEIVED A LETTER FROM MY HUSBAND. It seems he is still alive. The Turkish sultan captured him but released him on the promise of a ransom to be paid."

Michael sat silent, his mouth partly agape, perplexed by this new information. John Ducas stood next to Michael, his face a blustering red, while Psellus's eyes narrowed, calculating. No one spoke for several minutes until Psellus piped up.

"Thank you, Augusta, for providing this information to us. How sure are you of its veracity?"

"The letter is in his hand, so I am sure it came from him. He says he is on his way back to the city now. He was captured but agreed to a ransom in exchange for his release. He will be gathering what troops he can on his journey, to begin rebuilding the army."

Eudokia's voice was calm, but she had a more difficult time hiding her happiness at this news. Her words hung in the air, none of the three men responding.

Finally, Michael said, "Thank you for telling me of this letter, Mother. Uncle John and my other counselors and I will decide how best to respond."

He turned away, coldly dismissing his mother. Eudokia glanced at me, her lips closed tight against a thoughtless response.

Eudokia and I slipped out of the audience chamber. A Varangian shut the door behind us, almost too fast, as though willing us to be gone. We looked at each other, knowing without speaking that the meeting had not gone well for her or her husband.

※

EUDOKIA TRIED TO SPEAK WITH HER SON ALONE SEVERAL times over the following days but was given one excuse after another for why that was impossible. And yet John Ducas's sons, Michael's cousins Andronikos and Constantine, spent much time closeted with him and Psellus.

We were in the nursery with the younger children when Eudokia noticed a large number of imperial messengers leaving from the quay outside the palace.

"Anna, come with me. I can't wait any longer. I need to speak with Michael now."

We stood outside his audience chamber a few minutes later, Eudokia insisting on being admitted. Finally, the door creaked open. Michael was there, Psellus at his side.

"My son, you must tell me if you've heard any news from

your stepfather, Emperor Romanus. I saw messengers leaving and wanted to know if they had anything to do with him."

"M-m-mother," he began with a stutter, "n-n-no, I've heard nothing from him."

"Augusta, Emperor Michael has decided that it is time he rules on his own," said Psellus. "He has the support of the Varangians and the council. The failure of General Diogenes at Manzikert, his disgraceful capture by the sultan, and his unauthorized signing of an agreement to pay a huge ransom all mean he has forfeited his place on the throne. Your son sent out messages to all our cities and fortresses that any attempt by Romanus Diogenes to exercise any imperial authority is invalid and that his capture will be well rewarded."

Eudokia gasped. "But how can you do that? He is still an emperor crowned by the patriarch; he's still my husband. What do you mean by all this? It can't possibly be. Could I speak with the council, try to explain?"

"Augusta, the council already made its decision. The entire city will soon learn of the former emperor's dreadful dereliction of duty and that he has been removed from the throne." Psellus spoke those words with a smile of smug satisfaction.

I was angry at their condemnation of Romanus and my best friend's relegation to unimportant dowager. I grasped Eudokia's elbow and guided her out of the room, both of us shocked at this vicious attack on Romanus. Everything had gone wrong, horribly wrong.

Eudokia began sobbing when we got back to the privacy of her rooms. She took off her maphorion and flung it across the room.

"I hate Psellus. I hate John Ducas. Those two snakes are just evil. They could never do what Romanus did. They are so jealous of him. Fools, they're just evil, vicious fools. Anna, what can we do now?"

I was going to suggest writing to Romanus when I heard a clattering outside. A troop of the Varangian soldiers were crossing the courtyard in front of the Boukoleon, heading right for us. John Ducas followed close behind them. A sense of dread clutched at me.

"We need to get out of here now. Look at those men. We have to get away from them." My throat was dry as I choked out those words.

Eudokia looked out on them and made a strangled cry.

We took the back stairs used by the servants, down and out through a side door. Looking around, I saw an old building that had to be at least three hundred years old, dilapidated and sagging to one side. It held an underground room once used for storage that I hoped was forgotten. I pulled Eudokia behind me into the building, her fair hair flying, down its stairs to what seemed almost a crypt.

We heard sounds of men searching outside for us. Eudokia grasped my hand, tears streaming down her face. I put an arm around my old friend, trying to be strong while my heart beat painfully in my chest. It felt like we were mice hiding in this dark place, waiting for the cat to pounce. Perhaps it was a blessing that we did not wait long.

The Varangians soon realized where we were, making loud noises to get John Ducas's attention. The soldiers broke down the door when Ducas arrived and dragged us out onto the pathway in front of the building.

"Augusta," said Ducas with a sneer on his face, "sorry to disturb your rest. Not your usual rooms, I believe? No matter. You're here now. Your son has asked me to let you know that since Romanus Diogenes has been deprived of his crown, Emperor Michael has decided that the best thing for you is to enter a monastery. I've brought a razor to begin that change."

"No, I don't want to," she cried.

"Go ahead, resist if you want. But if you do, I will also use this to cut your sons with Diogenes."

He pulled out a razor and began chopping at her beautiful

hair. Eudokia did not, could not resist if that meant the small boys she had with Romanus might be made eunuchs.

I could not speak, horrified at John Ducas's raw hatred and threats. He slashed at her head, hacking at the hair to make it as short as he could. Blond hair scattered on the ground among the red autumn leaves. Even the soldiers, hard men from barbarian lands, looked shocked at the anger twisting in Caesar John's face as he worked.

He grunted out vile words as he chopped. "Whore." "Oath-breaker." and "Bitch."

Eventually, he finished and pushed Eudokia to the soldiers.

"See she's on the ship I have waiting at the quay."

Ducas bellowed at her as the two soldiers escorted her away, "And don't expect to ever see your filthy bastard of a husband again."

Eudokia stumbled at those words, held up only by the two soldiers who each grasped an arm.

Then he seemed to notice me. "Lady Anna, you can see the Augusta Eudokia no longer requires your companionship. You need to leave the palace immediately."

CHAPTER 12

NOVEMBER 1071 to July 1072

THOMAS HAPPENED TO BE PASSING NEARBY WHEN THE dreadful scene with Eudokia occurred. He grabbed my arm after the red-faced John Ducas marched off with his soldiers, not letting me fall when my knees buckled.

"Hush, Lady Anna," he said in a low voice. "Say nothing now."

I was too stunned to speak anyway. He guided me to my rooms in the Boukoleon, pausing to send one of the servants to collect my sons Alexios, Adrian, and Nikephoros. Inside, he sat me down and poured a glass of wine for me, adding only a little water to it.

I tried to pick up the cup, but my hands were shaking so that it spilled onto the table. I put it down and covered my face with my hands.

"Oh, Thomas, how could this have happened?"

He just shook his head while going to my clothes chest and beginning to pack it up. "The sooner you can get out of here, to anywhere the Caesar won't see you, the better." He paused and looked over at me. "I've never seen anyone look so angry, so crazed as he was. I knew he hated Emperor Romanus, but I can't even describe what I saw on John Ducas's face."

The three boys soon turned up, Alexios hot and sweaty from riding.

"You need to pack your things," I said in a shaky voice. "We are leaving the palace today, as soon as we can. I'll explain everything once we are back in our house."

Thomas accompanied us back home to Blachernae. The sun was close to setting when we arrived, surprising Thea and her two daughters and the servants.

"We have to talk," I said to my daughter-in-law. "Gather everyone. The servants need to know too."

Our household servants, my sons, Thea, and Thomas were assembled a few minutes later. I looked at their faces, most of them curious, some apprehensive. They stared at me, needing guidance. I took a deep breath.

"I'm sure everyone heard the news about the defeat of Emperor Romanus at Manzikert on the eastern frontier. You also heard that the emperor was not killed in the battle as we first thought, but was captured by the Turks and released on the promise of a ransom to be paid. Empress Eudokia and I expected Emperor Romanus would return to the city, but it does not appear that will be happening, at least not anytime soon."

Thea's eyes widened at this news of her father. This year had been storm-tossed for her, first with Manuel's death, then thinking her father was killed in battle, then learning he'd been captured. What I had to say next would be most difficult for her.

"Caesar John Ducas convinced Emperor Michael that he should be ruling on his own now, without the aid of his stepfather or mother. Messages have been sent to the governors of all the empire's themes that Emperor Romanus is not to be received or recognized if he approaches any city. In fact, a reward has been offered for his capture. Also, Emperor Michael decreed that his mother was to be tonsured and enter a monastery. Caesar

John cut off her hair at the palace before she left on a ship for that destination some hours ago."

Plain words for devastating news. Shock registered on the faces before me. Tears poured down Thea's face.

"I cannot predict what might happen now. I was Empress Eudokia's companion for many years, I am cousin to Emperor Romanus, he is Lady Thea's father, and my daughter Theodora is married to his son. I don't know what Caesar John might do to me or any of us because of those ties." I looked around the room until I caught Alexios's eye and gestured for him to come forward to stand beside me. My next words would echo the words my grandmother had said to her servants from her sickbed years earlier. Those words had placed a cloak of authority on my shoulders, as I must now place on my son's.

"If anything happens to me, I want every one of you to know that, despite his youth, I am leaving Alexios in full authority over the household in my absence. He has my complete confidence, and you will obey his instructions as though they were given to you by me."

I paused to let that sink in. I had a hand on Alexios's shoulder and felt him straighten at this announcement.

"To be clear, I want each of you to acknowledge your acceptance of my instructions in this matter, that Alexios is to have the exact same authority over the household as I do, even though he lacks a year to full maturity," I repeated.

Martina started by standing and saying, "I accept your instructions." Then the cook and kitchen boy, the gatekeeper and stable hands, the women helping Thea in the nursery, the washerwoman. They all stated their acceptance and began to rise to leave. Thea made a nod of acceptance, too upset to speak.

"One other thing: What I have said this evening cannot go further. Speak to no one of what I've said." The servants nodded.

Thea pulled me aside, her eyes red-rimmed and face tear streaked.

"This is terrible for my Papa, isn't it? It's so unfair."

I wrapped an arm around her waist and pulled her to a corner.

"I won't lie to you; it is. Your father's a strong man, and if anyone can overcome the Caesar's plans, he can. But he has mountains to climb to accomplish that."

Thea seemed to shrink, close in on herself. Losing her husband and possibly her father in the same year were terrible blows. She knuckled away tears with a shaking fist.

"I'll do what I can, but you need to focus on your girls," I said. "That's what Manuel and your father would want."

She nodded. Thea was a sweet young woman, a good mother, and had been a wonderful wife to Manuel. Perhaps if they'd been together more years, she would have grown stronger. Life had thrown too much at her at only twenty-two. She shuffled away to her room.

I approached Thomas then, pulling my seamstress, Martina, into the conversation.

"Thomas, I think it would be unwise for me to visit the palace now. I'd like to send Martina to visit you from time to time to learn what is happening with Eudokia and Emperor Romanus." Ducas may have demoted my cousin from emperor, but I would hold onto the title.

Thomas appraised the seamstress and seemed to approve of what he saw.

"Of course, Lady Anna. You know I'll do what I can."

Martina met the eye of the beardless eunuch and nodded her consent. "Whatever you need."

"Excellent. Thank you both."

THE NEXT DAY, I DECIDED TO WRITE TO ROMANUS TO GIVE him what news I had. The letter was not long, only reassuring him of the health of his family, letting him know what happened to Eudokia, and of our prayers for his well-being. I did mention that Caesar John, Emperor Michael, and many of the dynatoi appeared to be allied against him, but he would certainly have guessed as much by now.

I folded the letter, dribbled hot red wax onto the papyrus, and sealed it with my signet ring. It would be more difficult and expensive to get a letter to Romanus now that I wasn't in the palace. It would take at least two silver coins to hire a messenger willing to venture so far to find an emperor who might not be emperor any longer. I sent the coins and letter with Alexios to the Theodosian Forum, where I knew men willing to carry out such errands congregated, waiting to be hired.

Isaac returned home from Bulgaria that same day.

"Irene was waiting at the palace when I arrived there and told me you had returned home," he said.

"Irene?" I asked, confused.

"The woman from Alania, who came with her cousin, Empress Maria," he said, his cheeks flushing.

"Oh," I said, curious about how matters stood with them, before other concerns pushed that thought away.

"I had no idea just how bad things have gotten. Romanus really is no longer the emperor? After all he's done?"

"It is what John Ducas wanted, and he convinced Emperor Michael that he could reign alone. Of course, with his dear uncle's close counsel and that of Psellus. Otherwise, it's clear Michael wouldn't know what to do," I said, shaking my head. "I know you've always been friendly with him, but it is ridiculous how unsuited to being emperor that poor boy is."

He nodded reluctant agreement. "You're right about that. I know him well enough that I know he can't manage that job. I can't be angry with him either. He has the independence of a rabbit, huddled close to its hole for safety. The Caesar seems like that safe spot now. I'm sure Michael would never have sent his mother away on his own."

Alexios walked in then, back from the errand I'd sent him on.

"Isaac, it's good to have you home again," he greeted his brother. "Maybe you can sort out this mess Thea's father is in."

"What? I'm surprised you didn't manage it yourself," he joked.

Alexios grinned but then turned serious. "Mama, I found someone to take your letter, but. . ."

"But what?" I asked.

"Well, I'm not sure. Maybe I'm just nervous after everything that's happened. I didn't see anyone follow me, and the messenger I found seemed ordinary enough. Just felt strange, like I was being watched or something."

"What letter?" asked Isaac.

"I wrote a letter to Romanus, letting him know what happened to Eudokia and that his children and grandchildren are safe." My stomach started churning then. Had I lost my mind in sending it?

"I should have suspected John Ducas might keep an eye on me," I admitted. "But I've made my move; nothing more to do except see what happens."

We did not have to wait long.

Loud banging on our gate started as we were eating dinner in the twilight hour. The light Advent meal included bread, lentils, walnuts, and raisins. I could eat little aside from a spoonful of lentils.

Isaac rose and went to the window looking out to the court-yard as the gatekeeper let the visitors in.

"Varangians," he said, his voice just above a whisper. "At least a dozen of them. Looks like Hafdan is in charge."

"Who's he? What's he like?" Alexios asked.

"Tough guy, not friendly, but reasonable."

Isaac and I went out to greet the soldiers. The man leading them saluted Isaac.

"Isaac," said the burly blond man standing before us, "I've been instructed to arrest your mother, Lady Anna Dalassena, and any other men of your family in this house."

Isaac raised a surprised eyebrow at this.

"My mother? On whose orders?" he growled.

"Caesar John told us Emperor Michael ordered it. Since you are of adult age, the order includes you. Do you have any other brothers who have reached maturity?"

"No. I'm sure you'll have heard that my older brother, Manuel, died in April. My younger brothers are still quite young."

"Then come along. The Caesar wants the arrests confirmed soon."

"You'll have to wait while I retrieve my mantle from my room," I said. Try as I might, I still heard a quavering note in my voice.

Hafdan nodded. Isaac and I retreated back into the house.

Thea sat on a chair, huddled with her two daughters, shaking and unable to cope with this latest assault. Alexios stood nearby.

"Alexios, I'm leaving you in charge in my absence, no matter how long I am gone. Do you understand?"

"Yes," he said, although he had a worried frown on his face.

I embraced him then, whispering in his ear, "I know you can manage this."

I hurried to my room, but rather than take the usual winter wrap I used, I opened my clothing chest and dug down to the bottom where my Uncle Costas's mantle lay. I'd never used it in all the years since he'd given it to me, but the lavender and fennel leaves tucked between its folds to deter moths had worked —there were no holes in its heavy wool. This sturdy cloak was the kind used by soldiers on winter duty. My uncle had been a great general and suffered exile in Egypt and unjust arrests by two emperors. I unfolded it and something fell out, clattering metallically to the floor. A gold cross with the enameled face of Jesus in its center gleamed up at me. Uncle Costas must have left it in a pocket when he was tonsured and entered the monastery. It was likely too fancy for Stoudion, whose monks wore only plain wooden crosses. I picked it up and tucked it into my bodice, wrapping the mantle around me.

Isaac waited downstairs for me, having retrieved his cloak as well. I kissed a tearful Thea and her daughters good-bye, as well as the sons I was leaving behind. I put on a calm face, but inside I felt as taut as a lute string about to be plucked. I knew the innocent do not always get justice. We stepped outside where the Varangians waited and began the walk back to the palace I had left only the day before.

❧

ISAAC AND I WERE HELD IN THE SAME CHILLY ROOM Romanus had been held four years earlier, when awaiting his own trial. He had survived that trial, been pardoned, and married his empress before being flung aside. Now he was being hunted down.

I spent the next two days contemplating how to defend myself and Isaac from the charges Psellus told us we would be accused of. That oily bureaucrat had been gleeful on his visit, telling me it was now forbidden to even contact Romanus. Isaac agreed to let me speak for us both at the trial.

The trial was held, as it had been with Romanus's, in the old Senate building. It seemed John Ducas wanted a public demonstration of his family's power and authority before all the dynatoi. Easier that way to intimidate anyone else who might think to oppose him.

I wasn't sure how well I would speak in our defense. I had no training in law, no experts coaching me in the best way to fashion an argument before judges, only what my grandfather and Uncle Costas had taught me so many years earlier. I said a quiet thank-you to them for always pushing me, even though they never expected I would be in this spot. I doubted I could get a sympathetic hearing, nor did I know what the punishment might be if Isaac and I were judged guilty. I only knew what was true, and I would speak those words.

The eparch of the city stood before the assemblage and read out a charge of treason for writing to the deposed emperor, Romanus Diogenes.

"How do you both plead?"

"We plead innocent," I said.

That flustered the eparch. "Isaac Comnenus, how do you plead?"

"As my mother said, we are innocent. She speaks for us both," he said and stepped back.

Eyes wide with surprise turned to me; none expected a woman to speak in her own defense. I stood quietly, eyes downcast, sweaty palms resting on the railing, waiting for the judges' signal to speak. One of them nodded his head.

"Your Majesty Emperor Michael, and Empress Maria, eminent judges, senators, Caesar John Ducas, thank you for this opportunity to defend myself and my son Isaac from the unjust accusations of treason leveled against us.

"This is my testimony, that I swear before this court and before God is true. I have known Emperor Michael since he was a baby. He is the son of my dear friend, Augusta Eudokia. I have known the emperor's wife, Empress Maria, from the first day she arrived in our magnificent city. I believe they can both say I have shown them true affection and devotion during all those years. My son Isaac has had a wonderful friendship with Emperor Michael. That close affection means that neither of us ever spoke a disloyal word about Emperor Michael to anyone. There is no one who can truthfully testify to us showing any disloyalty to the emperor."

I looked at Michael, who nodded agreement with my words. He was a good lad in some ways.

"We have also been loyal to the former emperor, Romanus Diogenes. As many of you know, he is a distant cousin of mine, and he is the father of my daughter Theodora's husband, Costas

Diogenes, and the father of my son Manuel's widow, Theophano. He is the only living grandfather of my son Manuel's two young orphaned daughters. I understand Emperor Michael has reached an age where he decided to take on the reins of government fully, without the benefit of my cousin's advice and military experience. That is his right. I also understand the shame that falls on the Roman Empire when an emperor is defeated in battle and dishonorably taken captive by those we consider barbarians. That is a terrible blow to the empire, and its penalty should be terrible.

"Despite that drastic change in the position Romanus Diogenes holds in the empire, he remains in my family thrice over as cousin, father-in-law, and grandfather. Do I have the right to turn away my grandchildren's grandfather? I don't believe so. Every man here in this building has ties of blood and marriage. Would any of you turn away a family member even if they suffered setbacks?

"My letter to Romanus Diogenes contained only family information and assurances of my prayers on his behalf. I had no idea that even writing to him was considered treason when only a few days earlier he had been emperor himself. I was ignorant of this new law. My son Isaac was not even in the city when I wrote the letter, so clearly he is innocent. Was I wrong to write to my cousin Romanus? But isn't this something that any one of you might send to a family member in disgrace? I hope that my simple words would be something each of you could manage to send a family member and not be judged guilty of treason."

My hand slipped into my pocket and grasped the item in it.

I raised my hand high with the cross that Uncle Costas had left behind all those years ago, making sure they could all see the brightly enameled face of Christ.

"Here is my judge and yours. Think of Him before deciding and take heed that your decision is worthy of that supreme judge who knows the secrets of men's hearts."

I turned so that each part of the assembly could see the cross, eventually reaching where Emperor Michael fidgeted beside his frustrated wife, Empress Maria. Maria's cousin, the fair Irene, sat beside her. Irene was looking beyond me at Isaac. John Ducas sat beside Michael, his face bloated and red with rage. I would not let him see the disgust I felt for him. Psellus, nervously tugging at his gray beard, stood behind the Caesar.

I looked back to the judges, my heart thumping in my chest. The four of them appeared uncomfortable, glancing at each other, Ducas, and the emperor. There was a strong chance Ducas had told them what the verdict should be. The penalty for treason was often death, and although I had never heard of a woman being executed, I was concerned about Isaac.

The judges withdrew to a private chamber, leaving us to await their verdict.

"You did well, Mama," said Isaac. He put an arm around my shoulders. "Everyone was paying rapt attention to what you said. It felt like they trusted your words."

"I hope so," I said.

We stood in the accused's box, guarded by Varangians, for over an hour while the judges deliberated. Isaac and I chatted quietly, discussing the people in attendance at the trial.

"Hey," he said, gesturing to a man sitting in a corner, dressed in plain clothes and huddled under a bulky mantle that shadowed his face, "isn't that the judge Michael Attaleiates? The one who was on campaign with Romanus?"

"Why, yes, it is." The red hood trimmed in gold that judges wore had given him a stern appearance in court. Now, in common clothes and half-hidden under a brown hood, his face was gray and he looked haggard. "Perhaps he knows what happened at Manzikert. Andronikos Ducas is nothing more than his father's puppet. I know he planned to make trouble for Romanus. I'd love to speak with Attaleiates. Find out what really happened."

Just then, the judges returned.

"We have reached a decision," said the judge in the center.

"It is clear that Lady Anna Dalassena wrote to the former emperor, Romanus Diogenes, a treasonous act that was forbidden by Emperor Michael. Of that, she is clearly guilty, and her son, as head of her household, bears equal blame. The penalty for treason is death. At the same time, she testified before this court and God that she was unaware of the new law and that she has always been loyal to Emperor Michael. Her late husband was brother to Emperor Isaac Comnenus, and her eldest son died this past April while in service to the Roman Empire. Her testimony and loyalty, her son Isaac's years of service to the empire, indicate that the death penalty should be mitigated. Instead, we recommend that Lady Anna Dalassena and her son Isaac be tonsured and live out their lives in monasteries of the emperor's choosing as a nun and a monk."

I caught my breath at his words. Ducas had wanted us to receive the ultimate penalty, execution, and only my impassioned defense had turned away that sword. I looked up at where Michael sat in the emperor's seat and he nodded agreement with the judge. John Ducas glared daggers at the judges while Psellus whispered frantically in his ear. Irene and Isaac were staring at each other in dismay at the sentence.

Varangians soon escorted us back to our prison to await word on where we would be sent.

The cold weather penetrated the cell in which we were held and aggravated the chilblains on my hands, now a painful bright red. I noticed Isaac suffered the same way, but chilblains were the least of our problems.

"Mama, I don't want to be a monk," he said, holding his head in his hands.

I sat next to him on the old stone bench. "Isaac, you must do whatever you need to do to survive. If you can avoid taking the monk's oath, do so. But if you must take it, then do so. If we live out our lives there, we might as well begin doing so with God's blessing. If we are ever freed, we can be released from the oaths since they will be forced on us. The key is to survive for another day. That's what my grandfather and Uncle Costas taught me, and I've never forgotten it."

There was a noise at the door to our cell. The door opened, and a hooded figure entered.

"Irene," said Isaac, happiness radiating when he saw her.

"I can't stay long," she said, breathless. "The empress let me go so I can tell you that you'll both be sent to monasteries on Prinkipo. She was miserable about this persecution. And Michael didn't really want it either, but the Caesar convinced him you were both threats. The empress hopes in time to convince Michael to release you, but her opinions carry little weight with him at present."

Prinkipo was the same windswept island in the Sea of Marmara that Empress Zoe had been sent to all those years ago. Close to the city but isolated.

"Isaac, I just wanted to see you one time before—" Irene stopped.

Isaac stepped close to her, cupping her cheek in his hand. "Dear heart, I know. You most of all know I am not cut out for the monastery. Don't give up on us, please."

"I won't." She turned her face to kiss his palm, then swept out of the room, the door clanging shut behind her.

I looked at my red-faced son with a raised eyebrow.

He had the grace to admit, "Sorry, Mama. I should have said something to you about her."

⚜

THE NEXT MORNING, WE WERE BUNDLED ONTO A RICKETY fishing boat for the passage to Prinkipo. It was almost as though Ducas's ill will hoped a winter storm would rush through, capsizing or sinking the old boat with us on it, accomplishing what the judges could not bring themselves to do. We made it across without difficulty, though, and were loaded on a wagon. I was deposited at the gate of the monastery of the Dormition, while Isaac went a little farther down the road to the monastery of St. George.

Isaac, his face creased with concern, was my last sight as the heavy wooden gate squeaked shut on its iron hinges. A pale-faced nun of indeterminate age gestured for me to follow her. All was silent here, unlike the city where even the darkest part of the night echoed with life. Winter's browns and grays dominated the courtyard we passed through and added to the day's bitter flavor. That last farewell to Isaac, the deathly quiet, and bleak landscape produced a sudden sense of hopelessness. Irene and her cousin held so little power, so little influence over the emperor that I wondered if Isaac and I would ever be allowed to leave.

Hegoumena Thekla greeted me in her austere office, informing me that the bishop would soon arrive to tonsure me. I was shown to the nun's cell where I would sleep, a small bed its only furniture and a curtain hanging at its entrance. The bed's ropes groaned when I sat down and waited for the summons to the church where I would take my vows, thinking about how swiftly my circumstances had changed. My beloved son Manuel had died only a few short months ago. I had been companion to an empress, cousin to the emperor, and living in the Great Palace in the greatest city in the world just a week earlier. Empress Zoe must have had similar thoughts during her short stay thirty years earlier, but in her case the citizens of the city had risen up and demanded her quick return. No one outside our own family would dare plead for our release.

I shook my head, trying to push back the self-pity threatening my sanity. Romanus was somewhere in Anatolia, trying to reclaim the throne. Eudokia had been forced into a monastery far from here, surely worrying for her husband and children. My daughter Theodora was married to Costas Diogenes, Romanus's eldest son. My son, Alexios, just fourteen, had the responsibility of Thea and her daughters in Blachernae. I fell to my knees praying for them all.

1072

MY LIFE AT THE MONASTERY WAS QUIET, BUT INSIDE I seethed with anxiety for my children, grandchildren, Eudokia, and Romanus. I wore the same black dress I had worn since Manuel's death, and the new black scarf covering my tonsure was little different from the usual maphorion women in the city kept on their heads. I worked in the fields the monastery farmed as I had worked in the gardens at home, but there was little to do in those first winter months. Talk was permitted at meals following the readings of the day, although I had little to say. The most comforting time of the day was in the church, reciting the prayers generations had said in times of need. I wept and prayed throughout the dark and silent nights.

Little information from the outside world seeped through the monastery's thick stone walls. It was a surprise, then, in the week after Pascha in early April that I was called to meet with the hegoumena.

"Sister Anna, there is a person here who asks to meet with you," she said.

"Did this person give his name?"

She looked slightly uncomfortable. "He's a eunuch. Gave his name as Thomas, said you know him from the palace."

A wave of gratitude washed over me. Thomas had not forgotten me.

I met with him in the courtyard, sitting on a bench warmed with the spring sun.

"I've wanted to come out here before, but the palace is full of the Caesar's spies, eager to betray anyone for a handful of coins. He and his underlings traveled outside the city for a few days, so I decided to try to visit. I was fortunate to even speak with your seamstress, Martina, a few times. She's a brave woman."

"She had to be to survive her journey to the city. Tell me, are Alexios, Thea, and the rest doing well? Safe?"

"They're safe. The Caesar believes he rendered the Comnenus family harmless with you and Isaac tonsured and on Prinkipo."

"And what of Romanus? Any word on him? And Eudokia?"

"Romanus Diogenes is fighting back, trying to regain what he lost. He's gathered a goodly number of troops, mostly Frankish mercenaries and men from Cappadocia. The Caesar isn't giving up, even though the western army in Bulgaria refuses to fight Romanus, said they've sworn oaths to him. Ducas sent his two sons to wage war on him, but they'll need more troops. So Romanus has the upper hand at present. There's no news about Eudokia, but if anything happened to her, I'm sure the emperor would be told."

"And what of Emperor Michael?"

Thomas gave an ironic grin. "I would say he is tiring of his uncle's incessant pestering, as well as Psellus's tedious lectures. It took him a while to realize that when they told him he could rule on his own, what they meant was that they would rule for him. Michael hasn't said anything, just rolls his eyes when they're telling him what to do but they can't see his face. The servants think it's hilarious."

Thomas promised to return when he could.

The news of Romanus's efforts to regain the throne and that Michael was tiring of his uncle and tutor sounded good. I would keep praying that all would come aright somehow.

৩৵৯

THOMAS DID NOT RETURN UNTIL THE END OF MAY.

"Matters have not gone well for Emperor Romanus." At least he still called my cousin "emperor".

We sat in the shade of a willow tree, out of the sun on a warm day, but his words were chilling.

He frowned and looked down at his hands, trying to find the words.

"The Ducas boys, Andronikos and Constantine, recently defeated Romanus in Cappadocia. Romanus and what's left of his army escaped to a fort for a time. Last I heard, he was taking his army to Cilicia."

Cilicia was the wrong direction, away from Byzantium, toward Syria. A retreat.

"How did this happen? When you were here last month, it sounded like he had a large army. Romanus has led many armies, and those Ducas boys never have."

"Mercenaries go where the pay is greatest," Thomas said. "One of them, Crispin, had a problem with Romanus two or three years ago. I'm not sure what."

I recalled then what Manuel had written about Psellus causing a problem between Romanus and Crispin.

Thomas continued, "But the Ducas boys paid Crispin and the hundred and fifty men he commanded quite well and allowed them to take the lead in battle."

I closed my eyes, praying, but felt discouraged at this news.

⚜

THE NEXT TIME THERE WAS ANY NEWS ABOUT MY COUSIN IT came through Hegoumena Thekla. She called me to her office on a hot July day.

"Sister Anna, I've received a missive from Emperor Michael that I must share with you."

I looked at her kind face and saw a deep sadness in her eyes.

"The emperor's letter says that the former emperor, Romanus Diogenes, was captured by Emperor Michael's cousins, Andronikos and Constantine Ducas, on June twenty-sixth. Diogenes offered to be tonsured so that he could avoid execution."

My heart sank, but I asked, hoping for the best, "So he still lives?"

The nun glanced down at the parchment with the emperor's words. "I believe he does still live. But. . ."

"Yes?"

"I'm sorry but there's no honey that can sweeten this news," she said in a mournful tone. "It seems the emperor's cousin Constantine Ducas instructed his men to blind Diogenes on June twenty-ninth. The man doing it was. . .inexperienced. The former emperor has an infection. He's very sick. Emperor Michael wants you to know the blinding was not done on his instructions."

I stumbled out of her office and the building, retching. I reached a rosemary bush and threw up, sick at the thought of my handsome and brave cousin blinded, feverish with a killing infection. Bitter tears rolled down my cheeks, and I sat down in the grass, the smell of my own vomit overcoming the sweet herb. I'd seen the blinding of another emperor, Michael V, when I was seventeen. It was horrible, watching men hold him down as they stabbed at his eyes with a red-hot poker. Romanus would have fought like a bull. That other emperor suffered terribly and died of the infection the blinding caused. Romanus would too.

CHAPTER 13

August 1072 to November 1074

The Emperor Romanus IV Diogenes died on August fourth, five weeks after the blinding. The thought of what kind of suffering he must have endured left me sicker and sadder than I'd ever felt before. Nightmare images of his face with bleeding eyes woke me screaming in the dark of night. The news, when it came, was a relief, and dreams of him in a white silk shroud a blessing.

I received a letter from Eudokia.

Sister Anna Dalassena
August 10

My dearest friend, Anna,

My son, Emperor Michael, gave his approval for an imperial funeral for my beloved husband, Romanus Diogenes. He will be buried where he died at the monastery of the Transfiguration on the

Island of Prote, near Prinkipo, where you now reside. My son also gave his approval for you to attend this funeral, as will Romanus's son Costas and his daughter Thea. Please accept this invitation. I've arranged for a boat to bring you here.

The two sons that Romanus and I had will not be there, being judged too young to attend. I am grateful that Michael's wife, Empress Maria, now cares for them as her own. I miss them every day but after such a long absence I fear they may have forgotten me. My only release is in quiet contemplation and prayer, and completing this final task for my beloved husband.

Sister Eudokia Makrembolitissa

THE FUNERAL WAS AS MAGNIFICENT AS IT COULD BE ON A small island in the Sea of Marmara, separated from Constantinople by miles of water. Attendees came from Cappadocia in the east and Bulgaria in the west, and more than a few dared to come from the city. Romanus had been respected and loved by many, and they would pay their last respects.

For the last time, I stood as companion to Eudokia during the services that saw her husband's burial in the crypt of the monastery's church. A carved white marble gravestone covered his casket.

"You were so strong," I told her afterward. "I could not stop crying."

She looked at me, as composed as a luminous icon staring down from a church wall. "I'm done with crying. I'm grateful Romanus is not being hunted like a criminal or a wild animal. I'm glad he is no longer suffering. His time on this earth, struggling against the relentless demands of petty creatures, is done. I was blessed to have him as my husband, even if for such a short time."

"What will you do now?"

"Return to the monastery after the fortieth-day observance. It is my home now."

I embraced my friend, feeling the bones in her back pushing through her black gown. She'd become a pale wraith in the months since I'd last seen her.

"I do have one request of you," she said, a shadow of concern crossing her face.

"Anything," I answered.

"If you, or someone in your family, could watch over our sons, Leo and Nikephoros? Maria loves them the way she would her own sons if she and Michael had any. But if she ever does have a child, my little boys could be forgotten." Eudokia's eyes teared up now, thinking of the sons she would never see grow up, who would never remember her.

"Of course. Those boys are part of our family. We'll do whatever we can to keep them from harm."

Romanus's two oldest children, Costas and Thea, arrived together. They'd spent the past year being unobtrusive so as to escape the wrath of John Ducas and were a subdued presence. Costas looked almost embarrassed to be seen attending the funeral of a deposed emperor, while Thea shrank back into the shadows whenever possible. Still, they greeted me warmly and assured me of the good health of my children and grandchildren.

One man I saw standing alone was the judge Michael Attaleiates, tears streaming down his face.

"Thank you for coming," I said in greeting.

He nodded, then looked at me with troubled eyes. "I had to be here. He was a great man, and what happened to him was a tragedy—and a crime."

"I think we need to sit down and talk about what happened at Manzikert," I said.

He rubbed his eyes, as though trying not to see something.

"Maybe, someday. I'm still trying to sort it out myself, get answers to all my questions," he said before turning to leave.

The one surprise attendee at the funeral was fair Irene, as I called her to myself. Perhaps she hoped that Isaac would be there.

"I'm so glad to see you, Lady Anna," she said. "It's been almost a year."

Interesting that she used my secular title rather than my religious one.

"It's good to see you, as well. And how are matters in the palace? Your cousin and Emperor Michael are well?"

"Yes, they are. There have been some staff changes, though," she said, a smile lifting the corners of her mouth. "Caesar John recalled a eunuch named Nikephoritzes that his brother sent into exile five years ago after some disagreement with Empress Eudokia. He's proven to be a great help to Emperor Michael. The emperor no longer has to rely so much on his uncle now."

Irene likely didn't know that the story was Nikephoritzes had tried to pass on some nasty rumors about Eudokia to her first husband, Emperor Constantine. To Constantine's credit, he never believed them, and Nikephoritzes got kicked to some remote outpost for his trouble.

Irene and I soon parted, and I returned to the monastery on Prinkipo.

⚜

THE FALL WINDS HAD BEGUN TO BLOW WHEN ISAAC appeared at the monastery, not wearing monk's robes and accompanied by the fair Irene.

"Mama, it is time to go home. Irene has done it—we are free to leave Prinkipo."

The story tumbled out like bits of tesserae into an elaborate mosaic over the next few hours on the journey home. Michael missed his friendship with Isaac, was fond of me, and did not understand the need to exile us for the plain letter I had written. He had also grown resentful his uncle's domination, and Psellus's constant fussy corrections annoyed him.

John Ducas's fatal mistake, however, was bringing back the little eunuch Nikephoritzes. It turned out Nikephoritzes had taken the blame for the rumors about Eudokia all those years ago when John Ducas had actually started them. Then the eunuch got stuck in the hinterlands with not a word from the Caesar for over five years, which was plenty of time to build up a load of resentment.

Nikephoritzes arrived at the palace and soon wormed his way into Michael's favor. Irene whispered into his ear that he could best get revenge by convincing Michael to bring us back to the city. It would thoroughly anger John Ducas and prove he'd lost the influence he thought he had over his nephew. Psellus, who had always looked down on the uneducated little eunuch, would also be expunged from the emperor's circle. Gold did change hands, and Nikephoritzes got his revenge.

Irene was a determined woman and set about reaching her next goal—marriage to Isaac—like a general on campaign. Easygoing Isaac had been friendly with Michael since they were babies, so this was not difficult.

After our return, Michael found himself hunting in the park outside the Blachernae walls with Isaac. Isaac often joined Michael and his wife and Irene for dinner. There were many chess games played that Isaac tactfully lost. Michael invited Isaac to join his council when a seat became available following John Ducas's departure in January. The Caesar was not exactly sent into exile, but he was encouraged to return to his estates in Bithynia.

Isaac came home one day in late January with a smile on his face.

"Mama, you are invited to the palace to meet with Michael."

I raised an eyebrow at that but said nothing.

He picked me up and whirled me around the room, glowing. "Yes, it's to discuss the terms of a betrothal with Irene."

"So tell me what happened," I said.

He laughed. "Irene and Maria planned it all out. Maria brought up the subject of whom I should marry. Very casually, almost like she was joking about it. Then I teased her that I'd have to find someone willing to marry me. Michael was feeling pretty good about himself, having just won a game of chess from me. Irene was sitting right there, looking demure but smiling at Michael. And so he decided I should marry Irene. Thought he came up with the idea on his own."

The two of them—good-natured Isaac and single-minded Irene—would be a good match.

1073

MICHAEL ATTALEIATES VISITED ME IN EARLY MARCH, a year and a half since that terrible day at Manzikert. Rumors, whispers, and speculation had run through the city since we'd learned of that defeat. Some said it was betrayal, some incompetence, and others saying the Turks could not be defeated. I just wanted to know the truth.

Alexios joined us; Isaac was busy and I wanted another witness to this testimony.

"I would have come sooner," the judge said, "but I was trying to find out what really happened that day. Of course I was there, but where I was behind the battle lines I saw only a small piece of it. I tracked down every person I could to learn the whole story. Even then, some refused to speak to me. Some from fear, others from embarrassment or guilt about their role."

Attaleiates looked gaunt, no longer the well-fed, esteemed judge of the highest courts of Constantinople. This was a different man than the one who had presided over Romanus's trial for rebellion almost seven years ago.

"Please tell me what you know," I asked.

This is his story.

Romanus had one hundred thousand soldiers under his command. He wanted to make an end to the Turks that year and could have with those men he had trained so well. The army spent the summer marching deep into the eastern borderlands to take the fight to the enemy. They moved often because trying to keep that many men fed was an awful strain on the local people, many of whom had already suffered from devastating raids. There were small problems—the fire that killed the emperor's horses and destroyed much of his equipment that no one could explain, the usual quibbles with locals when trying to buy food. Then there were the lands they passed through, many of them ravaged by Turkish attacks. They journeyed through the valley where my son, Manuel, had fought the prior year. The sight of the rotting dead bodies of those soldiers frightened the superstitious in the emperor's army.

"Did Emperor Romanus look intimidated by these things?" I asked.

"No. He grew only more determined."

They arrived at the fortress of Manzikert on Lake Van in August to find it occupied by only a few Turks. Romanus was determined to take it back. The Roman army emptied the town and fort of the Turks in a day or two, but this place could not provide the food needed by a hundred thousand men and their beasts. Romanus sent thirty thousand to the nearby town of Chliat under Joseph Trachaneiotes so that recalling them would be easy if he needed them. Reports from our spies said that Sultan Alp Arslan was in the south, in Aleppo. However, once he realized the emperor had gone north, he raced to Manzikert with his men and surprised Romanus. Even so, the Romans were ready for a fight when they appeared outside Manzikert's walls. The two armies skirmished a few times, feeling each other out. The emperor and sultan tried negotiating for a day, but the emperor was determined to end the raiding permanently. He sent word to Joseph Trachaneiotes to bring his army from Chliat before the battle started.

"And what happened then?" I asked.

"Nothing. They never showed up. Romanus worried something terrible must have caused them not to come." Attaleiates's eyes flashed; his face reddened. "If they had encountered a larger force, then those might be coming to reinforce the sultan. He thought he had to start the battle soon or risk losing any chance of success he had."

"Had something happened to them?"

"No. Trachaneiotes got word to come, but he decided to retreat. The Frankish mercenaries with him, led by Roussel de Bailleul, wanted to come. Trachaneiotes refused. I only learned all that when I tracked down Roussel."

"Why did he refuse to come?"

"According to Roussel, Trachaneiotes said it was no use. Romanus was doomed. There was no way he would survive."

"But how could he know? Do you think Roussel was telling the truth?" I asked, feeling sick.

"I don't know about Trachaneiotes. I tried to speak with him, but he refused to see me. He just told Roussel to get his men ready to leave to return to the city. No other explanation. I do believe Roussel; he had no reason to lie to me."

Romanus still had an advantage over the sultan, with about seventy thousand men. Alp Arslan had far fewer, so the emperor sent about half of his army into reserve, to be called when needed. The man leading that part of his army was Andronikos Ducas.

I stopped Attaleiates then.

"Eudokia and I tried to warn him about Andronikos, but he could not believe the boy would be disloyal."

The judge nodded slowly, a frown on his face. "I wish he had paid attention to you. There were many things about this campaign that were. . .not right."

The battle went well for Romanus at first. They chased the Turks off a long distance but had raced so far from where they were camped that they risked being cut off. Romanus signaled for his banner to be reversed, indicating a return to the original battlefield. He also sent a man to Andronikos, instructing him to bring the reserves he commanded into the fight as he continued the battle.

"I don't know exactly what happened then. Some men said they saw the emperor fall; others said he never fell but was full into the frenzy of fighting. I can't say if some truly thought the emperor was dead or if they are lying. I just know someone called out that the emperor was dead and began abandoning the field. I was in camp, as usual. I'm a judge and no good with a sword. First, it was just a few men fleeing, but soon it looked like the entire army panicked and was grabbing what they could before leaving.

"I learned later what happened with Andronikos Ducas. He rode out alone to meet the emperor's messenger with the instructions he was to join the battle. Ducas handed the fellow a bag of gold, told him to keep quiet about it, and sent him away. He then turned back to the soldiers he commanded and told them the emperor was dead. They must retreat."

"How did you find out all those details about the messenger from Romanus?" I asked.

Attaleiates looked as though he would be sick. "I spoke with the man himself. He was loyal to Romanus until that bag of gold hit his palm. He's been quietly drinking himself to death since then."

I looked out the window, where a few starlings swooped over our garden, graceful as though all the world was in harmony. All the betrayals and treachery that those men could accomplish had been done to Romanus.

"I scurried off to Trebizond along with many others after the battle. Found ships to bring us back here. Every day, I've learned more and more about what happened, what I witnessed but didn't see enough of or understand properly. I can barely fathom how horribly the emperor was treated by his own officers—far worse than how he was treated as the sultan's captive. I can't stop thinking about how he must have suffered with his terrible blinding. It's been a nightmare for me, and the many others loyal to Romanus Diogenes.

"I've been an impartial judge my whole life. Tried to be calm and measured in my decisions. But I want to kill that bastard Constantine Ducas, kill him in the most painful way imaginable, so he receives in full measure the agonizing death he gave an honorable man. And I want the same for his traitorous brother, Andronikos Ducas, and their miserable father, John Ducas."

The judge's eyes brimmed with tears and he could not speak anymore.

Alexios escorted Attaleiates out. Cold fury washed through me. John Ducas had bought the souls of so many weak and greedy men and destroyed the one good and strong man in their midst.

"Mama," said Alexios, standing in the doorway, shock still bold on his face. "What do we do now?"

"We do what we can but trust God to extract vengeance in His own way and time."

⚜

Isaac and his Irene were wed in early February, before the start of Lent. Emperor Michael promoted Isaac to be the Domestic in charge of all the empire's forces in the east, in Anatolia. It was a great honor, and Isaac was a good soldier, but at only twenty-three he had never led an army, much less all of Romanus's remaining eastern forces. Alexios would join him, in this his first campaign.

The wedding was a lavish affair since it was for the empress's cousin. John Ducas and his sons did not attend and were not missed. Even so, others from the Manzikert battle were there— Joseph Trachaneiotes, Basil Maleses, Nikephoros Basilakes—and were among those who had abandoned and betrayed Romanus. John Ducas had arranged promotions for all of them, with

Trachaneiotes becoming dux of Antioch. I gritted my teeth and made polite greetings to them.

Lovely Irene became pregnant almost immediately. She and Isaac were elated about the child, but I could see deep envy, or perhaps grief, in the empress's eyes. The beautiful Maria of Alania spent most of her time mothering her husband's younger siblings, including his two half brothers. It was a poor substitute for having her own children, though. According to Thomas, the gossip was that the twenty-three-year-old emperor had not yet consummated his marriage.

Thomas was on good terms with Michael's favorite, the eunuch Nikephoritzes. Michael may have counted Isaac as a friend, but he relied on Nikephoritzes for anything related to governing and they were together from morning to night. I visited Thomas with a suggestion.

"Do you think Nikephoritzes could convince the emperor to. . ." I began.

Thomas looked amused at my polite reticence. "To do his husbandly duty?"

"Yes," I said. "Maria looks miserable, seeing her cousin with child almost immediately after marrying, while she's had none after seven years."

"He would be the only one to push Michael that way. No one else could." Thomas looked down, embarrassed.

"What exactly do you mean—the only one?" I asked, then stopped. "You can't mean. . ."

Thomas reddened and raised his hands in protest. "I have no proof, not seen anything specific myself. Just rumors, but reliable rumors."

The unspoken allegation explained Michael's years of reluctance, though.

"Nikephoritzes must know Michael's position would be strengthened if Maria has a son."

Thomas nodded. "Maybe, or he may worry Maria's position

might be better. He knows palace politics." He looked thought-ful. "I wonder what his price would be?"

I sighed, resigned to the situation. "See if you can find out. Maria may be willing to pay it."

"He'll have to convince Michael that seven years is really too long to wait for an heir. Michael is perfectly happy with how things are. It may take some time."

"Whatever we need to do."

Thomas nodded but then pursed his lips together and gave me a long look.

"Is there something else, Thomas?"

"As a matter of fact, there is. It's about Martina."

"Martina? My seamstress?"

"Yes," he answered, looking down. "We got to know each other while you and your son were on Prinkipo last year. She's a strong woman, a good woman with wonderful children. She overcame a terrible disaster to provide for them. We have become. . .fond of each other, in a way."

I blinked at this revelation.

"Of course, we cannot marry since I am a eunuch. But I want to adopt her children. I have no other family, and I do have the means to provide a dowry for Thekla and an apprenticeship for George. Eunuchs are permitted to adopt orphaned children, but I still wanted your blessing before I did so."

I'd known for years that Thomas yearned for a family.

"You have my blessing. Congratulations on your new chil-dren," I said. "Let me know when the ceremony will be held."

"Thank you, I will. And with any luck, we'll make sure the emperor has a child too."

Isaac departed with his army and Alexios, right after Pascha, in the first week of April. I hesitated about allowing them to serve together, where both might be lost, but there was no one else I could trust him with as much as Isaac. He pleased Alexios, who turned seventeen that summer, by allowing him to lead a phalanx for the first time. Isaac had to focus on rebuilding the imperial armies that had dissipated in the three years since Manzikert, recruiting and training men. Sultan Alp Arslan who had defeated Romanus, had himself been killed by a rebel, leaving the Turks fighting like jackals over the territory he'd claimed. Otherwise, the empire's weakened army would have had little chance against these invaders.

The army included the Frankish mercenary Roussel and four hundred soldiers loyal to him. Isaac wrote often, complaining about Roussel's typical Frankish greed. Mercenaries were a necessary evil due to the depleted army ranks. Like all Franks, Roussel never felt paid enough and groused endlessly about it. My son lost all patience with him when the Frank made one too many nasty remarks about Emperor Michael and sent him and his soldiers away.

Isaac wrote that he was leading his army to Caesarea in July after learning Turkish troops were gathered there. I hoped his ranks, diminished with the loss of the troublesome but experienced Franks, would suffice against the Turks.

Thomas appeared at my gate a few days into August with an anguished look on his face. He came into the garden, where I was watching my granddaughters playing in the sunshine.

"Lady Anna, there's been news from Caesarea. Your son Isaac's army fought a battle there, and he was captured. He wasn't wounded, but the Turks are demanding ten thousand gold solidi for him."

I sat stunned for a minute before asking, "What about Alexios? He was there too."

"Alexios wrote the emperor with the news, so he's free. He said he's negotiating with the Turks since he speaks their language. There was no one else to do that with the rest of the army scattered."

I raised an eyebrow at that. Alexios had always been able to talk the other children into mischief, but this was different—his brother's life might depend on it. Most lads at seventeen would not know how to take control of that sort of situation.

I spent an anxious two weeks waiting to hear any news of Isaac before Alexios blithely wrote me that Isaac was free and gathering his men back together. They would be home in the fall.

Isaac and Alexios returned to Byzantium in mid-October after a few more battles with the Turks. Isaac was at the palace when Irene gave birth to their first child, a son they named John. The experiences of battle, captivity, and perilous escapes that they shared that summer created as solid a bond between Isaac and Alexios as I had seen between their father and his own brother, Isaac. Alexios carried himself with a mature confidence, and Isaac treated him with the respect due an equal, not a brother six years his junior.

"Mama, I cannot imagine how matters would have turned out if Alexios hadn't been with me this year," Isaac said when I was at the palace visiting my new grandson. "I know a lot of sunny-day soldiers who would have given up and gone home after I was captured. Alexios just kept pushing and pushing. The emperor probably would have come up with the gold eventually, but not so soon as Alexios did by sweet talking the eparch of Ancyra."

"So he's not just the little brother who teased you mercilessly, talking you into trouble?" I asked.

Isaac laughed. "No, he's the little brother who always has my back. And as for talking, I wonder if he could persuade the devil himself into abandoning hell. At one battle, Alexios gave a little speech about honor and duty and fighting the empire's enemies to a bunch of dynatoi boys who hadn't ever gotten their soldier boots dusty and were quivering at the thought of the Turks outside the city walls. You could almost see those boys growing a spine as he spoke. They weren't the best soldiers in battle, but we needed every blade we could find."

1074

THE GREEKS OF HOMER'S DAY BELIEVED THE PAGAN goddess Nemesis flew on immortal wings to bring balance and justice to the world, punishing the arrogant and wrongdoers. I am Christian, but if I were pagan I would have seen Nemesis's correcting scourge in the events of this year.

The dux of Antioch, Joseph Trachaneiotes, one of the traitors of Manzikert, died at the hands of a band of thieves outside Antioch. The emperor, or possibly Nikephoritzes, decided Isaac would be the best replacement as the dux of Antioch.

Isaac asked Theodora's husband, Romanus's son, Costas, to join him, which he eagerly did. Costas and Theodora had had bitter arguments over his visits to brothels for the past few years, followed by tearful reconciliations. A few weeks after my son and son-in-law departed, Theodora joyfully announced that she was pregnant. Sadly, though, young Costas was killed in the fighting with those bandits, making my daughter Theodora a widow, and her unborn child fatherless.

Anatolia was a festering sore. The Frankish mercenary Roussel made trouble for the emperor wherever the Turks weren't doing so. That rogue managed to convince cities and towns from Amasea in the north to Charsianon in the south to acknowledge him as their ruler and pay their taxes to him rather than to the emperor. Emperor Michael, or more likely his favorite, Nikephoritzes, decided to enlist Caesar John Ducas to lead the army against Roussel. He was joined by his son, Andronikos.

John Ducas had been a low-ranking soldier in his youth. He had commanded the soldiers who guarded his brother when Constantine had been emperor, but he had never led an entire army at war. A few years earlier, he had railed against Romanus's supposed incompetence as my cousin struggled to build an army in the east from almost nothing. Ducas had no idea of the serious challenges faced by a true general. He had never convinced men to join battle against a deadly serious foe. He had forgotten the terror of thousands of arrows raining on your head, swords slashing at arms, spears finding the one deadly opening in your armor.

John Ducas, brother to one emperor, proud uncle of another emperor, harsh critic of Romanus Diogenes, went into his first battle against the mercenary Roussel, a man making his living by his sword, and he was defeated and taken captive. Andronikos Ducas fought to stop his father's capture, instead getting wounded so badly that Roussel just sent the boy home since he would have little ransom value if he died, as appeared likely.

Alexios, by then commanding several forts along the main road from Dorylaion to Nicomedia, encountered the party of Turks escorting Andronikos back to Constantinople. He took over the care of the wounded man with the aid of a military surgeon from one of the forts, and returned with him to the city.

"He looked pretty bad," Alexios said when he made a brief stop at our house. "Face gashed, and he might lose a leg. Surgeon had to cauterize slashes on his arms. Passed out most of the way back here; I only knew he still lived from his groaning."

"How was his wife when she saw him?" I asked. Marie of Bulgaria, as I still thought of her.

"I sent a messenger ahead to expect us. She was prepared, had a physician from the Hospital of Sampson already there. She looked shocked at his condition but didn't cry or scream the way some might. She did have to shoo a little girl back in the house. The child looked about eight but had the presence of mind to thank me for bringing her father home."

"That's probably Irene, their oldest child. I'm afraid I frightened her the last time I saw her."

"You, mama?" Alexios laughed in feigned shock before continuing. "The emperor better do something to get the Caesar back soon. Roussel is bound to make even more trouble if he doesn't."

Emperor Michael dithered about what to do, finally deciding that it would be best to send the Caesar's younger son, that vile Constantine, who had overseen Romanus's blinding, to rescue his father. Horrible Constantine accepted the task and went home to make ready before falling violently ill, dying that same night. He was only twenty-eight and healthy until then. No word of poison was ever spoken about his sudden death, but he had few friends and many enemies. Not many shed tears at his passing, except perhaps his father, languishing in chains in Roussel's castle through that long winter.

The death of one Constantine Ducas was followed not long after with the birth of another Constantine Ducas. Yes, Emperor Michael finally consummated his marriage with the beautiful Maria of Alania, who almost immediately became pregnant, giving birth to a son in November.

CHAPTER 14

1075 to 1077

MICHAEL DUCAS, SON OF MY DEAREST FRIEND, EUDOKIA, and Emperor of the Romans, was an idiot. I never wanted to believe that, but over time it became clear. He was not just weak, he was an idiot.

Thomas still kept me abreast of the emperor's foolishness after he acquired a house near mine for his new family. He was there most nights, escorting Martina to and from my house each day. One morning he surprised me with news about John Ducas.

"The emperor received a most unexpected messenger yesterday," he said.

I looked up from my desk where I had been eyeing the coins paid at my warehouse. "Who sent the messenger?"

"Roussel de Bailleul. The Frank announced to Michael that he has declared Caesar John emperor. He said he expects Michael to vacate the Great Palace and allow his uncle to rule since he can't come up with the ransom."

My jaw dropped at that demand, bold even for a trouble-maker such as Roussel.

"What is Michael going to do about this?" I asked.

Thomas raised his eyebrows, managing to look both dismayed and amused.

"He doesn't trust any of his own generals to retrieve his uncle, since they all loathe his beloved Nikephoritzes. Instead, he's planning to hire the Turkish sultan, Artouch, to retrieve Caesar John."

I screwed up my face, trying to see the logic in this. "But that will cost him more than if he'd paid Roussel the ransom."

"I know, but maybe he thinks Artouch won't notice how the coins have been debased," Thomas said, gesturing to the coins on my desk.

"That's ridiculous," I said. "Anyone, even a Turk, would know the difference between the old and new coins. These look so dull that it's as though the gold was mixed with dirt."

Thomas shrugged and bid me farewell. There was nothing either of us could do.

Artouch quickly attacked Roussel and captured both him and Caesar John. Roussel's wife immediately paid the ransom demanded, but John Ducas had to wait several more weeks before the emperor scrounged up sufficient additional funds to satisfy the wily Turk.

I had to laugh when, while visiting Irene and my grandson, I saw John Ducas back in the Great Palace dressed in the robes of a humble monk and with a shiny new tonsure on top of his head. He must have thought Michael would suspect him of conspiring with Roussel for the throne. So, instead of returning in the fine attire of a Caesar, he had found a monastery on his way back to the city and convinced the hegoumenos to tonsure him, before presenting himself to the emperor as a monk.

MICHAEL'S TROUBLES WITH ROUSSEL DID NOT END WITH John Ducas's release. The mercenary returned to Amasea and continued ruling the territory he claimed and collecting its taxes. Michael tried convincing his wife's family in Alania to send soldiers to assist in Roussel's capture, but once again, he couldn't pay them. They returned to Alania. The emperor's options dwindled.

"Lady Anna, I need to speak with you," said Thomas.

"Yes?"

"I believe the emperor will ask your son to make an end to the problem with Roussel. At least, that's what I heard at the palace this morning."

"But Isaac's in Antioch! It would be weeks before he could get there, and he's got Turks lurking in that area to deal with. That's ridiculous."

"Not Isaac. They want Alexios to go."

"Who wants me to go where?" Alexios was home for a few days from Heraclea, on the Black Sea where he'd been stationed. He must have been passing my office on his way out.

I was horrified. Alexios was eighteen years old, Roussel a seasoned leader more than twice his age. My son would be slaughtered.

"Absolutely not. I can't permit that. I'll speak to Michael, to Maria. He's much too inexperienced to deal with Roussel, scheming Frank that he is."

"What? What are you talking about?" asked Alexios.

Thomas raised an eyebrow in a silent question. I answered.

"Thomas says the emperor will ask you to lead the men you're commanding to take care of Roussel. I suppose it means either kill him in battle or bring him back to the city as a prisoner. It's ridiculous, of course. Roussel has hundreds of men, more than you command, and fought in more battles than he can count. I won't have you risking your life when there are other men who could and should do it. What about Bryennios? Why not him?"

Alexios looked thoughtful for a minute or two before a grin grew across his face. He leaned toward me.

"Mama, you mustn't stop me from this. I know there'll be risks, but I know Roussel, how he thinks. He's so arrogant he thinks he can get away with anything. That kind of man takes chances he shouldn't."

"Alexios, I've said no. I'll tell the emperor that too."

"Mama, please. I want your blessing, but I'll tell the emperor I'm willing even if you're not."

His eyes held a glint of steel when he said that. My son had grown up and wore a man's beard. He was from a long line of soldiers and he would be one too.

I sighed but gave him a stern look.

"If you insist on going, then you have my blessing. Just promise me you won't get yourself killed."

Alexios laughed. "I promise. I'll make you proud."

As Thomas warned, Alexios was called to the palace and tasked with ridding the empire of Roussel's threat. He gathered a few dozen men, believing a small group would not attract attention, and departed the city late in May.

I heard nothing until I received a letter from him in July.

LADY ANNA DALASSENA
July 3

MOTHER, I CAPTURED ROUSSEL. IT WAS EASY CORNERING HIM *and a few of his men, with the help of the Turks I'd hired. I returned to Amasea with him and convinced the citizens there to give me the gold I needed to pay off the Turks. They were happy to do so as long as I blinded the scoundrel before taking him to the emperor. We will be returning to the capital soon.*

Your son,
Alexios Comnenus

. . .

I WAS LIVID AT THIS LETTER. HE KNEW HOW I FELT ABOUT blinding anyone, even a treacherous Frank like Roussel. I'd seen men blinded and knew how Romanus suffered in his last agonizing days. I could never condone that brutal punishment. And yet he'd still poked the man's eyes out. I could not believe any son of mine would do something so heinous. I berated myself for allowing him into this terrible mission.

Alexios returned home a few days later, strutting into the house as though he had conquered the world. Until he saw my face.

"Mama, what's wrong?"

I glared at him before spitting out an answer.

"I thought I raised you better than that."

His eyes widened in surprise, and he backed away from me, the cocky grin wiped from his face. "Better than what? What did I do wrong?"

"You know what you did. You blinded that man. When I raised you to know that is something you are never to do. *Never*. How could you? I thought I had made it clear that no child of mine would ever, *ever* blind anyone."

He relaxed a fraction and let out a breath.

"Oh, that. Mama, I'm sorry. I didn't mean to upset you, but I didn't actually blind him. I just made the people in Amasea think I did. It was a trick. It was the only way they would let me bring him back here."

"What? That's not what you wrote in your letter."

"Suppose the letter got into the wrong hands? I couldn't take a chance. I didn't think you'd really believe I would do that." He looked honestly surprised and apologetic. "Sorry."

I glared at him, my anger still boiling.

"Next time, don't write."

JUDGE MICHAEL ATTALEIATES PAID ME A VISIT THAT FALL.
He looked haggard but gave me a forced smile in greeting.

We exchanged pleasantries, and he asked after my daughter
Theodora.

"Theodora is well, delivered of a little girl she named Anna,
but we're calling her Anita to keep her from being confused with
her cousins. That's the third granddaughter I have named Anna.
Nicknames minimize confusion when they're all here."

"I must call on her to offer my congratulations," he said
before pausing, a sorrowful look passing over his face. "The third
granddaughter of the emperor. It's sad that none of his three
granddaughters will grow up knowing him or even their own
fathers."

"I know," I said as I passed him a cup of wine. My heart hurt
thinking about all the men lost.

He stared down into his cup for a minute in contemplation.

"I wondered if you had heard the news from Raidestos?" he
asked.

"Raidestos? No, should I have? I recall it was hard hit about
ten years ago when we had all those earthquakes."

"That was terrible, but more easily overcome than the problems they have now."

"What happened?"

"Did you know I own property there? Lots of fertile land
and prosperous farms growing wheat. At least, they were prosperous until recently."

I frowned, wondering what the problem could be. Attaleiates
searched my face before continuing.

"The emperor decreed that a phoundax, a central warehouse,
be established for wheat for sale in Raidestos. Or I should say
Nikephoritzes decreed it; Michael just signed the order."

That sounded odd. I had inherited a warehouse from my
grandparents that brought in a good income, but I'd never heard
of a central warehouse.

"So what's wrong with it?"

"It's more than just a warehouse. The farmers can only sell their wheat to the merchants in the warehouse, no one else. There are just three or four of them, and they set the price lower than what the farmers sold it for before. If a farmer tries to sell it himself elsewhere, the merchants send out thugs to beat him up and his land and property are confiscated. All legal according to the emperor's decree. The merchants then ship the grain here to sell at a huge profit."

"Why would Nikephoritzes do this?" I asked, before realizing the obvious.

"Lady Anna, of course it's all about the money," Attaleiates said. "Each merchant pays that eunuch sixty gold solidi for this right. The merchants also pay the emperor to rent the space in the warehouse, and I guess the emperor gets some additional taxes that the farmers may have avoided paying in the past, but it can't be a lot more. So the emperor gets some more taxes, but Nikephoritzes gets even more through the back door. And the farmers, they've started calling the emperor "Parapinakes," or "minus a quarter", since they've lost a quarter of their income."

Many farmers barely eked out a living as it was. This would devastate them.

"Several of them came to me to see if I have any influence at the Great Palace," he said. "But I've avoided it since Romanus died. It's too depressing to watch all the endless corruption. I wondered if you might be able to speak a word for them on my behalf?"

"Judge, I don't have that kind of influence either. Besides, if they are doing this in little Raidestos, they've got to be doing it in other places too. Then we're talking about a lot of gold under the table. We both know Nikephoritzes won't give that up, and the emperor can't afford to give up what he gets. The treasury was almost empty, last I heard."

He looked disappointed but not surprised.

"I had hoped with Isaac married to the empress's cousin, you might have some chance. I knew it was a small chance, but I had to try."

"I wish I could help, but the only thing that would really help would be getting rid of Nikephoritzes."

1076

MICHAEL ATTALEIATES'S STORY ABOUT THE PHOUNDAX IN Raidestos was only the beginning. The price of bread rose higher than it had ever been in the new year. The farmers could not make enough profit selling their grain to the central warehouse to both feed their family and buy seed for the next sowing. They fed their families, bought less seed, grew less wheat, sold less wheat. It was a downward spiral. The phoundax merchants had less to sell in Constantinople but still had to pay Nikephoritzes, so the price of bread grew beyond the ability of the poorest to afford, and even some of those a little less poor went hungry. The thousands of refugees from the raided and wrecked areas of Anatolia only worsened the situation.

Our house, with its location in the quiet Blachernae suburb, usually saw few beggars or wandering monks. Now, though, they were as plentiful as on the Mese, asking for food. My grandmother had taught me to never turn anyone away, and we never did. But business was slow at the warehouse I owned, and my son Adrian had joined Isaac's army in Antioch. The cost of outfitting him had been enormous, and my youngest, Nikephoros, would be ready for the army in another year or so. I had always been frugal, but never so much as now.

Emperor Michael's slavish devotion to Nikephoritzes continued unabated. The two of them, protected by loyal Varangians, were oblivious to the cries of desperate people outside the palace walls. It was no surprise to me when the rebellions began.

"You'd think the emperor would be concerned when he sends someone as loyal to him as Nestor is, out to lead his army against rebels, and then the man turns into a rebel," said Thomas.

"Too bad Nestor wasn't successful at getting rid of Nikephoritzes. I'd love to know how the eunuch explained to Michael that Nestor just wanted to get rid of him, or how he explained why the rebels burned down the Raidestos phoundax," I said. "Too bad they couldn't burn down all of them."

Thomas rolled his eyes at that. "Don't look at me for that answer. I'm not around when they have their private meetings. It was bad enough when the soldiers from Macedonia appeared, looking for their pay."

I shook my head in disbelief. "I still can't believe the emperor set the Varangians on them. Romanus used to have to beg every year and get just a part of what was owed, but they were never as desperate as those Macedonians were. Does the emperor expect men to fight for him without their pay? And getting beaten for asking for it? Romanus would never have let this happen."

Thomas looked around to be sure we would not be overheard before saying in a low voice, "The worst of it is that there's plenty of money in the treasury, but Michael never wants to spend anything."

"You're serious?" I asked, shocked to my core.

"Absolutely, I made a quiet visit down there myself. I'm not sure why he's hoarding it, though. He doesn't even give the empress much of an allowance."

He then looked at me like a cat with a bird in its mouth, feathers sticking out. "Have you heard the latest?"

"The latest?"

"You won't believe the latest idea that Michael and Nikephoritzes came up with."

"What?" I asked, leaning in.

"The emperor has proposed betrothing his son to a daughter of Robert Guiscard and wants to give him a title as well."

"That Frank who spent years defeating all our armies in Italy? He controls everything we had there. Why would Michael agree to that?"

"The emperor's like a cart bouncing from one side of a rutted road and back to the other. He hired the Turks to free his uncle from the Norman Roussel, now he's hiring the Norman Guiscard to get rid of the Turks. And he thinks Guiscard will do it for the honor he'll get with the title and as the father-in-law of an emperor since Michael doesn't want to pay him any actual gold to attack the Turks."

It was my turn to roll my eyes. "Could Michael be humiliated any more than this? I've never heard of a greedy Norman mercenary doing something like that without a chest of gold in hand. He'll never do it unless Michael comes up with it."

"We both know that, but the emperor hasn't figured it out yet."

ﷺ

It was in early September that Marie of Bulgaria called on me. I had always been fond of her but had rarely seen her in the years since her husband, Andronikos, had betrayed Romanus at Manzikert. Andronikos still lived but had never fully recovered from the wounds he received fighting Roussel, although he and Marie had had several more children during those years. I wondered if he suffered as much as Romanus had, but I considered his punishment to be in God's hands.

"Lady Anna, it is so good to see you. It's been too long," Marie said in greeting.

"Marie, you are looking well."

Our conversation meandered through the usual pleasantries, family updates on her children and my grandchildren. She had been a sweet child, always ready to help in the palace nursery, and was a warm and friendly young woman. I realized I enjoyed talking with her more than I expected.

"There was one thing I would like to speak with you about," she said. "It's about your son Alexios."

"Alexios?"

"Yes, I was wondering if you have given thought to a possible bride for him. He is getting to the age where I thought you might be contemplating a betrothal."

I could not speak for a moment, trying to think what might have caused her to bring this up. Her oldest child, Irene, was about ten years old. Was she thinking of Irene? How could Marie think I would let a son of mine marry a daughter of Andronikos Ducas? I had to think of how to dissuade her from pursuing Alexios.

"As a matter of fact, I have been discussing a betrothal for him with one of the Argyros girls." Not a lie, but not exactly the truth. I'd had a brief conversation with the girl's mother the previous week about it, but no agreement had even been discussed, much less reached.

"Ah," she said. "He seems such a fine young man. I'm sure you've received many inquiries."

"Were you looking for someone for Irene?"

"Yes, but. . ." she paused. "Really, this is all because of Irene. Alexios has been her hero ever since she saw him bring her father home. She's asked me many times to see if he might be available. She pestered me so much that I promised I would call on you to inquire. I didn't even tell Andronikos or his father about this."

"I see. Now you can tell her that I already have plans for him. I'm sure there are many other young men who would be eager for the hand of the emperor's cousin," I said.

"I know, Lady Anna. She just has her heart set on him. Alexios is almost all she talks about. She will be disappointed at your news, but she'll get over it, I expect."

"Young girls can get such ideas in their heads, not understanding how the world works." I recalled Theodora's girlish dreams of marriage to Costas Diogenes and the disappointment that marriage had ultimately been for her.

"That's so true," she said.

Marie looked relieved as she bade me farewell, glad she had kept her promise to Irene. She must have expected that her request might not be received well. She was not to blame for Romanus's death, but he would always be a ghost hovering in any room with a Ducas in it as far as I was concerned.

I then went to my office and wrote a quick note to the Argyros family, asking to meet with them the next day. I would have to see the girl again and get to know her better. It would be impolitic of me to turn down an offer of Irene Ducaena unless I had some other offer in hand, so the sooner this was finalized, the better. I had never imagined that a proposal for one of my children would come from the family of John and Andronikos Ducas.

⚜

ALEXIOS AND HELENA ARGYROS WERE BETROTHED IN November when he was home for a few weeks. She was a pretty girl, almost fourteen, but the wedding would not be for over a year as her family preferred their daughters to be at least fifteen when married. Her family could claim two emperors from the past, while ours had Isaac and Romanus. The young couple seemed fond of each other. It was a good match for both families, and it kept Alexios from a marital alliance with the Ducas family, something I could not tolerate.

The day after the betrothal ceremony, Alexios took ship to meet with Michael Maurex at Heraclea. Our old family friend was now the empire's senior admiral and had let Alexios know he had soldiers available in the fight against the hordes of marauding Turks pushing north to Bithynia. Alexios was in dire need of the additional men to clear the roads and valleys of the relentless invaders. It was times like these that showed the

benefit of the friendship and help my husband and his brother
had shown Maurex all those years earlier, and I was grateful.

1077

My youngest, Nikephoros, whom we called Niko, my
only child still at home, and a muscular young man, accompanied me on a visit to his sister Theodora's one spring day. In the
past, I had often hired a sedan chair to get to her house, but the
weather was fine and I decided the walk would clear my mind.

"Mama, are you sure you want to walk? I can get a chair for
you," Niko said as we prepared to leave the house. "The roads
can be filthy."

"It rained during the night. They should be cleaned a bit."

I soon regretted my decision as I skirted around the second
human turd I encountered only to run into a ragged man
gripping the neck of a scrawny stray dog. Niko's strong arm
pulled me past those two. We saw beggars fight for the right to
seek alms at a street corner and the loser skulk to a less
promising spot. Priests stood outside of churches doling out
small loaves of bread to the hungry. There had always been
some beggars, the poor and needy, but it felt like half the city
had sunk to that level. My city, the city of Constantine, the
Queen of Cities, had become a sad wasteland, a place I didn't
recognize. It had not been as bad even just a week earlier on
my last visit.

"What is that man with a club doing on the street?" I asked
my son.

Niko looked over to where the man stood. "He's guarding
the bakery. The price of bread is so high, that gangs will sometimes rush in and steal everything. A guard is cheaper." His hand
on my elbow kept us moving at a quick pace. "So many came

here trying to escape the Turkish threat, but the city's not much better."

Theodora still lived in the house she inherited from her husband, the one that I had grown up in with my grandparents until they died and I sold it to Romanus and his first wife. It was just her, her daughter, and a few servants. Her husband, Costas, had been dead for almost two years, leaving her with little income and a baby. I wanted her and the child to move in with me. Niko would be joining the army soon and there was plenty of room for them. The miserable scenes we passed on the way to her house left me worried about her safety.

We arrived to find Michael Attaleiates there.

"Lady Anna, it's good to see you," he said, looking a little flushed.

"You as well," I said, curious about his presence.

Her baby, little Anita, was just starting to walk, with toothy grins every time she managed a few steps without holding on to something. She was the center of our attention until she began rubbing her eyes and fussing, and her nursemaid scooped her up for a nap.

"Theodora, Niko and I walked here today, and I have to say I was shocked at what I saw going on in the streets. I am extremely concerned about you living here alone."

"Mama, I warned you, I tried to get you a chair," said Niko as his sister glared at him.

"It's not that bad. I'm sure I'm fine here," Theodora said. "Besides, I'm not alone. I've got the servants here."

"Yes, it is that bad and getting worse each day. I want you to move back home with the baby. Niko will be leaving for the army in a few weeks, so I have the room. Baby Anita can grow up with Thea's two girls, and you won't have the expense of maintaining a household."

"Mama, I. . ." she began before being interrupted.

"Theodora, I think you should listen to your mother," said Attaleiates, leaning toward her, his voice urgent. "You know I agree with her that you'd be better off living with her. You can't afford the taxes on this property and there are desperate people about in the city these days."

Theodora glared at me. "Mama, how much better off are you, especially once Niko is gone? Just you, Thea, and her two girls? I'm happy where I am."

"The difference is that I have an income and can afford two gatekeepers, a stableboy, and a kitchen boy. Your gatekeeper, Eugene, is ancient, and he also takes care of your miserable little donkey. He wouldn't be much help if someone tried to break in. After what I saw today, it could happen anytime."

I paused and took Theodora's hand. She looked ready to cry.

"Things wouldn't be this way if Costas or his father were still here. I'm sorry about that; we all are. I just don't want anything to happen to you or little Anita."

My daughter nodded and sniffled, knuckling back a tear. "I'll think about it."

☙❧

I THANKED GOD EVERY DAY THAT MY GRANDMOTHER HAD urged me to keep a kitchen garden, fruit trees, and a few chickens. The food situation in the city grew worse daily. Wheat was in short supply because of the emperor's phoundax decree as well as the Turks in Anatolia. Meat usually came from Thrace, but the Pechenegs raided often and eagerly stole cattle and sheep before burning down the farmers' houses. That meant more despairing, hungry people entering the city. They looked to the emperor for help—in vain. He sat far behind the palace walls on top of his pile of gold, ignoring their cries. Even the city's great orphanage, built by Constantine the Great, found itself without the generous donations our emperors had always provided.

Theodora and baby Anita moved in with us a couple of weeks after my visit. My daughter was not eager, but she saw no point in remaining after they opened their gate one morning to find two emaciated dead bodies outside it. The house was sold for a fraction of what it would have been worth just a few years earlier—if people couldn't afford food, they couldn't afford a house.

I was helping them to get settled the day they arrived when an old friend appeared at my gate—General Nikephoros Botaneiates.

"It's good to see you again, Anna. Not many of us left from the old days when Isaac was on the throne. Just you and me, I think," he said.

"And John Ducas, we can't forget him."

He grimaced at that. "Have you been over to the palace?" he asked, a tracery of furrows and lines of age on his tanned face. He was over seventy years old.

"No, it's been a few weeks since I last left my gates. My sons tell me it is too dangerous to go out these days. I can't even repeat the horrible things I saw last time I ventured out."

"So you know it's bad. People are truly dying in the streets from hunger, and the emperor does nothing," he said, shaking his head in disbelief. "I came to speak to the emperor about the situation in Anatolia, but it's almost worse here. How can Michael keep ignoring this? Things were bad twenty years ago when I joined your brother-in-law to get rid of that old Emperor Michael, but then at least no one was starving."

"I know. And twenty years ago, the treasury was truly empty, and now, while it may not be full, I hear that it's far from empty."

"Is that so?" said Botaneiates, with an eyebrow raised.

"That's what I've learned," I said. "The money's there; he just won't spend it. You spoke with the emperor, then?"

"Yes, I had to try and get him to realize he must take action against the Turks. He refuses to see the problems. Claims I exaggerate." The old general stopped for a moment, looked around to be sure we weren't overheard before continuing. "Also, I received a letter from his mother."

I blinked in surprise. I didn't think Eudokia even knew him that well.

"She says her monastery has taken in many women and children who have nowhere else to go, but they're reaching the limit of how many they can accommodate. The Turks seized her corner of Anatolia, but she says they're leaving the monastery alone for now."

"Why did she write to you? Why not to her son?"

"She did write to Michael, got nothing back. Don't know if it's because of that nasty eunuch, or maybe he doesn't care to respond to his own mother. I couldn't tell if she's desperate or angry or both, but she said if he won't send help, then the empire needs a new emperor."

My jaw dropped. I swallowed hard and asked, "You didn't tell Michael about Eudokia's letter, did you? What did Michael say when you spoke?"

He frowned. "No, I wouldn't betray her confidence. I pressed Michael hard for military help, but he absolutely refused to send anyone. Says he's got no money, but if what you heard is true, that's a lie."

The old soldier looked down at his hands, still strong and tanned but with the veins and spots of age.

"Michael's left me no choice. I'm going to have to go down the same road Isaac did twenty years ago."

"General, you were with us when Isaac took the throne, so you know the kind of effort it takes to do that. Do you have the resources? Could you manage that at your age?" I asked, my voice low.

He puffed out his chest like a rooster, hooked his thumbs in his belt. "I've got some money and ideas to work around that problem. As for my age, I'm fit enough to lead an army. Besides, it doesn't look like the emperor plans to field an army himself. I may have an easier time of it than Isaac did. I do have a request of you, though."

"Yes?"

"Your son Isaac is dux of Antioch and married to the empress's cousin. How loyal is he to the emperor? If Michael told him to try and stop me, would he?" he asked. "When his Uncle Isaac took the throne, we fought other Romans for it. Never liked that, but we had to. I want to avoid it, if that's possible."

I sat back and thought about his question. Antioch was a strategic Roman outpost, often attacked by the Turks. It should never be left undefended, but Emperor Michael was not one to think strategically. Niko would be leaving soon to join his brother there.

"I'll do what I can so that you won't have to worry about my Isaac."

Botaneiates departed with my assurance and my best wishes for his success.

Niko left a few days later with strict verbal instructions on what to tell his brother. I would not make the same mistake in a letter again.

Botaneiates returned to his estates near Ikonion and began assembling an army in June. Some were the empire's soldiers, ill-paid and equipped by the emperor, and some were Turkish mercenaries. I could not imagine what he promised to pay the Turks, but it would have to be substantial. In early July came word that his army had declared him emperor, clothed him in imperial purple and had begun a slow march to Constantinople. The people of the city were ecstatic to the point that even Michael could not ignore their glee at this rebellion.

In the meantime, another rebellion bubbled up in the west. Twenty years earlier, before the rebels had chosen Isaac to lead them against the previous Emperor Michael, the general Nikephoros Bryennios had been chosen. He had been arrested and blinded before the uprising had gotten very far and my brother-in-law had taken over. Now, his nephew, another General Nikephoros Bryennios, had become tired of Michael's ill treatment and began leading an army to the city.

The city of Constantinople was being pinched between rebels in both east and west, both named Nikephoros. The two armies were still some distance away, but even in the harvest season food was scarce.

⚜

ALEXIOS HAD BEEN CALLED BACK TO CONSTANTINOPLE FOR a few days and so was home when I received a distressing letter from the Argyros family. Their daughter Helena had taken ill and died.

"I'm so sorry to hear this. She was such a lovely young woman. We must attend her funeral."

"I am, too," said Alexios with a frown. "We enjoyed being with each other and she laughed at my jokes. Her parents must be heartbroken."

"I'm sure they are," I said, remembering my own grief at losing Manuel.

There was a crowd at the Argyros house offering condolences when we arrived. A face in the crowd waved to me. Marie of Bulgaria with her daughter, Irene.

"Lady Anna, we were so shocked to hear of Helena's death. She was so young," said Marie. "I had to come to offer our sympathy."

"Yes, we were as well. It was very sudden. We had no idea she was in ill health. Alexios was fond of her and looking forward to their wedding."

Irene was looking straight at Alexios, a shy smile on her face. Alexios ignored her, focused on Marie's conversation. Irene was pretty enough, eleven years old, with dark hair and an oval face. She looked giddy at being in the presence of her hero. I should have realized we might encounter Marie, but there was nothing I could have done differently. I silently prayed that Marie had betrothed Irene to someone else since I'd last seen her.

We parted and made our way to the grieving family, said our

prayers beside her bier, and promised to join them for the girl's burial the next day.

It was the day after the burial that Marie again visited me.

"Lady Anna, Irene is still eager for a betrothal with Alexios. Since we last spoke about this, I have tried to interest her in other young men since she will be twelve next year and of marriageable age, but she will have nothing to do with them. This time, before I came today, she and I spoke with my husband and his father about your son. They both agreed it would be a good match."

"Marie, I think this is too soon for us to consider it. Helena has only just been buried, and we are grieving for the loss of her young life."

"I know, and I don't mean to rush you, but I wanted to be sure you knew that we were still interested. And you should know that Irene will have a substantial dowry to bring to the marriage."

I looked at Marie, realizing I needed to put an end to this persistence. Excuses were not working.

"Marie, you know I am very fond of you, always have been, since you were a child. Irene seems a good girl too. But I have to tell you that, given the involvement of your husband and his family in what happened to my cousin Romanus, I cannot countenance a marriage for my son with a child of your husband's or a grandchild of John Ducas's. I have hard feelings for them. I will always remember what they did to him."

She looked at me, flushing a bright pink, then bowed her head.

"I know, but if—"

"If what? John Ducas conspired against Romanus, your husband betrayed him, your late brother-in-law murdered him, and then John Ducas tried to get me and my son Isaac executed for treason. Can you explain how am I supposed to put all that aside?" I could not stop my voice from rising in anger.

She looked deeply embarrassed. "I know, I know," she said,

her voice cracking. "I am so sorry for all that, but we can't blame a child for a parent's or grandparent's mistake, can we?"

I took a deep breath to calm myself. "I don't blame Irene, but every time I look at her I see her father and grandfather. I cannot see beyond them. And I am surprised your husband and John Ducas have any interest in a son of mine for Irene."

Marie slunk away looking like a whipped puppy. She had done nothing wrong herself, but I had to tell her the honest truth of the matter to end the conversation.

But this was not the end of it.

Two days after that, another visitor was announced. Caesar John Ducas.

"I understand you refused the suggestion of a marriage between my granddaughter and your son Alexios," he said.

I sat looking at him, seeing a lifetime of bullying and greed writ large on his fleshy face, his scowling mouth. His thinning hair was a dingy gray, his beard scraggly. I had rarely seen him since the trial. He had once been an attractive young man but had aged badly.

"I am surprised you would even consider a marriage to a son of mine. I, whom you accused of treason. I, who was cousin to the emperor, the one you conspired against and had executed."

His face took on an expression of a child trying to wheedle his way out of trouble. "Now, Anna, that was all a long time ago. Can't we just let it go? Forget about it? You know a marriage between Alexios and Irene would benefit both."

I stared at him impassively and did not speak until the silence between us became deafening. "No."

His head sank, bowed onto his chest. When he looked up again, his blustering face was gone, replaced with a grief-stricken face.

"Anna, Andronikos is dying. He's been dying for a long time, never recovered from the battle with that miserable Roussel. Irene's his favorite, and he's promised her a marriage to Alexios.

The surgeons say he doesn't have long to live. I'm asking, could you please reconsider this request?"

"Caesar John, only God knows how much time each of us has. Your son could live many more years. He's already survived his injuries for at least four years, while Romanus has been dead now five years. I have given the request absolutely as much consideration as it warrants, and the answer is still no."

He stood up, his bullying face back on, and took his leave.

I wondered if he was lying about Andronikos's condition. John Ducas would have no compunction about lying to get what he wanted. Even so, the rumors said the young man would never walk again and he had little use of his right arm. I did feel sympathy for anyone in that condition, but it was a minor atonement for betraying his emperor.

I hoped the matter was done, but I soon learned otherwise.

Alexios rushed into the house three days after that interview, breathless and pale.

"Mama, I am so sorry."

"Sorry for what? What's happened?" I asked.

"I can't believe how stupid I was to fall into such an old trick," he said, pounding his head against the door post. "I was on my way home from the palace when John Vatatzes stopped me and asked me to join him on a visit to Andronikos Ducas. He's not doing well and since I did drag his miserable carcass back here a few years ago, I thought it would be the courteous thing to do."

A sense of dread began to weigh on me.

"When I got there, they asked me to wait in the garden until Andronikos was ready. I was there for a few minutes when this girl appeared, all by herself. It was the girl who was at Helena's funeral with Lady Marie. We chatted for a few minutes and then she started screaming at me to stop, to leave her alone. She was pulling at her dress so it fell from her shoulder; her hair came loose. I thought she had gone mad. The next thing I know, Caesar John and Vatatzes are running into the garden, yelling at me to unhand the girl. I was nowhere near her."

I was ready to weep. "Then what happened?"

"John Ducas pulled me back inside, into his office, accused me of dishonoring his granddaughter. Told me I had to make things right by marrying her, or he would make sure word got out that I assaulted her, and Vatatzes was his witness. No decent family would ever let me marry one of their daughters if the two of them spread that story."

My blameless son's reputation would be ruined if this concocted story got out. That wretched man had found a way to try and force Alexios to marry Irene. I could not understand why he was being so persistent.

I spent the night pondering what to do. Alexios and I went to their house at dawn.

"Caesar John, you and I both know my son did nothing to your granddaughter, so I think we should stop acting as though he did."

"I know only what I saw, and John Vatatzes saw it as well. And my servants will also attest to it. Irene looked as though your son had badly used her," he said, looking as pleased as a cat that had just gobbled down a baby bird. "Alexios's actions stained her honor."

"If Alexios treated her so badly, then why would she want to marry him? Why would you want your granddaughter married to someone like that?"

"If a woman does not have her honor, then she has nothing. I cannot let Alexios stain Irene's reputation," he said piously, giving Alexios an appraising look. "Besides, I think it was only a temporary aberration. He was driven to it by her great beauty."

"She's a child," said Alexios, pounding a fist on the table. "I have no interest in children, certainly not to the point of assaulting them."

"So you say, but witnesses say otherwise."

"Caesar John, you said Irene's reputation would be in tatters if this came out. If we walk away, the stories might follow Alexios for a while, but they would fade in time. Irene, though, would be hard-pressed to ever find a husband. Why shouldn't we just walk away?"

"Your son has a promising future ahead of him if he stays in the emperor's favor. Do you want his career in ruins? Irene is Michael's cousin, and it would benefit your son to have that connection. Many men would find the handsome dowry she'll take with her to be attractive."

He then proceeded to describe the houses she would be given, the properties that provided an income, many thousands of gold coins—the old coins before Michael debased them—she would bring Alexios when they married. I had to admit it was impressive

I thought about asking to speak with Irene and her mother but realized they could add nothing to the discussion. Irene would have been coached about her story, and Marie was thoroughly intimidated by her father-in-law.

We soon left, and as I sat in the curtained sedan chair bringing me home, I thought about why John Ducas was so intent on marrying his granddaughter to Alexios. He had no more love for my family than I had for his. So why?

Sounds from the street kept distracting me, voices commenting at the sight of Alexios, hailing him. My son followed us on horseback, responding to the friendly greetings from shopkeepers, some cheers from soldiers passing by, even blandishments from a few prostitutes leaning out of brothel windows. It reminded me of how people had loved and trusted my Uncle Costas because of his loyalty to the emperor and his bravery in battle. He was their young hero.

I finally realized I had been blind. It was the connection with my son that John Ducas wanted. The man who had captured Roussel, the young general, the wily hero of battles that John and his own sons would have lost. It was convenient that Irene was infatuated with him, but Caesar John would have ignored her wishes if he hadn't seen something in Alexios. Courage or audacity or some other spark that I, his own mother, had been too close to recognize.

I emerged from the chair once we were back inside our gates and watched my son joke with the gatekeeper and greet the stable boy as he handed his horse over to the lad. Alexios was only twenty-two and not especially tall, but he walked with an easy confidence his own father had never had. He was leading men the way his Uncle Isaac had, and with his youthful victories, people saw him as a champion, the way they had seen my Uncle Costas long ago.

Inside, he said, "The girl's dowry is far more than any other's would be."

"It is, but you'll be the one married to her. Life can be miserable if you don't find your wife agreeable," I said, remembering his Uncle Isaac's conflicted marriage. "I hate to admit it, but the connection to the Ducas family, as much as I dislike them, would be valuable to your career. Turning down Irene again, after all of John's scheming, would hurt you."

Alexios sat opposite me, smoothing down his red beard as he thought about the proposal.

"If I don't marry her, I'm certain someone else will for that kind of dowry. That man, whomever she marries, could become an enemy if he decided I did dishonor his wife. That could be a problem."

"What do you think of the girl herself?"

"Hard to tell since she's only eleven. Coming from that kind of money, I'd bet she's spoiled and gets whatever she wants. I don't like that she put herself into a compromising situation to force my hand, but she is a child, and I'm certain Caesar John coaxed her. Still, it's not good. She is pretty enough, though. How many children does her mother have?"

"Marie has had seven children since she wed Andronikos about a dozen years ago." It sounded like Alexios was mentally toting up the pluses and minuses in an account book or thinking of his next chess move, not deciding where his affections lay.

"You can sleep on it and we'll talk again in the morning. You know Theodora and Thea wouldn't be pleased about it," I added, thinking about the rift it might cause. "And Isaac hates John Ducas almost as much as I do, even though I doubt he'd make a fuss."

My son thought for a minute before speaking.

"Mama, I've made up my mind. If you can tolerate the connection to John Ducas, then I can agree to the betrothal."

⚜

JOHN DUCAS TRIED TO RENEGE ON SOME OF THE DOWRY items he had listed at our meeting, but my reminders made sure they were put back into the betrothal agreement. It was ready to be signed by mid-September at the Ducas residence. Alexios returned home from Thrace, where he'd been fighting the western rebels, in time for the signing.

The Ducas family preferred large opulent celebrations of events like that to demonstrate their wealth, power, and influence. This gathering, though, was modest. I hadn't seen Andronikos Ducas since the trial that sent Isaac and me to monasteries on Prinkipo. Then, he'd been a handsome and energetic young man, eager to wield his sword, for his father if not for Romanus. Now, he was carried into the room, flat on his back on a pallet. His legs had shriveled, and the recent pain-filled years marked his face. John Ducas had not lied about his son; Irene's father had little time left in this world.

Irene, with her narrow nose, and brown eyes and hair, resembled her father more than her dark-haired mother. She came to the ceremony bedecked in jewels, dangling gold earrings, and jingling bracelets. Gold embroidery weighted down her deep blue gown, just a few shades away from purple.

Alexios and Irene made their promises, my son signing for

himself and John Ducas for his granddaughter since Andronikos could no longer hold a quill. They exchanged rings as tokens of their promises.

Irene looked up with childish eagerness into her betrothed's face, pleased that she had gotten her heart's desire. I don't know what she thought she saw in Alexios's face, but it looked like little more than the ordinary courtesy I had raised him to show. There was no affection in his eyes such as I recalled seeing in his father's eyes at our betrothal. Irene had been so sure that Alexios was what she wanted that she had not realized that tricking someone into marriage did not build a solid foundation. The wedding date would wait until after she reached the minimum age of twelve, and I would not rush it.

Thea and Theodora had not been pleased at Alexios's betrothal to Irene. In fact, none of us were, but we understood the calculations that went into it, not the least of which were to Alexios's reputation.

It was not a surprise when we learned a few weeks later that Andronikos Ducas had finally died of his wounds. Alexios could not get away for the funeral, so I represented the family. The traitor of Manzikert was dead, and I shed no tears when I paid my respects. Rose-scented oil lamps burned around Andronikos's body, lying shrouded in the finest white silk on a bier at his house. His father greeted the mourners, while Marie of Bulgaria and her children including Irene, stood nearby. My mind wandered as I knelt for prayers, wondering how the world might have been different if Andronikos had answered Romanus's call for help and led his men into battle at Manzikert. Instead Andronikos, urged on by his father, had betrayed us all.

Andronikos Ducas's death was the final accounting for Manzikert that John Ducas paid. Nemesis had exacted her revenge. God's justice was accomplished.

CHAPTER 15

1078 - 1079

THE DREARY WINTER DAYS, COLD AND RAINY, LIFTED NO
one's spirits. It was just after Epiphany that more rumors circulated about Botaneiates. Emperor Michael was still on the throne, but the rebel troops had again acclaimed Botaneiates emperor. They'd again presented him with the purple robes and shoes of a ruler after their bloodless capture of Nicaea. His slow progress in Anatolia, gaining supporters as he went, was indeed avoiding the divisive battles that my brother-in-law had fought.

The rebellion in the west was a different story. Bryennios's supporters took up arms against their fellow Romans, who were led by Alexios. They scurried through the countryside from Dyrrachion to Thessalonike to Adrianople battling in their bid to unseat the emperor. Bryennios did not gain supporters the way Botaneiates did. The rebels burned one village to the ground in anger after they arrived to find it emptied of people and the supplies gone that they had hoped to expropriate.

The weary and hungry people of Constantinople cared little where relief from their incompetent ruler came from, whether from the west or the east. Emperor Michael belatedly became aware that his seat on the throne was becoming precarious. At the end of January, he sent an army of men to Nicaea to stop Botaneiates. Those men promptly threw in with the rebels. The army Alexios led in the west, on the other hand, remained loyal.

Alexios came home in early February for a few days, looking for money and equipment from the emperor. He returned from the Great Palace with an unexpected guest.

"Mama, let me introduce you to an old acquaintance of mine. Roussel de Bailleul."

This infamous Frank stood a head taller than Alexios, with sandy-colored hair and a red beard. His clothing was shabby, and he carried no weapons. He was thin, his wrists red and scabbed. He didn't resemble the fearsome warrior I'd heard so much about.

"Lady Anna, it is a pleasure to meet the woman who raised such a clever son. If it weren't for him, I would have long since ceased looking upon the world," he said in his barbarian-accented Greek.

"Lord Roussel, he's an obedient son, and he knows how I feel about blinding men," I said. "How is it that the emperor released you?"

"I suggested it," said Alexios. "I told Michael that Roussel was a brilliant fighter who could help us stop Bryennios. Michael agreed after Roussel swore an oath that he will join me in this fight. If you approve, I thought he could stay with us for a few days until I'm ready to leave, to get him some clothes, armor, weapons, a horse. I've space to put a camp bed for him in my room."

The Frank remained with us for less than a week, keeping close to Alexios. He did spend one afternoon with Judge Attaleiates, reminiscing about Romanus's last campaign against the Turks and what had gone wrong that fateful day. Both of them felt some remorse over those events, although neither had done wrong themselves.

The judge had become a frequent visitor to our house, serving as a kind of grandfather to the three granddaughters I shared with Romanus. It was also evident that he and Theodora had become fond of each other, but with Attaleiates already twice widowed, the Church would not permit a marriage between them.

Alexios and Roussel left the second week in February, with snow swirling around them, leading fifty men and dozens of wagons full of weapons and other supplies. I spoke with Alexios just before they left.

"How much do you trust this Frank?"

He shrugged. "He gave me his word. He's beyond grateful to be out of the emperor's foul prison and the shackles he was kept in, so I'll trust him for now. But he hates Michael for keeping him in chains. He'd rather have been dead, I think."

⚜

I VISITED THE PALACE AT THE END OF FEBRUARY, TAKING A ferry to the quay at the Boukoleon harbor, with the excuse of seeing Isaac's wife, Irene, and her sons. She had given birth to her second boy a few weeks earlier. He was named Alexios after his uncle. Thomas had told me Emperor Michael paid little attention to Empress Maria, leaving her adrift. As the mother of Irene's husband, I was probably the only woman from outside the palace to whom she could turn for advice. The two young women were in the nursery with their sons, speaking in hushed tones, when I arrived. Irene gave me a look of relief when I entered the room.

"Lady Anna," she began while snuggling her baby, "the empress and I know so little about what's happening beyond the palace walls. Is it true what they say about rebels approaching the city?"

I looked at Empress Maria, her pretty heart-shaped face wearing a worried frown and circles under her eyes.

"Augusta, Irene is correct. The rebels get closer every day."

"But isn't my husband doing anything about it?"

I reached for my grandson, John, a sturdy four-year-old so much the image of his father, and held his warm body close. "He's trying, but he ignored the problems for far too long. You haven't been outside the palace walls in months; you haven't seen the people suffering, the starvation I've seen. The emperor did nothing to help them, and now they want him gone."

"It's that wretched Nikephoritzes," she said, frowning. "Michael listens to no one but him, never to me. I hate that eunuch."

"Lady Anna, what would you counsel the empress to do?" asked Irene, putting a calming hand over Maria's.

I sighed and smoothed the soft fine hair that rubbed against my cheek. Little John stared up at me before wriggling away to play with Maria's son, Constantine, whom everyone called Tino.

"Augusta, I have seen the downfall of several emperors in my life. I cannot give you hope that Emperor Michael will rule for much longer." In truth, Michael had never truly ruled at all since he'd had either his mother, Romanus, John Ducas, or Nikephoritzes ruling for him. "As a mother, though, you know you must protect your son, do whatever you have to do for him."

Maria looked down at Tino, a handsome child of three who had inherited his mother's good looks. "What do you suggest?" she asked.

"Augusta," I said, "is your loyalty with your husband or your son?" I had to hear her say it.

She flushed pink but looked straight into my eyes. "With my son."

"I can't be sure, but I can tell you what I think will happen. I believe General Botaneiates will reach the city and claim the crown first. You know he was recently widowed and has no children? I suggest writing to him to let him know you will support his bid for the throne if he marries you and agrees to make your son his heir. He's from a noble family, wants no bloodshed, and the prize of a purple-born heir would ease his path to the palace."

She rubbed her hands nervously on her fine embroidered silk gown, trying to decide. "How can I be sure such a letter won't fall into the hands of Nikephoritzes? He has his spies, and he'd use it against me."

"Write the letter," I told her. "I've got someone I can trust to get it to him safely."

Michael Attaleiates left for Nicaea with Empress Maria's letter, along with one from me, vouching for him. I knew the esteemed judge would make a favorable impression on Botaneiates. He would be gone for two or three days.

In the meantime, I received a letter from Alexios recounting his battle against Bryennios outside a town on the coast of the Sea of Marmara. Roussel fulfilled his oath to Alexios in the battle, but then that rogue slipped away during the night with what he considered was his share of the plunder. Bryennios also managed to escape, making his way back to his family's stronghold in Adrianople.

Attaleiates returned from the errand to Botaneiates with other news.

"The general appeared favorably inclined to the empress's letter. He wouldn't commit to anything, but he said the empress's offer was a good one, one that would help him."

"That's the best we can expect. Any difficulties on the journey?" I asked.

He raised an eyebrow at that. "We had no trouble on our way to Nicaea, but on our return we were stopped by men loyal to the emperor."

"Who?" I asked, surprised anyone still was.

"Your son-in-law, Niko Melissenos, and his men. Fortunately, I had your note to show him, so he let us through. But he says he's holding true to his oath of loyalty to Emperor Michael. Honor-bound to it."

"Honor is important, but the emperor is also honor-bound to care for his subjects. He's not doing that. Michael is not capable of doing that. I hope for Donya's sake that Niko comes around."

"He seemed the stubborn type," said Attaleiates.

BOTANEIATES'S RESPONSE WAS NOT STRONG ENOUGH TO completely allay the empress's anxiety. Crowds began gathering outside the palace by the middle of March, calling the emperor "unworthy," calling to "dig up his bones" and throwing stones at the walls, even into all hours of the night. No one called him by his name or title anymore, just by his nickname that meant "minus a quarter," Parapinakes. Maria lived in fear that a mob would break through the gates and slaughter everyone in their path.

Alexios was back in the city, summoned by the terrified Michael. He arrived in mud-splattered armor, irritated by the emperor's demands.

"I don't know what he wants me to do. Stay here to stop the rioters from throwing rocks or go to Adrianople and make an end to Bryennios? I can't be everywhere. Shouldn't the Varangians be scaring off the mobs?"

We sat in my office, trying to warm up next to the brazier on a chilly spring day.

"They tried, but it's no use. They scatter for a time before starting again," I said.

Alexios looked thoughtful. "Maybe Parapinakes should just leave the palace for a while? Go someplace no one expects him to go? Let the mobs die down, then return?"

Even my own family called Michael by that unfortunate nickname. "Son, that won't fix the problems he's created."

He bent forward, elbows on his knees, looking me in the eye. "Mama, I know Parapinakes is an awful ruler and that his ridiculous Nikephoritzes could not be more of a thief. I know all that, and I wish he wasn't emperor. But I've sworn an oath of loyalty to him, and breaking my word, my oath, would make me into something far worse than he is. It would make me into a man with no honor. I can't do that."

Alexios was the man I'd raised him to be. I was never more proud of him than I was at that moment. And yet Michael's fate was already a boulder tumbling down a mountainside.

"Then you must get him off the throne without breaking your word. The people don't want him as emperor. Michael is a frightened and foolish boy. And Botaneiates does not want to shed blood unless he has to. The usual answer to this problem is the monastery."

৩৵৩

ALEXIOS WAS FORCED TO HIRE A BOAT TO TAKE HIM TO THE Boukoleon harbor since the mobs controlled the streets in front of the Great Palace. It took a couple of days before he could convince Michael to leave.

He arrived breathless at the house just after dawn the next morning.

"He's at the hunting lodge here in Blachernae."

"That's the farthest you could get him to go? I hope no one saw you," I said. It took no more than a few minutes to walk there from our house.

"We sailed at night. He was unwilling to go farther," he said raking a hand through his red hair. "He insisted Nikephoritzes come with us, more worried about that miserable little eunuch than he was about his lovely wife and child."

Alexios had never described a woman as "lovely" before. "Where are Maria and her son, Eudokia's children, and Irene and her boys?" I asked.

"Back at the palace. I told Maria I'd be back today. Not sure what to do with them, though. They can't stay there with the mob getting wilder all the time."

I thought for a minute. It would be best to have Empress Maria and the rest close, should they have to leave together. "I'll come with you. We'll bring them to the Petrion monastery. Old Empress Theodora lived there for a long time after her sister Zoe pushed her out of the palace. They'll have rooms suitable for the empress. Should we go now or wait till dark?"

Alexios frowned while he considered the risks. "Go now. Clouds are blowing in. I think a storm's coming, and it won't be safe for them to wait longer. The Varangians still control the seawalls near the palace; no one will notice a few women and children. We can be back by midday."

"One more thing, or rather, two more things."

Alexios looked at me quizzically.

"We need to send out two messengers. One to John Ducas, telling him he's needed at the lodge. Send the other messenger to the Stoudion monastery. We need the hegoumenos at the lodge to be ready to tonsure Michael."

We sailed in one of the ordinary ferry boats that ply the waters of the Golden Horn. The sky was an ominous gray, and the gusting wind almost blew my maphorion off my head several times. Irene was waiting on the quay outside the Boukoleon when we tied up there.

"The children are almost ready. The littlest ones were just napping when I saw you."

Maria stepped out, bundled in a heavy mantle and holding the hands of two little boys, her son, Tino, and Irene's son John. She was followed by three others—Zoe, Eudokia's thirteen-year-old daughter with Constantine Ducas, holding the hands of her half-brothers, Leo and Nikephoros Diogenes. Alexios paid solicitous attention to Maria, helping her and the two toddlers into their seats on the rocking boat while I assisted Zoe and the Diogenes boys. Irene had her new baby held tight in her arms.

We wrapped blankets around the children when rain began pelting us.

The swelling sea churned as the ferry slowly made its way into the Golden Horn's waters. The sea spray and rain drenched me to the skin, and my maphorion hung limply around my face. A mist rose, a blessing that veiled us from those who might try to stop or follow us. By the time we reached the Gate of St. John the Baptist in the seawall, Tino and John were soaked and whimpering in panic over the violent rocking of the boat. Zoe and her little brothers shivered in the cold and damp, but they were calm.

Alexios paid the ferryman and we hastened to Petrion, a few minutes' walk from the watergate. Irene carried her mewling baby son in her arms in the pouring rain while Alexios picked up and carried young Tino for Maria. Zoe grasped the hand of Leo Diogenes, while I held John's and Nikephoros's. Before long, our bedraggled party reached the monastery, and Alexios pounded on its gate.

The door hole opened to reveal the sallow face of a rawboned nun looking surprised that any would be knocking in such a storm.

"Sister, we must speak with your hegoumena," said Alexios.

The nun gazed at Alexios with suspicion. "On what business?"

I spoke up then. "Sister, we have the empress and the imperial children with us. They are in need of shelter." I pulled Maria forward. Her aristocratic bearing, exquisite face, and fine garments gave evidence of her high position, even if the nun had never seen the empress. She took stock of us all before deciding we posed no threat. She grudgingly pulled back the two bolts securing the gate.

"Wait here," she said after escorting us to an entrance hall where we could stay out of the rain.

The nun returned a few minutes later with a companion who looked at Maria with recognition. She nodded to the first nun and said, "Sister Alethea, wait here with the others. I'll escort Empress Maria to the hegoumena."

The two of them disappeared around a corner.

Irene was sitting in a chair, hugging John and the baby to her and trying to warm them.

"Irene, would you want to come with me and stay at our house rather than here?" I asked.

She flashed me a grateful smile but shook her head.

"I've been Maria's companion since we were children. I can't leave her now."

Maria returned with the hegoumena's decision.

"Irene and I may stay here with our children and with Zoe. But she says that Leo and Nikephoros are too old for the monastery."

"They'll come home with us, then," I said. "They'll be with their sister, Thea, there."

The fatherless boys had rarely been outside the palace walls without Zoe and almost wept when bidding her farewell. They were like driftwood, fallen into strong currents pushing them toward rocky shores. My house would be a safe harbor for them.

❦

THEA GREETED US ON OUR RETURN, QUICKLY TAKING charge of Leo and Nikephoros. She also handed me a message from Thomas telling me that the rioters had gone to the Hagia Sophia, compelling the patriarch's presence, and in that church of Holy Wisdom he had acclaimed Nikephoros Botaneiates our new emperor.

The messenger sent to John Ducas waited in our hall with the news that the Caesar was at the emperor's lodge. Alexios and I changed into dry clothes before leaving again.

"This is when you'll need to persuade Michael to abdicate," I told him before we left. "He thinks you're loyal to him, but you are fighting for the empire, the Roman people. Michael has forgotten about them. Think of this as just a chess game where the king has lost all his men except one knight—you. Michael's lost his queen, his castle, his bishop, and he's cornered. It's checkmate. He cannot win. His game is finished."

Alexios set his jaw and gave me a reluctant nod of acknowledgment. "Yes, it is finished."

The rain had stopped outside and the wind blew scudding clouds across the sky. It was midafternoon when we reached the hunting lodge where Michael had taken shelter. Inside, we found John Ducas pacing irritably in a reception room, growling at the servants for more wine. The hegoumenos from Stoudion waited quietly in a corner.

"I don't know why I'm here. My nephew refuses to see me," John Ducas said.

"He'll see you," I said. "Alexios will convince him to see you, and then you must tell him to abdicate."

"Abdicate? Why should he? He's not that bad," Caesar John said, waving me off as though unimportant.

"That's what you think? That he's not that bad?" I said in an angry outburst. "When people all over Anatolia are swarming into the city to escape the Turks he can't be bothered to fight, when people are starving to death in the city's streets? Don't you realize that your nephew, your precious brother's oldest son, will be destroyed by the mobs rampaging in the streets the way the caulker's son was destroyed? Do you want to see Michael blinded the way that other Emperor Michael was? Blinded to die the way Romanus did?"

"Why do you always have to bring up Romanus? Just let him rest in peace," he grumbled.

I stared at John Ducas in stony silence while Alexios put a hand on my arm.

"Caesar John," he began, "my mother is correct. We all know the mobs at the Great Palace are calling for the emperor's death. He can't even enter the Hagia Sophia without worrying he'll be attacked. We just received the news that the patriarch acclaimed

Botaneiates emperor in the Hagia Sophia today, and the new emperor is just across the water in Nicaea. If something happens to him, there's Bryennios rebelling in the west and camped in Adrianople. You know those two weren't the first to rebel, and if neither of them succeeds, others will rise up to replace them. We can end the fighting now. We all know Michael was never suited to being emperor. The hegoumenos can tonsure him, and Botaneiates will let him live out his days safely in Stoudion as a monk. You know it will be the best for him and everyone else."

"No, it won't be for the best," said John in a voice that quavered. "I can't agree."

"I do agree," said another voice. "The emperor must agree to the tonsure. The sooner the better, before anyone finds out where he is and there is bloodshed," said the hegoumenos, Michael Kourkouas. The respected priest in his black robes and long gray beard looked sternly at Caesar John. "If we do it quickly and a new man takes the throne, then Michael will be forgotten and he can live undisturbed. If we wait, people will be killed, and Michael will be one of them."

"Botaneiates told me he does not want to shed Roman blood, and so far he hasn't," I said. Then I dangled a carrot before Ducas. "I know he's also prepared to be generous to those who help him take the throne without a fight."

Caesar John blinked, looking at each of us in turn. The truth of Michael's plight stood in stark contrast to the lies John Ducas had told over the years to prop up Michael. He looked suddenly shattered, like an urn fallen to the ground and broken into small pieces. He nodded finally.

"So we're agreed, then. We'll persuade Michael to be tonsured," said Alexios. "I know he's waiting for me, so when I see him, I'll convince him to agree to see you, Caesar. We won't push him, just make him understand he has no other choice."

"I'll come with you," I said. "Michael is fond of me; he won't mind if I come with you."

John Ducas gave an irritated grunt at that but said nothing.

The emperor's apartments had the feel of a deathbed watch. A few servants hovered about, watchful as vultures trying to decide whether to leave their still-breathing prey or remain to feast over the corpse.

Michael's face held the same blank look it so often did, as though he was always unprepared for what was happening. Nikephoritzes stood nearby, gold bracelets jangling on his wrists and a jeweled collar around his throat that I had last seen years earlier on Eudokia.

"Your Majesty, I've received word from the palace that the rioters went to the Hagia Sophia and acclaimed Botaneiates emperor in the presence of the patriarch who confirmed it," said Alexios. "The word is they are prepared to fight in the streets to remove you."

Michael gulped loudly, taken aback at this. "But, Alexios, you have soldiers; you can stop them, can't you?" His voice sounded pitifully plaintive. He reached out a hand to grip the eunuch's arm.

Alexios appeared to consider this request. "Of course, Your Majesty, I could do that. It will end up in much bloodshed, many Romans killed in the fighting, I'm sure. If you desire that, I can do it."

Michael looked hesitant.

"Your Majesty, I saw your Uncle John when we came in. I think his advice would help you come to a decision," I said.

Michael's face turned red, but then he nodded and sent a servant to fetch his uncle.

Nikephoritzes's feral eyes darted back and forth between Alexios and myself, judging his situation. He then made the excuse of needing to relieve himself to depart.

"Caesar John," said Alexios when John Ducas arrived, "the emperor seeks your opinion on whether I should take my troops to the Great Palace to stop the rioting. I told him there would likely be many people killed if I did that, and he was concerned about so many deaths. It does him great credit that he is so disquieted at the thought of killing his own people despite their fickleness."

John Ducas looked thoughtful for a minute before speaking.

"Your Majesty, my dear nephew, General Comnenus is right in saying your care for your people does you great credit. You have always had such a kind soul, more like that of a monk or saint of old. I think if the people of the city acclaimed General Botaneiates as their emperor, then perhaps it is time for you to set down your burdens and allow him to rule."

Michael rubbed his forehead, trying to understand what he was being urged to do. "Where's Nikephoritzes? Someone get him and bring him to me. Immediately. I need his advice."

A servant scurried off in the direction the eunuch had taken.

"Nephew, it happened that on my way here I encountered the hegoumenos of the Stoudion monastery. You recall that that's where Emperor Isaac lived out his final years? The hegoumenos is waiting just outside the door here. It would take just a few minutes for the tonsure. All your cares will drop away as your shorn hair falls to the floor."

The servant returned without Nikephoritzes. "I-I can't find him anywhere," he stammered.

Michael looked panicky. Nikephoritzes had always been at his side for over five years, but John Ducas would not wait any longer.

"Bring in the priest," said Caesar John to the servant.

Michael's mousy brown hair was soon scattered on the floor around him. The hegoumenos led him outside, where, as a new monk, he was given a donkey to ride to his monastery of Stoudion.

"Do we have any idea where Nikephoritzes is?" I asked.

"If I had to guess, he's off to some far corner of the world where he can enjoy whatever wealth he's managed to carry with him," said Alexios. "Good riddance."

BOTANEIATES ENTERED CONSTANTINOPLE TWO DAYS LATER, the proud bringer of victory riding a magnificent stallion and attired in the imperial purple garments of an emperor. The patriarch crowned him in the Hagia Sophia, and the new emperor moved into the Great Palace. Nikephoros, the third emperor of that name, soon discovered the bulging treasury that Michael had hoarded. Thomas said he believed Michael had no idea how much was there, allowing Nikephoritzes to squander it as he wished. The new emperor used it to buy the affections and gratitude of his army, the city's dynatoi, the palace servants, and the Roman fleet, bestowing the largesse on one and all. The new ruler was hailed as peace-loving and generous.

Unfortunately, my daughter Donya's husband, Niko Melissenos, refused to accept the new emperor and even dared to oppose him while he was still in Nicaea. Donya came to me in tears.

"Mama, Niko was just being loyal to Emperor Michael. He'd sworn an oath of loyalty to him. Now, we're being exiled to the island of Kos." She wiped back her tears.

I put an arm around my daughter, trying to comfort her. I hated to see her and her son leave the city.

"Botaneiates probably doesn't see it as being harsh. New emperors don't want to encourage opponents, and Niko was an easy target to make an example of. Give it a little time; he could reconsider after a year or two."

It was difficult to send them off, but I consoled myself that I had suffered exile and survived. Kos was much closer than Amasea had been for us. They would survive too.

Donya left in mid-April, and the next day a visitor arrived at my door. Eudokia. Emperor Nikephoros had sent word to her that she was free to return to the city. The seven years spent in the remote monastery had added lines to her face, but she wore her widow's black dress and maphorion with the same grace she'd worn an empress's jeweled gowns.

"The emperor is considering remarriage," she told me. "He

wants the legitimacy that a marriage to me or my daughter-in-law would give. I told him to marry Maria. I have no wish to marry again. I'm done with that. I was glad to return, though. I've missed my children."

"You've seen Zoe?" I asked. "You know your sons, Romanus's boys, are here?"

She nodded and started to cry. "I didn't think I'd ever see them again. They were just babies when Michael sent me away. They won't remember me. I'm afraid they won't forgive me either."

I embraced my old friend, patting her back. "They remember you. I often tell them about you and their brave father. They know you had no choice; they know their father was a hero. Let me bring them to you."

Eudokia nodded, teary-eyed.

I retrieved Nikephoros, now almost ten years old, and Leo, who was eight, from the room where they studied with their tutor and brought them to her. I pulled the curtain across the doorway to give them privacy for their reunion, but it was no barrier to the sounds of this joyful homecoming.

Eudokia stayed with us for a few weeks that spring while she found a new place to live with her sons and Zoe, a new place that held no painful memories for her. At the same time, Botaneiates married Empress Maria. John Ducas pushed the new emperor to choose her and name her son, Tino, as his successor since Botaneiates had no children of his own. Beautiful Maria, a woman of twenty-seven, was now married to another emperor, a man old enough to be her grandfather. Her one consolation was that her son would not lose his right to the throne.

Alexios was still in the field with the army the rest of that spring, trying to defeat Bryennios, who persisted in his efforts to take the throne. The emperor tried to appease this stubborn rebel by offering him the title of Caesar with all the rights that involved, including the right to succeed Botaneiates on his death, something he had earlier promised to Maria's son. Bryennios refused the offer.

"The empress was livid when she learned what the emperor offered Byrennios," said Thomas one warm June morning after escorting Martina to our house.

"I can't blame her. Maria married him with the understanding that Tino would succeed his stepfather. I've known the emperor a long time, and he's not one to make promises he won't keep. Maybe he didn't expect Bryennios to take the offer."

Thomas scowled. "Maybe. Did you know the emperor brought a couple of servants with him to the palace, name of Borilos and Germanos? They're the usual Scythe types—big and hairy, loud and crude. I don't know what he sees in them. They're constantly whispering in his ear, and he seems to trust them, but no one else does. A couple of court jesters, really."

"How are relations between the emperor and empress?"

Thomas paused and looked me in the eye. "Uh, not warm. He's polite with her, respectful, but no more. I don't think they've shared a bed more than a couple of times. The two Scythes make fun of her. In fact, I think the empress is afraid of them. She insisted that Lady Irene, as well as Tino and Irene's boys, sleep in her rooms whenever the emperor doesn't, which is all the time now."

✦

Roussel was dead. I had no great fondness for the man—he'd done the Roman Empire no good—but the final twist to his story almost beggared belief.

The Frank made for eastern Anatolia after abandoning Alexios, to the castles where his men and family were, aiming to reclaim the territory he had before my son arrested him. He was there just a few weeks when who should turn up at his gate but Nikephoritzes, carrying what bags of gold he'd managed to purloin from the treasury. The wily eunuch thought Roussel would be the perfect man to lead an army back to Byzantium, rescue Michael, and put him back on the throne. He had somehow forgotten that Michael left Roussel in chains moldering away in prison for three years. A man like Roussel would always remember that painful humiliation, and he declined, with great clarity, to do anything ever to restore Michael to the throne.

So what did that miserable eunuch do? He poisoned Roussel, killing him. Roussel's men were livid at this treachery, tied up Nikephoritzes, and turned him over to the emperor's soldiers. They dragged him to the island of Prote in the Marmara, where the emperor's men tortured him until he revealed where his large stash of gold was hidden at Hebdomon, a few miles outside Byzantium. The greedy little man eventually died under torture. I suspect the new monk, Michael, was the only one who mourned him.

And so ended the lives of two troublesome men.

⚜

ALEXIOS SENT MESSENGERS AHEAD TO LET THE EMPEROR know he had finally defeated Bryennios in mid-August and was sending the rebel back to the city. The emperor sent his Scythe servant Germanos to take charge of the prisoner and return him to the city. Germanos blinded his captive before they even reached the city, without the emperor's authorization. The emperor forgave his servant's premature action and still permitted Bryennios and his family to retain their estates.

My son was miserable at this news. He had promised me to never allow such a punishment, and his captive was now deprived of his sight.

"I should never have let that barbarian take possession of Bryennios. I could tell he was a brute when I met him. He's not the kind of man I expected Botaneiates to put his trust in," he said.

I shook my head. "You couldn't have known what he would do. You hardly know Germanos."

I felt sick about Bryennios—blind and the only family he had left was his late brother's young son, also named Nikephoros. How would they end up after this? Emperor Nikephoros Botaneiates was turning out very different from the general I once knew.

Empress Maria was even more frightened when she learned what happened. Germanos had made the decision to blind Bryennios on his own, without the emperor's consent, leaving her to wonder what he might do to her or her son.

We were sitting in one of the palace's gardens, watching Tino and my grandson John running and kicking a ball back and forth. The joy on their sweaty faces as they played made me realize they were each other's best friend. Servants brought us iced pomegranate juice to enjoy on that hot summer day.

There were dark circles under Maria's eyes.

"I feel like I'm constantly in danger," she said, tears streaming down her face. "The two of them take turns trying to frighten me. They pinch me or throw things at me when the emperor isn't watching, ridiculing me to him. The emperor says I exaggerate, they're only teasing me, so I think he cares nothing for me. I try avoiding them, but I can't always do that. It's worse than when Nikephoritzes was still here."

I put an arm around Maria, trying to reassure her, but I could feel her trembling.

"How is the emperor with you?" I asked. Maria was a beautiful woman, patient and affectionate, with the perfect manners of a woman raised to be an empress.

Maria blushed, but her cousin spoke for her.

"The emperor is an old man with an old man's abilities." Irene winked at me.

My eyes widened when I realized what was wrong. He was a proud man, a leader of men, and embarrassed because he could not perform in the bedroom at his age. Like many proud men, he blamed the woman for his own failing. I felt bad for Maria, her first husband uninterested, the second one incapable.

"Isaac will be home soon. We can continue to live in the palace. That should deter them," said Irene, patting her cousin's hand.

I sipped the bright red juice, trying to avoid the inevitable pomegranate seeds. Like life's troubles, the seeds were always there. I looked at Maria's troubled face. I could think of only one viable solution to her situation.

"Augusta, it sounds like you need someone to protect you from these Scythes. Your son is not old enough to take on that responsibility. But suppose you had another son?" I asked.

"Another son, Lady Anna? What do you mean?"

"You need someone who will intimidate those two barbarians into leaving you alone. Your husband is disinclined to do so. You have no father or brother close by. You need a son, one who is old enough to protect you."

Maria raised a curious eyebrow.

"What would you think about adopting my son Alexios?"

Maria and Irene gaped at me.

"Before you discount the idea, as your son he could be here at the palace at any time. He's a soldier, physically strong and experienced at war, leading men in battle and frightening enemies. The emperor values him. He's betrothed to your son's cousin, Irene. If the emperor questions this, you can tell him it is to bind the two families closer." I didn't really want to bind the two families closer, but it was a convenient reason she could give the emperor. "Or tell him you wanted an older brother for Tino to rely on should anything happen to you."

The young women looked at each other, their faces both skeptical and hopeful.

"Have you spoken to Alexios about this? You know he's only a few years younger than Maria," Irene asked.

"No. I know it isn't common to adopt someone so close in

age, but it does happen. I'll explain why he needs to do this, and the two of you will have to convince the emperor."

"If you can get Alexios to agree first, then I'll approach the emperor with the request," said Maria.

Alexios looked at me as though I had lost my mind when later I told him my suggestion. We sat alone on the terrace behind the house, catching the evening breeze after supper. Thea and Theodora were putting their daughters to bed.

"You know she's just five years older than I am, don't you? It's ridiculous to think of her adopting me," he said.

"Attaleiates has spoken of court cases he's judged where there were adoptions between two people close in age. It's usually for matters related to inheritances, but it does occur," I said. "The empress is terrified of those two barbarians the emperor keeps around him. She's worried they will hurt her or her son. She has no father or brother or son to stop them. Do you have a better idea?"

He sighed and walked over to a rosebush whose branches climbed the sides of the trellis above our heads. I needed to water the red flowers; they looked a little wilted from the hot days we were having. Alexios brushed his hand against the bush before pulling it back sharply and sucking on the blood a thorn had drawn.

"You don't think she's exaggerating?" he asked.

"Irene agreed with everything Maria said. And as bad as Nikephoritzes was, Maria said she never felt frightened this way when he was still around."

Alexios eyed the little scratch on his hand, gave it another suck, and turned to me, his eyes in dark shadows.

"Mama, if this is the best solution, the only solution, then I will agree to it."

☙❧

EMPEROR NIKEPHOROS WAS DISTRACTED WITH ANOTHER rebellion when Maria came to him with her request to adopt Alexios. The new dux of Dyrrachium, Basilakes, was making an attempt to seize the throne.

"He just said, 'Of course, I have no objections,' and turned back to the report he was reading," Maria said a few days later. "I've arranged for a priest to officiate at the church of Saints Sergios and Bacchus tomorrow."

The next day, we stood inside that little church, a quiet miniature of the much larger Hagia Sophia, situated just outside the palace walls. A glittering mosaic of the Theotokos in blue and gold robes sitting with her Son on her lap gazed down on us from the dome. A gold-clad icon panel of St. Sergios in his armor was on one side of the royal door in the iconostasis, and one of St. Bacchus similarly clad was on the other side. The capitals on the columns held the monograms of Emperor Justinian and Empress Theodora, who had built this gem of a church five hundred years ago. The bright summer morning light shone in the arched windows.

A gray-bearded priest entered in his red vestments, lavishly embroidered with gold crosses and other holy symbols. Acolytes followed him carrying heavy lit candles, standing on either side of the priest as he began intoning his prayers. Alexios and Maria faced each other in front of the royal door. First, the priest asked Alexios and Maria both to consent to the adoption.

"I do," responded Alexios, pale and staring at his adopted mother.

"I do," said Maria, looking into her adopted son's eyes, a slow flush rising on her cheeks.

Maria reached up to slip a chain with a jeweled cross pendant over his head, a symbol of her care for her new son. Alexios then put his two strong hands between her delicate ones, and swore his oath to be an honest and true son to her, with all the rights and obligations that entailed.

The priest said a final blessing on them, and the brief service was done.

⚜

It wasn't long before Alexios had to demonstrate his protective devotion of his adopted mother. He stopped to see the empress on his way to meet with the emperor about preparations for the army being sent to end Basilakes's rebellion. The emperor's two Scythe servants, Borilos and Germanos, were tormenting her.

"They were making fun of her accent, taunting her," said Alexios, "and grabbing little Tino, scaring him and throwing the child back and forth between them, just out of his mother's reach. The boy was sobbing, and Maria was begging them to stop."

"What did you do?" I asked.

"I came up behind Borilos, grabbed him by the neck, threw him so he banged his head against the wall. Hard. That took the fight out of him. Germanos had the boy and was looking pretty surprised to see me. He put Tino down and started mumbling some excuses for what they did. Said it was just fun. I told him I didn't want to see or hear of them ever bothering the empress again. Then I made sure he had a few bruises to help him remember."

I held his face between my hands and eyed the side of it that had a new purplish tinge. "It looks like he didn't want that help remembering."

Alexios grinned and waved it off. "He hardly touched me."

"Thank you for doing this, son. I'm sure Maria appreciated it."

"She did, she thanked me many times over," he said and paused. "Mama, she's such a beautiful woman. It's terrible she was wed first to someone like Michael Ducas with no interest in

her, and then to Botaneiates who is so old that he can't. . ."
Alexios looked at me with anguished eyes.

Too late I realized he was in love with her, probably in love
for the first time in his young life. In love with an empress,
someone he could never have.

"Alexios, she's the empress, she's lived a good life, and she's
the mother of the emperor's heir. That would be enough to
satisfy most women. Marriages are complicated; I don't know
that she's unhappy with her lot in life."

He shook his head and turned away. "I don't know either."

۞

ISAAC RETURNED FROM ANTIOCH IN MID-OCTOBER AFTER
two long years away in that easternmost outpost. The fighting
there was a constant low-level thrum, with spurts of more
intense battles with the Turks. The empire had held it for over a
hundred years, but it wasn't clear how much longer it could
afford the men and money it required. The emperor was pleased,
though, with his accomplishments.

Isaac lived at the palace since Irene continued as Maria's
companion. Isaac and Alexios spent the next couple of weeks
catching up before Botaneiates sent Alexios to fight the new
rebellion led by Basilakes. The two brothers stayed up late into
the night during those few days, talking and enjoying the
company of Irene and Maria. The emperor joined them two or
three times, but at his age he was more inclined to sleep than talk.

Alexios was walking on air for those weeks before he left. He
was happy to see his brother, but their evening gatherings with
the two women put him in a more euphoric mood than I had
ever seen him in. I had to talk to him.

"There had better not be anything happening between you
and Maria," I said in my sternest voice.

He blanched. "No, Mama, of course there isn't."

"You don't think I'm blind, do you? I'm your mother. I can see perfectly well what is right in front of me."

"Mama, I wouldn't ever. . ." he began, backing up from me, voice quivering.

"Do you have any idea what would happen to you if anything did? And what would happen to Maria would be even worse. I would be so ashamed, *so ashamed,* if a son of mine got into trouble like that with the empress. How happy do you think those two barbarians the emperor clings to would be to tell him some story that compromised both of you? You are never to be alone with her. *Never.* Am I clear?" I had never had to speak to one of my children like that before, but I was frightened to think what the consequences could be.

He flinched at my words.

"Mama, we aren't ever alone." But his guilty look said that it wasn't for lack of desiring it.

"I would hope not. You haven't seen Irene Ducaena since you've been back," I said, bringing up his betrothed. I had no fondness for the girl, but she would distract Alexios from Maria. Or so I hoped. "You need to see her today. Remind yourself of whom you will be marrying."

My son looked pale and nodded at me before scrambling to get away.

1079

ALEXIOS SPENT THE WINTER MONTHS CHASING THE REBEL Basilakes around Greece until the man finally holed up in Thessaloniki. The man unwisely ventured out one night only to have Alexios and his men capture him. He was quickly put in chains and returned to Constantinople by the end of March. My son had no choice but to send him to the emperor, even though it was a foregone conclusion that the man would be blinded. The emperor rewarded Alexios with the title of Grand Domestic of the West, putting him in charge of the Roman army in the west. At the same time, he named Isaac the Grand Domestic of the East.

My sons' promotions to these highest of military titles were great honors but came with great risks. I had no doubt Alexios and Isaac earned the recognitions bestowed on them through their diligence on the battlefield, and their loyalty to Emperor Nikephoros. It meant, however, that for them to rise in the emperor's favor, others fell. Borilos and Germanos fought back with a fury, using every opportunity to criticize my sons to the emperor, especially Alexios.

৩১৩

MARIA AND IRENE MET ME WITH TIGHT-LIPPED expressions in the palace gardens when I visited one June day.

"There's a new child in the palace," said Irene. "The emperor brought his nephew, Synadenos, here."

"Oh?" I asked.

Maria and Irene exchanged a glance.

"The boy, the son of the emperor's sister, is almost fourteen. A handsome boy, but he has the manners of a peasant. He's never lived in the city, just in Chonai, where it seems he spent most of his time hunting, with little time in the schoolroom. I'm not sure he can even read," said Maria with a sniff, barely disguising her outrage.

Irene smoothed a wrinkle out of her skirt and added, "We believe he is being groomed as the emperor's successor."

I winced at that. The emperor was trying for a second time to supplant Maria's son with another candidate of his own choosing despite the oaths he'd made to Maria before their marriage a year earlier. The two women had nowhere else to turn since Alexios was in Bulgaria repelling a Pecheneg incursion into the empire and Isaac was fighting Turks in the east.

"Lady Anna, there's more," she said. "I've only been married to the emperor for a year, but he's not the man he was even then. He gets up during the night, wandering the halls. He looks at me as though he doesn't recognize me sometimes. He's bent over when he walks and now he's never without a cane. He's always spending time with those two Scythes."

The two women looked at me for an answer I didn't have.

"There may not be anything we can do. The emperor has not announced the change, has he?" I asked.

"Not yet," said Maria. "But I expect it any day."

"I recommend you continue as though nothing is amiss and that you be sure to befriend the Varangians, give them gifts, especially their leader. If the emperor dies, you'll need them to protect Tino."

Maria put her hands to her head, rubbing the sides of her face in frustration. "Caesar John said to marry this man, said he'd protect Tino. Instead, I have more concerns than before."

The poor woman was in an impossible situation.

The emperor summoned me to the palace a week later. I hadn't seen him in almost a year, and I could see what Maria meant when she'd described his growing infirmity. Botaneiates was in the old office that my brother-in-law, Isaac, had used, and that Romanus had used. The emperor's face was that of a soldier —but an old one: a set jaw, rheumy eyes, the line of an old scar half-hidden beneath a sparse gray, almost white, beard. His shoulders were still square, even though his back was noticeably bent beneath his purple robes. A tremor in his hand. Time had sliced away at him in a way a sword never had.

"Lady Anna, you may have heard I've summoned my nephew, Synadenos, here," he began.

"Your Majesty, yes, I did hear about your nephew."

"Yes, well, I've decided to name him as my successor. He's fourteen and a fine young man, sits a horse well, but lacks the polish of the city-bred men. That's where you come in, if you agree."

I peered at the emperor, wondering what he needed from me.

"You have several granddaughters, I believe. Granddaughters of Romanus Diogenes who live with you. I want Synadenos betrothed to one of them. It would help him to be married to another emperor's granddaughter, not just succeed as my nephew. You can decide which one."

I blinked at him in astonishment. "Your Majesty, that is such an honor, but I thought you designated the empress's son as your successor."

"That boy's too young; he's only five years old," he said in a gruff voice, as though trying to ignore the subject.

In truth, it was clear the subject was as much the emperor's age as it was the boy's age. Even he, with his infirmities and spotty memory, knew a man in his late seventies could not expect to live long enough for a five-year-old to reach manhood. The emperor had to be feeling Death's hot breath on his neck, and this nephew was close to maturity. Looking at Botaneiates, though, I was not sure he would live even long enough to see Synadenos ready to rule.

"I understand."

"Yes, and I want him to move in with you once they are betrothed. You'll see to the raising of Synadenos, teaching him what he needs to know. My sister didn't have the best teachers available for him in Chonai. Your boys turned out well. Just keep doing what you did with them."

His choice of one of my granddaughters as a wife for his nephew spoke well for the trust he had in my family's loyalty. The empress would have a very different opinion.

"Thank you, Your Majesty." I made my obeisance and departed.

Maria wept when I told her the news. She had done everything she could for her son, and it was burning into ash. I thought of Maria's plight, all her dreams coming to naught, as I rode in the jostling sedan chair on the way home. She'd been born a beautiful princess and had married two emperors, and was faced with disillusionment and disappointment at every turn.

I sat down later with Thea and Theodora to discuss the situation.

"This is a great honor the emperor has bestowed on us." I looked at Thea. "Since your Anya is nine and the oldest, her age makes her the most likely candidate. How do you feel about that?"

Thea frowned and rubbed her hands together. She had no love of palace intrigues. "She's still so young. I'd rather not see her betrothed yet at all, but she would be the most acceptable choice. Even so, I don't like the idea of him living in the same house as our girls."

Theodora looked at her sister-in-law with a crafty expression. "I think our house would need to add another wing for this boy. The emperor's nephew and heir would need servants of his own as well as his own private rooms. You can tell the emperor we will need to add that space before the betrothal is finalized."

"That's a reasonable request," I said, looking at Thea. "It may not delay the betrothal for long, but it would solve your concern about the boy's presence in the household."

The emperor quickly agreed to the request and saw that builders were at our property within a few days. As I had expected, though, the construction was completed quickly and the two children betrothed by the end of November.

CHAPTER 16

THE EMPEROR'S NEPHEW, SYNADENOS, MOVED IN WITH US after Epiphany. He was a likable boy with a slow smile and a mop of brown hair. Phillip Mouzalon, a young tutor Attaleiates had recommended to the emperor for his heir, joined him in the new wing of our house along with another servant. They kept to themselves for most of the day, only enjoying their evening meals with us. The boy was young and more interested in games than in his studies. His tutor persisted, though, and he did make some progress, beginning to learn the rules of palace etiquette and rhetoric. My own sons had learned to fight first from their father and then in practice with their brothers, but now we were a household of women, and I hired a retired Excubitor to train Synadenos.

I escorted the young heir to Emperor Nikephoros twice a month so he could evaluate the boy's progress. The emperor had initially provided money to cover the cost of the boy's presence in our household, but by March those funds had run out and I had to speak with him about that. After I repeated my request since he couldn't hear me the first time, he refused to look at me, instead making excuses for why the money was not forthcoming.

"Your sons have had exorbitant expenses in the field that I needed to cover," he said, blaming Alexios and Isaac for the shortfall. "You'll have to wait a few weeks before I can give you more." He rose from his seat to leave the office and grabbed his cane, almost falling backward into the chair again. He called for one of the eunuchs, not realizing the servant was at his elbow.

I gazed after the Roman Emperor Nikephoros III Botaneiates as he shuffled his way down the hall, escaping the uncomfortable conversation we'd just had. He was an old man worn out by life's storms. He was a good man, had been a good soldier and a good leader of men, but was gone bad like an apple forgotten in a cupboard corner—shriveled and rotting, ready for the trash heap. The empress's son, a boy of five, and his own nephew, a fourteen-year-old, did not have the maturity to rule. An empire beset on all sides needed a vigorous ruler, not an ancient or child.

⚜

THE DUCAS FAMILY INVITED ME, ALEXIOS, AND ISAAC TO A celebration of the betrothal of Irene's younger sister to the son of one of Caesar John's partisans. George Palaiologos was about twenty and eleven years older than his intended, Anna. Their marriage, like that of Alexios and Irene, would take place in a few years when their brides were older. The dark-haired nine-year-old Anna looked overwhelmed in her silk finery, an elaborate maphorion on her head, soft, childish hands poking out through her sleeves.

The women's festivities spilled out into the elaborate garden overlooking the Marmara. I stood with Isaac's wife, Irene, and Empress Maria enjoying the warm spring day while Marie of Bulgaria greeted her guests between her two daughters. I watched as Alexios's intended, Irene, welcomed the ladies of the dynatoi with well-practiced courtesy. I could not complain about the manners Marie had taught her oldest daughter.

"I haven't had such delicacies in months," said Empress Maria as she nibbled at a few morsels. "The emperor says we must not spend so much, but Caesar John must have plenty to afford all this."

Her cousin Irene's mouth twisted, an irritated look on her face. "He blames Isaac and Alexios for spending too much, but Isaac says he receives barely anything from him. I keep my mouth shut, but it's so unfair."

Few of the other ladies in attendance hovered around the empress, unlike in previous years. Many of them would have been disappointed and unhappy about the cut in the salaries paid to their dynatoi husbands at Easter, down from the heady first days of the emperor's reign two years earlier.

I stayed a courteous if perfunctory amount of time before moving to leave. Alexios and Isaac were in the men's party and planned to escort the empress and her cousin back to the palace later. Marie of Bulgaria caught my hand to walk with me to their courtyard, where a sedan chair waited with its chairmen.

"Lady Anna, I am so glad to see you and your sons. I asked Caesar John to be sure and introduce Alexios to George since they will soon be brothers-in-law. In fact, I was wondering if it might be time to set a date for the wedding of Alexios and Irene. She's begun her courses and is eager to become a wife."

I raised my eyebrows. Yes, they were betrothed and she was now fourteen, two years beyond the minimum twelve years. It was probably time. But the truth was neither Alexios nor I was ready for that final step. I think we both hoped for some impediment to appear, although we had different reasons.

"Marie, I don't think we can start planning that just yet. Alexios must return to Bulgaria tomorrow. We'll have to discuss it later this year, perhaps when he's home for the winter."

Marie's pleasant smile stayed painted on her face. "Of course, I understand."

I returned home and waited up for Alexios. He knew better than to try and spend more time with the empress, but I needed to be sure. He slipped through the gate just after sunset, whistling a popular tune I'd heard on the streets. He saw the lamplight in my office and stopped in before heading to bed.

"Mama? Staying up late?" he asked.

"Waiting for you," I said. "Were you delayed at the palace?"

"I spent no time with the empress aside from escorting her back with Isaac and his Irene, if you were wondering. I did stop to speak with Thomas for a long time, and then we walked back here to Blachernae together."

"What did you learn?"

He shook his head. "The servants at the palace have had enough of the emperor. He pays them late, if at all. The treasury is empty, and they have to cajole merchants to extend credit to the palace to buy foodstuffs. And everyone there hates those two louts, Borilos and Germanos. I don't know how long this can go on."

"Did you see the emperor?" I asked.

"Briefly. He looks bad." Alexios glanced in the direction of the wing where Synadenos and his tutor lived. "I'm not sure he'll last long enough for that young pup to grow to a wolfhound."

I nodded. "I expect you'll be glad to return to the easy life of a soldier rather than politics in the palace."

He gave a short laugh. "I suppose. I'm off to bed now; early start tomorrow."

A LOW LEVEL OF DISCONTENT SIMMERED IN THE CITY THAT summer. Merchants grumbled, food was expensive, and the eparch diligent in his tax collections. It felt like a stewpot ready to boil over. Then it did.

My son Adrian arrived with a letter from Donya in early September. Her husband, Niko Melissenos, had had enough of his exile and of Botaneiates. He decided he'd done enough penance for misplaced loyalty. He had assembled an army and begun heading for Constantinople and the throne. Donya asked only that Isaac and Alexios not be forced to confront him in battle.

I looked up at Adrian after I finished the letter.

"Do you know what this says?" I asked.

"Donya told me. I don't blame Melissenos. He would have been loyal to Botaneiates if given half a chance. I think that if he and Isaac had each been leading armies the past couple of years, we might have rid ourselves of the Turks."

I smiled at my son. I doubted it would have been so easy to be rid of the invaders, but he was still young and optimistic.

"Isaac's at Heraclea on the Black Sea. It should take you a day to get there to tell him what this letter says. Tell him I said to tell the emperor that he can't fight his sister's husband. The emperor will understand if he pleads family loyalties. Then you must go to Alexios in Adrianople and tell him the same thing."

"Yes, Mama."

It was midafternoon, too late to leave today. "Go down to the harbor now and arrange for a ship to leave at first light. Your brothers need to know this before the emperor tries to involve them."

What were we all caught up in? My granddaughter Anya was betrothed to the emperor's heir. My son-in-law, Niko Melissenos, was rebelling against the emperor. My sons Isaac and Alexios were the emperor's two most experienced generals, but with secret loyalties to the empress and her son, to whom the emperor had once promised the throne. It felt like an avalanche threatened to slide down a mountainside and destroy us all. I looked at my icon corner with its images of angels and saints, the Theotokos and Christ, and prayed we would all get safely through this dangerous time.

THE EMPEROR RECALLED BOTH ISAAC AND ALEXIOS IN November in an effort to convince them to take up the fight against their brother-in-law.

"Botaneiates wasn't too upset when we declined to lead his army against Niko. But those two barbarians of his were nasty. Said we were traitors and turncoats ourselves."

Alexios and Isaac were with me in my office, recounting their meeting at the Great Palace. The two of them bore a strong resemblance to their father, especially with John's red hair. Alexios was the more irritated of the two, pacing restlessly in the room.

"I've done everything the emperor ever asked me to do without complaint, and then to have his two henchmen imply I can't be trusted is insulting." Alexios drew a hand through his hair, his anger still blazing.

"Alex," said Isaac, the calmer one, "the emperor didn't say that. Just those two thugs. The emperor accepted our decisions. Even so, I am still worried about what sort of poison they're pouring into his ears."

"I know. What are they saying to him when we're gone? That old man looked so confused when we spoke. I don't know if he'll even remember what he told us."

"Alexios, the emperor entrusted his heir to me. The boy is betrothed to your niece. I know he'll remember that."

"Mama, I'm not so sure. Every time—"

"I know," I interjected, "he's not well. But he's still the emperor to whom you've sworn oaths." The day was mild, and I had the shutters open to the courtyard for the fresh autumn air. I glanced outside and saw a familiar figure hurry through our gate.

"Thomas is here. He's not usually here this time of day."

My old friend was soon in my office with us, sweating profusely and out of breath.

"Lady Anna, your sons need to leave the city immediately."

"What's happened?" I asked.

He sat down, wiping his face on his sleeve before continuing.

"Anthemius the cook told me he saw Borilos and Germanos lurking outside his kitchen. He overheard them plotting to arrest Isaac and Alexios tonight and blind them. They plan to convince the emperor your sons were plotting rebellion to justify it. They need to leave now."

I sucked in my breath, frightened at the thought of their possible arrests and blindings.

"I knew those two Scythes were ready to put a knife in our backs," said Alexios, pounding a fist on my desk. "How much longer do we have to put up with this ludicrous situation?"

Isaac frowned but was more thoughtful. "What worries me is they think they can convince the emperor of that right after we saw him. Who's really in charge anyway?"

"Whether the emperor is or not, you both need to be gone. Pack your bags and head out now. Make sure you keep men around you that you trust implicitly when you're back in camp," I told them.

My sons had soon departed, Alexios to Thrace and Isaac to Heraclea on the Black Sea.

"Thank you for coming so quickly," I said to Thomas afterwards.

"I'm glad I could let you know," he said. The eunuch had no beard to go gray, but the hair on his head was combed through with it. We'd known each other for over twenty years now. "The palace servants are fond of your sons. Many of them have known your children since Emperor Isaac's days. And they detest Borilos and Germanos."

"I can believe that," I said.

He paused, gave me a hard look, moved closer and continued more quietly, "In truth, the emperor is not capable of ruling any longer. I see him constantly, and he's more frail every day, in body and mind. I'm telling you, Anna Dalassena, you can't let this continue."

I raised an eyebrow. "What do you mean, 'I can't'?"

Thomas leaned in even closer, raised a hand to stop me speaking, his brown eyes piercing with unexpected intensity.

"Looking at this chessboard, the emperor, the black king, is almost in checkmate, even if he doesn't realize it. You, however, are the white queen and can move in any direction—your sons, your granddaughter's betrothed, even your son-in-law. No one else, not the emperor or the empress, not John Ducas, no one else has as strong a position right now as you do."

Those sharp words hung in the air, severe in their clarity.

"You, Anna, you need to think about who should be ruling and make plans to get it done before the Roman Empire is utterly destroyed. This is your decision, your destiny."

"Thomas—" I began before he interrupted.

"Isaac leads the army in the east, Alexios in the west. Your sons are the strongest contenders for the throne. Which of them do you want to rule? You must make it happen. You."

1081

COLD AND RAINY WINTER WEATHER KEPT ME INSIDE MUCH of the time, giving me time to consider Thomas's words. I'd never forgotten the dismay I'd felt as a girl when Uncle Costas decided his age and the risks to his children would be too great if he married Empress Zoe. Instead, she married that spendthrift, Monomachos. I thought back to how angry I'd been with John when he declined his brother's offer of the throne twenty years earlier. That time that vile Constantine Ducas had been crowned. I had loved Uncle Costas and John dearly, but the Roman Empire had suffered when they refused the crown. The disappointment from both those days still stung deep even if the anger had faded. Now, though, I could, with my sons, correct those mistakes. I shook my head in disbelief that I, just a woman, could hold that kind of power. But I did.

Would my sons want that burden? They would think so, as brash young men so often do, without knowing its true cost. Would it be Isaac with his calm intelligence or the clever and charismatic Alexios?

Thomas had spoken of the chessboard, but this was not a game. Things could go wrong. I had seen enough rebellions in a lifetime on the fringes of imperial power to know you needed supporters in the dynatoi and the Church, as well as money to be successful. Our family had connections and money, but not enough. The patriarch was a Ducas appointee and likely loyal to them. I didn't want my sons to have the same problems my brother-in-law had when he was ruling. As much as I was loath to admit it, the only family with enough supporters and gold to succeed was the Ducas family.

I decided it was time to discuss with Marie of Bulgaria a date for the wedding between Alexios and Irene.

The morning of February first dawned clear and cold. I dressed in my customary black, as I had ever since I had been tonsured at the monastery on Prinkipo. A sedan chair brought me to the Ducas family residence at midmorning.

Marie greeted me with nervous surprise, curious about the purpose of my call. We sat alone in a small room on the main floor sipping a hot milky beverage flavored with cinnamon. I wrapped my cold hands around the polished silver cup, trying to warm them.

"Lady Anna, I didn't expect to see you today."

I looked at her sweet face and realized I had to be completely honest with her. I'd known her since she was a small child; it wouldn't be fair to her to dissemble about what was happening. She would have as big a stake in my plans as I did.

"Marie, I came over about setting a date for Alexios and Irene's wedding, but in truth, we have much more to discuss."

I proceeded to tell her what I knew about the emperor's

diminishing capacities, the immaturity of the two designated heirs, the vicious schemes of the emperor's two favorites, and the question of who could be, or would be, the emperor's successor.

Marie's face changed as she listened, from the timid widowed mother dominated by her father-in-law to one of a confident woman, sure of what she wanted. It was like a mask slipping off. She sipped her drink and tucked a stray lock of hair behind her ear before speaking.

"I was coming to the same conclusions, Lady Anna. There really are no alternatives to Alexios or Isaac. Of course, Caesar John and I obviously prefer Alexios since he is betrothed to my daughter. What are your plans now?"

Her frankness took me aback, but the quiet ones can do that.

"We will need to be ready for the next opportunity. It could come at any time. Alexios and Isaac will need an army behind them, and they'll need the money to pay the soldiers."

"Lady Anna, you and I both know John Ducas will not put out money for Isaac since he has no connection to the Ducas family. Will Isaac allow his younger brother to be crowned? And Alexios and Irene will need to be properly married."

I felt my stomach turn over. My plans were not just in my head, they were turning to reality. I held my hands tight, trying to dispel the nervous excitement I felt.

"They'll see the wisdom of it when I tell them. I'll make sure Isaac understands that Alexios will be the one crowned."

Marie looked thoughtful. "I'll have to let Caesar John know what we're planning; he's at his villa on the Bosphorus. And I'll let George know too. He's in Anatolia with the army the emperor sent to stop Melissenos."

"Your other son-in-law? You think George Palaiologos needs to know?"

"Yes. I know, I know, he's young, but he's more capable than you might think for someone so young," she said with confidence. "He'll be a great help to Alexios when the time comes."

It appeared Marie and I were in perfect agreement on how to proceed. I could almost see the chess pieces lining up on the board.

WE DID NOT HAVE TO WAIT LONG. THE EMPEROR SENT urgent messages to Isaac and Alexios, recalling them to the city. They arrived at home on February eleventh, uncertain as to the reason for their presence and concerned about the threat Borilos and Germanos might again pose. I realized when they rode through our gate that the time had come for our plot to be set in motion.

I was in my office when they came in and sat down opposite me before leaving for the palace.

"The emperor did not say why he needed you both here?" I asked.

"No," replied Alexios. "We were surprised when we saw each other arriving at the same time."

Isaac glanced at his brother. "Don't know about you, but I'm going in with a knife tucked in my boot. I'm not giving those two thugs a chance to try anything."

Alexios winked at his brother. "Wouldn't go in there without one myself."

I stood up, walked to the window, and took a deep breath.

"I know you both realize too well the emperor's abilities diminish each day. Thomas tells me he can barely manage to handle the most urgent matters that reach him. He isn't capable of even lasting long enough for his nephew to be of age, much less the empress's son."

They both sat up and leaned toward me, surprised at the heavy tone of my voice.

"The empire cannot continue with either an old man or a child on the throne. We are threatened on all sides. We need a strong, capable man ruling. We all know Niko Melissenos is a good man, but if he hasn't managed to reach the city after almost five months, then he's not the one."

I paused, letting them take in my words.

"I think you both realize that the two of you are the strongest candidates. Of course, only one can wear the crown."

They sat silent, looking at each other uncomfortably.

Isaac cleared his throat and spoke first, "Whom are you proposing?"

"The one who takes the throne will need the support of the dynatoi, the patriarch. He needs money, more than I can provide. Isaac, you are the older brother, married to the empress's cousin from Alania. Your Irene does not bring much money or any dynatoi connections to help you. Alexios, you are the younger brother, but you are betrothed to Irene Ducaena, with a large dowry and family connections, as well as the support of the patriarch. I'm not saying which of you should take the throne, but Alexios has clear advantages."

Neither of them moved as I spoke. Alexios's eyes were bulging out at me, while Isaac had sucked in his breath.

"As I said, the two of you are the strongest contenders. But what's important to me is family, our family. Taking care of each other no matter what. I would rather that no son of mine is emperor if it means there's bad blood between you. If you can't look at each other and swear an oath to me that you will serve unconditionally whomever is on the throne, then I don't want a son of mine ruling."

"Mama, that goes without saying," said Alexios in a squeaky voice.

"I agree," said Isaac after glancing at his brother. "But are you certain of John Ducas's support?"

"Yes. I met with Marie of Bulgaria and she was clear about that."

Isaac sighed and glanced sideways at Alexios. "It sounds like you're going to be the lucky one."

Alexios was pale, his hands gripping the armrests of his chair. "I'm not sure how lucky I really am."

Isaac gave him a playful punch. "You'll be fine. I'll be there with you."

I let out my breath. I'd expected Isaac to accept the situation, but I had to be sure.

"What about the empress's son?" asked Alexios. "He is a Ducas."

He spoke of the boy, but his face said he was thinking of the mother. "What do you want to do?" I asked in a soft voice.

"I want to name her son my co-emperor. I have no children yet, no guarantee I will with Irene."

Isaac cocked an eyebrow at that suggestion. "Seems reasonable. It's the best she and the boy can hope for now."

I nodded agreement.

Isaac stood up and slapped his brother on the back. "Come along, Emperor Alexios, we need to get over to the palace. We can discuss what my exalted title will be on the way there."

๑๑๑

THE CLATTER OF HOOVES AND THE GATEKEEPER'S GROGGY voice announced that Alexios was home two hours after sunset. He would be alone since Isaac was staying at the palace with his wife and sons. I was in my office with the shutters closed against the cold, squinting at the account books from the warehouse I owned. The twin oil lamps provided just enough light to work, and the drop of rose oil I'd added gave off a pleasant scent. A jug of warmed wine, wrapped in a towel to keep it heated, a pitcher of water, and two polished silver cups sat on shelf nearby.

Alexios's footsteps came straight to my door. He entered and removed his heavy mantle, shaking off glistening snowflakes.

"I didn't realize it was snowing," I said. "Would you like some wine?" I turned to pour wine, mixing in water, for us both.

"You might have warned me," he said in a tense voice.

"You think I should have sent you a letter?" I asked incredulously.

He took the cup I offered, lifting it to his mouth for a long drink. Shadows flickered across his strong face with his young man's beard.

He put the cup down and wiped his mouth with the back of his hand. "No, I suppose not. It's just a shock to come home and have my mother tell me I'm to become the next emperor of the Roman Empire."

I folded my hands on the desk. "It was a surprise? Alexios, you know what's been happening. You've seen the emperor grow decrepit. You know who can lead armies, who can get the most support. The time has come."

He scowled and raised the cup to his lips again before speaking. "Well, you're right about that. I certainly realized that today."

"What happened?"

He and Isaac had arrived at the palace and were invited to dine with the emperor. That was usually a high honor, but the emperor had been in a foul mood, snapping at servants and complaining about everything.

"Isaac and I were sitting opposite each other at the table, looking at each other and wondering if we were going to be arrested. Here we were, just having left you and a discussion about overthrowing him, and already we were caught. It made no sense. I mean, how could he find out so quickly, but that's what we were thinking. Then one of the servants whispered to Isaac that there was bad news from Cyzicus."

Cyzicus was an old city in Anatolia on the Marmara coast, half a day's journey by ship from Constantinople.

Alexios started to chuckle at the memory. "Isaac mouthed 'Cyzicus' to me, and I realized the emperor was upset about some news from there, not us."

"Then what happened?"

"We met with the emperor and he told us to assemble our

armies, east and west, and go after the Turks who had just captured Cyzicus. His two thugs made sure they were there in the room with us and the emperor. I have to say, I think the emperor, decrepit as he's gotten, has not completely lost his mind. The fact that he recalled us was a surprise to them. Then they tried convincing Botaneiates that we're plotting against him, while we were sitting right there. Isaac kept quiet while I, sweet as honey, convinced him otherwise."

I did regret having to plot the overthrow of Nikephoros Botaneiates. He'd been a friend to the family for many years.

"Alexios, I don't want you harming the emperor. He can retire to a monastery like your Uncle Isaac did. He's a good man, just too old and not well. He'll never be a threat to you after that."

"I know. He shuffles around, holding on to a cane, a servant always at the ready in case he loses his balance and falls. I swore an oath to him, but we need an emperor who can lead an army. When there's news like what happened in Cyzicus, he needs to be out there, pushing back. Botaneiates is just the ghost of an emperor, even though he's still on this side of the grave."

I finished off the wine in my cup, placing it softly on the desk.

"We spoke with the empress," he said almost casually, his face lightening at the mention of her.

"What did she say?" I asked. He tried to hide his feelings for Maria, but I knew my son.

"She supports us, or at least will not oppose us or betray us. She's grateful that her little Tino can continue as co-emperor."

"I know she wants the best for her son," I said. "It's getting late. There'll be much to do in the morning."

It is no easy thing to overthrow an emperor. I'd seen many attempts go awry, even with the best military leaders. A lucky spear thrust, a sleeping guard, betrayal by an ambitious bureaucrat, an angry empress, any of those could undo the best plans. I would go to bed and say my prayers that my sons would be blessed with success.

☙❦☙

ISAAC, ALEXIOS, AND I MET THE NEXT DAY AT THE DUCAS house with Marie of Bulgaria to make our plans. Isaac was supposed to be returning to Anatolia to start marching on Cyzicus, but instead he and Alexios would go together to Thrace. Marie would send a messenger to George Palaiologos letting him know that Alexios was making a bid for the throne and to keep the emperor's army that was chasing Melissenos away from the capital.

Isaac and Alexios decided to leave the morning of the fourteenth.

"What about your mother, your sisters?" asked Marie. "The emperor will find out what you're doing. What happens to them?"

I didn't think Botaneiates himself would hurt us, but those Scythes were another matter.

"We've got the little girls to protect. I know the boy's tutor would certainly ask questions if we all suddenly left," I said.

Alexios was quiet for a moment, then grinned. "Stay in plain sight but untouchable. You need to stay completely in the open, so anything they might try would be seen by everyone."

"What exactly do you mean?" I asked, feeling suspicious of his sly grin.

"You take Thea and Theodora and their girls and leave during the night when we do. You'll go to the Hagia Sophia and be there by dawn. Then you'll claim sanctuary from the emperor and cling to the royal doors before the altar. You'll say your sons have been unjustly accused of rebelling. You're just women and children who demand the emperor's protection because of threats from the Scyths. Demand to be allowed to go to Petrion under the emperor's protection. Do it loudly," he said. "You have to be bold as a general going into battle. You want everyone in the city to see you, including the patriarch. The emperor and his thugs won't dare do a thing to hurt you, and you'll be safe once they find out what we're up to."

My mouth hung open. I eyed my son, wondering where he got crazy ideas like that. He threw his head back laughing at me and took my hands in his.

"Mama, I know you can do that. It will be great fun. I only wish I could be here to see it."

Marie stared at Alexios and then at me, considering the suggestion. "You know, that might just work. Then, after he promises his protection, you'll be safe. Not even Borilos and Germanos would desecrate a monastery to try and arrest a few harmless widows and children."

"I really don't think—" I began before Isaac interrupted me.

"Mama, you defended us before the whole Senate, defended us both against a charge of treason. You can do this; I know you can."

"That was to save our lives!" I protested.

"There will be a lot more lives depending on you now," Isaac said. "Just be bold and don't back down. Alexios is right, you can do it."

☙❧

A SLIVER OF WANING MOON HAD JUST RISEN IN THE EARLY hours of February fourteenth when we embarked on our perilous journey to the throne. Everyone went to their rooms after eating dinner, Synadenos and his tutor to their wing of the house that was fortunately behind the main house and with no view of the courtyard. We all dressed in traveling clothes and lay down to sleep as best we could until two hours before dawn. I rose then and woke the others and barring the door to Synadenos's wing. It would not stop them, but it would slow them down.

The horses Isaac and Alexios rode were ready, with old canvas wrapped around the hooves to muffle their clattering noise. Not even my usually chattering granddaughters spoke as we exited the gate. The gatekeeper had oiled the hinge the day before and it made barely a squeak as it closed behind. The lock gave a soft clink when Alexios turned the gate's key, a noise that seemed to echo on the empty street.

My sons walked with us as far as the church of St. Polyeuctos on the Mese road where we split up.

"Mama, just remember what I said. Be bold and they won't dare do anything to you," said Alexios.

He and Isaac stood before me, as nervous as a couple of race-horses waiting for the moppa to drop in the hippodrome signaling the race's start. I could see them in my mind's eye in the carceres next to the other horses, all stomping and ready. No others in this race could compete with them, but that never guaranteed victory.

"My sons, remember what I've told you. You are to be loyal to each other always, no matter how it goes. Avoid doing any harm to the cities and towns you pass, be faithful to the Church, and resolved in our purpose. I have every confidence in you both."

I embraced them both, kissed them, and gave them my blessing. They mounted and headed north to the Charisius Gate, soon swallowed up in the night's shadows. I turned to Theodora, Thea, and my granddaughters, and we walked south in the pale moonlight toward the Hagia Sophia.

We reached the Forum of Constantine with the first gray light of dawn. A statue of the first Emperor Constantine stood atop the porphyry column in the center, scarred now with a dull black slash where lightning had struck it a few months earlier. We had just passed the Senate building with its statue of Athena, helmeted and an owl perched on her shoulder, when I heard a familiar voice calling my name.

"Lady Anna, Lady Anna," called Phillip Mouzalon, Synadenos's tutor.

Thea, Theodora, and I froze and looked at each other, unable to believe our ears. I turned to face the young man, assuming an expression of calm innocence.

"Phillip, I didn't expect to see you here. We were just on our way to the Hagia Sophia for morning prayers, and then to see the emperor. I must tell him how wonderfully your pupil is doing at his studies."

He looked at our party with curiosity and confusion. I often rose early to attend Divine Liturgy, but the others did not.

"I heard a noise, and when I rose I found everyone gone, and we were locked in. I climbed out a window, then over the wall, and thought to find you," he said.

I put my hand to my cheek in a display of sadness at this oversight.

"Oh, I do apologize, that was so thoughtless of us. I'll be sure that never happens again. Would you like to accompany us? Perhaps you can go ahead to the emperor to announce us while we attend to our prayers in the church?" I said.

He blinked, his brows knit in bewilderment. "Well, yes, I'll walk with you and let the emperor know you'll be arriving soon."

I hoped the prospect of a meeting for any reason with the emperor would distract the tutor from wondering what we were actually doing.

We continued together for the next fifteen minutes to the entrance to the Great Palace as the sun rose higher. My heart was beating so hard I thought Mouzalon could hear it. The city was just waking up, cocks crowing, a few cookshops opening their doors, the scents of baking bread and sizzling sausages filling the air.

"Be sure to tell the emperor we will be there soon," I told Mouzalon when we parted at the gate of the Great Palace.

"Of course, Lady Anna," he said as he again eyed us before stepping back, his mouth tight.

I knew he would be letting people in the palace know of our unusual early morning visit to the church as soon as he got inside the walls. The emperor would guess that perhaps the suspicions of his two Scythes were correct.

We hurried to the Hagia Sophia and entered the outer narthex that was always open. In front of the great bronze doors to the inner narthex, still closed at this early hour, sat a pair of yawning black-robed priests with long gray beards, keeping watch.

"Kind fathers," I began, "could you please allow us in to pray? I realize it is early. I desire to make my prayers to the Mother of God and I have little time for our visit."

The priests looked uncertain.

"Father, my family is from Cappadocia, and we wanted to be sure to make our prayers here," said Thea, whose father's family was, in fact, from Cappadocia.

The two men exchanged a glance, one of them shrugged, and the other one spoke.

"It is not so early, and for devout pilgrims such as yourselves, we can make a small exception."

I sighed in deep relief, fearful the emperor might be sending someone to take us from the church before I was ready. The heavy door groaned open, and I stepped onto the marble floor made smooth with the footsteps of centuries of faithful worshippers. The dawn's pink sunlight spilled through the many glass windows onto the floor. Ahead was the sparkling silver-and-gold iconostasis with its many painted icons of saints on either side of the royal door, my goal. I walked slowly, afraid to show the urgency pounding in my blood. We were nearing the royal doors, with their gold painted arch and carvings of angels, when the sounds of running feet echoed across the great church's vast expanse.

I reached the doorway to the sanctuary, prostrated myself

and grabbed hold of its sacred doors, turned to my pursuers, and spoke in a clear, loud voice.

"Unless my hands are cut off, I will not leave this holy place except on one condition: that I receive the emperor's cross as his guarantee of his protection of me and my family."

Soldiers sent to arrest me and bring me to the palace stopped, staring at me, dressed in my nun's attire. I claimed sanctuary in the holiest church in Christendom, and I was a nun. Beside me huddled my daughter and daughter-in-law, my granddaughters, a covey of women that men usually counted as lacking in importance. The men looked at each other, reluctant to treat us as roughly as they would men.

The regular early morning visitors to the church had begun to arrive by this time and were avidly watching the drama unfolding before the iconostasis. The crowd grew larger every minute as word spread. The soldiers talked amongst themselves, trying to determine the best solution. Finally, the ones who appeared in charge left, leaving me gripping the arch.

The great church filled with thousands of people from the city, curious about what the day's event meant. I could hear some of them saying that I was the mother of the Comnenus boys, which was greeted with approving nods. The emperor would not be able to imprison or hurt us without starting a riot.

An hour after the soldier left to speak to the emperor, he returned with two of the emperor's secretaries, one of whom said the emperor was granting me sanctuary and handed me a small cross that fit in the palm of my hand. I stared at this trinket and knew it meant nothing to the emperor. I needed a large display of him granting his protection.

I sniffed and handed the small cross back to the emperor's messenger.

"This small display of mercy is not enough. I cannot leave here without a cross of distinction, a cross that truly and completely displays the emperor's mercy to me," I cried out, my voice echoing against the marble walls. "My sons have been conspired against by the emperor's two Scythe favorites, Borilos and Germanos, with the threat that they will be blinded. I require a larger symbol of the emperor's mercy. This will not suffice."

The two men who'd brought the cross turned pale, glanced at each other, and departed.

My hands became stiff as I gripped the royal door's entrance. Patriarch Cosmas appeared, and I explained the dilemma I and my sons had—they were conspired against despite years of loyal service. I feared for myself and my daughters' and granddaughters' safety during this time when accusations were lodged against them. He said little, Marie of Bulgaria having warned him beforehand of what we were planning.

The scene resolved piecemeal. I would, from time to time, make vociferous calls for God's mercy, the emperor's mercy in the face of the unjust accusations against my sons. The hours dragged on as the emperor must have tried to figure out what I and my sons were doing.

Finally, sometime after midday, an imperial secretary appeared carrying a large cross, one that was easily half my height. Christ's image was painted on a gold background that was brilliant in the sunlight. Thousands of people now filled the Hagia Sophia, women leaning over the balcony, men thronging the nave, priests listening from behind the iconostasis. Some of the onlookers made sounds of approval at the sight of this striking icon.

The bureaucrat bellowed out his announcement, "Lady Anna, the emperor sends this cross to demonstrate his trust in you and your sons, who have always been loyal to the empire and its emperor."

I grasped the cross to my chest, holding it high so that all could see.

"My daughters and granddaughters and I will leave now and go to the Petrion monastery where we will remain in peace with this sacred sign from the emperor," I said in a loud voice.

The crowd parted before us as we proceeded from the Hagia Sophia, up the Mese, on a return journey toward the Blachernae district and the Petrion monastery. We were followed and watched by what seemed like the entire city as our party of women moved through the Forum of Constantine, past the ancient churches of St. Polyeuctos and the Holy Apostles where so many past emperors lay in its mausoleum, and finally to Petrion, overlooking the Golden Horn.

I walked through the city, carrying the cross like a beam from a lighthouse, and realized Alexios was right. Boldness will get you far in this world.

⁂

THE SAME THIN, SALLOW NUN WHO HAD GREETED US THREE years earlier when we'd arrived at Petrion with the empress and her son opened its gate for us now.

"They're waiting inside for you," she announced as she secured the gate behind us.

"Thank you, Mother," I said.

We passed through the corridors to the rooms that had housed Empress Maria. This time it was Marie of Bulgaria, along with her two daughters, Irene and Anna, who awaited us.

"You're finally here," Marie said in relief. "I thought you'd have been here hours ago."

My hands shook as I leaned the cross the emperor had given me against a wall. The anxiety of the day was catching up with me, and I could not even think what to say yet. I sat down on the first chair I found.

"Mama was wonderful," said Theodora, putting a hand on my shoulder. "Alexios will be so proud of you. You should have seen her—first the emperor sent her a little cross, but she rejected it as too small to signify his promise of sanctuary. The emperor's secretary looked like she'd thrown him a thunderbolt when she sent him back with it. Finally, he came back with this one. It looks like they had to convince a priest to relinquish it, like it came from one of the churches inside the palace walls."

"She was so brave," said Thea. "I could never do what she did. You should have seen her when Phillip Mouzalon called to her in the Forum of Constantine, she looked as untroubled as a sleeping baby when she turned to face him, while I could hardly move."

Soon everyone was talking at once, recounting the adventures of the day. I sipped at the cup of wine someone thrust into my hand, able to relax a little after so many hours on edge. Now, Alexios and Isaac had to move their pieces into position to checkmate the emperor.

THE NEXT DAY, ISAAC'S WIFE IRENE AND HER TWO LITTLE sons moved into Petrion with us.

"I've been with my cousin in the Great Palace since we were small children. But I need my sons to be here under the emperor's protection in case this fight goes wrong for Isaac."

The emperor sent guards to maintain a watch around the monastery, ostensibly for our own protection.

The monastery permitted Marie to order foodstuffs from her own house for our group. Marie, coming from parents who had left her a wealthy woman, and her marriage into the affluent Ducas family, expected only the best, even during the long weeks of Lent that began a few days after we began our stay at Petrion. We ate often of shellfish, thick lentil stews filled with onions, carrots, and mushrooms, honeyed almonds, the softest breads, raisins, and dates. The food was so abundant one day that I suggested we offer the remainders to our guards.

The bored soldiers eagerly partook of the delicious provisions and began sharing all they heard of what was happening with my sons' rebellion. They told us that in early March Alexios and Isaac's army had gathered in Thrace and was marching to the capital. A few days later came word that the army had acclaimed Alexios as emperor, as had every city and town the army marched through on its way to Constantinople.

A side benefit of the servants coming and going each day was that they carried messages to and from Caesar John. That was how we learned that Alexios had been chosen emperor by the army. Isaac had graciously conceded, even strapping the purple sandals on his brother's feet.

I became better acquainted with Alexios's betrothed, Irene Ducaena, during these weeks in Petrion. The girl was still just fourteen and had grown up with every privilege her family's great wealth could obtain. Now, she would be the next empress of the Roman Empire, the consort of a young and handsome emperor. She made sure everyone, but especially my granddaughter Anya, who was betrothed to Synadenos, with the now lost prospect of herself being the next empress, knew that. My granddaughters soon created their own small clique, while Irene and her sister coalesced into another, until their mothers noticed and tried to reconcile them all. Thea, Theodora, and Marie made sure the girls learned to demonstrate congenial manners, but there would never be affection between them.

It was obvious, though, that Irene was not just in love with the idea of being empress; she was desperately in love with Alexios. She hung on every scrap of news that came to us about him and insisted we spend hours everyday in the monastery's church praying for his safety.

Like my granddaughters, I found it difficult to be affectionate with Irene, even when she shyly asked me for stories of Alexios when he was a child. Her eyes lit up at every amusing tale of teasing his older brothers and sparkled with admiration at his prowess in battle. I could not fault her for being indifferent to my son. The problem was not just her spoiled and haughty behavior, although that did not help matters. The true problem was her growing resemblance to her father, Andronikos, that left me as cold as the grave Romanus lay in.

CRIT

MARTINA, MY SEAMSTRESS, VISITED THE CONVENT ON THE pretext of providing clothes for the children living with us while bringing us news from the palace that Thomas gleaned. The emperor was reaching a sad end, unable to muster the determination to fight either Alexios in the west or Melissenos in the east. He was pinched on both sides but vacillated between offering the throne to one or the title of Caesar to the other. He hated losing the throne he had claimed so late in life, but he had lost the ability to rule it. Every move my sons made brought the end of his reign closer.

The guards told us toward the end of March that Alexios's troops were at the walls of the city. One of the guards, an agreeable young man from Cappadocia, Elias, had so appreciated the meals we provided that I thought to ask him if he could escort me to the ramparts of the city walls to see what was happening.

He looked nervously at me. "Lady Anna, I don't think I should be doing that."

"Has anyone told you I shouldn't go for a short visit on the walls?" I asked.

"Not exactly."

"You'll be with me, and I promise you I won't stray from your side. But it would make me so happy to see my son, even if only from a distance. We won't be long. No one will be the wiser," I wheedled, putting a handful of honeyed almonds in his palm. "I'm sure Lady Marie will have more delectable foods for you when we're back."

He shoved the almonds into his mouth, chewing hard on them. "If you promise we'll be back quickly." His words were garbled, but I understood.

"Of course. I long to see my son, as any mother would. Just a few minutes there."

Elias and I slipped out that morning when Marie was busy heaping food into the bowls of the other soldiers then on duty.

The walk over to the northern Mese took about twenty minutes, and then from there north to the Gate of Charisius that Alexios and Isaac had exited when leaving Constantinople in February. We climbed the steep old steps to the top of the high inner wall that gave us the best view. The walk up the stairs left me winded, and I leaned against the stone parapet. A pair of hawks circled in a clear blue sky, searching for prey. I could see far into the lands beyond the walls from this height, fields green now and lush with new spring grass. A large army camped in the distance, with tents and campfires and men milling about. The breeze still held the clean crispness of winter, while the sun encouraged the spring buds to reach up.

The men guarding the Gate of Charisius spoke a rough Greek, coming from lands to the west around Dyrrachium.

"Are these the only soldiers guarding the walls?" I asked Elias.

His mouth twisted while thinking. "No, Varangians guard from the Marmara and the Porta Aurea, the Golden Gate, to the Gate of Rhesios, while tagmata troops are in the section from Rhesios to the Fifth Military Gate. These men, the Nemitzi from Serbian lands, guard the walls to Blachernae and the Golden Horn."

Two figures below us walked through the grass bordering the moat, the outermost barrier of the walls, and just beyond the range of an archer's arrow. One was helmeted and dressed in armor, the other in monk's robes. The soldiers on the walls shouted down rude comments to the monk, who ignored them. I watched them walking and recognized the stride of Alexios in the armored man, while I thought the monk's movements resembled Caesar John, perhaps attired in his monk's robes to avoid suspicion of attempting to gain the throne for himself. They didn't notice me, so engrossed in conversation were they.

"Thank you, Elias," I said. "We can return now."

MARTINA VISITED AGAIN ON MARCH THIRTY-FIRST.

"Thomas says the patriarch visited the emperor, told him to abdicate. The poor man was so confused he didn't understand at first. Then he decided to send a message to Niko Melissenus, offering to make him emperor."

Marie and I exchanged a glance. That was not the result we were looking for.

"That doesn't make any sense. Alexios is right outside the gates. Why not him?" I asked. "Does he have any idea what's really going on?"

"I'll send a message to George," she said, referring to her daughter Anna's betrothed. "He'll take care of it."

We spent the day alternating between praying in the church and returning to our rooms, trying to distract ourselves. Irene and her mother had a decided fondness for frivolous novels full of romantic stories about beautiful maidens, brave heroes, and terrible creatures who threatened destruction. I did not care for such silly stories but sat politely while Irene read aloud, listening instead for any commotion coming from the street. But all was silent that day.

Raucous noises began reverberating through the city at dawn. The sounds coming from outside, though, were not so much the sounds of fighting between soldiers as they were of households trying to fend off robbers. Theodora and I walked out of our rooms toward the front gate of the monastery to learn what was happening. The guards the emperor had sent us were outside, pushing back against the marauders.

"Whose men are they?" I asked the nun standing just inside the entrance. The poor woman was wringing her hands.

She just shook her head and scurried down the corridor to the hegoumena's office.

I went over to the gate and opened the door hole to see what was transpiring. A handful of men in armor were harassing the soldiers, who were pushing back against them. Were they Alexios's?

I shouted out at the men in the loudest voice I could muster, "Whose army are you from?"

The men kept their squabbling up. I opened the gate and went out.

"I said, whose army are you from? Who is your general?"

The shouting stopped and the men glared at me. One spoke up saying, "We're with the new emperor, Emperor Alexios Comnenus."

Relief flooded through me.

"I am the Lady Anna Dalassena, and I am the mother of your new emperor. What are you doing attacking this holy monastery? You should be ashamed of yourselves. I am residing here with Emperor Alexios's sisters, nieces, his betrothed wife, and mother-in-law. If you want to continue in service to my son, you will cease harassing us and leave this place immediately. Otherwise, if you continue this unwarranted intrusion, I am confident that your service to my son, and possibly your lives, will be dramatically shortened. Do you understand?"

The men looked at each other, then back at me, and decided it would be best to leave. They apologized and departed.

"What on earth happened with Alexios? How did all these men start running loose in the city, thinking they can just push their way into a monastery like that?" asked Theodora.

"I have no idea, but this is not good," I said, outraged at this abysmal behavior. I watched the troublemakers leave, but the sounds of other attacks going on elsewhere in the city could be heard.

I went inside and spoke with Marie.

"You must send a message to Caesar John immediately. There are soldiers from Alexios's army rampaging through the city. I can't tell for certain, but I think they are looting. This must be stopped now."

Marie sent her message, but we heard nothing until the next day when a note arrived from Caesar John.

"He says Alexios is emperor and Botaneiates abdicated and

moved into the Peribleptos monastery," she read. "Some of the soldiers were out of control once they were inside the city walls but they've been rounded up and won't be a problem in the future. Alexios will be here tomorrow."

⁂

ALEXIOS ARRIVED AT PETRION MIDMORNING ON APRIL third, accompanied by Isaac and an entourage of soldiers. My two sons embraced me, together lifting me off my feet in their enthusiasm.

"Mama, we did it," Alexios said.

Tears were in my eyes at his words.

"We must give great thanks to God for this victory," I said. "But what happened with your men? They were running rough over the people in the city. Terrible stories about murders, thefts, women being violated."

Alexios exchanged a glance with Isaac. "Caesar John promised them booty when they signed on. I didn't realize until too late."

"They know better now," agreed Isaac.

I shook my head at them, disappointed in those events.

"The reason why we came is to bring you to the palace for my coronation tomorrow," said Alexios. "We leave now."

"And my wife and boys too," said Isaac. "Thea and Theodora. The whole family."

I frowned, thinking of his betrothed and her family. "And there's also your Irene, her mother and sister here."

He shrugged, distracted.

"They can come, but my wife will be crowned later," he said, looking preoccupied.

⁂

MY SON ALEXIOS I COMNENUS WAS CROWNED EMPEROR OF the Romans the next day, April fourth, by the patriarch, in the same solemn service that emperors had been using since Constantine the Great. He stood in the line of men such as Augustus, Marcus Aurelius, Constantine the Great, Theodosios the Great, Justinian and Theodora, Basil the Bulgarslayer, and his own uncle, Isaac Comnenus.

I stood surrounded by my sons and daughters near the green marble circle in the Hagia Sophia where his coronation took place. My own husband had declined the throne when his brother's ill health forced his abdication, a choice that angered and disappointed me for many years. Alexios now stood where his father should have stood. I prayed my son would have the strength to rule wisely for many years.

He stood dignified and regal as Patriarch Cosmas anointed him with holy chrism, clothed him in the emperor's purple raiment, and finally placed on his head the golden crown with jeweled pendants of a Roman emperor.

This time, there was no Constantine Ducas standing behind him coveting the throne, as there had been when Isaac Comnenus was crowned. John Ducas was here now, but he was standing with the other dynatoi, not in the prominent position he'd held when his brother was crowned. Then, too, in those years Isaac had faced terrible problems with the patriarch Michael Keroularios. The patriarch today, Cosmas, had been appointed by Michael Ducas when he still reigned, and he'd opposed the marriage of Botaneiates to Empress Maria when Michael abdicated. He had encouraged Botaneiates relinquishing the throne, and had made no problems for Alexios taking it. Still, I didn't want Alexios having the same problems his uncle had experienced. I knew now, as I had not twenty-three years earlier, that he needed a supporter in the patriarch's seat.

It was like the games of chess I played as a child with my grandfather and Uncle Costas. The king needed his castles, his knights, and his bishops as support when he went into battle. Cosmas's loyalty to the Ducas family might conflict with my son's efforts to rule. Perhaps he could be convinced to retire.

I then suddenly remembered the last of the powerful game pieces. The queen.

CHAPTER 17

April 1081

Patriarch Cosmas approached me before everyone sat down at the banquet celebrating the new emperor.

"Lady Anna, you must know of the atrocities your son's army perpetrated in the city the day they entered its walls," he said. His words were somber, but his eyes would not meet mine.

"Your Beatitude," I said, bowing my head to him. "I did know of it. My son was appalled at the way they ran riot, but he understands his men may have misunderstood Caesar John. They believed John Ducas told them they would be free to loot once they were inside the walls."

The patriarch glanced across the room. He was staring across at Caesar John, who was glaring at us. The priest had the grace to look uncomfortable, swallowed and then continued.

"That was an unfortunate misunderstanding. Even so, they were your son's men. Restitution and penance must be made."

So that's how John Ducas wanted matters to be. He would control Alexios through the patriarch. I looked hard at the patriarch and resolved that he would soon, one way or another, be retiring from that position.

"I understand. I will speak with my son."

⚜

I MET WITH ALEXIOS AND ISAAC IMMEDIATELY AFTER THE celebration. He and Isaac were outraged at John Ducas's attempt at manipulation.

"Mama, this only reinforces something I've wanted to speak with you about," Alexios said.

We sat in the office that had once been his uncle's in the Daphne Palace. The sun was setting on that promising spring day.

"John Ducas is a snake and I really do not want to marry his conniving granddaughter. I know I'm betrothed to Irene, but betrothals can be broken."

I sighed, not surprised. "You want to marry Empress Maria, don't you?"

Isaac watched us, keeping quiet.

"Yes," he answered. "I have for years. You know that." He looked at me, eyes glowing with hope and desire for the beautiful empress.

Isaac sat forward with his opinion. "I think we should concentrate on what the patriarch said. He wants penance and restitution. We need to find out what that means. Then bring up the idea of a different wife for you."

"Isaac, you and I will visit the patriarch in the morning to find out exactly what he wants," I said.

⚜

WE SAT IN PATRIARCH COSMAS'S OFFICE BEHIND THE HAGIA Sophia two hours after dawn the next day.

"I believe at least forty days of penance on the emperor's part would suffice to demonstrate his sorrow for the actions his men committed. The penance should include fasting and sleeping on the floor, not a bed. And making payments to those who were robbed or otherwise damaged, of course," he began.

"Of course," I said cautiously. The way he spoke made me think this was only his opening bid.

"There's also the matter of the emperor and his betrothed being wedded, and of her crowning."

John Ducas might not have been in the room with us, but he was the one negotiating.

"We had planned for a wedding in a few months. In fact, I spoke with Irene's mother about that just a few weeks ago."

He nodded thoughtfully. "Yes, that may be true, but you have to admit circumstances have changed. Your son is now emperor and can marry Irene at once and see she is crowned."

Isaac leaned forward. "Your Beatitude, with all due respect, I'm not sure my brother still believes Irene Ducaena will make the best wife for him. He has been contemplating other choices, perhaps a marital alliance with a foreign ruler. The empire is beset on all sides, and we need alliances to stop the attacks."

The patriarch's fist hit the table.

"Absolutely not. Emperor Alexios signed a valid marriage contract with Lady Irene's grandfather. He cannot set her aside even for reasons of state. The marriage must go forward. The sooner that happens, the better."

Isaac persisted for his brother. "Sir, I know there was a contract signed, but surely the safety of the empire is a concern that rises above the Lady Irene? Empress Maria's family rules in Alania and have been loyal to the empire."

Cosmas looked at Isaac as though he had lost his mind. "You can't possibly be thinking of her, can you? Empress Maria has already been married twice, and both of her husbands still live, even if in Holy Orders. You must know the Church does not permit third marriages. And not only that, she is the emperor's adopted mother, the adopted brother of her son. A marriage between the emperor and Maria cannot, I repeat, absolutely cannot occur under such unorthodox circumstances."

Isaac backed down at the patriarch's vehemence.

"Your Beatitude, thank you for your time. We will return to the emperor and inform him of what we've discussed," I said, bowing respectfully.

⚜

ALEXIOS WAS MISERABLE AT THE NEWS WE BROUGHT HIM, but soon the misery turned to anger. It simmered for a few days, disappointment written on his face. He stormed around the palace at odd hours, disgusted at being coerced again by the devious John Ducas. Finally, he sat down with Isaac and me.

"Of course, I will agree to do the penance, as will my entire family. In fact, I'll personally do the penance for eighty days. I will also agree to marrying Irene and seeing her crowned. However, I must receive the patriarch's promise that he will resign his post immediately after she's crowned so that I can choose a patriarch more to my liking. Mama, I want you to choose one who will be best for us."

"That's all?" I asked.

"No. Irene and whatever Ducas relations she drags into the Great Palace with her will not be living in the Boukoleon with me. They can all live in the Aetos Palace. Besides, if I am to do penance, I can't be having carnal relations with her, can I? No point in having her close by in that case. Of course, I'll be leaving on campaign soon, I may not be back before November."

Isaac raised an eyebrow. "Getting Cosmas to retire sounds like an excellent idea. He's clearly not an ally of ours. But putting Irene and her family in that old building?"

"I've been inside. It's decent enough, not the worst of them. I've put the servants to work cleaning it up," Alexios said, looking smug. "This way John Ducas will know exactly where he and his scheming granddaughter stand with me. I refuse to let them think I am their puppet. I refuse to be bullied by them."

Patriarch Cosmas paled at Alexios's demand for his retirement from office, but in the end, he agreed. My son and Irene were wed in a small ceremony in an ancient chapel on the palace grounds, followed by Irene's crowning. It accomplished what John Ducas wanted, but without the great pomp and ceremony he expected, and with the loss of the patriarch's influence. Nor was the marriage consummated since Alexios was still doing his penance when he left the city for Dyrrachium.

In the end, Irene realized her dream of marrying Alexios, along with gaining an imperial crown, but she slept alone on the top floor of the Aetos palace, surrounded by her Ducas kin. This would not be the marriage of her young girl's dreams.

ALEXIOS LEFT BY JUNE ON CAMPAIGN AGAINST THE Norman, Robert Guiscard, who had gained control of all of southern Italy and had now crossed the Adriatic and was laying siege to the city of Dyrrachium. Before Alexios departed, though, he issued this Chrysobull, an imperial proclamation, that finally closed the door to any aspirations to power that John Ducas, or even Irene, could ever have.

"WHEN DANGER IS FORESEEN OR SOME OTHER DREADFUL occurrence is expected, there is no safeguard stronger than a mother who is understanding and loves her son, for if she gives counsel her advice will be reliable; if she offers prayers, they will confer strength and certain protection. Such at any rate has been my experience of myself, your emperor, in the case of my own revered mother, who has taught and guided and sustained me throughout my earliest years. She had a place in aristocratic society, but her first concern was for her son and his faith in her was preserved intact. . .

"But now I am preparing with God's help to do battle with Rome's enemies; with much forethought an army is being recruited and thoroughly equipped; not the least of my cares, however, has been the provision of an efficient organization in financial and civil affairs. Fortunately, an impregnable bulwark for good government has been found—in the appointment of my revered mother, of all women most honored, as controller of the entire administration. I, your emperor, therefore decree explicitly in this present Chrysobull the following: because of her vast experience of secular affairs, whatever she decrees in writing shall have the permanent validity as if I myself, your Serene Emperor, had issued them or after dictating them had them committed to writing. Whatever decision or orders are made by her, written or unwritten, reasonable or unreasonable, shall be regarded as coming from myself. In years to come they will have the force of law permanently. Neither now nor in the future shall my mother be subjected to inquiry or undergo any examination whatsoever at the hands of anybody, whomever he may be. It shall be absolutely impossible in the future to demand account of any action taken by her under the terms of this present Chrysobull.

Alexios Comnenus, Emperor of the Romans

I MIGHT NOT WEAR A CROWN OR HAVE THE TITLE OF Augusta, but in the absence of my son Emperor Alexios, I would rule the Roman Empire. I would be the queen on this chessboard.

AUTHOR'S NOTE

First, thank you for reading my novel. I hope you have enjoyed this adventure with Anna Dalassena and the other Byzantines of her era. The part she played in the history of the Byzantine Empire was critical, and one I thought deserved to be told.

Next, while this is a work of fiction, I am a stickler for historical accuracy and do my best to stay close to the historical record. Fortunately, there are three contemporary historians who wrote about this period: Michael Psellus, Michael Attaleiates, and John Skylitzes. In addition, Anna's granddaughter, Anna Comnena, wrote a history of her father's reign, "Alexiad," which overlaps for a few years with the earlier three historians. These sources provided a wealth of information about the events in my novels. I've also been fortunate that there are many historians these days researching and writing about the Byzantines. My book, "Byzantine History in the 11th Century: A Brief Introduction," includes a listing of many of my sources among modern historians. I have immense respect for all their work.

I strayed from the historical record a couple of times. One area where I did was for Anna Dalassena's grandfather, Adrian Dalassenus. The record says he was the son of Constantine (Uncle Costas in my novels) Dalassenus, but given Uncle

Costas's ten years imprisoned by the Fatimids in Egypt, it seemed more likely that Adrian was his much younger brother. I've also seen Eudokia Makrembolitissa's birth as listed in the 1020's, but given that she was still giving birth in 1070, that also seemed unlikely.

There is no record of a friendship between Anna Dalassena and Eudokia Makrembolitissa. However, they would certainly have known each other well. Constantine Ducas's first wife was a Dalassena (I've made her a cousin of Anna's); Ducas was a supporter of Isaac I Comnenus's rise to the throne; and Eudokia's second husband, Romanus I Diogenes, was a cousin of Anna's.

The Battle of Manzikert was a pivotal event in Byzantine history. It was one the Emperor Romanus IV Diogenes could have won but for the treachery of John Ducas and his son, Andronikos, and their supporters. The tragedy of that betrayal echoes even into modern times.

Michael Psellus, the historian and bureaucrat, recedes from this novel with the arrival of the eunuch, Nikephoritzes. It appears that after he was removed from imperial service John Ducas commissioned Psellus to write his history of the 11th century's emperors to the time of Michael VII Ducas. He likely died during Michael's reign since his history ends with fulsome praise of that inept ruler, probably in the vain hope of returning to the emperor's inner circle. My website (eileenstephenson.com) includes three blog posts about Psellus.

One question that often comes up with historians is why Anna Dalassena allowed her son Alexios to marry Irene Ducaena, the daughter of the traitor of Manzikert and the granddaughter of John Ducas who had had her (Anna) tried for treason. The family connection she had with Marie of Bulgaria was a clue, but still didn't seem to be enough that Anna could overlook Andronikos and John Ducas's betrayals. My idea of the manipulative John Ducas tricking Alexios and Anna into accepting it seemed plausible, but we will never know for sure.

Thomas the eunuch was completely invented. I've read that the use of eunuchs diminished during the Comnene dynasty, so I thought Anna's sympathy for Thomas's plight might have played a part in that.

Blindings of rebels and former rulers was commonplace in the Byzantine Empire until the Comnene. We also know from Anna Comnena's "Alexiad" that her grandmother was adamantly opposed to the use of that punishment. There was only one recorded blinding that occurred in the reign of Alexios I Comnenus, and it probably broke Anna's heart to order it. That's a story, though, for the next book.

I have many people to thank for their help with this novel. First, the editor and cover designer for all my books, the wonderful Jenny Quinlan. There's also Julie Witmer who created the beautiful map at the start of the book. Hal Stull and Bruce Bustard gave me regular and invaluable feedback in our writers' group. And then there were my beta readers: Tinney Sue Heath, James Conroyd Martin, Scott Hieger, and Jane Rawoof. Each of them looked at the story from a different perspective and gave it the tough love it needed. Thank you to all of you!

Finally, thank you to my husband, Ken, and our children and grandchildren. You've kept me from becoming a reclusive hermit obsessing about people who lived a thousand years ago!

One final, final note:

Reviews are critical for all authors, but especially for indie authors who are not traditionally published with all the marketing staff those big publishers have. Please consider leaving a review or a rating at Amazon, Barnes & Noble, Goodreads, Bookbub, or other reader websites you might frequent. I am always grateful for feedback from my readers. Thank you!

ABOUT THE AUTHOR

Eileen Stephenson was born in Fort Worth, Texas, but has spent most of her life in the Washington, D.C. Area, earning a living in the finance industry before discovering the enthralling world of the Byzantines. She has degrees from Georgetown University and George Washington University, and is married with three daughters. Her first book, *Tales of Byzantium*, is a collection of short stories of love, war, and finding your destiny in medieval Byzantium. Her second book, *Imperial Passions - The Porta Aurea,* is the early life of Anna Dalassena, the mother of Alexios I Comnenus, through the years until Isaac I Comnenus becomes emperor. Her third book, *Byzantine History in the 11th Century - A Brief Introduction,* showcases the leading figures and events of those pivotal years and the drama of a century of rebellions and murders, romance and political scheming.

You can visit her website, eileenstephenson.com, and blog to learn more about the Byzantines. She can also often be found commenting in Byzantine history Facebooks groups, and you can follow her on Twitter, @Byzyeileen, and on BookBub.

facebook.com/eileenstephenson

twitter.com/byzyeileen

bookbub.com/profile/eileen-stephenson

ALSO BY EILEEN STEPHENSON

Tales of Byzantium

Imperial Passions - The Porta Aurea

Byzantine History in the 11th Century - A Brief Introduction

Made in the USA
Monee, IL
10 May 2025